PRAISE FOR STEPHE

BY THE SAME AUTHOR

Stephen Aryan

THE WARRIOR

QUEST FOR HEROES, BOOK II

ANGRY
ROBOT

ANGRY ROBOT
An imprint of Watkins Media Ltd

Unit 11, Shepperton House
89 Shepperton Road
London N1 3DF
UK

angryrobotbooks.com
twitter.com/angryrobotbooks
Be Your Own Hero

An Angry Robot paperback original, 2022

Cover by Kieryn Tyler
Edited by Eleanor Teasdale and Gemma Creffield
Map by Tom Parker
Set in Meridien

ISBN 978 0 85766 958 2
Ebook ISBN 978 0 85766 959 9

Printed and bound in the United Kingdom by TJ Books Ltd.

9 8 7 6 5 4 3 2 1

MIX
Paper from
responsible sources
FSC
www.fsc.org   FSC® C013056

For David Gemmell

He paused, an hand on the wooden and.

CHAPTER 1

Kell Kressia, King of Algany, and two-time saviour of the Five Kingdoms, cursed as his opponent's sword clipped his fingers. He managed to hold on to the wooden practise blade, but only just. His opponent today was the same as yesterday, and every day before that, for months.

Odd Heinla was a member of the Raven, one of twelve elite warriors, who were his sworn protectors. Each of the Raven would sacrifice their life to save his, only not today. Today, he and Odd were just two men, stripped to the waist, sparring with wooden blades.

Kell's torso was dotted with fresh purple bruises. There were also a few green and yellow ones from a few days ago. There were scrapes and cuts on his shoulders, and now the fingers on his right hand were starting to swell up like fat sausages. Amazingly, he was actually getting better with a blade. Six months ago, he would have been one giant bruise, instead of sporadic welts. Now, he was managing to parry half of the attacks.

Odd was the best swordsman in Algany, but also an incredibly private person, which suited Kell. Odd barely spoke, didn't comment or offer his opinion on current affairs unless asked, and he never gossiped. After two years of sparring, the only things Kell knew about the man was that he was lethal with a blade, and that he was respected by his peers. Even among the Raven, Odd was regarded as the best

1

of the best. He wasn't a fawning sycophant, or someone who let Kell win because he was the King. He was relentless and utterly focused. Every time they set foot in the circle, they both fought as if their life depended on it.

As always, Kell and Odd were in a private courtyard in the palace, far away from prying eyes. They were just two anonymous men fighting in a chalk circle.

"Again," said Odd, swinging his arms to loosen his shoulders, gesturing for Kell to do the same. "You're too tight."

Kell tried to relax his body, anticipate Odd's next move, and not stare at his feet. Even now, there was so much to remember. It was coming, gradually, but it still wasn't easy. Kell had hoped that, by now, his skill would have overshadowed the famous heroes he'd admired as a boy. For all of their faults, of which there had been many, they had been talented fighters.

Kell signalled that he was ready and then moved to meet Odd in the middle. The man was so damn quick that Kell barely saw his blade coming. He sensed it though, managed a rough parry and quickly lunged, trying to maintain his balance. He missed, of course. Odd wasn't there anymore, but Kell didn't overextend. When Odd riposted, Kell was able to shift his weight and adapt, blocking a series of blows. But he still had no time to go on the offensive. He barely had enough time to breathe.

His lungs were burning, his shoulders ached and his swollen hand screamed at him to drop the blade. Kell held on grimly, blocked on his left, but then felt something thwack him across the ribs on the right. The blow left him winded and light-headed.

Odd stepped back, waiting for Kell to catch his breath before they continued. The man was barely breathing hard, but his dark skin glistened in the noonday sun. At least Kell had managed to make him break a sweat.

"Your Majesty, I'm sorry to intrude, but there's urgent court business," said a wheedling voice. Follis. He dressed in garish colours that sometimes made him think of his old friend, Vahli. Sadly, Vahli was gone, and Follis had none of the charm or wit of the bard. The others were gone too. As far as everyone else knew, they were dead, and once again Kell had returned as the sole survivor from the Frozen North. But when he came back this time, he'd paid close attention to how the new saga had been written about his quest. If anything, there was a lot more at stake. He had to protect his friends, and the secret about what they had really found in the castle of the Ice Lich.

As he had anticipated, the new Vahli saga had been an enormous success. It was far more popular than the old one, written by Pax Medina. Much to the annoyance of certain people in the church, bards across the Five Kingdoms had been singing all about his new adventure. Kell didn't mind. His only wish was that Vahli was still alive to see it.

Most days, it felt to Kell as if the quest had been part of another life. For two years he had been king of Algany. Even now, he was still getting used to the idea. It often felt like a joke. He almost expected someone to tell him there had been a terrible mix up, take away his crown, and put someone else on the throne instead. In fact, he often hoped for it.

Damn that cunning old bastard, King Bledsoe. He'd trapped Kell into this new royal life. Kell thought he had wanted fame and fortune, only to realise that what he'd really yearned for was the peace and isolation of his farm. He still missed his old life. He missed the quiet. These days, he was surrounded by people and rarely had a moment alone.

Follis was one of many unctuous aides that had been foisted on him since becoming king. If there was a more annoying person in the Five Kingdoms, Kell had yet to meet them.

"Can't the Queen deal with it by herself?" asked Kell. Sigrid was more than happy to look after the day-to-day issues of running the kingdom. Kell didn't enjoy the responsibility, didn't want it and hadn't been born into it. Not like her. She'd been training for it her entire life. She knew her way around court etiquette. Kell tended to blunder along, and then apologise when he inevitably made a mistake. It was a dance far more intricate than fighting with a sword, and one he had no desire to master.

"I'm afraid Her Majesty requires your help with this task," said Follis. He didn't want to be here either. They both knew he would rather be dealing with the Queen. Follis knew better than to intrude on his private time. That meant it was serious.

"Fine," Kell conceded. "We're done for today," he said, saluting Odd with his blade.

"Majesty," said Odd, giving him a short bow.

"Any improvement?" asked Kell, hopeful.

Odd see-sawed a hand. "Maybe."

At least he wasn't getting any worse. "I'll see you tomorrow."

Kell poured a jug of water over his head, letting it run down his chest, then wiped a towel down his body. He scrubbed most of the water from his short-cropped hair and left the rest to dry. Turning up slightly dishevelled would annoy his wife, but it couldn't be helped. Besides, it seemed there were few things about him that didn't annoy her.

It wasn't Kell's fault that Sigrid's late father had chosen him as heir. It also wasn't his fault that tradition in the Five Kingdoms dictated that only a boy could inherit the throne. As an only child, Sigrid had been forced to marry him in order to become queen. It also wasn't his fault that their baby daughter had died after three months of a rare disease. Not that it mattered. It felt as if she blamed him for that, too. It had been the final blow which tumbled their house of cards.

Some mornings, before he was fully awake, he thought their daughter was still alive. She'd been so tiny. So perfect. He used to think all babies looked the same, until he'd stared into her eyes for the first time. The grief could have brought them together, but instead it had driven them further apart.

As was their duty, they had produced another heir, their son Marik. He was an utter joy, and a glorious bright spot in a life which Kell otherwise felt trapped by. But the birth of their son had not changed their relationship.

Now they slept in separate rooms and did their best to avoid each other as much as possible. Unfortunately, despite the size of the palace, it wasn't always possible, and the times where they crossed paths felt awkward.

But they still had jobs to do. These days, Kell didn't bother trying for a kingly façade. He dealt with everyone as himself. It was simpler and more honest. The Honest King of Algany. That's what some had taken to calling him. There were worse monikers in the history books.

The royal court was a far cry from Kell's farm in Honaje. It had been hard physical labour with long hours, but at least it had been honest work. He didn't know if anything he did these days actually made a difference to the lives of others.

When he'd finished dressing in his uncomfortable royal finery, he gestured for Follis to lead the way. Kell's boots echoed along the corridors of the palace. It was nice and quiet in this part of the building, far away from the daily bustle. There were always so many visitors in the palace, with people coming and going.

Every day he tried to find a little time for himself, away from his duties as king. It was difficult, but he always managed it. Without that break, he became cranky and impatient. More so than usual.

Over the last two years, everyone around Kell had learned about his need for solitude. They didn't understand it, but they made an allowance. Most found peace in prayer. For him it used to be the farm. Now, Kell found it honing his skill with a blade. It allowed him to block out everything and focus only on the moment. To forget everything that existed outside the chalk circle. It made the rest of his life bearable.

By the time he reached the heart of the palace, Kell had settled into the mantle of his new role. He smiled and nodded when people greeted him. As far as anyone outside the palace knew, he was a happy and enthusiastic king. Over time, he'd become adept at putting on a mask and playing to the audience. If he were still alive, Vahli would have been proud.

Kell diverted from the most direct route to the throne room, so that he could speak with the petitioners. As ever, there was a line of people waiting to have their grievance settled by someone in authority. Sigrid hated it when he did this, focused on the small stuff, so it was a good thing she wasn't around. Follis tutted at the minor delay, but held his tongue.

Today there were thirty people standing or sitting in a line. All of them could have been one of his old neighbours; farmers, labourers, craftspeople and a few merchants. Their faces lit up with genuine warmth as he approached. Such an honest reaction was missing from his daily affairs.

Kell shook hands, listened to a few stories, traded a couple of jokes and was disappointed when, a few minutes later, someone tugged on his sleeve.

"Majesty, we must be going," insisted Follis.

The atmosphere instantly changed. The people stepped back, remembering he was someone special. For a brief moment, he'd been one of them again. An ordinary man, talking with his neighbours about their daily struggles. Now, they were looking at him in a way he didn't like.

Kell quickly turned away so he didn't have to see the adoration and awe. It was the kind of look he'd dreamed about receiving as a young lad. One reserved for heroes and figures from legend. Now it made him feel sick.

What's wrong, hero? whispered a voice in his head. If Kell squinted he could almost see Vahli, striding down the corridor towards him. He would have loved being a member of the royal court. All of that power and influence. All of the political wrangling and verbal sparring that hid people's real agenda. Kell could have appointed him as the Royal Bard, and forced him to perform the Medina saga out of spite.

"Something amusing, your Majesty?" asked Follis.

"No. Nothing," said Kell.

Two members of the Raven were on duty guarding the doors to the throne room. They were always stoic. Kell had never seen one of them lose their temper. Today, both guards were visibly unsettled. A strange form of relief washed over their faces as Kell approached. Before he could ask, they pulled open the doors and practically shoved him inside.

The room had been cleared of all non-essential people, making it feel cavernous. With only five people inside, Kell had never seen it so quiet. Queen Sigrid was sat on her throne, and lurking off to one side was Lukas, the King's Steward. Two more members of the Raven were on duty inside the room.

As Kell entered, Sigrid rose from her seat. Much to his surprise she was pleased to see him. Her eyes flicked to the stranger in the room and then back. There was a question there as if, somehow, she expected him to have the answer. As if he'd known this day was coming.

Even before the figure turned around, Kell knew who it was. There was no mistaking the pale, blue-grey skin, the long bony limbs, the white hair and tapered head. It was Willow, the Alfár.

Many times in his dreams, Kell had seen her yellow-on-black eyes, but it was still a shock to see them again in person.

As they stared at one another across the room, his mind flooded with memories of their journey together. His return to the Frozen North. Their battle with deranged beasts and evil spirits. The ever-changing maze inside the huge castle, and the second death of the Ice Lich. Inevitably, he thought about the friends who had accompanied them.

Kell had liked to imagine that when he was old, and had only a few teeth, they would meet up again and talk about the good old days. Now, he wondered if anything like that would ever happen. He hadn't heard from the others since his return to Algany. They were probably just busy, dealing with affairs of state as rulers of the Summer Isles.

Willow's presence, and the urgency of the summons, had put everyone on edge. Since the time of Kell's grandfather, everyone had heard the stories, but few had seen an Alfár in the flesh. There had been no new sightings of Willow for two years.

Her return was an ominous portent of bad tidings.

"Hello," said Kell, maintaining eye contact as he approached. Willow had saved his life many times over. Unlike the others, he wasn't afraid, but today Kell sensed there was something else between them. An uncomfortable pressure. A question she wanted him to ask. "Are you well?"

Willow tilted her head, not avoiding the question, but visibly agitated in her own way. She rarely shouted or screamed. She had all of the same emotions as humans, but the physical tells were small and slight. He tried to work out what was upsetting his old friend.

Vahli's famous saga about Kell's second adventure barely mentioned the Alfár. The modified version was easier for people to understand. No one really knew what to make of the Alfár and, as a result, didn't care about them. Kell understood the reasons for the omission, but he didn't like it. Although he was sure Willow didn't care about fame or even a reward.

Looking at the startled faces, Kell remembered that as far as most people knew, Willow had died in the Frozen North with the others. All heroism in the story had been laid solely at his feet, which in turn, had led to great fortune for the kingdom of Algany. To see her again, alive and in the flesh, was causing quite a stir. Kell could see why Sigrid had emptied the throne room. The fewer people that knew Willow was still alive, the better. But he didn't think it was their shock and alarm that had upset her. As one of few Alfár in the Five Kingdoms, she experienced that wherever she went.

And then it came to him. Willow's exclusion from the saga had cost him little. Just a promise that one day, in the future, if she needed his help Kell would give it, no questions asked.

"I made you a promise," said Kell, crossing the room and gripping one of her hands. Her skin was just as warm as he remembered. "Do you need my help?"

It was the right question. Relief showed in every angle of her body and a smile touched the corners of her mouth. Willow squeezed his hand in thanks.

Whatever the reason for Willow's visit, Kell was pleased to see her. It was a reminder of who he used to be. A person that, over time, he had grown to like and better understand.

"My people are in danger," said Willow. It had been a long time since he had heard the Alfár's peculiar sing-song voice, but it was not something he would ever forget. The others in the room were already shocked, but now they looked worried about what was unfolding. Even Lukas, the King's Steward, who was rarely lost for words, was off balance. There was no formal court etiquette for dealing with an Alfár. It was unknown territory for all of them, except Kell.

"What do you need me to do?" he asked.

"Come with me, to my homeland," said Willow.

"Can you tell me what's happened?" said Kell, hoping for more details, although it was a risk. Often Willow didn't feel comfortable talking about personal matters in front of strangers. However, there were only four other people in the room and it seemed she was willing to share.

"Do you remember how the beasts of the Frozen North had been altered?" asked Willow.

"How could I forget?" said Kell.

The Ice Lich had used her stolen powers to change their nature. Some had been driven into a frenzied rage, so severe, that the beasts had maimed themselves in their attempt to kill him and the others. Sometimes in his nightmares, Kell would run across those ice fields again, trying to escape the beasts. The ice would break beneath his feet and he would sink into freezing cold water, only to be torn apart by the savage bone sharks.

Sigrid was staring at Kell as if he was a stranger. From the beginning, he had told her the truth about his return to the Frozen North and the power of the Ice Lich. Maybe a small part of her had thought he'd made it up. Or maybe, like everyone else, she'd just never seen an Alfár.

A side door opened and Odd came into the room, dressed once more in his Raven uniform. He observed the strange tableau but said nothing, then took up his post beside the throne. If he was rattled, it didn't show.

"I remember that the beasts were driven berserk," said Kell, turning back to Willow. "It was the Lich's influence."

"At first, I thought it was something else. It's why I've been here for so many cycles," said Willow, turning both hands in a tumbling circle. Kell didn't know if she meant months or years. "My kinsman, Ravvi, and I came here, searching for the Malice."

"What is that?"

Willow tilted her head back and made an awful keening sound which echoed off the walls. The Raven were immediately on edge, drawing their weapons, but Kell waved them back. It was a cry of anguish and suffering. When the echo had faded, Willow stared at Kell again, her eyes burning with fury.

"A long time ago, my homeland became infected with a blight. At first, the changes were small and no one noticed. It trickled through the soil, slept beneath the sand, the bark of trees and even our skin. Over time, it showed in the plants and then the animals. We named it the Malice. The twisted versions that it produced were cruel. Beasts were driven into a rage, consuming their own and taking glee in their savagery. Plants tricked and trapped their prey. Poisoned fruit created madness and horrors in the mind.

"The Malice consumes and remakes all that it touches. It is relentless, and all of our attempts to stop it failed. Ravvi and I came to your Five Kingdoms in search of a cure. When I heard of the changes, in the weather and the beasts, I feared the Malice had spread."

"Is it here?" asked Sigrid. Her face was pale, and Kell knew that her first thought concerned the safety of their son.

"No. It was the Lich," said the Alfár, tilting her head to one side, regarding the Queen at an angle. "I was worried we had brought it with us, but it cannot pass through the doorway. The Five Kingdoms are safe."

"What happens if your people can't stop the Malice?" asked Sigrid.

Willow didn't need to say it. Kell could see the answer in her eyes. If left unchecked, the Malice would consume the Alfár's homeland and then continue to spread.

"Our search has been long and difficult. Ravvi has finally lost hope. Now, he clings to the idea of a cure that comes from a dark ritual." Willow turned her head to one side and spat on the floor. He'd never seen such a visceral response of disgust from her. Kell was certain he didn't want to know the details of such a ritual. "It will fail," she continued. "And could even make it worse. He must be stopped."

Kell didn't hesitate. "When do we leave?"

Some of the anguish eased from Willow's features and her half smile returned. Perhaps she had thought he would not honour his promise to her.

"Now," said Willow, gesturing towards her belongings on the far side of the room.

"I'm ready," said Kell.

CHAPTER 2

If she were alone, Sigrid would have said something out loud. Ordered herself to stop staring at the Alfár, and contribute something to the conversation. Instead, she pinched the skin on her right hand until the pain gave her a jolt. Willow was alive. Sigrid, like everyone else, had believed that the Alfár was dead. The Vahli saga had been very clear about Kell being the only survivor.

Kell was discussing plans for the journey, as if the Alfár was just another person. A small part of her had believed they were just a myth. A childish fairy tale, like flying horses.

Her mind was struggling to come to terms with the most obvious fact.

Willow wasn't human.

The shape of her skull was all wrong. Her eyes were terrifying, and then there was her voice. It sounded as if two people were talking at once.

Sigrid was slipping again. She dug her fingernails into the palms of her hand until she was sure they bled.

"How long will the journey take?" Sigrid asked, making Kell and the Alfár turn towards her. She flinched when the Alfár's yellow-on-black eyes looked at her. They were unlike anything she'd ever seen in her life. "Aren't you going to introduce me?"

Sigrid moved to stand beside them, even though her instincts told her to run screaming from the room. One half of her mind was teetering on the edge of madness. The other half – where rigid formality defined all encounters – took over, which came as an enormous relief.

Kell sighed, clearly frustrated by her need for decorum in all circumstances. Sigrid wasn't about to apologise. It was a part of who she was. It provided her with structure to cope with difficult situations, just like this one. It was one of many reasons they were an imperfect match.

"Sigrid, this is my friend, Willow. Willow, this is my wife, the Queen," said Kell with exaggerated care.

Sigrid raised a hand towards the Alfár, but then faltered as Willow focused on her. Willow looked down at Sigrid's hand as if she didn't know what to do with it, glanced at Kell and gave him a lopsided smile.

Sigrid lowered her hand, hoping that her husband would say something to fill the awkward silence. Instead, he kept his mouth closed. At first, she thought it was his way of getting back at her for insisting on the appropriate decorum. Then she realised it was something else. He didn't know what to do either.

"Wife?" asked Willow.

"We are bound as a couple," said Kell, talking to the Alfár as if she were a child. He even mimed the joining of their wrists from the marriage ceremony. It had taken months of planning, but in the end, it had been a wonderful day. The cathedral had been packed with people, and Sigrid thought it an auspicious start to their relationship. It hadn't taken long to fall apart.

"We pair together," said Kell.

"Ah, I see. Have you mated?" asked Willow, and this time it was Kell who smiled. Sigrid couldn't tell if the Alfár was mocking them, or she simply didn't understand. Sigrid's instincts were of no use. Willow's body language gave nothing away about her thoughts.

"We have a son," said Kell, beaming with pride. Despite his faults, Sigrid knew that Kell loved Marik and would do anything for him. She knew that his own father had been absent during his childhood. Kell was determined that it wouldn't be like that for their child. He wasn't interested in state affairs, but he was an active participant in their son's upbringing.

"We must leave soon," said the Alfár, apparently finished with small talk.

"I just need to gather supplies for the journey," said Kell.

"You can't just leave," said Sigrid. She wouldn't exactly be sad to see him go, but he was still the king of Algany. He couldn't disappear for days, or even weeks, to go on an adventure. Some days, he seemed to forget that he wasn't a farmer.

"Why not?" asked Kell.

Now she knew he was mocking her. "You have responsibilities."

"Lukas, don't rulers sometimes go on diplomatic missions to other nations? To encourage trade and broker peace?" said Kell, bringing the King's Steward into their conversation. Lukas slowly approached, uncomfortable at intruding, and nervous about being close to the Alfár.

There was a long, awkward pause before Lukas finally answered. "Yes, they do." The Steward backed away a few steps, giving them a modicum of privacy.

"There. You can tell people I've gone on one of those trips. Besides," said Kell, lowering his voice so that the others in the room couldn't hear, "we both know you're better than me at this."

"That's not the point," she said, not exactly disagreeing. "You shouldn't leave."

"But this is what you've wanted since the beginning, right?" he continued whispering. Sigrid glanced at Willow, the only one close enough to overhear their intimate conversation. The Alfár was watching them, but her expression remained blank.

"You haven't thought it through. You don't even know what you'll be facing, or where you're going," said Sigrid, ticking items off on her fingers. "Or even what the weather will be like."

"It doesn't matter," he said stubbornly. "I made a promise and I intend to keep it, no matter the cost."

At that moment, she hated him for his loyalty to the Alfár. Kell had never shown her the same level of devotion. Their relationship had been awkward from the start. After the birth of their daughter, it had improved, but then rapidly declined when she'd died. It was far easier to hate him and mourn in private. Sigrid knew he wasn't to blame for what had happened; mostly she blamed her father for going along with tradition. But she couldn't tell Kell that. A wall had grown between them that wouldn't be breached with an apology. It would be too little, too late.

From his expression, she knew Kell's mind was made up. Compromise was always difficult for him but there were some issues where he would not be moved. Those conversations always ended the same. Jaw clenched. Furrowed brow. Grinding his teeth. It was easier just to walk away.

"How long will this journey take?" she asked, turning to the Alfár.

Willow was so still and silent, it would have been easy for Sigrid to forget she was even there, if not for the seed of anxiety in her stomach.

"Many cycles. It will be some time," said Willow.

"How long is a cycle?"

"She doesn't see time as we do," said Kell, "but I think it could be a few months."

Kell had always told her the Alfár weren't human, but she hadn't really believed him. She had thought they were just another tribe of humans. Only now, being face to face with one, was she beginning to understand how wrong she'd been.

"Well, you can't go by yourself," said Sigrid, trying a different approach. "It wouldn't be safe or appropriate."

The moment the word appropriate was out of her mouth, Sigrid knew it was a mistake. Kell flinched as if slapped. It was one of the things he hated the most about being king.

Being appropriate. Only doing what was right for someone of his station. She knew he still thought of himself as a common man. Most of the time, he didn't seem to notice how people looked at him. He was a hero in their eyes.

Kell folded his arms and, without moving, the distance between them grew.

"If it's going to be dangerous, then you should at least take some protection," she added, hoping he'd listen to reason.

"Four can make the journey. Four is hallowed. Four is cunning," said Willow, startling everyone. There was a strange rhythm to the words. As if it was part of a ritual or prayer.

Without turning her head, Willow pointed a finger at one of the Raven by the throne and then another by the far door. The first was Odd. He was a good choice for a bodyguard. His skill with a blade was remarkable, even amongst the Raven. Besides, there was something about him that always made Sigrid feel a little uncomfortable. She would feel more comfortable with him out of the palace.

Sigrid thought Willow's second choice was a bad idea. Like all members of the Raven, Yarra had earned her position by excelling far beyond a normal soldier. However, she also had blood on her hands.

"Agreed. We'll leave tomorrow at dawn," said Kell.

Sigrid wanted to talk him out of taking Yarra, but now wasn't the time. Kell left the throne room with the Alfár in tow. Lukas was visibly torn with whom to follow. He opened his mouth to discuss what had just happened, but he also needed to make preparations for the journey. She gestured for him to see to the king's needs. Their conversation could wait a little longer.

Sigrid stared at her son asleep in his crib. She'd always known that children would be an important part of her life, but she'd never felt a yearning for them. Her friends had told her that it would come. That it would be different when it was her own flesh and blood, but she hadn't believed them. Holding her daughter for the first time had changed everything.

Now, her first thought in any situation wasn't about herself. To live that way was selfish when she had someone who relied so heavily on her. Every decision had to be carefully weighed, with all risks considered. She knew that most parents went through something similar but, as queen, the outcome of her choices had wider-reaching consequences. Now, she often thought about the impact on all children in Algany, not just her son.

Marik fussed in his crib, vigorously kicking his legs. Sigrid calmed him with a gentle touch, stroking his forehead with two fingers. His furrowed brow, a mirror of his father's expression, relaxed and he settled down.

Kell was being selfish. Even if she didn't need him, their son would in the years to come. Every child wants to know their father, if only to know what to rebel against. Without Kell around, people would tell Marik stories about him that were full of heroism and sacrifice, danger and adventure. The truth, of course, was always more complicated, and full of contradictions.

The door to the nursery opened and Bessy, one of Marik's nursemaids, came into the room. Sigrid had carefully screened every person who would be looking after her son. Bessy had a wide, kind face and her huge laugh filled the room. She had three grown children and one grandchild on the way. Sigrid knew that Marik would come to adore Bessy, just as she did.

Leaving Marik to his rest, she crept from the room. Lukas waited in the corridor outside. Sigrid took a deep breath, then led the way to her study. It wasn't long ago that it had belonged to her father. It was where he'd conducted all of the daily business that didn't require the formality of the throne room.

As she sat down behind the desk, Sigrid could still picture her father in the same worn leather seat, pouring over an urgent message or writing in his journal.

Despite having prepared for the role her entire life, it had still been a daunting task to take over from him on a permanent basis.

"What news?" she asked.

"Another group of missionaries from–"

"The King, Lukas," she said, cutting him off. Other matters would have to wait. "What's happening with the King?"

"Nothing we say will change his mind, Sigrid," said Lukas, dropping all formality.

"Tell me something I don't know."

"Apparently the Alfár's homeland is in the east, across the Narrow Sea."

Well, that was new. No one really knew where the Alfár came from, although there had always been speculation that it was somewhere far beyond Corvan. Some of the land in the east was inhabited, although few people from the Five Kingdoms had ever travelled that far. Other than merchants, not many found a reason to cross the Narrow Sea. It would explain why there had been so few sightings over the years.

"We have to change his mind about taking Yarra. He should choose someone else," said Sigrid. If she couldn't stop him from going, then the best way to give him a fighting chance of coming back was better protection. Sending all twelve of the Raven would be the ideal solution, but she knew no one would agree to that. "Suggest Semira or Hanno. Either one of them is a better choice."

"I'll speak to him about it," promised Lukas. Sigrid couldn't approach Kell directly. He wouldn't listen to her. Slow and subtle worked far better with him.

"Thank you, Lukas."

"You seem distracted. Are you worried that he won't come back?"

"Of course I am," said Sigrid. "Whatever our personal problems, he's still my husband and the father of our child."

Kell's fame had a number of political benefits, but right now she didn't care about any of that. Her job was to focus on the bigger picture. Her personal relationships and feelings should have no bearing on the situation.

If only it were that simple.

"And if Kell dies on another adventure, he will become a martyr. That will cause more problems with the Holy City and Reverend Mother Britak," said Sigrid.

The old priestess took every opportunity to highlight the apparent blasphemies and inconsistencies in the Vahli saga. As Kell was the only survivor, the Reverend Mother often insinuated that he was a liar. She believed that the improvement in the weather was part of a natural cycle. That it had nothing to do with the death of the Ice Lich. Britak was dedicated to bringing the teachings of the Shepherd to the Five Kingdoms, and she saw any form of hero worship as idolatry.

"So, that's the real reason you want him to come back?" said Lukas.

"No. Marik will need his father."

"What about you? What do you need?"

Sigrid considered the question but couldn't find an answer. Lukas gave her an infuriating grin on his way out. He knew that the questions would rattle around in her head until she found the answers. She needed Kell, and didn't want him to leave.

Kell had sacrificed a great deal for his country, but then so had she to become queen. Perhaps things would have been different if they had been given a chance to get to know one another. Instead, they'd been married a few weeks after her father's funeral. While she'd been struggling with her grief, Kell had been filled with resentment for being trapped in a life he didn't want. In such a barren wasteland, with no shared moments of joy, there had been no time for affection or even mutual respect. Their coupling had been dispassionate and almost formal, to produce an heir.

In spite of everything that had happened, she knew that

Kell was a good man. He wouldn't be here, otherwise. He could have ignored her father's dying wish, abandoned her and gone home to live on the farm. If he hadn't taken the throne, without an appointed successor, the country would have been thrown into disarray and civil war. Kell had stayed. For Algany, for her father, but also for her.

What she really needed was simple, honest, yet painful to admit. She needed him. Doing this by herself was difficult. It was a daily struggle, and worst of all, it was lonely. Sigrid didn't know how her father had done it for so many years after her mother had died. The thought of doing it all for the next forty or fifty years, with no one to confide in and no one to share it with, filled her with dread.

Perhaps, when Kell returned, they could try to start afresh? Raise their baby son together, and develop new positive memories. Love might not be possible but perhaps, in time, there could at least be some affection between them.

A few hours later, Sigrid found herself pacing back and forth outside Kell's door. She'd run through what she wanted to say to him several times, about a fresh start and working together. There was a lot she needed to tell him.

Before she lost her nerve, Sigrid knocked and waited. When Kell opened the door, all of her prepared statements vanished from her mind. He stared at her expectantly, waiting for her to say something. Instead of talking, Sigrid kissed him.

Much to her delight, she felt a spark between them. Once Kell's surprise had faded, he kissed her back. She shoved the door closed and then she was pulling at his shirt, tugging it off over his head. He fumbled with the buttons on her dress and she helped, grinning like a teenager, while he laughed and kicked off his boots. They fell onto the bed and the next hour disappeared into a haze of intensity she'd not felt in a long time.

Afterwards, they lay together staring at the ceiling. She could hear him breathing deeply, but didn't think he was asleep. When she touched his chest, he shifted around and laid a hand on top of hers. His skin was still warm and she moved closer to him, sharing body heat. She didn't want to spoil the moment, but her mind wouldn't rest. It inevitably turned towards his departure.

"It wasn't like that before, right?" she asked.

"Oh, no. I think I'd remember," said Kell. She could hear the smile in his voice. "Not that I'm complaining, but, why now?"

Sigrid shifted around until she could see his face. "I'm sorry. I was blaming you for things that weren't your fault. That wasn't fair."

"I'm sorry as well. I was angry at your father for so long," said Kell with a sigh. "I shouldn't have taken it out on you. We should have talked about this at the start. Why didn't we?"

"Shock. Grief. Pride. Take your pick."

A comfortable silence settled between them.

"This wasn't to try and make you stay," said Sigrid, gesturing at the tangled sheets and scattered clothes. "I had a speech planned."

"What kind of speech?"

"When you get back, I want to start afresh. I want us to do all of it together. Raising our son, being a family, ruling Algany. How does that sound?"

Kell smiled and Sigrid's creeping fear eased away as he pulled her close. "I would like that more than anything."

There was more she wanted to say, but the bond between them was as delicate as a spider's web. If she pulled on it too soon, it would break. Instead, she said nothing and decided to enjoy their remaining time together.

CHAPTER 3

Odd had been given the rest of the day off to see to his affairs because, in the morning, he would be riding out with the king.

Odd seriously thought about refusing his orders, but he knew the repercussions would be grave. He would lose his position as a member of the Raven, but even worse than that would be the questions. They'd want to know why he rejected the command, and he wouldn't be able to give them a satisfying answer. Then, of course, he'd be locked up in a cell, and that would be a death sentence.

The other alternative was to run. Build a new life somewhere in the Five Kingdoms, but he liked that idea even less. The only sensible thing he could do was travel with the king and hope for the best. For someone who was normally so risk-averse, it made his skin itch.

They were going to visit the unseen lands of the Alfár. Kell had told them that it was somewhere across the Narrow Sea. They would find out the rest in due course. He knew nothing about the terrain and, under such circumstances, it was difficult to prepare.

The biggest problem Odd faced was that no one knew how long they would be away. The king had estimated it would be at least two to three months. The King's Steward would pay his rent until his return, so that didn't concern him. Some of the Raven lived within the palace grounds, but a few like him, and some with families, preferred to be in the city. Odd lived alone and craved isolation. Most thought his solitude was spent in prayer. Out of the twelve members of the Raven, everyone believed him the most devout. The truth, however, was more complicated.

From an early age, his mother had warned him that others wouldn't understand. Shortly after his twelfth birthday, Odd had realised that he was different from other children and that his family was atypical too. Most of them had two parents. Like him, a few had only one, but a missing father wasn't what separated him from the others.

It was always there, lurking in the back of his mind. The hunger had been quiet of late, but it was never sated, only asleep. Sometimes he thought of it like a bear, and when it awoke after hibernation, it was ravenous. If he didn't feed the hunger, the complaints would get louder and more intense, until it felt as if he were being torn apart inside.

Odd loved routine. It provided safety. A framework so he knew how to act in any situation. People relied on him to be in uniform, and on duty, at a certain time of day. There was no room for negotiation or discussion, which was perfect.

Outside of work, he'd created his own structure so that he could function. He had carefully allocated slices of time for reading, sleeping, exercising, eating meals and even socialising with others, as long as it was done in a controlled environment. There was also time for prayer, or at least the semblance of it, for the benefit of others.

He didn't believe in the Shepherd, but the hour he spent every day in a silent imitation of prayer provided him with clarity of thought. Without it, he would become lazy and likely to make mistakes. If that happened, the cracks would begin to show in his stories. That would lead to more questions which would get him into trouble.

Odd always hurried everywhere. Time was precious, and today that was especially true. There was much to do before the morning. There were some personal issues that could not wait. Whatever lay ahead, he needed to do this now. It increased the risk, but he didn't have a choice.

Two small children playing in the street saw him coming and immediately began to imitate his fast gait. Their exaggerated version of his walk wasn't amusing, but he knew a smile was required. He'd become very adept at pretence. Sometimes it still took him a while to work out the appropriate response, but most of the time it had become a reflex. He didn't understand much of it, but it was necessary for his survival. He had to blend in with everyone else. If he didn't, they would find out his secret, then they would kill him.

He'd seen it happen before.

It had been drilled into him, from an early age, by his mother. He was special, but if others found out, they would be scared and try to hurt him. So, he'd done nothing to stand out, even when his abilities far exceeded the people around him.

His mother was like him. She had the hunger. But one mistake had cost her life, leaving him alone in the world at fifteen. Thankfully, by then, he'd already become skilled at being unremarkable. After only two years in an orphanage, he'd been able to join the army. From there, he had gradually risen through the ranks, eventually earning his position as a member of the Raven. Demonstrating a fraction of his abilities had been necessary in order to progress, but unlike some, he didn't like showing off.

The two boys in the street soon grew tired of imitating him and quickly fell away. On the stairs up to his room, Odd ran into his landlady, Madam Ovette, which required him to make appropriate small-talk.

"Hello, Madam. Are you well?" he asked, forcing a smile.

"Oh, I'm well, thank you, Odd. Very well. Just heading to the market before it closes," she said, brandishing a basket. Madam Ovette always tried to get a few bargains at the end of the day.

"How is the family?" he asked, knowing that she had a

growing number of grandchildren. He didn't enquire after anyone specific, as it would only highlight her flagging memory.

"They're good, growing up so fast. It seems like only last year that Tommen was born, but now he's shaving!"

Tommen was eleven, so hadn't hit puberty. She was talking about Barden, a different grandson, but Odd didn't correct her.

"That's good. Well, I must go, king's business," he said, giving her another smile.

"Of course," she said, gesturing for him to go ahead. Odd knew she liked him as a tenant because he never caused any problems, and always paid his rent on time. As a landlady for one of the Raven, his presence had also improved her standing in the local community. It meant she never questioned him too closely, and made no comment about the irregular hours he kept. As far as she knew, it was all official business.

He gave her a final wave and went up to the top floor of the building.

Finally alone, Odd double checked the door was locked, stripped out of his uniform and hung it up in his wardrobe. Standing naked in the centre of the room, Odd took a moment to study his reflection in the mirror. Every inch of his dark skin shimmered with vitality. He was almost thirty and he'd never been stronger or fitter. Odd wasn't as tall or as broad across the chest as some, and his features were considered plain by many, but apparently he had a friendly smile. He tried it out, feeling the muscles shift across his face, but the warmth didn't reach his grey eyes. When in civilian clothing, it was easy for Odd to disappear into a crowd, which made things simpler.

Made from a local hardwood, his bed had taken four strong men to carry upstairs. But with one hand, Odd lifted one side of the bed. He nudged open a floorboard beneath with his foot and, with the bed still held aloft, he bent down and pulled out a set of clothes.

The garments were cheap and, most importantly, plain. The boots were worn, but the soles were thick and sturdy. Normally

Odd planned such trips well in advance, but it might be several months before he came home. It worried him a great deal but, as there was nothing he could do about it, he put it from his mind. Today's problem was sating the hunger. Tomorrow, he would deal with what came next.

Odd lowered the bed and quickly dressed. In the mirror he imagined a completely different man. Staring at his features, he saw them shift in the glass. The changes were slight – a tilt of his eyes, the width of his nose, a new cleft in his chin – but they dramatically altered his appearance. At first glance, a friend might think he was a relative to Odd, but definitely not the same person.

Today he didn't have an hour to spend collecting his thoughts. Instead, he meditated for ten minutes, going over the location in his mind, the people he'd seen and the name of the tavern. He'd been preparing for this visit for almost a month.

Feeling calm, Odd left his building and headed southwest across the city. Two streets away from home his gait changed, becoming a rolling limp, as if one of his hips was locked. He imagined it had been caused by a mishap with a horse, or a defect from birth. His shoulders slumped and he made a point of avoiding eye contact. The people who saw him felt pity, or they were offended by his disability. None would remember his face, or how he was dressed. If questioned, they would only remember that they'd seen a cripple with a limp. He'd become invisible in plain sight.

Odd was forced to slow his pace as the crowd thickened and the streets became choked with people. The taverns in this part of the city attracted those with little money, so the drinks were cheap and the food was plain. This wasn't the kind of place one would visit for the ambience. The modest tavern he'd chosen was called *The Gallows Glee*.

The crowd inside was a blend of manual workers, merchants with only one or two ribbons on their tricorn hats, and a shifting sea of faces passing by. In addition to locals, there were a couple of Hundarians, a pair of broad-faced Seith, and even a table of pale-skinned Corvanese from across the Narrow Sea.

Odd took a stool at the bar, bought a mug of frothy ale and kept his head down. Breathing in the hoppy fumes, he let his mind drift, looking about the room.

The mix of conversations washed over him. Most of them were people sharing their worries. Money was the biggest gripe, and second was a spouse. There was some laughter in the room, but it was harsh and often cruel. There were no hookahs on the tables, but a few customers were chewing tobacco, their teeth stained yellow and brown.

A few people idly met his gaze. He ignored them and went back to his drink. The one he'd come for wasn't a bold man. It took a while for Odd to find him amongst the crowd.

When a game of cards sprang up in one corner, Odd drifted over, keeping a watchful eye on the rest of the room. It wasn't a high-stakes game, but several people stood observing in companionable silence.

Odd stood beside one of the Corvanese merchants. He was slightly shorter than Odd, and his clothes were dusty from travel. Even his black tricorn hat was mostly grey, the two ribbons bedraggled and frayed. The skin on his pink cheeks was marked with old scars from a childhood pox, and his eyes were deep green.

They exchanged a friendly nod and refocused on the game.

"Do you gamble?" asked Odd.

The merchant regarded him with unfriendly eyes. "No."

"Me neither. Too much risk. I've learned my lesson."

The merchant grunted and Odd waited for the inevitable. One of the players was doing much better than the others. A tidy stack of coins sat in front of him and the other three eyed him suspiciously. As far as Odd could tell, the man wasn't cheating; he'd just had a very good run of cards.

"Lose some money?" the merchant eventually asked.

Odd slowly shook his head. "Wife. She found out about the girlfriend."

One of merchant's blond eyebrows lifted in surprise. "Two women?"

Keeping his eye on the game, Odd shrugged. "Now she wants money every week, otherwise she'll tell my foreman. He's devout, so I could lose my job."

The merchant grunted. Odd knew it wasn't the promiscuity that interested the merchant, but there was a distinctive frisson of energy. "A bad deal," he commiserated.

"Worst part is, the girlfriend left me too. Now I have to listen to the wife endlessly scold me. She never shuts up."

"Sounds like my wife," said the merchant, taking a sip of his beer. "Likes to remind me of my mistakes."

"Maybe we should just kill them for a bit of peace," whispered Odd. He laughed and the merchant joined in, although there had been a slight hesitation. "At least it would be quiet," he added. Odd knew he was rushing, so he had to get the balance just right. The merchant was nervous but interested.

"I'll drink to that," said the merchant and they clinked mugs.

The winning player at the card table was starting to look worried as he scooped another hand. The other three were scowling. It wouldn't be long before someone accused the winner of cheating.

"Maybe I should become a merchant," mused Odd. "More time away from home sounds good to me."

"The problem is she's always there when you get back," grumbled the merchant. "Mine saves up her bitterness, like pennies in a jar, then smashes it when I get home."

"Yours sounds worse than mine. Maybe I should kill her as well. Do you a favour!" Odd nudged the merchant and chuckled, but the other man didn't laugh. Odd felt as if he were balancing on a razor's edge. "What?" he asked, feigning ignorance.

"You've thought about it, haven't you?" asked the merchant.

There was a familiar look in his eyes that Odd recognised. Another person would be shocked, or appalled. The merchant was curious.

"It's just talk," said Odd, backing out of the conversation.

"Right, just talk," said the other man.

The winning player was doing his best to avoid a fight. He hadn't admitted to being a cheat, and yet had still offered the others their money back. Odd noticed the man sat on the winner's right was smirking. He'd been cheating the whole time, bottom dealing cards. Two of the players grabbed the winner, while the real cheat used the misdirection to pocket all of the money.

The tavern owner appeared with a wooden baton which he hammered on the table. The fight abruptly ended before it began and all four men were escorted to the door. Whatever happened on the street was their business. The crowd of onlookers dispersed and Odd drifted back to the bar.

Odd could feel the merchant's stare from across the room. The man was trying to act casual, but he was interested. He hadn't killed yet, but one day soon, he would. Out of convenience and because he hated her, it would probably start with his wife. After that, if he wasn't caught, it would be someone chosen with greater care. He would despair about his urges, maybe even consider taking his own life, but inevitably he would kill again. It would become a part of him, until it was the centre of his life, and everything else was a shadow.

When the merchant didn't approach him, Odd was certain he'd come on too strong. Normally it took several meetings, spread out over a couple of weeks, but there wasn't time. It had to be tonight. Just as Odd was beginning to worry, a familiar presence settled beside him at the bar.

"Buy you a drink?" said the merchant.

"No. I've got to get home," said Odd, turning away. "To my wife."

He paused once outside in the street, pretending to enjoy

the fresh air, but in this part of the city it smelled of cheap meat and stale beer. Behind him the front door of the tavern opened and closed. Odd wobbled as if dizzy from too much ale and someone steadied him from behind.

"Thanks," he said, turning to face the good samaritan.

"That's all right," said the merchant.

An uncomfortable silence settled between them. Odd let it stretch out for a while. He was just a man getting ready to go home. The merchant was the one with murder on his mind. "Forget what I said in there. I was just letting off steam," said Odd.

The merchant nervously licked his lips. "Of course."

"I'll see you around."

"What if it wasn't just talk?" asked the merchant.

Odd said nothing and kept his expression neutral. He pretended to consider it for a while. "All of our neighbours know that we fight," Odd said slowly. "The moment she turned up dead, everyone would know it was me." He shook his head but then paused as if an idea had just occurred. "Unless..."

"Unless what?" said the merchant, stepping closer.

Odd grabbed him by the elbow and together they quickly walked to a quiet side street. From there he guided the merchant to the mouth of a narrow alley, wedged between two rows of shops. The owners used it as a dumping ground for stale fruit, and he could hear the skittering of rats. The merchant wrinkled his nose at the smell, but he wasn't aware of the real danger. He was too excited by the prospect of murdering his wife and getting away with it.

"Unless what?" he asked again, desperate for more.

"Unless I was seen by lots of people when she died. Then I couldn't be a suspect."

"And my wife?" he asked, hopeful.

Odd shrugged. "Unfortunately, she was tragically murdered while you were away, where lots of people saw you conducting business," he said gesturing at the merchant's hat.

As the merchant's eyes widened in delight, Odd stabbed him.

He sank his dagger up to the hilt in the merchant's stomach. In the rush of excitement, it took a little time for the pain to register. When it did, he gasped and tried to pull away, but Odd quickly stabbed him four more times.

He finally released the man, who stumbled back, staring at the blood spreading across the front of his shirt. Slowly, so slowly, he realised that his death was imminent. Somehow, when people came this close, they knew instinctively. It was as if a door had opened in his mind. Odd envied the clarity he saw in his victim. The merchant would soon know the answer to the biggest question about life: what happened after death?

The strength began to leech from the man's body, and he would have fallen if Odd hadn't held him upright. The merchant tried to speak, but Odd shook his head. Now wasn't the time for regret or last words.

It was close.

The tingling down Odd's spine told him there was a spectral presence in the alley. The hair stood up on the back of his neck. The air became still. The city fell silent and the world was reduced to the two of them. A doorway opened and the merchant stared at something beyond this life.

Odd moved his mouth close to the merchant's and inhaled deeply at the moment of death. Energy flowed out of the dead man into him, passing down his throat. His chest swelled, his skin felt as if it was on fire, and his whole body thrummed with power.

All too soon it was over, and he was holding up a cooling sack of meat. Odd dropped him in the filth and took his money, to support the idea of it being a robbery.

He wanted to scream, to laugh hysterically and run all the way home. He could do it at a sprint, and would arrive without being out of breath. In the few seconds after, he always felt more alive than at any other time in his life. The energy he'd taken from the merchant made him faster, stronger and more resilient. Injuries healed more quickly, illnesses were shaken off and his body continued to adapt, gradually moving him towards his true self.

Far beneath the red, deeper than the marrow in his bones, on a level he didn't fully understand, Odd knew that he was changing. Becoming something else. Something more than human.

Hiding his true nature on a day-to-day basis was hard enough, but he also had to cover up the true range of his abilities. He was significantly faster than he let on. Whenever Odd sparred with anyone, he had to force himself to hold back, otherwise people would become suspicious.

Instead of running, he walked home at a sedate pace and maintained his limp. He took a winding route back through the city, sticking to quiet streets to make sure he wasn't being followed. His clothes were splashed with blood and, although the shadows were heavy, he made sure no one saw him.

Eventually he made it back to his street, at which point he dropped the façade and walked as himself. At this time of night Madam Ovette would be back in her rooms and, thankfully, he didn't meet any other residents.

Back in his own room, he locked the door, stripped out of his clothes and washed them carefully to remove all the blood. Normally he'd wait for them to dry, but today he stuffed the damp garments back in their hiding place. In the mirror, Odd readjusted his features until he was himself again. Then he searched inside for the hunger.

It was still there, buried deep, but for the time being, it was asleep. Hibernating, like a beast in winter. But Odd knew that, in time, it would awaken and he would have to feed it again.

CHAPTER 4

When he woke up the next morning, Kell's first thought was to sneak out, but this was meant to be a new beginning. Instead, he woke Sigrid by touching her on the shoulder. It took her a few seconds to fully come awake. Kell found he was holding his breath, waiting for her to realise she was in his bed. Much to his relief, when Sigrid noticed her surroundings, she smiled.

"I wasn't sure if you'd be happy to see me," he said.

"I don't have any regrets."

"I have, but not about last night," admitted Kell. "Mostly about agreeing to leave you and Marik behind."

"I know that the Five Kingdoms owes Willow a great debt. I'm not thrilled about you going, but what's the alternative?"

In the silence that followed it was clear that neither one of them had an answer.

"Hopefully it won't take too long." Kell reached for his shirt and started to untangle it.

"Just don't make any promises," said Sigrid, slipping into her dress.

"At least this time, I'll have good bodyguards." With two members of the Raven, and Willow watching his back, no one would get anywhere near him.

"I wanted to talk to you about that."

"I know what you're going to say," said Kell, "but I need someone who's good at thinking on their feet. Yarra is the best strategist in the Raven."

"She's lost faith in herself. You'll have to force the issue."

Kell helped Sigrid refasten the buttons on her dress. "Then I'll have to be brutal."

When they were dressed, a comfortable silence settled between them. "We have a lot to talk about, but it will have to wait until I get back."

"I'll see you in the courtyard," said Sigrid. She gave Kell a kiss and then let him go.

It was still early, but he knew the morning would soon slip away. He expected Lukas would suddenly find urgent business that needed his attention, but for once he could legitimately refuse. Besides, Sigrid was more than capable of handling anything in his absence.

In order to get to Willow's homeland, they needed to cross the Narrow Sea. Ships from Corvan docked at several places up and down the east coast, but the shortest stretch across the water was from the Holy City of Lorzi.

That required Kell and the others to dress in plain clothes to avoid being recognised. Willow would inevitably draw some attention, but even so, Kell hoped they could sneak through the city and board a ship without being detected. If King Roebus, or even worse, Reverend Mother Britak, found out Kell was there, it would cause a number of problems.

Once onboard, they would be in Willow's hands. She would take the lead and Kell would be happy to relinquish control. He'd only led in the past because of his prior experience in the Frozen North.

Willow had given them some ideas of what to expect in terms of temperature, but had been vague about everything else. When he'd asked her about potential threats, she merely said monsters, which was unsettling. She had promised to tell them more once they were underway, and Kell trusted the Alfár to keep her word.

Part of him was tempted to suggest taking more of the Raven, but remaining unnoticed would be difficult enough in the company of an Alfár, let alone a muster of soldiers. The larger the group, the more challenging it would be to slip through the Holy City without attracting any attention. Willow had been intent that four was a good number for whatever lay ahead, and Kell trusted her instincts. King Roebus had spies everywhere, but Kell was more concerned about the Reverend Mother and her goons.

When Kell entered the stables, it was clear that Lukas had been busy making preparations. Three horses were saddled and ready for a long journey. Sat beside each on the straw covered floor was a bulky pack, their contents almost overflowing. Peering inside one he found a sack of food, cold-weather clothing, a tent, flint and tinder, a herb pouch and other supplies for treating injuries. There was also a fishing kit and a dozen more practical items. Lukas had tried his best to plan for every situation.

When all of the horses began to shift about with unease, Kell knew that Willow was nearby. He didn't know why, but no horse could stand being close to the Alfár. There was something about her kind that unsettled the animals.

Sometimes, in his nightmares, Kell was chased by the monstrous Nhill – the thing that had once been a horse. The beast was another part of his second journey to the Frozen North that he desperately wanted to forget.

Kell walked out to meet Willow in the middle of the yard, then led her away to another part of the palace. In a private courtyard, where he practised most days with Odd, they sat together on a bench.

"Tell me the rest," said Kell. He still didn't like speaking in front of a crowd, but had developed a mental callous from doing it so often. On the outside he often looked calm, but inside his stomach would churn. Kell had noticed Willow's unease in the throne room, but only because he knew what to look for. The others were unfamiliar with her subtle expressions and probably thought she was cold and distant. She had all of the same emotions; they were just buried beneath a stony veneer.

"Once we cross the Narrow Sea," said Willow, in her peculiar sing-song voice, "we will make our way to the Dragon Tree. From there we will travel to my homeland. I must warn you, it will be dangerous."

"I expected that. But why do you need us to go with you?"

The Alfár glanced up at the sky but her eyes were far away, trying to find the words, or perhaps it was simpler than that. She was trying to put it into terms that he would understand. In the past, Kell had explained ordinary aspects of their world and she'd been baffled and amazed. It stood to reason that her country would seem equally strange to him.

"The Malice. It has infected everything in my homeland." Willow turned towards him and he saw a shimmer of tears. "It has infected my people."

If it poisoned everything it touched, then it would be difficult to avoid. Perhaps her people had been eating tainted food and drinking poisoned water.

"How badly?"

"Some time ago, the wise among our leaders said we had to run, so that we could live. We fled from our places of rest. Our great city," said Willow, clenching her fists with impotent rage. "Many would not listen. They said it would not affect them, and that those who ran were weak. They debated and argued, back and forth. While the leaders talked, many people continued living normally, oblivious to the danger. Some thought it was a fleeting disease that would pass without incident."

"What happened to those who stayed behind?" said Kell.

"They were swallowed by the Malice and remade. Whole lines of ancestry were gone in one turning. For some, it happened overnight. Others barely noticed they were infected, until it was too late. It trickled into their minds like a creeping fog."

"Did they die?" asked Kell.

"No, they live. But they are not Alfár. Not anymore." Willow's pain was so apparent that he took her hand to offer some comfort. She squeezed his fingers so tightly Kell hissed in pain and she eased her grip. He'd forgotten how strong she was.

"From the moment we enter my homeland, I will become infected again. Your people are different, here," she said, gesturing at his chest and then his head. "The effects will be slower. After a while, I will begin to change as the poison creeps into my body. Gradually, my mind will become fogged and slow. You will have to keep us on course."

"What will the Malice do to me and the others?"

"It will try to change you," said Willow. "It will be subtle. A prickle against your skin. An unusual bad thought that still feels like your own. A harsh word that comes out of nowhere. You must try to hold on to yourself, in here," she said, gently touching the side of his head. "Your eyes will deceive you. Your senses will lie. Listen to your heart. I will need you to tell me who I am and keep me true."

The idea of losing himself was far worse than anything they'd faced in the Frozen North. Beasts could be fought, but if his mind was addled, would he even notice they were in danger? Would he even care if his eyes and ears deceived him?

"I'll do my best," he said, not wanting to make a promise he couldn't keep.

"We must catch Ravvi, my kinsman, as soon as possible," said the Alfár. "He will be alone on his journey. Without a guide, he will succumb quickly to the poison and become…" Willow trailed off, struggling to find the right word. Instead, she swirled her hands with random, jerky movements.

"Chaotic?" suggested Kell, and Willow gave him one of her half smiles.

"Yes, chaotic. And dangerous," she said and her smile faded. "Will you make the journey to my homeland?" asked the Alfár.

The Malice wasn't his problem. It wasn't infecting his people, or his city. He had responsibilities and a family to think about. They would need him in the future, even if the kingdom didn't.

After his conversation with Sigrid he wanted to say no, but

Willow had been willing to sacrifice her life for his cause. How could he live with himself if he wasn't willing to do the same in her hour of need?

"I will travel with you," said Kell, and this time Willow's smile stretched all the way across her face.

A few hours later, they gathered near the stables to say their goodbyes. Kell, Yarra, Odd, Lukas, and a few others. Willow was stood off to one side, watching them with a slightly forlorn expression. Kell wondered how long it had been since she had seen her family, but he didn't dwell on it. The thought of being away from his wife and son for a few months felt deeply uncomfortable. He didn't want to imagine what it was like for Willow.

Since his first day in the palace, a part of Kell always expected it would come to a sudden end. Someone would tell him that there had been a terrible mistake. That he wasn't supposed to be King. Then he'd go back home to his farm and that would be it. He'd done his best to keep everyone at arm's length, learning the minimum about those around him. That would change in the days and weeks ahead. Soon he would know far too much about his companions, including if they snored and the regularity of their bowel movements.

Kell was surprised to discover that Yarra had a sister, called Lea, who had come to say her goodbyes. Yarra had lean, slightly northern features, despite being born in Algany. Her father was from Hundar and she had clearly accentuated her normal clothing to disguise her identity. With a shaven head, three silver earrings in both ears and a stud in her nose, few would think she was a member of the Raven.

Her younger sister must have taken after their mother. She had a softer, kinder face and was quick to smile. Yarra was doing her best to remain stoic, but Lea was teary-eyed, much to the embarrassment of her sister.

Odd was already standing by his horse, ready to depart. No one had come to bid him farewell. For the first time since they'd met, Kell pitied the man.

When Sigrid emerged from inside the palace, carrying their son in her arms, Kell's eyes became misty. The idea of being separated from Marik for weeks, possibly months, made him feel physically sick. But unlike grief, which could ease over time, the longer he was away, the worse the feeling would become. The only advantage of going now was that Marik was so young. Hopefully, he wouldn't remember Kell's absence. He spoke nonsense to his son and kissed him several times, before handing him to Bessy.

There was little chance of privacy, but Kell moved a short distance away from the others to speak with his wife. He stared at Sigrid, trying to imprint the image of her face in his mind.

"I won't ask you to make me a promise about coming home safe," she said.

He smiled. "I will try my best, regardless." For the first time, the thought of returning to the palace filled him with a sense of longing.

Getting used to living in a city, constantly surrounded by the noise of other people, was always going to take a long time. Then there was the politics and intrigue of court. The responsibility of running a country and trying to be a caring ruler that thought about the lives of others. As if all of that wasn't enough, he also had to work out how to be a good husband and father. The weight of it all would be crushing if he were attempting it by himself. Looking at the woman before him, he finally saw her as his partner.

"I've left you something in my room," said Kell. Then he lowered his voice to a whisper, "It's hidden behind a panel in my wardrobe." Lukas was out of earshot making a final check on the horses. He trusted the Steward, but he didn't know who else might be listening. "There are a few things I didn't tell you, or anyone, about the Frozen North."

"What sort of things?" she whispered.

"Vahli kept a second journal. It was written in code, but I translated it."

"What does it contain?"

"It's about what we really found in the Ice Lich's castle, and the real origin of the church." He leaned even closer. "The journal is dangerous, but the contents might prove useful for future battles with the Reverend Mother."

When they broke apart Sigrid was staring, desperate to know more, but she didn't ask. She gave him one last passionate kiss and then they were out of time.

"We must go," said Willow, getting to her feet.

Without saying another word, Kell mounted up and rode out of the western gate, leaving his whole life behind once again.

The city streets were quiet. There were no crowds, and no one really paid them any notice. Odd and Yarra had traded in their Raven uniforms and armour for something nondescript. The only concession was their weapons, but the scabbards had been swapped for plain leather and the grips bound with material. Kell carried his famous sword, Slayer, on his back, but it too had been wrapped to conceal its identity. Willow wore baggy clothing and had pulled up her hood to cover her face. At a distance, she might be mistaken as a tall Hundarian. It was the best they could do at short notice. She ranged ahead on foot, taking side streets to avoid prying eyes.

They made it across the city of Thune without drawing any attention to themselves, for which Kell was grateful. Now that he was committed to this journey, the idea of any kind of a delay made him uncomfortable.

Once they were outside the city gates, Kell nudged his horse into a canter and the others followed. Willow veered off, heading south on foot. Moving at a steady pace, it would take them three or four days to reach the docks in Lorzi. They had been lucky up to now, but Kell knew it wouldn't hold. There were spies everywhere from other nations, and probably from the Reverend Mother as well. The fewer people that knew about his journey, the safer it would be for those he'd left behind.

The Alfár would make her own way to the Holy City, travelling at night to avoid detection. Willow had assured Kell that she would be there soon after him, if not before, and he believed her. She had been travelling across the Five Kingdoms for years and knew the land far better than anyone.

In a few days' time, he would be heading across the Narrow Sea. Kell didn't know if the squirming in his stomach was anxiety or something else. Whatever it was, they were going to see the Alfár's homeland, and that thought filled him with equal parts excitement and dread.

Three nights later, they stopped a short ride from a small farming town. They set up their tents in the wilderness, their fire shielded by a dense copse of trees. The thought of spending the night in a warm bed was appealing, but Kell couldn't take the risk in case he was recognised. Living in the palace had also left him feeling a bit cooped up and it was a relief to be outdoors.

Odd had walked off into the dark to pray. Normally he did it in camp, but tonight he'd said he needed solitude. Kell hadn't been aware he was so devout. It was one of many discoveries that he was making about his new travelling companions.

As they were making camp, Yarra approached Kell by the fire. He'd been expecting this conversation since they'd left home, but she hadn't found the right time to talk with him.

"Majesty, there's something I need to tell you."

"Kell. Out here, my name is Kell," he said, adding more wood to the flames. The bark began to blacken and crisp, filling the air with the pungent aroma of pine.

"I shouldn't be here," said Yarra, ploughing on. "You've made a mistake choosing me for this journey."

"Are you a member of the Raven?" he asked, hanging the kettle on the hook over the fire.

"Yes."

"And did you earn that position honestly?" he asked, knowing the harsh trials each of them had been put through before. Being a member of the Raven wasn't just about physical prowess, or skill with a blade. Each soldier had to excel in several areas before they would be considered. Every year, hundreds took the trials and most of them failed.

"I didn't cheat," she said.

"Then you're exactly where you need to be. I need someone I can rely on to protect me."

"It's not that simple," said Yarra. "I made a terrible mistake."

"I know what happened," said Kell, looking her in the eye.

In addition to protecting the king, members of the Raven were also tasked with investigating potential threats to the royal family. A year ago, someone had overheard a group of religious zealots, led by a man named Marlen, who intended to kill Kell and his wife. Yarra had investigated the threat and had been eager to eliminate it. She'd led a group of soldiers into what she thought was an empty warehouse. It had turned out to be an ambush and, despite killing Marlen and the others, all of the soldiers under her command had died.

Since then, she'd obeyed every order without question and had not put a foot out of place, but Yarra refused to lead. Members of the Raven were not supposed to be meek followers. They were proactive thinkers and investigators who took charge. She had lost all confidence, become a sheep, eager to do as she was told.

"It's my fault that they died," said Yarra. "I should have been more careful. I shouldn't have rushed in. Their blood is on my hands."

"You need to leave it in the past. I need you for what lays ahead."

Yarra stubbornly shook her head. "I can't."

According to the old saying, time healed all wounds. Kell knew from personal experience that was a lie. Some black marks on the soul would never fade, no matter how much time you gave them. One way to erase them was to scrub them clean by diving back into the fray, but that didn't always work.

"There are only four of us on this journey. I've no idea what's to come, but I know it will be dangerous. So, my life will be in your hands," said Kell. "Without you at your best, we may all die."

The kettle began to whistle and Yarra hadn't flinched at its insistent shriek. "That's not–"

"Fair? Tell me you weren't about to say fair?" he said, talking over her. Kell removed the kettle and dropped some leaves into the pot. "Either you're a member of the Raven, or you're not. It's that simple. If I can't rely on you out here, then I don't want you slinking back home to protect my family, either. Here," said Kell, slapping a dagger in her hand. "You may as well cut your throat now. It'll save someone else the trouble of doing it later, when you refuse to fight back. Make a decision, and do it quickly."

Yarra stared down at the blade. The polished surface glimmered in the firelight. He waited in silence to see what she would do. She was balanced on a wire and could fall either way. He saw the muscles in her neck working as she tried to say something. Kell shook his head. The time for talking was over. The moment was upon her. There was no going back.

For a long time she merely stared into the flames. When Odd returned from praying, he saw the dagger in Yarra's hand, but didn't react. Nothing seemed to faze him. Instead of asking the question he just raised an eyebrow.

"So," said Kell, turning to Yarra. "What will it be?"

CHAPTER 5

Sigrid didn't waste any time. As soon as Kell's party left the palace she raced along the corridors, as fast as her legs would carry her, only slowing down when she heard a servant approaching. The moment they were out of earshot, she lifted the hem of her dress and resumed running.

She managed to arrive at her husband's room in record time. Servants hadn't even been in yet to make the bed – not that she'd slept in her room last night. The servants would notice that and gossip. Unfortunately, there were few secrets in her personal life. If she did nothing, then in no time the palace would be rife with rumours. She hated pretending not to notice the speculative looks people exchanged around her. Grabbing the bedsheets she ripped them off the bed, tangled them up and left them in a knotted lump. Kell moved around in his sleep a lot. It would have to do.

After locking the door to ensure that she wasn't disturbed, Sigrid went to the tall standing wardrobe in the corner. It was a monstrous thing, carved from a dark wood she couldn't name from somewhere in Hundar. There had been a fashion for it fifty years ago, and half of the guest rooms in the palace were filled with them. She thought they were ugly and wanted to change them for something more pleasant. It was on her list of many things she wanted to update.

Shoving his clothes to one side she felt around the wooden panels at the back, searching for something out of place. All of them felt identical. Next, she tried tapping them, but none were hollow. She thought about using a candle to get a better look, but she was just as likely to set his clothes on fire. He must have done it by touch, so there had to be something.

Moving more slowly, she traced the edges of the panels again. The top left panel had a small notch in one corner. It was so slight she'd missed it the first time. By pushing that notch, she heard something click and felt it shift. There was just enough light for her to see an opening at the top, creating a small pocket. From inside she retrieved the bard's journal and an accompanying notebook.

The journal was written in a series of asymmetric symbols she didn't recognise. In the notebook, she found pages and pages of Kell's untidy hand translating the coded journal.

Before she could read it there was a polite knock at the door. A servant, come to tidy the room.

Cursing her luck, Sigrid replaced the journal, resealed the hidden compartment and closed the wardrobe. She concealed the notebook in the small of her back and rebuttoned her dress before opening the door.

"Apologies, your majesty," said a young woman, curtseying when she saw who it was. "I didn't realise you were in here. I can come back later."

"It's fine. I was just taking a look around," she said, wishing the girl hadn't been so diligent in her duties. Despite Sigrid's best efforts to prevent them, there would still be rumours about her and Kell. Now they'd all think she was mooning after him. At least it was better than the truth. The potentially volatile contents of the journal weren't something she was ready to share. Not just yet.

"Go ahead," said Sigrid, gesturing for the girl to be about her duties. She'd have to read the notebook later, when she was alone. She hoped it wasn't going to be a long day, but Sigrid already knew that was wishful thinking.

* * *

"Thank you, ambassador," said Sigrid, smiling at the rotund, brightly dressed woman as she left the negotiation room. Since becoming Queen, Sigrid had been using this room almost as much as her study. The throne room was reserved for official court business. Pomp and ceremony, greeting important visitors, and moments that the people would be told about. In here, she got down to business, away from the gossips and hangers-on, the servants and even the Raven. She was safe from attack this far inside the palace, and the only injury she was likely to sustain was to her pride. The weapons used here were only words, but the effects could last a great deal longer than a bruise.

Lukas sent the ambassador on her way with a guiding hand and a fake smile, then locked the door. Once the sound of her footsteps had faded, he leaned against the wall and heaved a sigh, echoed by Sigrid.

It had been another difficult and painful negotiation. Despite the woman's soft appearance, Ambassador Gryce was ruthless and had a mind as sharp as a barber's razor. She would argue over every last detail if it meant she would receive a handful more coins. The Seith were masters of trade, but Gryce took it to the extreme. At least it was over. The grain shipments had been secured for another year and regular deliveries would continue without interruption. It had been over two years since the frost that had decimated the harvest, and the scars were still healing.

"What's next?" asked Sigrid, rubbing the bridge of her nose. A headache was forming. She was tired and, so far today, hadn't managed to eat anything. Sigrid poured herself a glass of watered-down wine and grabbed a few grapes. The sweet taste awoke her hunger so she cut up two apples, ate them and then grazed the remaining stalks until all of the grapes were gone.

"Do you want me to send for something more substantial?" asked Lukas.

"Yes, please," she said, draining her glass and pouring another.

When Lukas returned, they focused on the next item of business: the missionaries.

"Another request?"

Lukas nodded. "She's persistent, that's for sure."

"Is it bad that I just wish that the old windbag would die?" said Sigrid.

As the spiritual leader of the church, Britak gave others the impression that she was a benevolent and maternal figure who cared about everyone in the Five Kingdoms. In reality, she was more ruthless than any hired sword. Sigrid genuinely believed the old woman would do or say anything if it furthered her cause. And she would do all of it with a smile because, in her mind, it was for the greater good. Her belief was absolute. That was what made her so dangerous.

"If she died, it might make things a little easier in the short term," said Lukas. "Although from what I've been told, she's been grooming her replacement for years. The next person to wield the holy crozier could be equally difficult."

"The ambassador from Seithland is difficult. The Reverend Mother is like a tick. She's after blood. I saw that report yesterday. How many injuries have her 'holy servants' inflicted this week?"

"Her missionaries are responsible for three broken bones, one woman who was beaten unconscious but will recover, and the death of a young thief. Although, that was because of the horse and carriage, not the missionaries. When confronted for stealing, the boy ran and the driver didn't have time to slow down."

Sigrid gave Lukas a withering stare. "We both know she's responsible for all of it. And I know the boy was starving. They should have been helping him, not chasing him through the city for grabbing a loaf of bread!" She took a deep breath to calm down and came to a decision. "As you advised, I've been patient and generous. I've tried to stay neutral, keeping state away from the church. Negotiation is pointless because they're all zealots. There's nothing holy about the missionaries. They're thugs in cheap robes. No, Lukas, it stops here."

Their discussion paused while a servant delivered a plate of bread, butter, cheese and sliced ham.

"What did you have in mind?" asked Lukas, helping himself to some. Sigrid contemplated her answer as she chewed a fat slice of smoked ham.

"We need to send a clear message. Like my father, I've tolerated street preachers because they're harmless. People tend to scorn them, but these missionaries are something else entirely." Sigrid stuffed her mouth with some bread smeared with butter, savouring the taste. She was hungrier than she realised and filled a plate. "I think in order to preach within the city limits, about any religion, it should require a permit. We're supposed to be a fair and equal nation, so it wouldn't do to have representatives of one faith flooding the streets of the capital. That would be bias."

These days, faith had become a private thing for families to celebrate in their own homes. Whether they followed the Shepherd, or another faith, it didn't matter to her, or the rest of the kingdom. As long as they weren't hurting themselves or someone else, it wasn't her business. It also wasn't blasphemy or idolatry, despite what the Reverend Mother claimed in her sermons.

When her father had first taken the throne, every church dedicated to the Shepherd had been filled to the rafters. Those days were gone. Trying to get them back by beating people and calling them sinners, wasn't the right way to go about it.

"And how many permits should be issued to the missionaries?" asked Lukas, already knowing her answer.

"Very few. Barely a handful, in fact." She was tired of the old windbag trying to tell people how to live.

"I'll see that it's done."

"For now, they are to be escorted, politely, to the city gates. Make it very clear that any further attacks will be met with a severe reprimand."

"Yes, your Majesty," said Lukas, giving her a seated bow. They both knew there would be repercussions, but she'd been treading water for too long, hoping for a change. It was time to take action.

"Good. Now, what's next?" she asked.

When Sigrid had been a child, her mother had often read adventure stories to her. To begin with, she'd revelled in them, but after a few years she started asking questions no one could answer.

What did the monsters eat when they weren't gobbling up brave warriors? How did they survive through the winter? Did they lay eggs like birds or give birth like horses? Her mother had grown irritated, but her father had laughed, perhaps knowing that one day, her analytical mind would prove invaluable.

Finally alone in her rooms after another long day, Sigrid poured over Kell's journal, searching for answers. At the beginning the story was the same, although some of Vahli's observations about his travelling companions were more intriguing, and indicated an astute mind. From the start, the bard had known that Kell was struggling with his past. In fact, he'd known all of them were troubled by something. Over the course of the journey, his intuition was proven right. Gerren was searching for a place to belong. Malomir for courage, so that he could become the king his people needed. And Bronwyn to step out of her father's shadow and find her true purpose. Kell, of course, had been trying to let go of the past, and find an answer to the questions that had haunted him for ten years.

The bard's notes about Willow, the Alfár, were full of questions and puzzled observations. Why was she travelling with them? How did she benefit? Where did she come from? Vahli didn't understand her and couldn't read her body language or expressions. But she had a connection with Kell, and a strong bond of friendship had developed between them. Sigrid ignored the twinge of jealousy and kept reading.

The journal also indicated Vahli's first meeting with Kell had not been a coincidence. He'd been sent to protect Kell. Sigrid suspected her father was responsible, and that meant Lukas was likely involved too. It was something to ask him about later.

While the story gave her deeper insight into the people involved, it was only when she came to the last part that Sigrid nearly fell out of her chair. It was late and her eyes were already tired from reading, but sleep became the furthest thing from her mind.

Finding out the true history of the Ice Lich was astonishing, but it was dwarfed by the revelation that the castle was the Shepherd's tomb. At first, shock warred with disbelief, but she quickly realised why Kell hadn't told anyone. The potential damage it could do was enormous – not only to the church, but also to the Frozen North itself if people began to make pilgrimages. The Holy City would lose its appeal and its power as the holy centre of the church. The Reverend Mother's waning power base would soon evaporate. On the surface, that sounded good, but Sigrid didn't imagine that Britak would go down without a fight. It would be brutal and bloody, and the public would suffer.

With each new revelation Sigrid found she was becoming numb. She was astonished to find out that Malomir and Bronwyn were still alive, and had gone to reign together in the Summer Isles as King and Queen. Until Willow had arrived at the palace, everyone in the Five Kingdoms had just assumed that the Alfár was dead.

When she reached the end of Vahli's account there were more pages in Kell's hand, but these were different. They contained secrets about his heritage and connections to the Choate. Sigrid flew through the pages then set the journal aside, trying to process everything she'd just read.

A firm double knock at her door told her who was waiting outside. "Come in, Natia," said Sigrid.

Although she was dressed like a servant, Natia moved like a soldier, confident and with purpose. Her eyes were watchful and her spine erect, despite the touch of grey in her black hair. "He's finally asleep, Majesty."

Natia was her son's second nursemaid, but also his protector, although only Sigrid and Lukas knew about her dual role. Few people seemed to remember that many years ago, she had been a member of the Raven, before leaving to start a family. "Come in, close the door behind you."

Natia did as instructed and sat down when Sigrid waved her towards a chair.

"Something on your mind?" asked Natia.

She was ever forthright, which was something Sigrid needed. Too many people she spoke with on a daily basis wouldn't give her a straight answer to a simple question. Sigrid had known Natia her whole life. First, as a surrogate aunt and a member of her father's Raven, and now as her son's nursemaid. There were few people she trusted more in the palace.

Sigrid laid out what she'd learned about Kell, his connection to the Choate and the truth about the Shepherd. Natia whistled through her teeth and leaned back in her chair.

"I need a moment," said Natia, mulling it over. From her pocket she took a small knife and a lump of wood she'd been carving. It was starting to look a bit like a bear, although Sigrid thought it could also be a wolf. She began to carefully scrape off small pieces as she spoke, dropping the shavings into her lap.

"If the Reverend Mother found out about this, it might just kill her," said Natia.

"If only," said Sigrid. "I'd risk sharing it with her, if that was a guarantee."

"And your husband has been sitting on this for how long?"

"More than two years. He should have told me, but I can see why he kept it a secret."

Natia grunted. "He's not as stupid as he looks."

"No, he's not." They'd all underestimated Kell, including Lukas and her father. Sigrid wondered what other secrets Kell was keeping that he hadn't shared with her.

"So, what will you do with it?" asked Natia, without looking up from her carving.

"At the moment, nothing, but if the Reverend Mother tries to press forward with her crusade, I might have to leak some of the details. Provide the people with an alternative history of the Shepherd." It would be interesting to see how people reacted when they were presented with a different story.

Natia paused and glanced up at Sigrid. "That could be very dangerous for you."

"It would be done carefully, so it couldn't be traced back to me." The Reverend Mother might suspect the information had come from her, but she'd struggle to prove it. "I'd also have to omit certain details, about the Choate and the Frozen North." If she released the whole story, the Reverend Mother would paint the tribespeople as heathens and make them a target. Most people thought them godless sinners, like those who lived in the Summer Isles. "What do you know about the Choate?" asked Sigrid.

"Not a lot," admitted Natia.

"I think that might have to change," said Sigrid.

Kell had hinted that the Choate knew a lot more than he'd written in the notebook. The Choate mostly kept to themselves, rarely caused trouble and never held large gatherings in the Five Kingdoms. Whenever one of them settled in a town or city, it was usually by themselves or with a small family. As far as Sigrid knew, there were no Choate neighbourhoods in any cities in Algany, or in fact anywhere in the Five Kingdoms.

"Do you know how many are living here in Thune?"

"No, but I can find out," said Natia.

Sigrid shook her head. "That's not important. But I need a reason to speak with one of them that doesn't look suspicious."

"Have one of them arrested. The cells are the perfect place for a quiet chat."

"I was hoping for something a little less dramatic."

"It would be efficient," said Natia.

"I need to make a new contact, not upset them before I've even said hello."

"Maybe Lukas can help. He's more subtle than me." That was putting it mildly.

Given what she had discovered about the church, Sigrid was confident that the Choate people would have an opinion on what the Reverend Mother was doing. They were also another potential ally against her. Sigrid needed to talk to one of them, face to face and in private.

For now though, she'd done what she could to minimise the Reverend Mother's impact on her city. It would take a bit longer for the message to filter out into the countryside, but once Sigrid's people delivered an edict to her soldiers, and sent missives to town and community leaders, it would get through. There would be a significant limit on the number of zealots and religious attacks in her kingdom.

Very soon after that, the old crone would realise that Algany had become a hostile environment for her religious crusade. The next move would be up to the Reverend Mother.

Sigrid found herself grinning. She was looking forward to the fight.

CHAPTER 6

It had been a long time since Kell had been to Lorzi, the Holy City, but little about the place had changed in the interim. Security at the sally ports for travellers was still fairly lax. Soldiers kept an eye out for troublemakers, but mostly they were there to keep the traffic moving.

At the larger gates, broad enough for two carts to comfortably pass side by side, security was tighter. A vast array of goods flowed in and out of the Five Kingdoms from Lorzi. Every wagon coming into the city was thoroughly inspected, and all paperwork carefully checked.

The Seith were the masters of trade. It seemed as if every carrot and bean passed through their hands. As long as you had the money, they could get anything you wanted. Most people didn't ask where the items came from, and they didn't much care.

Every day, dozens of ships crossed the Narrow Sea, their holds full of cargo. Kell hoped that with so many ships coming and going, they could slip away unnoticed by King Roebus and the Reverend Mother.

As he thought about her, a huge edifice came into view, reminding him of the old woman's power and influence. Looming over the city, casting a vast shadow across the streets, was the Shepherd's cathedral. The massive, blue-domed structure was an impressive feat of architecture, especially as it had taken the best part of a century to build. Such dedication and commitment to a cause was remarkable. It was unfortunate that it was all built on lies.

Revealing the truth about the origins of the Shepherd would reshape the Five Kingdoms, most likely for the better, but it was also likely to spark a war. Kell had kept the secret for years, but in his absence, he trusted Sigrid to do what was best with it. He didn't want there to be any more secrets between them.

"Sir?" asked Yarra. She'd decided not to kill herself, but wouldn't make any other decisions. It was a small step in the right direction. She followed his gaze until she noticed the cathedral. "Did you want to pay a visit?" she asked, misinterpreting his stare.

"No," said Kell.

"We should keep moving," whispered Odd. They'd stopped a short distance from the gate, forcing other travellers to walk around them. The guards hadn't noticed them yet, but they would if they stood out in the crowd.

"Let's go," said Kell, glancing briefly at the other structure fighting for dominance of the sky: the palace of King Roebus. It wasn't long after his first journey to the Frozen North that he'd visited the palace. Some parts of that period in his life were just a blur of images. He remembered long corridors with identical doorways, marble pillars and gold decoration on the walls. There had been a huge party in his honour, with lots of important guests from across the Five Kingdoms. Kell was fairly certain he'd met King Roebus, but he couldn't be sure. Regardless, it wasn't long after that Kell had been sent home to the farm. Maybe he'd said something embarrassing to the king's face. Given the king's loyalty to the Reverend Mother, Kell certainly hoped so.

Odd led the way through the streets of the outer district. One hand was hidden beneath his cloak, and Kell knew it was resting on a dagger. Any thief who tried to rob them would have to be brave and stupid. Yarra followed a few steps behind, her eyes combing the streets for trouble. Kell tried to relax, but a part of him was certain that, at any moment, someone would recognise him. If he was identified, alone in the Holy City, there would be political ramifications. Questions would be asked about why he was sneaking around, and that would reflect badly on Algany. It would also stall their journey, which he didn't want to delay. The sooner they left, the sooner they could return home. Besides, Willow was desperate to catch up to her kinsman, so any delay could be critical for her people.

Thankfully it seemed the people in Lorzi were too busy to notice and had no interest in three more travellers. Kell was shouted at by merchants hawking their wares, waved at by whores looking for business, and generally ignored by everyone else who seemed to be in a hurry. Even so, they kept their heads down. Any number of spies for King Roebus, or the church, could be lurking amongst the crowd.

He was surrounded by a sea of faces from across the Five Kingdoms, but despite not knowing any of them, they felt familiar. Tall men and women with shaven heads from Hundar. Outlandish hardy folk from northern Kinnan. Wide-faced merchants with red clothing from Seithland in the west. Even the occasional tattooed Choate, although most people gave them a wide berth. Kell was tempted to smile at them, but he repressed the urge in order to remain incognito.

He was worried that when they arrived in Willow's homeland, wherever that was, nothing would be recognisable to him. On several occasions, he'd been forced to explain something about the Five Kingdoms to Willow that would be obvious to a child. Navigating through a foreign land where little made sense to him, while also trying to help Willow hold onto her identity, twisted his stomach in knots.

"Are you all right?" asked Odd, noting his distress.

"Fine," said Kell. He knew that worrying about it wouldn't change anything, but he couldn't help it.

They hurried through the outer district and entered the

spur, the main area dedicated to trade in the city. Half a dozen wide streets, like spokes on a wheel, converged at a huge open market. Hundreds of canvas stalls covered two thirds of the space, and the rest was filled with pens for livestock.

It would've been easier to skirt the market, but if anyone was following them, this was the place to lose them. Odd waded into the crowd and Kell kept him at arm's length, with Yarra a step behind. As they fought their way through the crush of bodies, his senses were overwhelmed with a variety of pungent smells and loud noises. The sheer number of voices made it impossible to hear what anyone was saying without shouting.

Butchers' stalls stood cheek to jowl with spice merchants and fruit sellers, creating a kaleidoscope of vivid colours. After only a few minutes, he began to feel slightly dizzy. Kell could understand why Willow refused to enter cities unless absolutely necessary.

Once they were free of the spur, they skirted the outer ring, avoiding the heart of the city. From there, they took a wide avenue straight towards the docks. It was a relief to be free. The noise had given Kell a headache.

By the time they reached the docks, it was early in the afternoon, and Kell was ready to leave the city. Almost a hundred ships were tied up, most of them cogs, sitting heavy in the water, while cargo was unloaded with cranes. There were hundreds of people: sailors, burly dock workers, soldiers to keep the peace, irate port officials and flustered merchants. Laden carts were walked to the end of the pier where dozens of horses waited, ready to transport goods to their next destination.

Moving in slow cartwheels, far above his head, were hundreds of white gulls. More were perched on the rigging of ships, diving into the water and fighting over scraps of food. There were a few fishing boats unloading their catch, but most of them were out on the water at this time of day.

The air was full of voices fighting for dominance, all of them overlapping to create a deafening cacophony of sound. That was something else he wouldn't miss about being king. On occasion it meant he had to venture into the city, and he still wasn't used to being around such large crowds. At least the palace was quiet. But, he supposed, if he was going to be King in more than name, then he would have to spend time among the people. Being in a crowd was, regrettably, something he would have to get used to in the future.

"Now what?" asked Yarra, shouting to be heard over the din.

"We wait," said Kell.

Odd settled with his back against a wall, at ease on the surface, hand still hidden in his cloak. Yarra just glared at anyone who wandered too close, daring them to try something.

After a while, it became apparent that no one cared who they were, as long as they stayed out of the way. Carts rolled past in both directions, moving up and down, laden with fresh produce. Mangy cats prowled the docks, looking for scraps, swiping at gulls that came too close.

One moment the space in front of Kell was empty and the next, Willow was standing there. Despite the hood that concealed her face, Kell knew it was Willow. There was no mistaking her distinct silhouette, but more than that, Kell could sense her. There was a faint pressure at the back of his mind. Theirs was a bond that went beyond friendship.

As she approached, Willow gave him a half smile, as if she knew what he was thinking. Then again, perhaps it was just his imagination.

She tilted her head back, peering down at them from the shadows of her hood. "I've booked passage for us on a ship," said the Alfár. "Are you ready?"

A dozen excuses rose in Kell's mind about not leaving his family, but he ignored them. If Willow had ever been afraid during their journey to the Frozen North, she'd never let it show. He owed her the same courtesy. "Lead the way," he said. The Raven followed two paces in their wake, still alert for danger.

"Every living creature knows fear," whispered the Alfár in her strange, echoing voice. Perhaps she really did know what he was thinking.

"Even you?" he said with a wry smile.

Willow turned away, her expression suddenly pained.

"I'm sorry," he said immediately. "That was thoughtless."

His fear was nothing compared to what she must be feeling about the threat to her homeland. In the time they'd been apart, Kell had fallen back into old habits. He'd started thinking like everyone else, acting as if the Alfár didn't have emotions.

"I'm sorry," he said again, because he should have known better.

They passed pier after pier, all of them bustling with activity, before she led them down one that was a little quieter than the others. The ships on their dock carried some cargo, but several of them had lines of people waiting to board with luggage. There were a dozen colourful merchants from Seithland, pale Corvanese soldiers, and a mixture of passengers from across the Five Kingdoms.

"That one," said Willow, gesturing at the last ship on the end of the stone dock. At first glance, the cog looked identical to the others, but as they approached, Kell saw that part of the deck had been converted into a temporary shelter, clearly designed to offer passengers some protection from the elements. The crossing would take less than a day, and the newly erected pavilion didn't give Kell hope that the voyage would be smooth. He didn't like the idea of being tossed about.

They joined the back of the line and Willow did her best to remain inconspicuous. A burly sailor from Algany with a bald head and broad shoulders was standing by the gangplank. He checked each person's name off the list before helping them onboard. Unlike the other sailors, he wore a black and red striped shirt which denoted his rank as captain. As they reached the front of the line, Kell was surprised when Willow pulled down her hood, revealing her face.

"Back again, I see," said the captain, grinning up at the Alfár. "How long has it been?"

"Many turnings, Ashvar," said Willow, smiling fondly at the man.

"Ha, yes. Many," replied Ashvar, gesturing at his bald head. "Last time, I had hair. So, is this everyone?" he asked, looking at Kell and the others.

"They are my friends. They will be no trouble," promised Willow.

"From you, Keelo, I would expect no less. You'd better get on board, we're casting off soon."

Kell and the others stowed their gear then exchanged greetings with the other passengers. Thankfully, none of them recognised him, but rather than press his luck, Kell found a space at the railing to watch their departure.

A short time later, the mainsail was unfurled and they slowly drifted out of the port. Once they were clear of the other ships, the captain adjusted course. The sails caught a strong headwind gusting through the Narrow Sea, and then they were on their way.

As the docks of the Holy City began to recede into the distance, Kell heaved a sigh of relief. Willow joined him a moment later. She stared out across the waves. Kell thought she looked pensive, but he was out of practise at reading her subtle expressions.

"Is he an old friend of yours?" asked Kell, gesturing at the captain on the bridge.

"Old," said Willow, musing on the word as if she didn't understand what it meant. Kell waited, knowing that any unanswered question would bother her and eventually she would reply. "Not so old to me," she finally added.

Despite the weight of the ship and its flat bottom, it began to pick up speed on the crossing. Kell held onto the railing with one hand, just in case.

"Why does he call you Keelo?" said Kell.

"The last time I saw Ashvar, he was young. He had trouble saying my name," said Willow. "When did you first hear of my people? Who told you about us?" she asked suddenly, turning to face him.

Kell took a moment and thought back to his childhood. "When I was a boy, my grandfather told me about your people. But his father had told him stories too."

"What did they say about us?" asked Willow.

There was a sense of urgency to her question that told him it wasn't idle curiosity.

"It doesn't matter. I know that most of it was wrong," he said. Now that he knew more about Willow's people, he was embarrassed by the stories he'd been told. There was little truth to them, and they must have been created from idle speculation. With so few Alfár in the Five Kingdoms to corroborate the stories, and because they were known for being taciturn, it was not a surprise that they had become so widespread.

Willow said nothing, waiting for him to answer. She became so perfectly still he couldn't even see her chest moving. "They said your people were nomads. That you lived alone and only came together to mate."

"I came here, to your Five Kingdoms, searching for something to help my homeland. To stop the spread of the poison. To heal my people and slow the rot," said Willow fixing him with one of her intense stares. "Ravvi and I are the only Alfár to have ever visited your people."

"So, you're saying, only the two of you have ever visited the Five Kingdoms? No one else? All the way back to the time of my great-grandfather?" he asked, waiting for Willow to correct him, but she said nothing. "That's not possible."

That would make Willow at least a hundred years old, if not

more. But then again, he was judging her by human standards.
Again.

"Time is different here." Willow made a circular motion
with her hands, slowly rolling one over the other. "A year in
the Five Kingdoms is not the same as a turning in my home.
Do you understand?"

"No," said Kell shaking his head.

"One day in my home, is longer in this place," said Willow,
trying again. "I cannot say exactly how long. A week. Maybe
two. But, it has been just the two of us. No one else has visited
the Five Kingdoms."

"You've been searching for a cure for all this time?"

"Yes."

"And you haven't found anything?"

Willow sighed. "No. Now you understand Ravvi's
desperation. But fear does not change the truth. His idea of a
cure could damn my people to a worse fate than at present. If
there is a way to fight the Malice, it lies elsewhere. After today,
I do not think any Alfár will return to the Five Kingdoms."

Once the Holy City had disappeared over the horizon, the
rest of the party joined them on the deck.

"Where are we going? And why?" asked Yarra. Up to now
it had been safer for them not to know all of the details, just in
case they were captured.

"To Corvan," said Willow, "and from there to my homeland.
We must stop my kinsman, Ravvi." Willow then proceeded to
tell the others about the Malice, how it had poisoned her home
and then her people.

"And it will poison us as well?" said Yarra, fiddling with one
of her many earrings. Odd was listening intently, but showed
no outward signs of being nervous.

"It will happen," said Willow.

"But the effects will be slower on us."

"Yes. Pain, in your joints, or marks upon on the skin. But
that is just the beginning. The lightest touch of the Malice,"

said Willow. "The further north we go, the longer it has to soak in it, and the worse it will become. Change will happen, inside and out. Right down to the root. It will also affect the mind. The doors will open and I could drift. You should all know the path, in case I become lost. You may have to lead me."

"Doors?" said Kell, turning to the Alfár. "What doors?"

"In time. Inside," said Willow, gesturing at her head. "What has been. Today. Tomorrow. All at once. Out of order. The reason for being in my homeland may begin to feel like a minor thing. A memory, so why struggle and fight? Easier to just lie down and sleep."

"Will it affect our minds in the same way?" asked Odd, speaking for the first time in hours.

"It is difficult to know," said Willow, "but if the journey is long, then you may also become lost in memory."

The rest of the voyage across the Narrow Sea passed without incident, but when the headland of Corvan came into view, Kell was eager to get off the ship. He was usually fine on a fishing boat, but there was something about the motion of the ship that upset his stomach. He had ignored the offer of food when it was made, despite being after midday. A few passengers had been vomiting off of the stern for most of the night. Thankfully, he'd managed to avoid that, but only just.

As a favour to his old friend, Captain Ashvar let them off the ship early with a skiff. One of his crew rowed them out to the beach on the coast of Corvan. Everyone else would continue inland to the capital city of Bayex. There were a few raised eyebrows, but Kell suspected the other passengers would put it down to nothing more than the peculiarity of having an Alfár onboard.

They crunched across the pebbled beach, and by the time they'd found a path up to the top of the cliffs, the ship had disappeared around the headland.

Kell glanced around for any signs of life, but there was nothing. Just grassy scrubland, windswept hills and the empty beach below. There were a few rabbit warrens dotting the headland, but they looked abandoned, and the seabird nests were empty. They were completely alone.

"Is it far?" asked Kell.

"Not far," promised Willow, gesturing to the south.

They moved only a short distance inland away from the cliff edge, but otherwise hugged the coast. After an hour of walking, Kell saw a faint silhouette in the distance. He knew it by reputation, but had never been there in person. The Ravens had confused expressions, but after another hour they at least knew where they were going, if not what it meant.

As the afternoon shadows began to lengthen, they arrived at the Dragon Tree. According to local history, it was over a thousand years old and the only remaining tree of its kind. While monstrous, it wasn't the tallest Kell had ever seen, but it was so broad around the trunk and roots that it created a skewed perspective. The Dragon Tree was easily the height of twenty men, and trying to see the top gave him a pain in the neck. The gnarled grey trunk was covered with a vast asymmetrical array of ridges and whirls, lumps and nodules, and the canopy of evergreen leaves and thorny spikes reached skyward. The air around the tree was unusually still, and no birds alighted on its branches.

Most surprising was Odd's awed expression. "It's amazing." He rested one hand lightly on the trunk and smiled, as if communing with it.

Yarra was less impressed. "Which direction do we take?" she asked, searching for the next landmark. There was nothing in sight. Just more scrub and grassland. Further inland there were farming communities and villages, but Kell thought Willow had something else in mind.

"I will show you," said Willow, moving closer to the tree. Off to one side, Kell saw the ground had recently been disturbed.

Kneeling down, Willow cleared away some of the top soil and then reached deeper into the earth with both hands. With a grunt of effort, she unearthed a large, heavy sack.

Reaching into the hole again, Willow retrieved a second bag as large as the first. It was lumpy and clanked when she moved it. The Alfár handled both with care before opening the first. From inside the sack, she produced a glass jar that had been sealed with wax. It contained dried black and purple leaves from a plant Kell didn't recognise. Glancing inside the sack, he saw dozens more jars, all packed with unusual items.

"They won't cure the Malice," Willow said, "but they will help with the symptoms and ease the pain. Ravvi didn't even take them with him." The Alfár's posture shifted. Kell had seen Willow angry before, but this was something else. Disappointment.

"We will get them to your people," Kell promised. "So, which way are we going?"

Willow carefully resealed the sack and then dragged both closer to the tree. "Here. The doorway is here," she said, resting a hand on the trunk.

The others looked at Kell for an answer, but he could only shrug. Drawing a dagger from her belt Willow made a shallow cut on her thumb. Rich blue blood welled from the wound, and she began to whisper words in her own language. Even though he didn't understand what was being said, Kell felt there was a rhythm to the words, as if it was a song or prayer.

"What's happening?" asked Yarra, pointing at the shadows. They were starting to swell, as if night had fallen. Willow had painted a series of symbols on the Dragon Tree with her blood. Nine swirling runes that formed a rough circle. As she continued to whisper, Kell saw them begin to glow.

Any remaining sunlight faded, and they were enveloped in shadow. They stood in a pool of absolute darkness that extended in every direction. All light from the symbols was suddenly extinguished. Kell could barely see his fingers in front of his face, but he could sense movement. The symbols on the tree began to glow again, more brightly this time. They cast waves of purple and red light across everyone's face. He could feel it moving over his skin, as if the light had weight. The Alfár's voice had grown loud and taken on an insidious tone. He could feel the words crawling inside his head. Scrabbling for purchase, as his mind tried to make sense of them.

Willow's voice rose in volume yet again. The symbols flashed once in response and then faded away. Everything turned pitch black once more and Kell found himself wrapped in silence. He couldn't see or hear the others, and didn't know if they were still beside him. With his eyes open or closed, everything was the same. The darkness was absolute. In the absence of light, imagined white shapes danced across Kell's field of vision.

A loud cracking sound, like the tearing of a tree branch, filled the air. The purple light returned, rising from the ground to form a line, and then the edge of a doorway, in the heart of the Dragon Tree. The outline of everything became clear again. The shape of the tree, his companions, the Alfár and the heavy sacks at her feet.

With a grunt of effort Willow leaned against the tree and the glowing doorway widened, revealing a shining portal like the surface of the sea. It was so bright Kell had to squint against the shimmering light.

With one hand shielding his eyes, he saw Willow shoving the heavy sacks through the door to whatever lay on the other side.

"Take my hand," said Willow. "Form a chain."

Holding on to Yarra and the Alfár's hands, Kell shuffled forward, following Willow towards the glowing doorway. His heart was pounding, but it was too late to turn back. Willow stepped into the light and vanished. Her fingers squeezed Kell's as his face made contact with the portal.

Much to his surprise, it was warm against his skin, but so bright he had to close his eyes. He couldn't see what happened when he passed through the doorway, but when the light had faded, he risked opening them again.

On the other side of the doorway was a place unlike anything he'd even seen before.

CHAPTER 7

Odd stepped through the doorway into a new world.

Everything was different. Overhead, a burnt umber sky was dotted with jet black clouds, and somewhere in the distance, an unfamiliar white sun was setting. If there were any stars in this place, he couldn't see them. The sky was utterly empty. The absence worried him on a gut-level, but he couldn't say why.

The air was sickly sweet, like molasses, heavy on the tongue and humid. Sweat covered his skin, and the others winced at the intense heat. Looking back at the way they'd come, Odd expected to see another tree. Instead, there was a huge, stone portal, more than five times the height of a human. The black slabs were covered with strange letters in a language he didn't recognise. The portal showed no signs of erosion. It was as if the doorway had just been built, but Odd could tell that it was ancient. It had a permanence that spoke of great age. He could feel it in his bones. It shimmered like water for a couple more heartbeats and then faded away, leaving behind only a solid wall. The way home was gone.

Off to one side were dozens of offerings. Trays of food that had withered away until they'd become unidentifiable brown husks. They were so old they no longer smelled of decay. Brightly coloured flowers, tied together with string, sat beside clumps of old withered stems. There were all sorts of random items that seemed to have little monetary value, but were clearly significant. A small painting of a figure. Jagged pieces of crystal and brightly polished rocks. A straw figure as long as his arm, dressed in real clothes.

It was a shrine, although to whom he couldn't say.

They were standing on a square platform at the top of a rise with a set of steps descending from three sides. The one in front curved down into a huge valley, at the bottom of which sat a sprawling city, unlike anything he'd seen before. The other two paths led to the slopes, which had been carved into terraces for farming. It was becoming too dark to see all the details, but Odd could just make out some kind of tall crops moving in the light breeze.

This wasn't just an undiscovered country. They were in another world. In spite of that, Odd was disappointed. Searching within, he realised that the hunger remained. He still carried it.

Yarra was visibly disoriented and Kell unsettled, but he was making an effort to mask his anxiety. Only the Alfár was unaffected by the doorway, but there was a deep sadness in her eyes. It was an unwanted homecoming.

"Where are we?" asked Kell.

"Your voice," said Odd, and then he heard it. His own words had taken on a peculiar resonance, as if two people with similar voices were speaking at the same time.

They didn't belong here.

"That is Yantou-vash. The last city of my people," said Willow, gesturing at the city below. Her voice had lost its peculiar timbre and sounded normal to his ears.

They'd only just arrived and yet, in this strange land, darkness was sweeping in fast. The white sun was falling towards the horizon with more speed than seemed possible.

"Come," said the Alfár. "We need to reach the city limits before it's too dark to see the path."

Willow led the way towards the city, but before they reached the outskirts, night had already fallen. They stumbled along, carrying the heavy sacks between them, which rattled and clanked in the dark. Several times, one of their party tripped or stumbled over an obstacle, but they managed to avoid serious injury.

Finally, as the path levelled off, the darkness was pushed back as light came from numerous buildings up ahead. This gave Odd his first real view of the city. He thought it resembled a monstrous series of giant anthills. The walls of each gnarled, conical building were pitted with dozens of small openings, like the cells of a beehive, but each had been filled with coloured glass. Light from within spilled out in a kaleidoscope of reds, greens, blues and yellows, blending together, creating new patterns and colours he couldn't name. There were no other windows and any doors were closed or hidden from view.

"This way," said Willow, leading them past the first clump of buildings. The city wasn't set out in a way that Odd recognised, adding to the feeling that they didn't belong.

After a while, Odd noticed the homes were grouped together in rough circles. Peering through the narrow spaces between the buildings, he could see tantalising glimpses of what was in the middle. Odd saw people moving around inside the homes, but no one came out to greet them, and no alarm was raised at their arrival, either.

"It's so random," said Kell, following the Alfár as she skirted another group of houses. The city had clearly not been built with a plan in mind. Odd guessed that over time it had been constructed out of necessity. The chaos of its design spoke to him of desperation.

Long shadows filled the spaces where the light from homes failed to penetrate. These dark pockets were bitterly cold, and Odd noticed their breath was starting to frost in the air. They needed to get indoors and find shelter soon.

"I can't feel my fingers," said Yarra, her teeth chattering. Kell was blowing on his hands, and even Odd was starting to feel a chill. He missed his uniform and its layers of warmth, as well as the protection the armour provided. Only the Alfár was unaffected by the temperature.

"In here," said Willow, gesturing towards another cluster of houses. Odd didn't know how she was able to navigate so well, as all of them looked identical in the dark. They walked down a narrow passage between two houses towards the centre. With his shoulders grazing the walls, Odd could hear conversations coming from within. The words were in a language he couldn't understand, but the tone of voices was gentle. A lullaby, or a lazy conversation between family members. Brushing one building with his fingers, he found the material smooth like pottery, despite its uneven appearance.

At the centre of the houses was a small garden. The thick branches of a single tree, laden with fruit, concealed the sky above. A single door in each home faced into the centre of the cluster. It suggested an intimacy that, once again, made Odd feel like an outsider.

Willow banged on a door and then waited, while everyone else tried to stay warm. The Alfár that answered the door was shorter than Willow, but otherwise the resemblance was uncanny. She had to be a close blood relative, or even a sibling. Her only distinguishing feature was a branching purple vein which ran down one side of her face. The skin around the blemish wasn't bruised, making Odd wonder if it was because of the Malice.

The two Alfár embraced and then, after pressing their foreheads together, whispered a greeting to each other. Willow gestured at each of them in turn and Odd heard Willow say their names, familiar sounds that stood out in an otherwise strange language.

"This is my sister-mother," said Willow. "Nyandar."

"Come inside quickly," said Nyandar, ushering them into her home. "It's not safe to be out at night."

The central room of the house was warm with heat coming from a generous fireplace. Odd glanced at the rest of the house as they congregated around the fire. He stared at the sloping ceiling, the curving staircase built into the wall, and the strange herbs hanging from a rack above their heads. Odd returned his eyes to the fire and its familiarity. The wood was glowing red and yellow. The ashes beneath the metal grill were grey and black. Finally, here was something familiar he could understand. Although the smell of the fire was a little unusual, he didn't care. The feeling was seeping back into his fingers and toes ,and for that, he was grateful.

Their host provided them with earthen bowls of stew and hunks of warm bread. Odd was famished and ate ravenously, savouring the tastes that were both peculiar and tantalisingly familiar. It almost tasted like potatoes and leeks, celery and carrots, but not quite. The food was filling and, like the entire city, he was curious about its origins. However, as with everything else, it could wait until tomorrow.

Whether it was from unexpected exhaustion due to their journey through the doorway, or because something had been added to the food, Odd began to doze by the fire. Gentle hands guided him up the stairs, supporting most of his weight. While he struggled to keep his eyes open, he felt himself being eased onto a soft bed. He was safe, warm and had been fed. All of his concerns would keep until morning.

A harsh sound woke Odd from his sleep. As he lay there, listening to his surroundings, he waited for the noise to repeat. When nothing happened, he slowly opened his eyes, poised for an attack, but there was nothing. Yarra was asleep next to him in a separate bed, her breathing deep and even. Kell and Willow were elsewhere. Slowly, his mind pieced together the noise and identified the source.

The sound had been in his sleep.

It had been a familiar scream from a recurring dream. His mother was being dragged away. She was laughing at the scattered, broken bodies of the soldiers around her and the savage wounds they'd inflicted, as if they were meaningless. Their blood was spattered across her face, between her teeth, splashed down the front of her dress. He saw again the shocked faces of neighbours on the street. They were ignorant. They didn't understand what she was, nor what she was becoming. Only he could see the light shining from every part of her skin. She was alive in a way they couldn't comprehend.

Sliding out from under the blanket, Odd was relieved that the floor beneath his feet was warm. It was covered with layers of reed mats, their geometric patterns barely visible in the gloom. Someone had taken off his socks, boots and jacket before stowing them and his pack beneath the bed. His sword and dagger were there too, but he left them behind. Sneaking around in boots was almost impossible, so on silent bare feet he crept out of the peculiar egg-shaped room towards the oval doorway. A thick curtain hung across the opening, blocking out the light, but also muffling sounds from the rest of the home. As he tugged the curtain aside, Odd heard a whispered conversation coming from below. He edged towards the stairs, until he could hear what was being discussed.

Peering around the edge of the railing, he saw Kell and the two Alfár sat together in front of the fire. The flames had died down to glowing embers, but heat was still pouring into the room. A half-empty bottle sat between them, and they were all sipping a plum coloured liquid from small glasses.

"–getting worse," he heard Nyandar say.

"Even here in the city?" asked Willow. "I'm surprised they would dare."

"They're desperate. Starving. But they still disappear down their holes when the sun rises."

"Something else for us to worry about," said Kell, before yawning.

"You should get some rest with the others," said Nyandar. "We can speak again in the morning."

"I'll go soon, I promise."

There was a strange silence and then Nyandar made an unusual huffing sound. It took Odd a moment to realise it was the Alfár's equivalent of laughter. "You seem at ease in our company, Kell Kressia. I am surprised."

"I spent a lot of time with your niece on a dangerous journey. I think we would call ourselves friends," he said.

"We are friends," said Willow. "I will tell you about it another time," she said to her aunt.

"Very well. Ask your question, Kell Kressia," said Nyandar.

"How is it that you know the human language so well?"

"You are not the first human to visit our homeland. Only Willow and Ravvi have ever travelled to the Five Kingdoms, but a long time ago, some of your people lived here. But that is not what you were going to ask me," said Willow's aunt.

"Did my people cause the Malice?" asked Kell.

A difference kind of silence filled the room. Odd was surprised when Willow embraced Kell, squeezing him tight.

"No. It was not you," said Nyandar, smiling at them both. "Your people are not to blame."

"Why would you think that?" asked Willow, still holding Kell's hand.

"You came to the Five Kingdoms in search of a cure. I thought we might have been responsible, because we failed in our duty to Govhenna."

"You know a great deal," said Nyandar.

Odd didn't understand what they were talking about, but it was clear that the Vahli saga about Kell's journey was only part of the story.

"No. The Malice cannot pass through the doorway. It's not your fault," said Willow. "Now, sleep and know that you are safe in this home."

Odd withdrew from the stairs and went back to his room before they noticed he'd been eavesdropping. Yarra was still asleep, oblivious to him sneaking about. He heard Kell come up the stairs, go into another room and settle down for the night. From below came an intense whispering as the two Alfár conversed in their own language. If he'd been able to understand the words, Odd suspected many secrets would have been revealed about this place, but their language was beyond his gifts.

Odd laid back down on the bed and, as he drifted on the edges of sleep, he wondered what other secrets Kell might be keeping from them.

The following morning, after a breakfast of fresh bread, fruit and nuts served with a peppery tea, Nyandar kitted them out with supplies for their journey. In daylight, the interior of the house was just as peculiar. Shafts of different coloured light criss-crossed the main room, bathing them all in strange hues. It made Yarra look as if she had a skin affliction. Odd was also able to see Nyandar more clearly. In addition to the strange veins on one side of her face, she had mottled patches of skin on the back of her hands and forearms. He wondered again if these were the effects of the Malice and what it would do to them.

While they waited for Willow to return from an errand, Odd watched Kell with renewed interest. Up to now, he'd always thought the man was fairly ordinary and of modest intelligence – that he'd survived both journeys to the Frozen North due to luck and being surrounded by skilled warriors. For the first time since they'd met, Odd questioned his initial assessment.

A short time later, Willow returned carrying four sets of unusual scale armour. The shirts were obviously made for Alfár, as it came down to Odd's knees when he put it on. But once they'd all been measured, Nyandar took the armour away to be resized.

With some time to spare, they were allowed outside. However, Willow discouraged them from going beyond the circle of houses for their own protection. All of the houses belonged to members of her extended family, and each Alfár Odd saw bore a passing resemblance to Willow. Although he saw no obvious physical deformities, each had been afflicted by the infection. Some had patches of discoloured skin, or black veins that stood out against their pale arms and faces. Some were obviously in pain, but they all did their best to conceal it. All of them were friendly, but Odd sensed that he and the other humans made the Alfár uncomfortable.

Odd had once seen an Alfár as a boy, and the image of it had haunted him. He'd seen the yellow-on-black eyes in his nightmares for months. Now they were everywhere and they still gave him a chill. Given what Nyandar had said last night, he wondered who he'd seen all those years ago, Willow or her cousin, Ravvi.

"How can you stand the heat? You're barely sweating." Yarra wiped sweat from her face and drank from her canteen. Even the water tasted different. It wasn't flat or metallic, just different. Softer, almost, and it had a faint floral odour that wasn't unpleasant. Odd ignored the question, letting the silence stretch out.

"Have you ever seen anything like it?" asked Yarra, looking up. Odd didn't know if she was talking about the strange tree they were sat beneath, or the city in general.

A short distance away, Kell and Willow were talking to an Alfár. The king seemed at ease on the surface, but after a couple of years, Odd could read his body language. As ever, Kell was anxious, but today he also seemed excited.

"Are you even listening to me?" asked Yarra. Odd hadn't been paying her enough attention.

"What?"

Yarra was staring at him expectantly. "There's just the two of us."

"I know."

"Then we need to be able to rely on each other."

"I agree," he said, not sure where she was going.

"What if I become dangerous or turn rabid?"

"If that happens, then I won't hesitate to kill you," said Odd.

Yarra's eyes widened in alarm. He'd made a mistake. She'd been talking about something else.

"You'd kill me?"

"Only if you threatened the king," he added.

She relaxed a little, but was still on edge. An awkward silence filled the space between them.

"What happens if both of us are infected?" said Yarra.

"Then the king may have to kill us."

"But what if he gets infected? Who will keep us heading in the right direction?"

"We will find a way," said Odd.

"How?"

No matter what he said, Yarra would not be satisfied. He'd seen this before with other people who'd suffered a loss of faith. Some turned to drink, others gambled. Her vice was self-doubt.

She was waiting for something to go wrong, just to be proven right. It was the easiest game to play in an imperfect world. She would have to break the cycle. Odd knew he should offer some words of encouragement, but he had none to give.

Leaving Yarra to stew over the future, he went to stand with Kell and Willow. Outside the circle of houses there was a flurry of movement and raised voices. He couldn't understand the words, but it didn't matter. Something had gone wrong. The clamour of many feet all moving in the same direction spoke of a gathering crowd.

"Stay here," said Willow, moving away to investigate, but Kell went after her. On impulse, Odd followed as well.

"You still need protection," said Odd, when the king noticed.

About forty Alfár were heading towards the source of the disturbance. He and Kell joined the back of the mob, and mostly went unnoticed. Odd realised every Alfár was armed, and many wore the same scale armour they'd been presented with that morning. They were clearly a people who were used to dealing with danger. These were warriors on a hunt, not a startled group of villagers.

"Blood," said Kell, pointing at the ground. There were spots of blue and then a trail, as if the bleeder had been running.

A little further on, there were noticeable pools of blood and splashes on the side of nearby homes. A vicious fight. The victim had been cornered and then fought for their life.

Not far away, the crowd had stopped and were staring at something on the ground. Willow eased her way to the front and they followed close behind. All of the Alfár stared at them, but no one barred their path.

When they reached the front, Willow had squatted down, giving Odd a clear view of the victim. The Alfár's torso had been torn open, revealing a jumble of organs that he didn't recognise. From the gaps, it looked as if some had been removed and possibly eaten. Other gnawed bits had been discarded and left beside the corpse. There were also defensive slashes on the victim's arms, but the wounds hadn't been made by any blade Odd recognised. The cuts were too uneven and jagged.

Dark-blue blood had soaked into the ground, making it soft. Around the body, he saw the clawed impressions of an animal. The spacing suggested a short creature with four legs, about the size of a large dog.

A flurried conversation started around them. Several Alfár were angrily pointing at the victim, their voices loud.

"What are they saying?" asked Kell.

"They're going to hunt it down. Dig it out of its burrow," said Willow, translating.

"What was it?" said Kell, pointing at the prints.

"A martok. A burrowing animal. They used to be harmless."

Even though he was in an unfamiliar land, filled with dangerous creatures, Odd felt reassured. Until now, he hadn't known how he was going to cope, but now he had an answer.

Although it had been some time since the victim had been killed, there was a familiar presence in the air. A doorway, one that only he could see, had opened and closed. That meant he could feed the hunger.

CHAPTER 8

Kell had been on edge since their arrival in Willow's homeland. The uncomfortable feeling in the pit of his stomach was a constant reminder that he didn't belong. After the familiarity of a warm fire, a hot meal and a good night's sleep, he thought it might have faded. Instead, it seemed worse than ever before. This was not his world and his body knew it.

His experiences in the Frozen North set him apart from others, but when meeting a stranger in the Five Kingdoms, it was possible to find something in common. Here, he would forever be an outsider. Someone who could never fully integrate with the locals, because he was fundamentally different from them.

Until that moment, he hadn't realised how much Willow must have endured by living in his world. He was ashamed to think about how she had been treated by everyone she'd encountered. It now made perfect sense that she preferred her own company, and would spend so little time surrounded by humans. Kell was keen to leave the Alfár's city and get away from so many strangers as soon as possible.

Although the thought of being away from his family was unsettling, Kell was glad to be free of the responsibilities that came with the throne. What he was doing here would actually make a difference. As king, it was more difficult to see the immediate impact of his decisions on the lives of others.

"This doesn't change anything," said Willow. He knew from

first-hand experience that Willow was incredibly tough. Even though she wasn't visibly upset, Kell knew she was distraught to see a dead Alfár.

"Are you sure a harmless animal did that?"

"Yes. It's this place. It changes everything. We have to leave as soon as possible," she said, leading them away from the crowd.

On the way back to Nyandar's house he saw a group of Alfár gathering weapons for a hunt. In a strange way it reminded him of Hundar. Over the centuries, the Hundarians had pushed back the wilderness, but every now and then a child would go missing. It was a harsh reminder of the brutality of nature. In the Alfár city, nature had been tainted, by something savage and inhuman. It also served as an unpleasant reminder of the Ice Lich and her power, which had corrupted the beasts of the Frozen North.

But unlike all Hundarian settlements, Yantou-vash had no defences of any kind. It was just a huge, sprawling collection of homes, clustered together for protection. If it was swarmed by tainted creatures, there would be a massacre.

When they returned to Nyandar's house, she was waiting for them at the front door with another relative. There was a passing resemblance between this Alfár and Willow, but the newcomer's skin was darker. His eyes were deep set, and there was only a slight mottling of the skin on his left arm. So far, Willow was the only Alfár Kell had seen without visible signs of infection.

"This is my kinsman, Maize," said Willow, introducing the newcomer. He said something abrupt in their native tongue. Kell guessed it was a complaint at the shortening of his name for the benefit of humans. Nevertheless, Maize gestured for him to step forward, before settling the armour over Kell's head.

All four of them had been measured earlier in the day, but final adjustments needed to be made to the scale armour.

"It's so light. What's it made from?" said Kell, not directing his question at anyone in particular. He was confident the individual plates weren't metal, but he couldn't identify them.

"They all come from an armoured beast. It died a long time ago," said Nyandar. A look passed between her and Willow. It was something else he wasn't supposed to ask about.

Maize finished making adjustments to Kell's shirt and then moved on to Yarra.

"Are we far behind Ravvi?" he said, hoping it was a safer topic. "Did he pass through here recently?"

"He was here not long ago," said Nyandar.

Maize barked something in their language and Willow practically winced. Kell assumed it was an insult or a curse about Ravvi.

Willow had spoken about her kinsman with sympathy and regret. She understood why Ravvi was disappointed and had lost faith in finding a cure. This was the first time Kell had seen genuine hostility directed at him.

The conversation dried up, and the rest of the adjustments to their armour were made in silence.

While the Alfár went to gather supplies for their trip, the group was left to rest beneath the spreading branches of the peculiar tree. The temperature wasn't uncomfortable yet, but it was still early in the day. He'd been told it was going to be another hot one, so he was glad of the shade.

"I wonder what it tastes like?" said Yarra, reaching towards one of the strange fruits. It was shaped like a small pear, but purple and fuzzy like a peach.

"It's probably poisonous," said Odd.

Yarra snatched her hand back and glared at him. "Of course it's not. They would have warned us."

Odd just shrugged, which only annoyed her further.

Leaving them to bicker, Kell took a short walk towards a makeshift clearing between two groups of houses. Today, the sky was pale grey and there was a light wind, bringing with it rich, earthy smells from the surrounding terraces. He could see many groups of Alfár tending to the crops, but something was bothering him about the peaceful scene. It reminded him of his old home town, Honaje, where he'd spent many long days working on the farm.

Turning around to survey the city, he realised what was missing. It had been right in front of him the whole time.

A short time later, Willow found him wiping unshed tears from his eyes.

"What's wrong?" she asked.

Kell's mouth was horribly dry. He knew the answer, but still had to ask the question. "Where are all the children?"

Willow sighed and Kell instinctively laid a hand on her arm. Her grief was palpable.

"There are no children. When the Malice first appeared, the young and the very old struggled the most. They were the first to die. While our Elders debated about what to do next, more of my people suffered and died. The wisest among our leaders left their homes and we followed. Sadly, many stayed behind in the old places."

"But wasn't that a long time ago? Many cycles?" said Kell, knowing that the Alfár didn't measure time in the same way as humans. "Surely some children have been born since then?"

"No. Not one."

Kell had already lost one child, and the grief of that had been crippling. It had left him numb for months, barely able to function. Deep inside him, there was a wound that would never heal. To lose every single child was a level of suffering he did not want to imagine. He couldn't begin to understand their collective grief.

It was far worse than he thought. Already cursed by a mysterious plague, the Alfár were now a dying race, and every death brought them one step closer to extinction.

They were supposed to be leaving the city straight away, but when Nyandar returned with their supplies, she was accompanied by a group of strangers. All of them wore armour and each carried a spear. So far, no one had mentioned a leader in the city, but from the way the others deferred to them, they must have had some kind of authority.

Willow and her aunt spoke with them at length. Even without being able to understand the words, it became apparent that it was not a friendly chat. Several times one of the strangers glanced or gestured towards Kell, as if he was responsible for something.

He wanted to ask what was happening, but knew better than to interfere. The Raven were alert, appearing to loiter nearby out of coincidence, but Kell knew they were prepared for a fight. When Odd touched the pommel of his sword and raised an eyebrow, Kell shook his head. They wouldn't make the first move. Whatever was happening in the city, it had nothing to do with them. He trusted Willow, but had no such loyalty to the other Alfár. He hoped they didn't attempt to take him somewhere against his will, as the result would be bloody.

Eventually, the tense conversation ended and the strangers moved away. Odd relaxed and Yarra went back to studying the tree.

"We cannot leave until tomorrow morning," said Willow, visibly annoyed at the delay. "Some of my people believe it was not a coincidence that a martok attacked so soon after our arrival."

"They think we're involved?" asked Kell.

"Not directly. Every time Govhenna's doorway to the Five Kingdoms is opened, there are ripples." Willow moved her hands through the air, wiggling her fingers.

"I didn't think you were superstitious," said Kell.

Willow cocked her head to one side in confusion.

"I mean that I didn't think your people believed in spirits and ghosts."

"No, we do not. But there are some things that we do not fully know. The doorway is one. The Malice is another. When the two meet," said Willow, sharply bringing her hands together, "something is felt. In the air and ground. We must wait until the hunters have found the martok. It shouldn't take them long."

"Then if we have time, can you tell us more about where we're going?" asked Yarra.

"Come. I will show you," said Willow.

She led them away from the relative safety of her family's home towards the far side of the city. It took almost an hour to reach the limits. During that time Kell was struck, time and again, by the differences between Yantou-vash and a human city. There were no clear streets and everything had a feeling of disharmony. Occasionally, they would run across what resembled a shop or a forge, but it was always on its own, surrounded by clusters of homes. A muscle twitched in Yarra's face at the chaos as she tried to cope with the random layout.

"It's too quiet," said Odd.

That was another thing that had been bothering Kell. Although there was a general background murmur of voices, the city had none of the familiar hustle and bustle. It felt more like a refugee camp.

"Where are all the birds?" asked Yarra.

There were none in the sky and no trees in the valley to act as perches. Many things which they took for granted, and expected to be part of the natural world, were missing from the Alfár homeland.

When they reached the outskirts of the city, there was no border. The collection of houses simply stopped. A short distance beyond that was the mouth of the valley. Looking out at the land beyond, Kell saw they were at a higher altitude than he'd realised. The land sloped away from them down to a wide plain dotted with occasional trees, but otherwise it was featureless. On the horizon he could see rising foothills.

Willow squatted down and the others joined her in a circle as she began to draw in the dirt with a finger. "Below us is the Vache, the Empty Plain. The name is a lie. There is risk, so we must be alert. We should post a guard throughout the night.

The plain leads to the Kolenn Mounds," said the Alfár, drawing
a straight line down to the distant lumpy foothills. "From
there, we travel inwards through Stejno, the slopes, to Riesla,
the Tangle." Her finger traced inwards and then began to move
in circles over and over, creating a blurred patch of earth. "It is
a dangerous place. Dark and hot with many threats."

"Enemies?" asked Yarra, suddenly alert.

"Yes, but not people. Not animals. Different," said Willow,
struggling for the right word. "They are–"

"Monsters," said Kell. The Alfár gave him one of her
unsettling half smiles, showing teeth.

"Tainted. Twisted things, changed by the Malice. It is difficult
to now recognise their start," said Willow.

"Is that what happened to the martok?" asked Kell.

"The Malice brought old darkness to the surface," said
Willow.

"I don't understand," said Kell.

Willow looked around, searching for something. She dug in
the ground with her fingers and eventually found a small black
stone. She dug around a bit more and found a white stone
which she held up as well.

"This is the martok," she said, pointing at the white stone.
"It is gentle. It lives in burrows and eats plants. It was a soft
creature, but then, the Malice crept inside. Deep within and
long ago, the martok was something else. Powerful. Hungry.
An eater of meat. It dreams of the old days, hunting and
killing. The Malice knows and brings forth the worst. The
teeth and claws grow long. The hunger returns. Now it is
something new and yet old," said the Alfár, pointing at the
black stone.

"The hunger?" said Odd.

It was the first time since they'd met that Kell had ever seen
him surprised. It was there for a moment and then it was gone.
But there had been something else on his face as well. A raw
emotion. Fear.

"For the hunt," said Willow, unaware of Odd's unease. "But its old prey is dead. Dust. So instead, it attacks whatever is nearest. Sometimes it hunts my people."

The idea that the Malice was almost aware, that it could use his desires against him, was deeply unsettling. The more Kell learned, the more he thought he'd made a terrible mistake coming on this journey.

"Think on yourself. Not the mask, but deep within," said the Alfár touching her chest and then her forehead. "Know your true self. Be aware, because if there is darkness inside, the Malice will find it."

"Where do we go after the Tangle?" asked Yarra. Her eyes were focused on the makeshift map, recording the details, perhaps building strategies in her mind. Maybe some of the old instincts remained. Kell hoped so, as they would need her skills if they were to survive.

"Then we will come to Robra, the Boneyard. It is a desolate place. The heart of what was my people's homeland – the abandoned city of Laruk. The ruins of the old. Now, it is a graveyard for many," said Willow, bowing her head for a moment in remembrance. Yarra was about to ask another question but Kell waved her off, giving the Alfár a little time.

"It is after that we will face the worst threat. The greatest horror."

The others looked at Kell expectantly, and eventually he had to ask. "What is it?"

"We came to Yantou-vash to rebuild our lives, but many of my people refused to leave the old places. We are just the remnants," said Willow, gesturing at the city around them. "But not all who stay were killed by the Malice. Many were corrupted. They are now perverse beings, and they will try to kill us."

Kell had seen Willow's strength. He knew what one Alfár was capable of, never mind hundreds or perhaps thousands.

"Where are they?"

"They were driven north, to the Choke. It is a narrowing," said Willow bringing her hands close together until they were almost touching. "We must find a way through the tainted horde. On the other side is the first place the Malice was found. Ravvi will be going there. We must stop him."

"We will," said Kell, but even he thought it sounded like an empty promise.

Before nightfall, which came unusually fast again, the hunters returned in triumph. When they passed Nyandar's house, Kell risked a glance at the crowd and caught a brief glimpse of the martok. The carcass was carried between two of the Alfár on a pole. Once, it might have been a harmless burrowing animal, with features that suggested both a rabbit and a mole, but the Malice had changed it into something brutal. It had distended front limbs, savage ripping claws and powerful back feet tipped with huge nails. Its snout was elongated, lined with a row of sharp teeth, and a green tongue lolled from its mouth. In death, it seemed rather pathetic, but he'd seen what it had done to one of the Alfár, and any sympathy faded in the wake of its savagery.

Now that it had been caught, they would be able to leave in the morning. Willow was still annoyed about the delay as it put them further behind Ravvi. One thing she hadn't mentioned, and he didn't feel comfortable asking in front of the others, was if her kinsman was travelling alone. If he had help from other Alfár, who believed in his desperate cure, then intercepting him would be even more difficult. However, if Ravvi was by himself, then apprehending him might be easier, but only if they could outpace him. He would face the same dangers as them, but without help from others. Kell thought Ravvi's chances of success were slim. It would require an iron will to stay focused during such a hazardous journey.

It took a long time for sleep to wash over him. As much

as what lay ahead plagued his mind, his thoughts returned to Sigrid. Their reunion had been joyful but brief. Kell truly hoped that when he returned, their life would be different.

There was Marik to think about too. If the journey took a few weeks of travel here, then it could be several months back home, or even a year. Hopefully, at his son's current age, such a period of absence would go unnoticed.

Kell was determined to be there for all of the important moments that his own father had missed. He'd died before Kell had turned five, so there had been no one to show him how to fish, how to shave, how to talk to girls, and how to be a good man. It was no wonder that he'd grown up wanting to be like the heroes.

There was so much Kell wanted to teach his son.

When he finally dozed off, Kell dreamed about staring at himself in a mirror, but no matter how he moved, the image was always slightly askew.

CHAPTER 9

Just as they had on the first night, Nyandar and Willow stayed up for a long time, talking quietly by the fire. Willow had been away for many years and they obviously had a lot to catch up on. Odd lay on his bed and waited for hours before they eventually retired.

In the dead of night, when he was certain everyone was asleep, Odd got dressed and crept out of the bedroom he shared with Yarra.

As Odd sat on the far side of the curtained doorway, he listened to the house. Most buildings creaked, ticked and groaned at night as they adjusted to changes in temperature, but whatever the Alfár had used to make their homes, they didn't respond in the same way. The house was utterly silent and still. He could hear the others breathing, snoring and shuffling about in their beds, but nothing else.

In the main room, he slipped on his boots and studied the front door. It had no lock, but a wooden bar lay across it on the inside. From what Willow had told them about her homeland, there were far worse things lurking in the darkness than martoks. Blocking the door at night seemed like a wise precaution.

Outside, the air was cold and Odd's breath immediately frosted in front of his face. He couldn't see anything moving in his immediate vicinity, and any sounds were muffled and indistinct. A low mist clung to the ground, adding to the feeling that he was in a dream, or a city full of ghosts.

Nevertheless, Odd proceeded with caution, sticking to the shadows. He found a dark corner between the house and its neighbour and stashed a spare set of clothing he was carrying, just in case. Despite the hour, he saw light in a few houses, but the majority were dark and shrouded in silence.

Even though he was unfamiliar with the place, there was a recognisable cohesion that came from so many living close together. Patterns formed without most even being aware. In a human city, people would stay up late into the night, drinking in bars and taverns. Criminals and prostitutes would prowl the streets, looking for opportunities. Then, in the coldest and quietest part of the night, right before the dawn, a city would echo with silence. But without any nocturnal activities, most of the Alfár went to bed early, and the empty night stretched on for hours until morning.

After a while, Odd became aware of an unusual and repetitive noise in the distance. Moving closer to the sound, he realised it was several people chanting in unison. He couldn't tell if they were singing, or it was some kind of ceremony. Curiosity drew him nearer, until he found the source of the noise emanating from a strange building.

All of the homes in the city were of a similar shape, which is why the squat structure stood out among the others that surrounded it. Odd crouched down a short distance away, noting the wide, sloping roof that was low to the ground. It also had a small door that was partly submerged in the earth. Any Alfár would have to crawl to get inside. A narrow plume of grey smoke rose in a continuous stream from a small opening in the centre of the roof. It had a floral and slightly acrid scent, as if they were burning flowers or herbs. Outside the door, he could just make out what looked like several piles of discarded clothing, but he didn't risk getting any closer to make sure.

The chanting voices, perhaps a dozen in total, rose in volume. While the Alfár's language was incomprehensible to him, it had a certain lilting rhythm that he normally recognised. This, however, was something else. A simplistic chant, or a short phrase repeated over and over. It was hypnotic and he guessed part of a ritual.

Odd found himself lulled into a daze by the sound and he struggled to stay awake. Eventually the chanting stopped, and a short time later the low door swung open. A dozen naked Alfár crawled out and quickly began to dress in the cool air. Staring at their naked bodies, Odd felt no desire or arousal, merely curiosity as he studied their unusual curves and angles.

The interior of the strange building behind them was shrouded with smoke, so he was unable to see inside. Once they were all dressed, the Alfár exchanged a few words and then began to disperse. One female remained behind to secure the building.

Willow had told them about what lay ahead on the journey. A landscape full of twisted monsters. The gradual erosion of their mind and grip on reality. Tomorrow morning would be too late. It was a huge risk, the biggest he had ever taken in his life, but Odd knew he wouldn't find a better opportunity.

Moving as fast as possible, while scanning the ground for obstacles, he came up behind the Alfár. Somehow, she heard his approach and turned around before he was close enough to strike. Her initial surprise faded when the Alfár saw that it was him. Their arrival was not a secret, and he was one of only three humans in the city, which made him a curiosity. She didn't see him as a threat, especially as he smiled and kept walking forward until he was close enough to touch her.

She said something in her language. It had the lilt of a question. Perhaps she was asking if he was lost.

"I was looking for you," he said, still walking forward. As she began to reply, he stabbed her in the chest just above the belly. With a human he would have gone for the heart, but the Alfár were different inside. There hadn't been much time to study the Alfár killed by the martok, but he'd seen enough. They had at least two hearts, and their other organs were arranged differently. With both hands on the hilt, he tried to drag the blade up and disembowel her.

Instead of screaming, she hissed like angry cat and lashed out, sending him spinning away, bleeding from the scalp. Something stabbed into the small of his back as he landed. Odd drew on the well of energy inside, fed strength into his limbs, and scrambled upright. Rich blue blood was gushing from the wound in her stomach, but the Alfár was still on her feet. He thought she might cry out for help, or try to run. Instead, she merely stared at him and waited.

Odd launched himself at her, using his weight to bear her to the ground with him on top. She landed badly and cried out, but as he tried to cover her mouth the Alfár head-butted him. Black stars danced in front of his eyes and pain shot up his nose. It was definitely broken. He tried to silence her again, and this time she bit his hand, drawing blood.

The dagger was slick and difficult to grip, but Odd managed to pull it from her body. They fought for control of the weapon, rolling back and forth on the ground. She bit and clawed at him and eventually managed to sink her teeth into his shoulder. Odd wanted to scream, but instead he ground his teeth together. She spat out a lump of his flesh and red blood mixed with blue on the ground.

The loss of blood from the chest wound he'd inflicted finally slowed her down a little. Using more energy to strengthen his limbs, Odd was able to wrestle the dagger away from her hands. Before she could scream again, he stabbed her in the chest, three, four, five times. Again, and then again. There was no chance of making it resemble a martok attack. He needed to slow her down, otherwise she was going to kill him. She was far stronger and tougher than he'd realised.

After stabbing her more than twenty times, the Alfár began to weaken. Her struggles lost their energy and she lay back, arms at her side, breathing heavily.

Dropping the dagger, Odd tried to ignore his wounds and

focused on staying conscious. Every second he sat beside the dying Alfár put him at greater risk of discovery, but he had no choice. The hunger was relentless, and he was its slave. All of this would be for nothing if he gave up now.

It took a long time, but eventually the moment approached. The familiar prickle along the back of his neck told him they were not alone. The Alfár's eyes widened as she stared at something far away. Something secret that no living being had ever seen before.

Moving closer, Odd took a deep breath and then placed his mouth over hers. As the light faded from her eyes he inhaled deeply, drawing energy from the dying Alfár into himself.

An unpleasant burning sensation ran through his veins. It started in his throat, then raced throughout his body, until it felt as if he was on fire. It shouldn't be like this. It should have been ecstasy.

The pain was so intense Odd fell back and began to convulse. His wounds were forgotten as a greater agony swallowed him whole. The world faded away and he fell into a pit of darkness. His flesh was burned away by the fire. His bones were melted down to ash, then ground to dust beneath a black slab of all-consuming pain.

He drifted, in a nowhere place, for a long time, caught between two worlds.

Slowly, so slowly, the agony receded. The fire in his veins ebbed away and eventually he was able to sit up. Touching his face, Odd realised his nose was back to normal and had been repaired. The wound in his shoulder was also gone. Looking himself over, Odd noticed that all of his wounds had been healed. He was still covered in blood, but his body was whole.

Somewhere, deep inside, an ember of the Alfár remained. It had not been completely extinguished, and even now he could feel it, like a thorn under his skin. Despite the lack of pain and injuries, Odd didn't feel euphoric.

Something was horribly wrong.

An intense jolt of pain ran through his stomach and he doubled up. His vision swam and then resettled. The pain faded away, but Odd was worried it might return. He could black out again and had no way of knowing if he had cried out during the fight. He had to get back.

He concealed the Alfár's body inside the sweat lodge, so that someone wouldn't stumble over it. It wasn't perfect, but it would do. He just had to hope they left the city before anyone noticed her absence.

With lurching steps, Odd retraced his route and retrieved his spare set of clothes. A short distance away he found one of the stone wells that were dotted around the city. After he stripped off, he drew up a bucket of water and rinsed as much blood from his skin as possible. The water was icy cold, and he shivered in the dark as he dressed.

His old clothes were a lost cause, caked in mud and soaked in human and Alfár blood. If he had more time he would bury or clean them, but Odd felt whatever thread of luck had been with him was wearing dangerously thin. Instead, he wrapped the garments up into a tight ball and stuffed them under one arm. He'd worry about them later. His first priority was to get inside Nyandar's house without being discovered. With every step he expected someone to raise an alarm, but the dark concealed much. Thankfully, this late at night, almost no one was awake.

Disorientated and still wracked with pain, Odd stumbled into the house and took off his boots. Mercifully, there was no one inside the main room. Getting up the stairs was difficult, as spasms of pain raced along his nerves. Eventually he made it to the bedroom and, to his relief, Yarra didn't stir as he crawled inside. After stuffing his filthy clothes to the bottom of his pack, Odd climbed into bed.

Despite warming up beneath the blankets, Odd continued to shiver, but it wasn't from the cold. Occasionally a jolt of energy ran through his body, making his limbs twitch uncontrollably. A stabbing pain blossomed in his stomach, mirroring the wounds he'd inflicted on the Alfár. It was just coincidence though, nothing more. After a while it ebbed away, but then something else took its place. A tingling across his scalp, then stabbing pains across the soles of his feet. The hunger had faded, but he didn't know for how long, or if it had been worth the risk.

He tried to get some sleep, but random pains continued to surface and then fade away throughout the night. When something crawled up his leg he kicked off his blanket and scratched at the skin on his thigh. There was little light in the room, but just enough for him to see a distinctive blemish on the skin. He'd not only absorbed the Alfár's energy, but also her sickness. He was now infected with the Malice.

Hours later, burning with fever, dripping with sweat and barely clinging to consciousness, Odd saw a figure enter the room. At first, he thought it was Willow, but as they drew closer their features coalesced into that of his mother.

She was younger than he remembered and more carefree. At the end, there had been traces of grey in her hair around the temples. It was nothing more than an affectation, to throw people off the scent, but it hadn't worked. They'd still come for her, with fire and wrath.

"Mother," he said, reaching out towards her.

"Sleep, my son," she said, looking down at him. Her gentle smile was like a soothing balm against his skin. There were so many things he wanted to ask her. About her life before he'd been born. About his father. About the hunger. "Rest," she said.

He felt her settle on the edge of his bed. She pulled up the blanket, tucked it beneath his chin, and laid a cool hand on his forehead.

"Mother."

"I'm here. I'll watch over you," she promised him.

He'd been trying to sleep for hours, and now he wanted to stay awake to be with her. Odd's body felt so heavy and tired. He tried to fight it, but a great weight settled on him. The last thing he saw before passing out was her gentle face.

Someone was shaking him by the shoulder. As Odd came awake and took in his surroundings, the events of last night came flooding back.

"What's happening?" he asked, fearing the worst.

"We're getting ready to leave."

Odd's head swam as he sat up and winced in pain.

"Are you all right?" asked Yarra.

"I just need a moment." His vision turned black but it quickly began to recede. He'd never experienced anything like this before in his life. It was almost like a hangover.

"You're a really heavy sleeper. I tried to wake you earlier, but you didn't move. At first, I thought you were dead. Breakfast?"

"I'll be right there," he promised.

Once she'd left the room, Odd checked his leg and wasn't surprised to see a grey patch of discoloured skin on his thigh. At least it hadn't spread, and so far it didn't hurt.

After washing the sweat from his body in a bowl of water, he dressed in clean clothes and joined the others for breakfast. They made small talk but Odd simply listened, his mind distracted by the images of his mother. It must have been the fever, and yet it had felt so real.

Feeling a prickle on the back of his neck, Odd glanced around and saw Willow staring at him. Her expression was impossible to read and her eyes gave nothing away, but he didn't think she was simply curious.

"Are you all right?" asked Kell, noticing he was distracted.

"Strange dreams."

Willow bobbed her head. "The Malice."

"Isn't it a bit early for that?" said Kell. "You said the effects would be slower on humans."

"Perhaps," conceded the Alfár, but Odd thought she was humouring him.

It was inevitable that all of them would become infected. Odd had merely accelerated the process. If the lines between vision and reality were already beginning to blur, then going forward, he would have to be extremely careful.

They ate a hearty breakfast of bread, fruit, boiled eggs, cheese and butter, but once again Odd noticed there was no meat.

"Do you have any cows or pigs here?" asked Yarra, echoing his thoughts.

Nyandar and Willow exchanged a look before their host slowly nodded, giving permission.

"No. We have no animals like that," said Willow. "Once, there was something similar. Cattle for herding, milk and meat. Now, all of them are infected and their meat is tainted."

"Then where does the milk come from?" asked Kell, holding up a piece of smoky orange cheese. It was slightly bitter, as if marbled with mould, but the surface was clear.

"It comes from a zhagvet. It is like a hairless goat."

Yarra swallowed the piece of cheese she'd been chewing and glanced at the eggs. They were slightly larger than a hen's and she didn't ask. Sometimes, it was better not to know.

"No horses, then," said Kell.

Odd had also been thinking about the journey ahead.

"No. We have none," confirmed Willow.

"That explains why they don't like you," said the king. He shared a smile with the Alfár, hinting at something from their shared past.

Nyandar filled their packs with as much food as they could carry, which Odd guessed would last a week. After that, they would have to forage, and the further they went, the greater the risk of infection. From what Willow had said, the spread of the Malice was much worse in the north, especially in the Tangle. Also, without any horses, he guessed that it would take weeks to reach their destination. Their odds of survival were getting smaller all the time.

"Thank you for letting us stay in your home," said Kell, making a point of honouring their host. Much to everyone's surprise, Nyandar embraced the king, which he slowly returned.

Outside, Odd noticed a small crowd had gathered. His first thought was they had come for him, but as he reached for his sword he saw they were Willow's family. All of them bore a passing resemblance to one another, and once again he was struck by the absence of children or old people. Kell had shared with them the awful toll the disease had taken on the Alfár people.

The crowd waved them all off, standing in the shade beneath the wide limbs of the strange tree, but they didn't leave the circle of their houses.

When they reached the edge of the city, Odd breathed a sigh of relief. No one had discovered the dead body from last night. It was possible that someone would pursue them once it was found, but he thought it unlikely. Murders had to happen. He couldn't believe that no Alfár had ever killed another.

They walked down a gentle slope out of the valley heading towards the wide, open plain. In the distance Odd could see foothills, but ahead only uneven grasslands broken by half-buried slabs of grey rock, scree slopes and the occasional withered tree.

"You seem relieved," said Kell. At first, Odd thought the king was talking to him. As he turned his head to answer, he realised Kell was speaking to Willow. "Did you not enjoy being among your people?"

At first the Alfár didn't answer, but eventually she spoke. "It is difficult, after being with humans for so long. There is much about my people that I had forgotten. Their suspicion of strangers. The poison that sings inside them. In the Five Kingdoms, all of that was left behind."

Odd felt a twinge of pain in response to Willow's words, but he knew it was nothing more than coincidence. Either that, or it was another mild hallucination like the vision of his mother.

"There's a great sadness in them," said Kell. "I felt it from the moment we arrived."

"They are dying, and yet they do nothing. Ravvi and I were seen as rebels," said Willow. "I had hoped that in the time I was away something would have changed. That others would have tried to find a cure on their own, but they have done nothing. It is as if they have given up."

Odd hadn't noticed the sadness Kell had mentioned, but he could see it in Willow's face. They were risking their lives to save her people, while they did nothing for themselves.

They'd been on their own long before they'd left Yantouvash.

CHAPTER 10

"So, what do you think?" asked Sigrid.

Natia looked up from the latest carving in her lap. It was a small bird in flight, although it was too early to say what species. "Do you want my honest opinion?"

"Of course," said Sigrid, running a hand down the dress.

"It's the same colour as something your son produced this morning, when he vomited up his breakfast."

Natia's brutal honesty was often welcome, but not always appreciated. Unfortunately, on this occasion, she was right.

"Help me with the buttons," said Sigrid, turning around.

Natia brushed off her fingers and then unfastened the top six buttons of the dress. Sigrid went into the next room to change, leaving the door open so they could talk. A royal-blue dress would be a safe choice. It was one she'd worn in the past while attending events, but the people wouldn't care. Besides, it was comfortable and warm.

"I'll be ready to leave in a few minutes. Please let my guards know."

"You should take more than two guards with you," yelled Natia from the other room.

"Too many would make me look weak and seem heavy-handed. It would also appear as if I couldn't trust my own people."

"At least take one of the Raven, or let me come with you instead."

"That might be a little difficult to explain," said Sigrid,

hanging up the vomit-coloured dress. It had been a gift from ambassador Gryce of Seithland. Sigrid suspected the ambassador had also received it as an unwanted gift. Despite the colour, it was exquisitely made. There was no way Gryce would simply give away something that expensive for free. She would expect something in return for such generosity.

"Why?" asked Natia.

"People might wonder why my son's nursemaid is visiting an orphanage without the prince." Sigrid shrugged into the blue dress and reached behind her back to fasten the buttons.

"You're the queen," said Natia. "Who's going to question you?"

She had a point. But there were always people looking for a way to exert pressure on Sigrid. Right now, the Reverend Mother was on the rampage after her missionaries had been summarily expelled across Algany. Too many questions might be asked if Natia accompanied her into the city.

"I'll be fine. Stop worrying," said Sigrid. Her two guards were loyal and competent. They would be more than enough protection, especially in her own city.

"Just to put my mind at ease, please take four guards," said Natia as Sigrid re-entered the room. "Much better," she said, nodding with approval at the navy dress.

"Fine. Four guards." Sigrid rolled her eyes, but part of her was pleased. It was nice to have someone care so much about her well-being. Her mother had been gone for a long time and Lukas, although he did his best, was no substitute for her father. In addition, Kell had been gone for three months and she was really starting to feel his absence. The palace was too quiet without him. She hadn't realised how much space he'd occupied. She hoped he was on his way home by now.

Before she started moping about her husband, Sigrid headed for the door, forcing a warm smile onto her face.

"And this is where the younger children sleep," said the

orphanage administrator, a lanky man called Ephram. The dormitory was cramped but well-kept, with bunk beds running in two rows down the room. A pair of small wooden chests sat at the foot of every bed. It wouldn't hold much, but before coming here, the children had been living on the streets. Sigrid was confident none of them would complain about having limited space.

She smiled and nodded at Ephram's running commentary, doing her best to pretend she'd never seen a child's bedroom before. The real reason she'd come was to find out how the older children were progressing. The crown funded several orphanages in the city, but this was the first to incorporate a workshop. Those who were interested could begin an apprenticeship in carpentry, metalwork or making furniture.

At the far end of the room, two of her royal guards were keeping watch. Two more were in the corridor a short distance behind. All of them were doing their best not to look too bored. Sigrid gestured for the two in front to go ahead down to the workshop. The biggest threat in the building was getting a splinter. Nevertheless, it paid to be cautious. A queen was never without enemies.

She followed the guards at a more sedate pace with the administrator, who insisted on describing everything in detail. They walked through the older children's dormitory and then down a narrow set of winding stairs to the ground floor. With the children at school, it was a lot easier for Sigrid to tour the building. The place was old, but in good condition, although she thought she could smell damp. It was something she'd have to mention to Lukas.

Downstairs, Ephram had a small office, and there was a bedroom at the back for someone to sleep on site. One member of staff was always available throughout the night. The ground floor also housed a large kitchen, games room, and a walled-off yard for the children to play in safety, away from the streets and those who might lead them astray.

Before coming here, some of the children had been pickpockets and thieves, forced to steal for someone else. A few had sold their bodies for money, but most had been beggars. The brutality of their lives had been severe, and many of them still bore scars, both physical and mental. Hopefully with time, and patient care, they would recover.

As Sigrid considered what they had endured, her thoughts turned to her son, Marik. He would never know such hardships, but part of her knew she could not remove all traumas from his life.

"Two of the children are currently apprenticing with a local baker," said Ephram, by way of apology for the flour scattered across the kitchen floor. He was nervous and kept staring at her in amazement. Sigrid was used to it. A lot of people had seen her at a distance, but few had the chance to speak with her face to face. It was almost as if she wasn't a real person in their mind.

"The workshop is through here," he said, leading her down a narrow passageway that opened out into a wide room. The walls were covered with carpentry tools. There was a small forge in one corner and two huge workbenches in the centre of the room. Scattered across the top were half a dozen unfinished projects, pieces of twisted metal and half-formed chairs. Despite the open windows the room smelled unpleasantly ripe, as if something was rotting.

"I'm sorry," said Ephram, tripping over something. Sigrid looked down, expecting a forgotten tool, but instead she saw that it was an arm. One of her guards lay face down on the floor. A pool of blood was spreading out from a wound across her throat. A short distance away the other guard was on his knees. He'd been disembowelled but was trying to hold in his guts, which spilled out around his fingers.

"I'm so sorry," Ephram said again, as he backed away across the room.

The door to the workshop opened and a large bearded man

entered from outside. His clothes were plain and his features ordinary, but Sigrid was focused on the sword in his hand. There were two more armed men outside, but they didn't come into the building.

From around one of the workbenches came a woman, armed with a pair of daggers. Both of them were already covered with blood.

"Go," said the big man.

"They have my wife," said Ephram, backing away towards the door. "I had no choice." At least he hadn't betrayed her for money. Given the situation, it was a small consolation.

"Go now, before I change my mind," said the big man. The administrator hurried out and the big man locked the door behind him.

Sigrid still had two more guards. If she screamed, they would definitely hear and come running. She glanced behind her, hoping to see them, but the corridor was empty.

The big man grinned. "No one is coming."

"I could scream," said Sigrid.

"Please do," said the woman. "It makes this more interesting."

Taking a deep breath Sigrid screamed at the top of her lungs until she ran out of air. The sound echoed around the room and then died.

If the guards were in the building, they would have heard her by now, which meant they were also dead. No one was coming to save her.

"Feel better?" asked the woman. With a casual flick of her wrist, she cut the throat of the injured guard. He choked for a few seconds and then slumped to the floor.

A scuffing sound drew her attention. Glancing over her shoulder Sigrid saw a rangy man, armed with a bloody mace, coming up behind her. Sigrid picked up a hammer from the workbench and tried to stay calm.

"No clever words? No threats or attempts at a bribe?" asked the woman with the daggers.

"I don't see that there's much point," said Sigrid, trying to keep an eye on all three of them. The man behind her was creeping up slowly. It was difficult to know who would reach her first. The big man stayed beside the door and seemed happy to watch.

"How about some pleading?" asked the woman as she inched forward. "I always enjoy a bit of that."

"Get on with it, Merle," said the big man.

"I'm just having a bit of fun," said Merle. She ran the point of her dagger across the workbench, scoring a line on the surface.

"Who sent you?" asked Sigrid, playing for time.

"Does it matter?" asked Merle. It did, but only if Sigrid got out of the room alive.

She feinted towards Merle with the hammer and then turned quickly, aiming a blow at the man behind her. In her panic it slipped from her grip, catching them both by surprise. Instead of hitting him in the head, she clipped his shoulder and heard something crack. His arm hung at a peculiar angle and he stumbled back with a scream of pain.

"Aggghh, she broke my shoulder!"

As Sigrid spun around, Merle was already rushing forward. Sigrid picked up a lump of wood from a workbench and tried to keep the woman at bay. Merle slashed with her daggers, forcing Sigrid back towards the injured man. Despite the broken shoulder, he was still conscious and angry. There was nowhere to go.

Merle grinned in delight as if Sigrid were a cornered mouse.

Something heavy slammed into the back door. It was so hard that it unseated the big man who'd been leaning against it. While Merle was distracted, Sigrid swung her wooden club, but Merle heard it coming and danced out of the way. As they faced off, something hit the back door again, heavy enough to rattle the hinges. The big man backed up a few steps, staring in alarm. The third blow was so powerful the door broke, falling into the room. It clipped the big man on the thigh and, with a hiss of pain, he stumbled back and fell to his knees.

Sigrid caught a brief glimpse of a Choate warrior dressed in leather armour, carrying a short sword in one hand. Outside on the ground, Sigrid saw two men with bloody wounds.

The big man had barely raised his sword before the Choate warrior was on him, moving past a clumsy swing. She ducked beneath a slash, moved inside his guard and stabbed him twice in the chest. Before he'd even realised what had happened, the warrior was heading towards Merle.

The big man coughed once and dropped his weapon. He put a hand to his chest and collapsed onto his face.

Merle actually grinned, apparently delighted at the prospect of a good fight. She turned away from Sigrid, not considering her a threat. Her smile faltered when Sigrid slammed her club into Merle's shoulder.

Merle howled in pain, realising too late that she was actually trapped between two enemies.

"A little help, Rek!" she shouted at the man with the broken shoulder. Something silver whipped past Sigrid's face too fast for her to see. Rek stumbled back with a dagger in his throat. He choked and spluttered, but it was already too late. Merle was alone, and the odds were against her.

"Drop the dagger," said Sigrid. Merle licked her lips, assessing her chances of escape. "You don't have to die."

"I'm not going to beg," promised Merle.

"I don't want you to," said the warrior. Her gaze never wavered from her opponent. When Merle feinted with her dagger, the Choate barely moved, angling her body to one side. Merle picked up a piece of wood and hurled it at the warrior, before she scrambled over a workbench. The Choate stabbed her once in the thigh and stepped back as Merle's dagger came back around in an arc.

"Don't be stupid," said Sigrid. "Tell me who sent you."

"Your blasphemy must end," said Merle.

Blood was pouring from the wound in her leg and her shoulder was injured, but Merle refused to give in. She hobbled towards the door on one leg, but the Choate warrior got there before her.

"Don't," warned the Choate, but Merle ignored her. Instead, she launched another frenzied attack, slashing wildly with her dagger, trying to create enough space to escape. Merle was losing a lot of blood and didn't have much time. Desperation gave her speed and she came close enough to elbow the Choate in the face. As the warrior stumbled back, Merle made a final run for the door.

Before she had put a foot outside, the Choate's sword punched through Merle's back. The point emerged in the centre of her chest and she stared at in surprise. Wasting no time, the warrior pulled the blade free, letting Merle's body drop to the ground.

"Are there any more assassins?" asked the warrior, addressing Sigrid for the first time.

"No," she said. "They're all dead."

"Are you sure?" asked the Choate.

"No, I'm not. Who are you?" asked Sigrid, staring at the triangular tattoos on the woman's face. They ran down her right cheek and there were similar designs on her neck. She retrieved her dagger from one of the bodies and quickly assessed the others. Everyone else in the room was dead. The stink of open bodies was steadily getting worse.

"I'm Gar Malina. Come with me," said the warrior, heading for the door. "I'll make sure you get back to the palace."

"How did you know I was in trouble?"

"I heard you scream," said Malina, studying the street outside.

"No," said Sigrid. "I mean, why were you nearby?"

"Kell told me to keep an eye on you."

"You know my husband?" said Sigrid.

"Of course," said the Choate. "He's my cousin."

* * *

Despite her protests that she'd suffered no injuries, Sigrid had to endure an hour of being poked and prodded by the royal physician. Eventually, he declared Sigrid unharmed and she was allowed to return to her rooms to change out of the blood-spattered dress.

Walking three paces behind her at all times were two members of the Raven, grim-faced and armed to the teeth. Sigrid had the feeling they would never leave her side for the rest of her life. The number of palace guards had been doubled and all of them were itching for a fight. Not just because of what had happened to her, but also for the murder of their friends. The attack had taken place in her own capital city. If there was anyone still tied to the attack in the country, they would soon wish they were dead.

Sigrid had not thought the Reverend Mother capable of sending assassins. This dramatic change of her style was both surprising and worrying. She usually preferred to operate in more subtle ways. Sigrid would not underestimate her again.

As Sigrid entered her study, Lukas and their special guest, Malina, came to their feet. "Please sit," she said, collapsing into a chair. The others followed suit. Her stomach rumbled, but right now Sigrid wasn't sure food was the best idea. The smells and images of dead bodies were still firmly lodged in her mind.

"I have two dozen palace guards scouring the city," said Lukas. There was little that made him nervous, but Lukas kept glancing at the Choate. "A number of agents are also investigating the attack using a more subtle approach. We will find out who was behind this."

"I already know. It was Reverend Mother Britak. One of the killers said something about blasphemy."

"I didn't think she'd be so obvious," said Lukas.

"Me either," said Sigrid. "I suspect there will be no proof she was directly responsible. People paid anonymously and so on, but she was definitely behind it."

"You must have made her really angry," said Malina. "Now that you're safe, can I leave?"

"Actually, I wanted to talk to you about something else," said Sigrid.

"What about?" asked Malina.

"I need your help. The Reverend Mother is determined that the Five Kingdoms follow the Shepherd's teachings. She will do anything to make sure that happens."

"You mean her version of the book," said the Choate, leaning back in her chair. Her eyes glowed with anger. Even though the Raven had insisted on taking away Malina's weapons, at that moment Sigrid thought it wouldn't make any difference. She was incredibly dangerous, even without a blade. The hate radiating from her was palpable.

"Her version?" said Lukas, raising an eyebrow.

"Govhenna," said Sigrid, confusing him further, but then Malina relaxed and even smiled. "There's something I need to tell you," she said, turning to the King's Steward.

CHAPTER 11

Not long after leaving the Alfár's city, they reached what Willow had called the empty plain. Kell could see why it had been given that name, despite her protest that the name wasn't true.

There was a certain rugged beauty to the desolate landscape. The sweeping hillsides were covered with umber, green and orange reed-like grass. A gentle wind stirred the fronds, creating waves and complex patterns, reminding him of the sea. Occasionally, the smooth earth was broken up by a rocky outcrop, a copse of trees or some low scrub, but otherwise it seemed devoid of life. As far as he could see in every direction, there were no structures of any kind and the sky was empty. The air smelled different than in the city, fresher, and yet it was still uncomfortably warm, especially wearing armour and carrying heavy packs.

They quickly settled into a routine that continued unbroken for two days. During the day, they walked north at a steady pace, watchful for danger despite the overwhelming impression that they were alone. They saw the odd burrow, and sometimes what resembled a rabbit's warren, but they never saw any evidence of the animals that had made them.

Willow remained on edge and, in turn, the Raven were equally alert, hands resting on swords. Staying that focused for long periods of time was draining, and when night would fall, sleep came easily for all of them.

The temperature dropped dramatically in the evening, and any wood or dry scrub they gathered was used for a cooking fire. Once the food was warm, they let the fire go out. Willow was afraid that if they left it burning, it might draw unwanted attention to their camp.

After eating, Kell huddled up in his blankets for warmth and went to sleep while someone kept watch. He took his turn every night, and those four hours were the worst part of being on the empty plain. There was nothing to distract him. Willow had assured him there were some animals out there, but no-one saw or heard anything. No insects, no nocturnal animals shuffling about, and no bats or birds. With nothing to see or hear, it was hard to remain alert, never mind awake.

Whenever he started to fall asleep from sitting still for too long, Kell would pace or make circuits of the camp. When his watch was over, Kell would fall into an exhausted dreamless sleep and the others did the same.

Every night before they ate, Odd walked a short distance away from camp to pray, which Kell found peculiar. One night he decided to ask Yarra about it.

"Has he always been so devout?"

Yarra shrugged. "As far as I know. I think his parents were religious."

"Do you know much about him? Friends? Family?"

"Not really. He tends to keep to himself. I think he prefers his own company."

Kell knew Yarra had worked with Odd for years, and yet she also knew next to nothing about him. He couldn't really criticise her though, as he'd known Odd for two years and knew just as little. As someone who had also been described by others as a bit of a loner, Kell could relate. He suspected Odd used the time away from their camp for prayer, but also to be alone. Even in this unusual situation, with so few people, it was difficult to break the habit of a lifetime and open up.

The isolation on the plain didn't bother him, but by the

second day, Kell began to miss the sounds of other people. Also, the absence of any native wildlife began to worry him. The only sounds in this world were the wind rustling through the long grass, the clinking of their armour and their own breathing.

When the painful silence became too much, and the ringing in his ears too loud, Kell and the others broke it up with conversation. They talked about everything and nothing, just so that they didn't feel so utterly alone. Even Willow was affected, and although she never started a conversation, from time to time she would contribute.

Every morning, Kell and the others checked themselves for signs of infection. So far none of them had any physical symptoms, but it was more difficult to judge if their minds had been affected.

On the third day around midday, Willow suddenly became very animated. In the distance to the west was a copse of trees, but something else had drawn her attention. She'd picked out something directly in front and ran ahead to inspect it. Kell and the others couldn't see what it was until they were almost standing on top of it.

It was the remains of a fire.

"It was Ravvi," said Willow, keeping them back so that she could inspect the camp site. The ashes were cold and had been scattered by the wind, but it was clear that someone had spent the night there. There were some scuff marks on the earth from his boots, and what could be tracks, but Kell wasn't sure.

"Stay. Make camp, and if you need to, build a fire for protection," said Willow, waving at the trees. Judging distances on the plain was difficult, but Kell estimated it would take over an hour to walk to the trees and back.

"Go. We'll be here," said Kell, dropping his pack to the ground.

"I will scout ahead for his path and return before dark," promised Willow, leaving her pack beside his. Kell noticed she held on to her peculiar two-headed weapon. With her strange, loping gait, the Alfár ran north and was soon out of sight.

"Yarra, would you mind gathering some firewood?" asked Kell.

"I don't mind," she said.

"We can use the time to spar," said Odd, and Kell groaned.

It was too cold to fight without their shirts, but they both took off their armour. Kell still wasn't used to the additional weight and found a few sore spots on his shoulders. Feeling much lighter than he had in days, Kell even fared a little better than usual. He still lost every time, but more than once he came close to scoring a hit.

"Were your parents religious?" asked Kell, when they took a short break to catch their breath.

"No," said Odd, with a small frown.

"I was just curious, because you pray every day."

Odd grunted but didn't answer.

"So, if it wasn't your parents, where did it come from?"

Odd said nothing for a long time. He scanned their surroundings, for danger or a distraction, but there were none. Yarra was more than halfway to the trees and would not be back for some time.

"I find it calms the mind," said Odd. It was obvious he didn't want to answer the question, but as it was just the two of them, he seemed more at ease. "Out here it's quiet, but I still need the balance it provides."

"That's something I need to work on," said Kell.

"You are making progress," conceded Odd, which was the closest thing to a compliment. "Are you ready to continue?"

They practised for another hour, by which time Yarra had returned with a large bundle of dry branches. It would be enough for a few hours and see them through the coldest part of the night. Just as she began to stack the firewood, something caught her attention.

"What's that?" she asked, looking back the way she'd come.

At first Kell couldn't see what she was pointing at, but then he noticed something moving towards them. It was partly concealed in the shadows beneath the trees, but soon detached itself and came forwards. At this distance he couldn't make out many details. He could see it was fairly low to the ground and about the width of two or three carts.

"What is it?" asked Yarra, squinting towards the approaching black mark.

"I think it's a herd of cattle," said Odd.

Narrowing his eyes, Kell could see several animals clustered together. They were roughly the same size and shape as sheep, but their coats were jet black. Their features were unclear, so he couldn't be certain about the resemblance.

"I thought Willow said they were no cattle here," said Yarra.

"She said there used to be, but they were tainted by the Malice," said Kell, reaching for his mail shirt.

"We should get ready, just in case," she said.

From what Willow had told them, it was safer to assume that everything they encountered was hostile. They scrambled into their armour and Yarra helped them secure the straps. The beasts never deviated from their path, but occasionally the lead animal would pause to inspect something on the ground.

Fresh sweat ran down the inside of Kell's armour making him itch.

"They're following Yarra's tracks," said Odd. His eyesight was remarkably sharp at long distances. "The lead beast keeps smelling the ground."

"Can you tell how many there are?" asked Yarra.

"Eight. Maybe ten."

All they could do was watch as the beasts marched closer and wait to see if they turned out to be hostile or not. An hour later, Kell had his answer.

The resemblance to sheep was fleeting. The beasts had the same thick woollen coat and curling horns, but their faces were more canine with long snouts and sharp teeth. At first glance, Kell thought they were as placid as sheep, but there was a level of cunning in their grey eyes that spoke of predatory intelligence. Yarra and Odd wanted to keep him out of the fight, but they relented as three swords were better than two. It was still hours until dark, and they had no way of knowing when Willow would return. They were on their own.

The beasts had slowed their approach and Kell could now count ten of them altogether. They tentatively shuffled forward. It seemed as if they'd never seen a human before and were genuinely curious, smelling the ground, staring at them expectantly. They barked and whined a few times, but Kell and the others remained silent. When they didn't respond, the beasts grew bored and their curiosity faded. They pawed the ground with their clawed feet and seemed to be working up to a fight.

The tips of their horns and teeth would be the most dangerous. If one of them fell to the ground, Kell guessed the pack would move in to rip them apart. The closer they came, the more he noticed a rancid smell. Their fur was matted and filthy, covered with dirt and rotting material, along with some kind of grease or fat.

"Focus on their legs and snouts," said Kell, remembering the maglau in the Frozen North. Their skulls had been almost impenetrable, and their weapons had been useless against them.

"We need to kill that one," said Yarra, pointing at one beast that was slightly smaller. "It's the leader."

Kell didn't have time to ask how she knew as the pack ran forward. Odd proved why he was arguably the best swordsman in Algany as he'd maimed two of the beasts in no time. His movements were faster than Kell's eye could follow. Odd had hacked the front leg off one with his first swing, and severed the back legs of another with his second. The animals began to bray like donkeys, their voices high-pitched and loud.

Two of the beasts barrelled into Kell, driving him away from the Raven. They were like wolves, separating the old and the lame from the rest of the pack.

For all of her reluctance to lead, Yarra showed no hesitation in battle. As one beast came towards her, she kicked it in the snout and slashed another across its face, severing its upper jaw and nose. Yelping in pain it skipped back as blood spurted from the gaping wound. Another then rushed towards her with its head down, trying to impale her with its horns. Yarra skipped to one side and slashed it across the body as it went past. Her sword sheared away a chunk of its thick coat, but it was so dense, the beast was unharmed. With what Kell thought was a sneer, it charged her again while another of the pack waited to trip her up.

Kell saw three more go after Odd, but right from the beginning, it was clear that it wasn't a fair fight. Between one blink and the next, Odd had stabbed one in the face and opened up the throat of a second. The third beast had no thoughts of self-preservation as it tried to grab him by the leg. Odd rolled over its back, dropped to one knee and lashed out, hamstringing its back legs. The whole fight had taken less than three heartbeats. Kell couldn't understand how Odd was moving so quickly.

Kell used one hand to vault over the backs of two beasts as they charged, ignoring his revulsion at touching them. Before they could turn around, he stabbed one of them in the flank and then kicked it hard in the hindquarters. It stumbled on its injured leg and fell, leaving him to face the other alone. That was when the palm of his hand began to throb from where he'd touched its mangy coat.

The beast spun around to face him, readying itself for an attack, but before it had a chance, Yarra and Odd were there, hacking at it from behind. While it was distracted, Kell stepped forward and swung his sword down in a chopping motion, aiming at its neck. Black inky blood gushed from the wound, and it collapsed to the ground.

There were three beasts remaining on their feet. The others

were dead or yowling in pain from severed limbs and gaping wounds. One of the three still upright was the pack leader. It nudged the other two forward with its head.

"Back-to-back!" yelled Yarra, until the three of them were facing outwards. The creatures circled them until each was standing opposite a human. Kell's shoulders were on fire, and his arms felt as if they'd been filled with lead. He'd been tired from his sparring, and now he just wanted to drop his guard. But the beasts were watching for any sign of weakness and he couldn't take the risk. The palm of his left hand was burning, the skin inflamed and red. He rubbed it against the material of his trousers, but it didn't help.

"Come on!" said Kell, daring them to attack. He just wanted it to be over.

Just as the beasts were readying themselves for another charge, Kell heard a familiar sound which made him smile. The creatures had heard it too, as one of them cocked its head to one side. A second later, Willow's mace slammed into the middle of its spine, snapping it like a twig. As the others turned to assess the new threat, Kell charged, knowing the Raven would be right behind him.

They made short work of the remaining animals, dismembering them quickly. Willow brought her axe down on the neck of the one at her feet, severing its head. More black ichor seeped from its body, staining the grass. It mixed with the blood of the others, creating a small inky reservoir.

"If that's the kind of thing we're facing, it wasn't too bad," said Yarra, slightly out of breath.

Kell dropped his sword and sat down on the ground. His hand was really painful and, just as he was about to mention it to the others, he noticed something worrying. Willow and Odd hadn't relaxed and were now watching the dying beasts.

"What's wrong?" said Kell, forcing himself upright with a grunt of effort. As he drew closer, Kell saw what they were staring at. "What's happening?"

Blood from several creatures had run together, soaking into the ground to create a shallow pool, which had started to bubble. As they watched, one of the beasts rolled towards another and they began to merge. The rancid fur broke apart and Kell had a brief glimpse of the horror beneath: a bony, pale thing with blistered flesh and a gaping maw. The merged beast didn't regrow its limbs, but now it had two snapping heads and six legs.

"Cut off the heads," said Willow, pointing at one of the beasts she had beheaded. It was completely inert. The maimed members of the pack began to twitch. Kell and the Raven started hacking them apart, spraying blood everywhere. It spattered across Kell's armour, but where it touched his skin, it started to burn.

Willow kept the two headed beast busy, until she had a chance to use her axe. Using her uncanny strength, she cut the muzzle off one head and, spinning her weapon around, used the mace on the other, smashing its skull apart.

"Just die!" screamed Yarra, sawing her blade back and forth on a beast's neck. Finally, the head came free and the twitching body was still.

When it was done, all of them were breathing hard, covered in blood and utterly exhausted.

"It burns," said Kell, dropping his sword as the pain in his left hand began to mount. He blacked out but came awake a couple of seconds after, cradling his hand.

"Sit down," said Willow, guiding him towards their temporary camp. She retrieved a glass jar from her pack and withdrew two long purple leaves, which she began to chew. Kell watched as the skin on the back of his hand began to blister, and white pustules formed before his eyes. Taking his hand, Willow applied a purple paste to the skin, gently rubbing it in. Almost immediately the pain began to ease. Some of the colour was leached from the paste and the blisters stopped bubbling.

"Let it soak in," said the Alfár. Kell sat back while she helped the others with their burned skin too. When that was done, she built up a fire. They had been carefully rationing their water, but now Willow filled the kettle. She added other herbs to the pot, and once the water was boiling an acrid smell filled the air.

The others had inflamed skin on their hands and faces, although Odd didn't seem to be in any obvious discomfort. One side of Yarra's face was badly affected. The skin was red and sore and she gritted her teeth. Once they'd all drank two mugs of spicy tea, the pain began to fade and some of the heat eased from her skin.

"What about Ravvi? Did you find him?" asked Kell.

Willow frowned. "No. He's many days ahead. The trail disappeared not far from here."

"Did he hide his tracks?"

"His mind could be drifting, paranoid. A part of him knows I will try to stop him, but that could be buried deep beneath fear and hallucinations."

"Then he could be drifting off course. We might be able to catch up with him?" suggested Kell.

"We have to keep going and hope for the best."

Kell raised an eyebrow but didn't say anything. It was a familiar phrase, but not one he'd ever heard Willow use before. After more than a hundred years of living around humans, she was now starting to talk like them.

As night fell, Willow built up the fire. Kell didn't want to camp so close to the bodies, but no-one was in any condition to travel.

"Did it burn you?" asked Kell, when Willow came to check on him.

"I'm not hurt," she said, peeling back the paste on his hand. The skin underneath was still a little red and sore, but it was already much better.

Once they'd eaten a hot meal and the warmth from the fire had seeped into his bones, Kell started to doze.

"I'll take first watch," said Willow.

Kell didn't argue and, wrapped up in his blanket, he quickly fell asleep.

At some point during the night, he woke to see Odd sat on watch a short distance away from the fire. Just as he was about to go back to sleep, Kell realised Odd was talking to someone. Raising his head, Kell saw the others were asleep.

CHAPTER 12

"Why are you here?" said Odd, keeping his voice low.

The others were still asleep and he didn't want to wake them. He'd slept for a few hours after the fight, but his eyes were still gritty. Being tired couldn't explain why he was seeing a vision of his mother. It had to be the Malice.

"I wanted to talk to you," said his mother. This time, her appearance was just as he remembered at the end. Older, with lines around the eyes, and a little grey at the temples to match her age. But when no one was looking, she had moved like someone in their twenties, enthusiastic and full of energy, not weighed down by decades of life.

Part of him wished that she was real. There had been so many times in his life, after she'd died, that he would have given anything to talk to her again, just one more time. No one else understood him. How could they? They didn't have the hunger. Even when he was surrounded by people, Odd was always alone.

He shook his head. "You're not real. The poison has crept into my head."

She looked at him with disdain. "Don't be ridiculous."

He knew it was all in his imagination, and yet, a part of him was still desperate to talk with her.

"If you're real, then why did you wait until now to talk to me?" asked Odd, struggling to keep his voice down. "Did you know they beheaded you and then burned your remains, just to make sure you wouldn't come back?"

His mother said nothing, because the illusion had no answers to give. Odd turned away, waiting for her to disappear. He flexed the fingers on his left hand that had been spattered with tainted blood from the beasts. The skin was still pink and a little tender, but he was in a much better condition than the others. The wounds on their skin would take several days to heal and then scab over. His hand was merely a little inflamed, and that would be gone by tomorrow. If he was injured again, Odd needed to be careful. Without thinking, he'd exerted some energy to speed up the healing process. If he recovered too fast from wounds, they might become suspicious.

Caution, in all things: that was the second lesson his mother had taught him about the hunger. The first was that he had to feed it. If he didn't, he would die.

When Odd turned back, his mother was still sat on the ground beside him.

"I'm sorry," she said in earnest.

Odd sneered at the phantom. "Now I'm certain you're an illusion. My mother never apologised for anything in her entire life. Ever. Not even at the end."

Blood on her teeth. Bodies with ripped out throats. Wild laughter at the horror on their faces.

"I'm not sorry for anything I did. I'm sorry that you inherited the hunger from me," she said.

Odd rocked backed on his heels and then laughed at his own naivety. He glanced over his shoulder to make sure the sound had not woken up the others. They were still asleep, their breathing deep and even.

He was so desperate to believe that she was real. Loneliness was something that he'd never been able to understand. He missed his mother, but he didn't find it difficult to spend time by himself. Some of his fellow Raven couldn't stand to be alone. They had to be surrounded by people all the time. Odd wondered, if they despised their own company, did that mean they hated themselves?

His mother's absence hurt, but until now, he didn't think he'd been lonely.

"You would say anything to get a reaction," whispered Odd.

"Your father didn't understand. He couldn't. When he found out what we were, he was scared. That's why he left us when you were a boy. It was easier to tell you that he'd been lost at sea."

His father had been a sailor, so her story made sense. Odd didn't remember his mother telling him, but the memory was there somewhere, buried deep. The Malice had merely brought it to the front of his mind. All he had were vague memories of his father from when he'd been very young.

"It's a gift. That's what my mother told me," said Odd, despite himself. The hunger had given him many things. In some ways, the hunger had shaped his entire life. Every single interaction with other people had to be carefully assessed.

"I was wrong. It's a curse," said his mother. "It keeps other people at arm's length. You can't risk them getting too close, in case they find out about your secret. That's why you've never had someone special in your life. Never taken a risk."

"I risk everything every time I have to feed," said Odd, shaking his head. He just wanted her to shut up. The Malice seemed intent on making him question everything about his past.

The phantom was ignorant. It didn't understand what he had to do in order to survive. He'd tried to ignore the hunger once and had nearly died. He had no choice if he wanted to live.

Odd scrunched up his eyes, willing her to go away.

"I meant a risk with your heart," said his mother.

Odd turned to confront her, but she had already disappeared.

In the morning, Odd was distracted and struggled to eat breakfast. The others were also having trouble and picked at their food. The smell coming from the rotting bodies didn't help. Willow had called them the calaparchei. Once, they had been passive herd beasts, but the Malice had turned them into something vicious by digging up their past. And now, it was rooting around inside his head.

More disturbing than the calaparchei was the recurring vision of his mother. If she came from his memories, it suggested there was much about his childhood that he had forgotten or buried, either by accident or on purpose. Until now, Odd hadn't thought there were any gaps in his memory.

"Are you all right?" asked Kell.

"Bad dreams," said Odd, before looking up to see who was in earshot. Yarra had moved a short distance away to relieve herself, and Willow was tidying up the camp. Kell seemed genuinely concerned, which was surprising. In the past they'd spent a lot of time together, but Kell hadn't filled the air with meaningless small talk. In between their sparring there had been a comfortable silence. It had been perfect.

"Do you want to talk about it?" asked Kell.

"No," said Odd. "Thank you," he added, trying to soften his abruptness because he knew it was required. Kell shrugged and moved away to pack his belongings.

Odd was glad to put the camp and the dead beasts behind him. They still had supplies for a few days, but Willow asked them to be alert for anything they could forage. There was little in sight beyond the endless sea of grass, but as the calaparchei had proven, the empty plain was deceptive.

After another day of trekking, where everyone remained constantly on edge, they finally reached the Kolenn Mounds. The undulating foothills made it hard to judge distance or see very far in any direction. Willow guessed it was only another day's walk through them to reach the Stejno, the inward sloping path. It was still light, but they were tired after yesterday's fight, so they walked for another hour before making camp early.

In search of a good place to stop, they followed a gully that eventually led to a stream. The further north they went, the wider and deeper it became until the water was waist high. Trees leaned into the water, overhanging branches sweeping the surface, but apart from a few leaves and twigs, it looked clean. With plenty of wood for a fire, and fresh water, Odd could almost forget what had happened yesterday. The fight itself didn't bother him. The beasts had been unusual and vicious, but the vision of his mother continued to worry him. He wondered if the others were experiencing any hallucinations.

"We should wash and gather water," said Willow as she prepared a fire. "The land to the north is very dry."

Odd was slowly getting used to the muggy air, but the thought of cooling off in the stream was appealing. Yarra hesitated, but Odd stripped off and waded out into the water. As a soldier, he was used to being naked around others and it didn't bother him. However, as he had a blemish from the Malice on his thigh, he made sure he was always facing away from the others to conceal it.

The stones beneath his feet were smooth, but the stream wasn't fast flowing, so there was no danger of being swept away. As the water closed over his hips, Odd sighed with pleasure, finally cool for the first time in days.

Kell followed and eventually Yarra took the plunge. Odd immersed his whole body and dunked his head, before scrubbing his skin with a bar of soap. After a few minutes his toes began to go numb, but he wasn't ready to get out of the water. He idly glanced at the others, looking for signs of infection, but couldn't see any discoloured skin or black veins. They all had bruises and abrasions from the fight, which were still raw, but nothing else.

When he felt someone's eyes on him, Odd turned to see Willow watching him. Her stare was slightly puzzled, but he was certain it wasn't his nakedness that interested her. He had a few injuries, but they weren't as pronounced as the others and were already beginning to heal. He would have to be careful. Willow was more astute than he'd realised.

The Alfár kept watch for potential threats while they bathed, and then took her turn upstream, out of view. While Odd dried off beside the fire, Yarra shaved her head and Kell tended to his sword. When a twig snapped loudly in the fire Yarra was immediately on her feet, dagger in hand. Kell was almost as quick, scanning the area for danger, but there was nothing. Their nerves were clearly raw from the previous attack.

After some time had passed, and Willow still hadn't appeared, Kell went to fetch her. He returned a short while later, leading her by the hand like a child. She was dressed, but her feet were bare.

"What's wrong with her?" asked Odd.

"I don't know. I found her just sitting by the stream."

Kell guided her to sit beside the fire to dry off. The Alfár remained immobile, staring into the flames without really seeing them. A few minutes later she blinked and came back to herself. It took Willow a couple of seconds to recognise her surroundings and their faces. Normally it was impossible to read her, but now her emotions were close to the surface.

"What happened?" asked the Alfár.

"You went somewhere else," said Kell.

Willow shook her head. "I was thinking about my mother. It was an old memory."

It didn't bode well if her mind was already being affected by the Malice. Until now, Odd thought he was the only one.

"Has anyone else experienced anything strange?" asked Kell.

Odd shook his head. He wasn't ready to share.

"Are you sure?" said the king.

"I've been hearing voices," said Yarra. She sounded ashamed, as if admitting that she'd been infected was a failing on her part.

"What kind of voices?" asked Willow.

"People I used to know. People I failed."

"The dead," said the Alfár.

Yarra nodded. "They whisper and blame me."

The Malice was targeting their individual weaknesses. Digging into their psyche and finding what would affect them the most. It made sense. Yarra's well-known failure had changed the course of her life. She wore her guilt like a heavy cloak.

If that were true, why was the Malice showing him a vision of his mother? What did it hope to achieve?

"What about you?" asked Odd.

"Nothing," said Kell, which was possible, but seemed unlikely if everyone else was being affected.

"We must keep a close eye on each other," said Willow. "If you see or hear anything unusual, tell someone." They all nodded soberly in agreement.

Normally, a fire was a source of comfort, but as night fell it was both a blessing and a curse. It kept away the chill, but it also made them a target for anything lurking in the foothills. Visibility was poor, as the land was so uneven. Anything could creep up on them and they wouldn't know until it was on top of them.

When Odd was on watch, he heard something moving about in the distance and a faint snuffling sound, but nothing approached their camp. Even so, he spent the hours until dawn waiting for an imminent attack that never came.

After another day of walking through the foothills, they reached what Willow had called the Stejno. The foothills gave way to a series of sloping gullies, shale covered pathways and jagged hunks of rock. The whole area was grey and featureless. Odd couldn't see a single weed to break up the monotony of the landscape. Whatever life had once dwelled in the area had been driven away, or consumed by the Malice, leaving a desert of stone and sharp rocks in its wake. Odd thought they might see a few bones from dead animals, but there was nothing.

There were also no obvious paths either, which meant

footing was treacherous. He didn't want to think about what would happen if they were attacked while sliding down a slope or clambering over rocks.

After two days of scrambling down and crawling up gullies, they were all utterly exhausted. Odd's legs and shoulders burned, and he could see the others were suffering just as badly. Each night, the silence was so deafening that even the slightest noise became incredibly loud. The scrape of every rock, the trickle of gravel and crunch of their footsteps echoed until all of them were suffering from tension headaches. Chewing willow bark helped for a few hours, but by midday they were all rubbing their temples again.

On the third day, they reached a plateau of sorts, which led them to a series of ragged cliffs, their faces crumbling and unstable. They would need ropes to descend to the bottom, but it wasn't that which had caught Odd's attention. Below the cliffs, stretching as far as the eye could see to the horizon, was a monstrous forest.

"The Tangle," said Willow. The revulsion on her face was clear as she stared down at the forest.

A creeping sense of dread washed over Odd, making his scalp prickle. The trees were massive, gnarled things, with branches knotted together like a strangled bramble bush. Normally, trees protected and supported one another, but here each tree was doing its best to attack and rip its neighbour apart.

Spiny thorns grew from every limb, which overlapped to create a vicious net. Most peculiar was that the skin of every tree was pitch black, as if rotting, and yet they were thriving. He could see bright-green veins through cracks in the bark, but there were no buds or fruit. Grey and brown coloured leaves grew from every tree, and the ground at the edge of the forest was covered with wilted foliage.

There were holes in the canopy, but in such a tainted landscape, he doubted anything growing on the forest floor would be pleasant. Odd had never seen anything so vicious.

"It's so quiet," said Yarra, shading her eyes against the sun.
"I can't see or hear any birds or animals."

"There are many beasts," said Willow. "Everything in there
will try to hurt us. There is no fresh water, and once we are in
its shadow, there will be no reprieve. It will take five days of
comfortable travel to pass through the Tangle, but we may not
be able to rest at night. We should make the journey as fast as
we can. Maybe we will manage it in three."

"No sleep for three days?" said Kell.

"Once the beasts of the Tangle have our scent, I do not think
they will let us rest," said the Alfár. "The stronger ones fed upon
the weak. It used to be a beautiful forest; now it is a jungle with
poisonous swamps. What remains is cruel and dangerous."

"There's still a few hours of daylight. Do you want to start
today?" asked Kell.

Willow shook her head. "We should sleep as much as we
can and begin tomorrow, at first light."

They stayed close to the edge of the cliffs and made camp as
best they could without a fire. While they laid down to rest,
Willow kept an eye on the Tangle in case anything crept out.

Odd napped throughout the afternoon and the others did
their best as well. His dreams were anxious, full of peculiar
images that quickly evaporated when he awoke, leaving
him uneasy. Everyone was thirsty, but they conserved their
water as much as possible. Given the ordeal that lay ahead,
Odd forced himself to lie down and try to sleep some more.
He managed a few more hours, but woke late at night with
sandy eyes.

Yarra was on watch, her back towards them as she stared out
at the Tangle. At first, he thought she was talking to someone,
but then Odd realised she was repeating a litany to drive away
the voices.

"You're dead. You're not real. You're just in my head," she
whispered, over and over, rocking back and forth.

Odd scuffed his boots to announce his presence before sitting down beside her on a rock. She'd fallen silent and refused to make eye contact.

"How are you feeling?" he asked.

"Fine," said Yarra, convincing neither of them.

A comfortable silence settled between them. Normally Odd would be the last one to break it, but he thought the unusual circumstances warranted he say something else.

"You've been carrying that guilt around for a long time," said Odd. "You need to put it down."

Yarra laughed. "You're awful at consoling someone. In fact, you're pretty awful at making any kind of small talk."

"That's fair," said Odd. "But, you know I'm telling the truth."

"I'm sorry. I know you're just trying to help, in your own weird way."

"Can you let it go?"

"I really don't know," said Yarra. "I thought I was getting better, but maybe I was fooling myself. Out here, there's nowhere to hide. All I've done for days is think about it."

"Have you found any answers?"

Yarra laughed again, but there was no mirth in the sound. "No. I'll tell you when I do."

"Get some sleep. I'll keep watch."

"Are you sure?"

"I can't sleep anymore," said Odd, rubbing the last of the sand from his eyes.

"Thank you," said Yarra, briefly resting a hand on his shoulder.

It took a while, but eventually her breathing deepened, and she slept.

"You can feel it, can't you?" asked his mother, nodding towards the Tangle. She appeared sitting on the rock beside him, knees under her chin, arms wrapped around her legs.

She was right. If he concentrated, Odd could sense the tainted forest below. It was as if someone was running their hand across the back of his scalp. The constant prickle spoke of life, of being watched, and something else. Something that was malicious and a threat.

"Take a look at what's lurking inside," she said. When he didn't respond she snorted in derision. "Don't tell me you're afraid. I didn't raise you to be a coward."

"I'm not afraid," said Odd, keeping his voice low. "I just don't see the point."

"Know your enemy. That was one of the first lessons I taught you. Look!" she said, gesturing with one hand.

Odd knew the phantom wouldn't leave him alone until it got what it wanted. To appease it, he drew the smallest amount of energy from the well inside. His eyesight, already better than average, sharpened again. He felt his pupils shift and then widen until he could see in the dark.

The shadows began to peel back beneath the trees, fading from black to grey. Lurking on the fringes of the forest was an array of creatures with misshapen, mangled bodies. All of them had sharp teeth and claws, a few even had horns. Others resembled two, or even three beasts, merged together into one body with flaccid surplus limbs. One creature had a second shrivelled head on the same neck as a strong skull. The cruelty of the Malice had no limitations.

All of the tainted beasts were waiting for them.

"You will need to draw on your power to stay alive in there," said his mother. Odd grunted but didn't reply. He was watching how the creatures interacted, snapping and occasionally clawing at each other if they strayed too close. There were visible differences between them, but each was acting as if it were part of a pack with a known hierarchy.

"What will you do when the well is dry?" asked his mother. Odd relaxed his eyes and let them shift back to normal before he turned to address the illusion. Speaking to it directly seemed to be the only way it would leave him alone.

"Why would it run dry?" he asked. The energy he'd taken from the Alfár was vast, twenty or even fifty times that of a human. He could still feel it coursing through him. The pain he'd initially experienced had been a concern, but now he put it down to the Alfár being so different. It had not returned, so he believed it had been a symptom of his body adjusting to such a huge amount of raw energy. In normal circumstances, he had to feed the hunger every two or three months. If he had been feeding on Alfár all of his life, it might only have been necessary to kill once or twice a year.

The ghost of his mother gestured at the Tangle. "That will tax you like nothing else. You will have to draw on your reserves."

"So will the others," said Odd. "But they'll make it."

His mother snorted. "Do you really think any of them will survive?"

In truth, Odd had thought the chances were already slim. While his companions were skilled fighters, he thought only Willow would prevail against such brutality, and only if she were lucky. The twisted beasts on the fringes of the forest were the weakest, which meant that further in, they would encounter whatever preyed on them.

"When the well runs dry, what will you do? How will you survive?" asked his mother, intruding on his thoughts. "Which one of your friends will you kill to survive?"

"I wouldn't do that. Besides, it would be impossible." They were never far from one another, and there would be no way for him to convincingly make it look like an accident. "What do you want?" asked Odd, tiring of her questions.

"I don't want to see you get hurt."

"It's too late for that. Look at where we are," he said, gesturing at the blighted landscape. "Everything out here is determined to kill us."

"You know what I mean," she chided him.

"I don't know why I'm even talking to you. You're not real."

"Not real?" said his mother, giving him a withering glare. "Then how would I know that someone is listening to our conversation?"

Odd turned his head and saw that Kell was staring at him. When he looked back, his mother was gone.

"Odd," said the king. "Who were you talking to?"

CHAPTER 13

A little after dawn and another cold breakfast, Kell packed up his belongings with the others. His breath frosted in front of his face, but he knew the temperature would soon rise and he'd be sweating inside his armour again.

As if what was waiting for them inside the toxic forest wasn't enough to worry about, the others were being affected by the Malice. Last night he'd caught Odd having a conversation with his dead mother. At first, he'd denied it, but eventually he admitted that he'd been speaking with her for a few days. Yarra was being tormented by the dead, and Willow was becoming vague and easily distracted. Her emotions were much easier to read, and she'd adopted a few human mannerisms, such as tucking loose strands of her white hair behind her ears.

Since the Alfár had told them about the possible side-effects, Kell had been bracing himself. So far, the only thing he'd noticed was a peculiar sense of nostalgia, as if he'd just come home after a long trip. It made him feel extremely relaxed, which was incredibly dangerous, given what lay ahead. The Malice was cunning. It was affecting each of them in a different way. It wasn't self-aware, and yet, it burrowed deep in the mind to find a weakness it could exploit.

He hoped that the building guilt he felt about leaving behind his wife and son was not artificial. The thought that it might not all be his gnawed at the back of his mind. He also wondered, with the time difference, how long he'd now been away from the Five Kingdoms. Surely, at this point, it was only a few weeks at most.

"Ready?" asked Willow, startling him. Kell realised he'd been lost in thought, staring at his sword, Slayer. He stood up and bit the inside of his mouth until the pain sharpened his mind. He couldn't risk drifting off like Willow had at a critical moment.

"I'm ready."

The two members of the Raven joined them on the edge of the cliffs.

"Can you see them?" asked the Alfár, gesturing towards the Tangle below.

"I saw them last night," said Odd.

Kell had noticed a few shapes flitting back and forth through the trees. Vague, lumpy creatures the size of a small dog, sometimes walking on four legs, sometimes on two.

"What are they?" asked Yarra.

"We call them fetch. Once, they were birds and beasts. Now they are nothing. Amalgams of flesh and bone. Mind and muscle." Willow hefted her two headed weapon. "Show no mercy and believe nothing you hear. Some of them can mimic voices, so stay in clear sight of each other."

In the trees, a simian fetch shoved its lumpy head between the branches towards them and laughed, showing off its big teeth. Kell had faced beasts that had been altered in the Frozen North, but nothing like this. These creatures had been remade into monsters, as if their flesh was wet clay.

Kell bit his mouth again and readied himself for a fight.

Another simian fetch flung itself at Kell and he slashed it across the face. With a squawk of pain, it fell to the ground, oozing grey blood. Shifting his grip, Kell stabbed downwards with both hands, pinning its head to the forest floor. His sword went through its skull and then sank deep into the earth.

Kell stumbled and nearly fell over backwards. His left leg sank into the soft earth, and he had to use both hands to yank it free from the bog. It came out of the hole with a loud squelching sound.

While the others were finishing off the last of the troop, Kell took a moment to catch his breath. The air stank of tainted blood and stagnant water. It was hot, sticky and all of them were sweating profusely. Clouds of insects followed them about. His hands and face were already itching from a number of bites. So far, the fetches hadn't caused any serious injuries, but dealing with them was proving to be exhausting.

A thorny vine crawled across the ground towards him. Kell sliced off the end before it came too close. It retracted, oozing ichor as it slithered away. Everything in the forest was trying to kill them. The ground was uneven, firm in some places and more like a swamp in others, with standing pools of water. None of it was fit to drink, and there wouldn't be any fresh water until they had made it through. Swallowing hard, Kell tried not to think about the limited supply of water in his flask.

With a grunt of effort, Willow swung her weapon at the last fetch, splitting it in two with her axe. The creature squeaked as it fell apart. She'd barely walked away from it when Kell noticed several vines scrambling across the ground towards the dead bodies. They dragged the pieces away to feed.

"We need to keep moving," said Willow, trying to catch her breath.

The others were too tired to talk, but they nodded and pressed on with the Alfár leading the way. Although there were gaps in the canopy, it was difficult to judge the time of day. Kell guessed they had been walking through the Tangle for a few hours, which meant midday wasn't far off. They still had at least another two days of this to endure.

In this part of the forest, the land sloped downwards and they moved carefully, looking for trip hazards. Kell wasn't the only one to have nearly broken his ankle. Yarra had stumbled over the entrance to an animal's burrow, and Odd had to be rescued from a sinkhole.

When the land levelled out again, the trees ahead were spaced out around large pools of water that were crawling with insects. There were several narrow pathways through the swamp, but all of them meant getting close to the water and whatever was lurking beneath the surface.

Willow put a finger to her lips and gestured at the water and then her eyes. All of them had their weapons at the ready. As normal, Willow went first, Kell second, Yarra third and Odd brought up the rear. So far, Odd was faring the best out of them all. He had a few bites, but no real injuries.

Placing her feet carefully, Willow led the way down one of the narrow paths. When the insects drifted towards her, she ignored them. There were more dangerous threats to worry about than a few more bites. Her eyes were focused on the surface of the water. When a few bubbles drifted up from one of them she froze. Kell saw her muscles tense in readiness, but nothing emerged from the pool. With his heart pounding loudly in his ears, Kell followed a few paces behind, stepping in each of Willow's footprints.

Something crawled down his neck, burrowing beneath his armour, but Kell ignored it. He wasn't sure if it was fear, an insect or sweat. Also, for no obvious reason, he was experiencing a rising sense of euphoria – as if he relished danger and found it wonderful to be fighting for his life. The Malice was testing him again, searching for a weakness.

Kell had just moved past a pool when Yarra tapped him sharply on the shoulder. He froze and turned his head, looking back the way they'd come. To his right the surface of the water had been disturbed, ripples moving out from something close to the bank. Odd was staring at it intently. Every muscle of his body was taut. Moving slowly, he gripped his sword with both hands, then raised it above his head. Kell sensed Willow moving towards him on his left.

The ripples on the water slowed and then settled. The surface became calm but none of them moved. Yarra was about to speak when Odd slowly shook his head, his eyes never straying.

A huge creature burst from beneath the surface, racing towards Kell with a open jaw full of sharp teeth. He glimpsed six churning legs, a long snapping mouth, and a heavy tail with a spiked club on the end.

Odd moved so fast his sword was a silver blur. His first swing bit deep into the creature's body, but it wasn't a lethal blow. Nevertheless, its charge faltered, giving all of them a moment to surround it and take a swing. They hacked at the creature while it tried to keep them at bay with its jaws and tail. It clipped Yarra on the shoulder and she stumbled to a knee, but before it could take advantage Willow brought her mace down on top of its head. The creature flopped down on the edge of the pool, leaking brain matter. At some point in the past, it might have been a swamp lizard, but it had been altered and remade into a horrific image.

"Look out!" shouted Odd, shoving Kell to one side. Another lizard snapped at the air where he'd been standing. Odd hacked off one of its legs, danced around its jaw, and sliced off the end of its tail. Snarling with rage, Yarra stabbed it in the head, blinding it on one side.

"And another!" said Willow, moving to stand back-to-back with Kell. He and Yarra jabbed at the half-blind lizard, while Willow and Odd fought the new one. On five legs the lizard was still incredibly fast. The injury didn't seem to bother it much. It feinted at Yarra and then rushed at Kell. Muscle memory took over and Kell dodged its attack, then slashed it across the side. He'd barely stepped back when the lizard's jaws came around, trying to latch onto his leg. Before he could swing his sword, it spun around, smashing its body into him. Kell's ankles clicked together, and he toppled over, dropping his weapon to break his fall.

While he scrambled around for his sword, Yarra began to scream. Kell dragged Slayer from a pool of water and charged back into the fray. The lizard was trying to crush her between its jaws, while she hacked away at its head with her dagger. Yelling at the top of his lungs, Kell brought his blade down on the back of the lizard's neck. It bit deep into the creature's flesh and black blood fountained from the wound. Its jaws eased and Yarra wriggled free before she and Kell stabbed it to death.

While the others finished the remaining lizard, Kell checked Yarra for injuries. Much to his amazement, the scale armour had held up against the crushing power of the lizard's jaws. Yarra was winded and would probably be bruised underneath, but she wasn't bleeding.

"Your arm," said Yarra, between breaths.

Only then did Kell noticed a long gash down his left forearm. He hadn't even felt it. It was shallow, but bleeding profusely. Willow also had a small wound on one leg. Both injuries were quickly treated and carefully bound, as the chance of infection was high.

"What's that?" said Yarra, pointing at something over Kell's shoulder.

The words were barely out of her mouth before Odd was moving past him in a blur. His sword swept left and right in a tight arc and something heavy splashed to the ground. Another lizard gurgled its final breath and lay still. Odd wasn't even breathing hard.

"How did you do that?" asked Yarra. "I've never seen anyone move so fast."

Odd just shrugged, as if it were nothing.

"You've been holding back," said Kell. "All this time we've been sparring."

"It's more than that," said Yarra. Kell thought she looked afraid. "How are you so fast?"

Odd didn't answer and a peculiar silence settled over the group.

"We should eat. Keep up our strength," said Willow, reaching into her pack. Food was the last thing on Kell's mind, but they all ate and then drank sparingly from their flasks. When they were done, they pressed on, leaving the dead bodies behind for something else to feed on.

Twice more they were attacked by vicious beasts that had once been gentler animals. A herd of bovines with small, deer-like heads and razor-sharp horns tried to overwhelm them with numbers. Several of the beasts drowned, or were trampled by the others, in their frantic attempt to kill. It didn't slow down the rest and they charged with their heads down, trying to impale their victims. By using the trees for cover, Kell and the others managed to break up the herd and pick a few off at a time, dodging and swerving, so the beasts didn't have the chance to pick up speed.

Once half the herd were maimed or dead, the others scattered, only to return a couple of hours later to try again. They cut down the rest until only three remained. That time the beasts ran and, thankfully, didn't return.

When darkness fell, Kell was bone-tired. There wasn't a part of his body that didn't hurt. Worst of all were his arms and shoulders; they ached so badly from fighting all day. His legs trembled so much he felt on the verge of collapse. He was light-headed from a lack of water, and his skin constantly itched beneath his clothing. There was no water to wash with or drink, and no relief from the heat. The trees soaked up warmth during the day and slowly released it at night. More insects appeared, and the air was full of peculiar sounds with creatures that called out to one another.

"Rest," said Willow, gesturing at a small dip beneath a clump of trees. Kell sat down and, despite the danger, was ready to fall asleep. He ate because it was necessary but didn't feel hungry. The moment he'd finished chewing he laid down and passed out from exhaustion.

Someone shook him awake and he almost complained until Yarra placed a finger on his lips. She shook her head and then moved a short distance away. At first, as he rubbed the sleep from his eyes, Kell thought it was morning. Beams of blue light filtered down through gaps in the canopy, turning night into day beneath the trees.

Peering through the branches, Kell could see the edges of a fat moon hanging low in the sky. It was so large he could see its surface, which was pitted and scarred. There were unfamiliar cracks and craters that looked ancient. It was a different moon to the one he'd stared at his entire life. Kell's mind quickly skittered away from what that meant.

This moon was almost full, and back home, he would have called it a harvest moon. One that burned late into the night, making it easier to gather crops during the autumn.

Not far away, Willow was hunkered down, her eyes focused on something in the distance. Yarra and Odd were alert, swords held at the ready, kneeling down beside the Alfár. Moving quietly, Kell knelt down beside the others.

"What is it?" he whispered.

Odd didn't respond. His eyes were locked on something.

Yarra turned her head towards him. "There's something out there. I saw a pack of maybe a dozen creatures. Something we've not encountered before, but they looked vicious. Then they started mewling, as if they were being attacked."

"What happened?"

Yarra swallowed hard. "Something worse ripped them apart."

It was hard to judge distance in the forest as it was so quiet, and sounds carried easily. Kell heard crunching and then lots of snapping, as if someone was tearing branches off a tree. This continued for a while before an eerie silence returned.

"I see you," murmured Odd, raising a hand. He pointed slightly off to the right, but even when he squinted Kell couldn't see anything between the trees.

"There," breathed Willow.

At first, Kell couldn't make it out. The only thing he could see was a tangled knot of bent trees, twisted vines and scrub. Shapes were indistinct and slightly blurred at such a distance.

Then it moved.

It was wider than a man, taller than an Alfár and it walked upright on two legs. Something that big shouldn't be able to move so fast, but it was gone in the blink of an eye, disappearing between the trees. Kell caught a glimpse of a shaggy hide and cold, green eyes, in a vaguely humanoid face.

They waited in silence for a long time before Willow finally relaxed. The others kept their swords handy, and together they moved to where Odd had first caught sight of the creature.

Kell had seen dead animals before, but nothing like this. The tainted beasts of the Frozen North had been driven into a savage rage by the Ice Lich. Their every thought and instinct had been overridden, until they were essentially mindless slaves. The tableau in front of him spoke of intelligence and cunning, far beyond that of a beast.

The creatures had all been torn limb from limb, until there wasn't one left with its head or legs. Dozens of organs had been ripped out and scattered around the edge of the clearing, like grisly flower petals. Next to that, the legs of the dead beasts had been laid out, end to end, arranged into a ring. And stacked in the centre of the circle, in a grisly pyramid, were the heads.

Even in death they looked cruel, with sharp teeth, jagged horns and barbed skulls, but Kell still felt a stab of pity. Whatever had done this was sending them a clear message about its intent.

And now, it was stalking them.

CHAPTER 14

It had been two years since the attempt on Sigrid's life, and since then, at least two members of the Raven always stayed with her. They even stood watch outside her bedchamber at night. No one was willing to take any chances, and security in the palace remained tight. Every visitor was carefully questioned, every delivery thoroughly searched. At times, it did make Sigrid feel as if she were living in a prison, but she understood the reasons so didn't complain. She was also grateful that it meant no one would ever get near her son.

As she walked into the negotiation room, the Raven took up their positions outside the door. Normally, her inner council were talking amongst themselves when she entered the room, but today there was a deathly silence. All three members rose to their feet, Natia and Lukas bowing, while Gar Malina placed a hand over her heart instead.

"Blood of my blood," murmured Sigrid. It was an old Choate expression reserved for close family. While not exactly blood relatives, they had become very close since Malina had saved her life at the orphanage.

"What's happened? Why are you all so quiet?" said Sigrid, gesturing for everyone to sit down.

"I've just received a message from a contact in the Holy City," said Lukas, showing her a tiny scroll from the aviary. "Rumours about the training camps for missionaries are true."

"We already knew the Reverend Mother was building an

army of zealots," said Malina. "She's been pulling in her people from all over the Five Kingdoms."

"It was only a rumour up to this point, ambassador," said Lukas.

Use of her title made the Choate warrior frown. She hated it, and had baulked at the formality, but it had been necessary to explain her continued presence in the palace. Malina had refused her new position, until she'd been given an order by the Choate War General. Sigrid had never met the man, but she had the impression he was fearsome, given how quickly Malina changed her mind.

Thanks to Malina's efforts, and after several months of careful work, Algany had become the first nation in the Five Kingdoms to open official diplomatic channels with the Choate people. It was a significant step forward, as just over two hundred years ago they had been at war with the tribespeople. Not that anyone was focusing on that, particularly King Roebus and the Reverend Mother. They were too busy doing their best to drag the Five Kingdoms into another pointless war. Sigrid hadn't persuaded the Choate to allow an ambassador into their territory, but she was confident that in time, it would happen.

"We knew about the zealots. What else has happened?" asked Sigrid. "Has the army of missionaries–"

"Thugs," said Natia.

"–left the Holy City?" said Sigrid.

"No. It's worse than that," said Natia, clicking her tongue in annoyance. "She's on her way here."

Sigrid raised an eyebrow. "The Revered Mother is coming to Algany?"

Natia actually put down her carving and looked up from her lap. Today's project was a sleeping circle of cat. "The last time she made the journey, she was already infirm. She must be decrepit by now."

Sigrid remembered the visit very well. It had been just after Kell had set off for the Frozen North on his second journey.

Her father had refused to see the Reverend Mother, claiming ill health. Sigrid had been forced to entertain the old windbag, playing the role of both a good host and dutiful daughter. It had been an exhausting charade.

"If the journey could kill her, why is she taking the risk?" asked Malina.

"Because she has something to gain," said Lukas, mirroring what Sigrid had been thinking. "Something very important."

"How long do we have until she arrives?" asked Sigrid.

"I'd guess six to eight days," said the Steward. "If they want her to survive the journey, they won't travel far each day."

"Is my army ready?" asked Sigrid, looking around the table.

"Yes," said Lukas.

"They're soft," said Malina.

When Natia didn't immediately defend them, Sigrid raised an eyebrow. The former Raven had nothing to do with the army, but all of the generals listened when she spoke. They respected her experience and knew that she had the ear of the Queen.

"They're out of practise," Natia agreed.

"Then what do you both suggest?"

"Drills. Toughen them up a bit," said Malina.

"Also, it wouldn't hurt to have them shore up the city's defences," added Natia. Thune wasn't a city designed for a siege. It had some fortifications, but it wouldn't hurt to improve what was already there. It would also send a clear message to anyone watching – Algany was readying itself for war. Hopefully it wouldn't come to that, but Sigrid knew it was important to prepare for the worst.

Nine days later, Reverend Mother Britak and her entourage arrived in the capital city, with all of the expected pomp and ceremony. A path had been cleared through the streets, extra squads of soldiers were on patrol, and a suitable welcoming committee had been arranged in the palace. Typically, there would be a banquet for such a distinguished guest of honour, but as she had made clear in the past, Britak hated displays of gluttony. Instead, a modest meal would be served for Sigrid, the Reverend Mother and ten carefully selected guests from the city. One for each of the twelve pillars of Britak's faith.

Sigrid drummed her fingers on the arm of the throne. She had been waiting over an hour for the Reverend Mother to appear. She was surrounded by her distinguished guests, ambassadors from all Five Kingdoms, and Malina. Every person in the room kept their distance from her. The other ambassadors were also doing their best to ignore the newest member of their cadre. While the ambassadors had made an effort to dress for the occasion, the Choate wore her leather armour as usual. Her only concession was to go unarmed. The only people allowed to carry weapons in the palace were members of the Raven.

Four stood on duty inside the throne room, resplendent in their colourful dress uniforms, armed with halberds and swords. The walls were lined with minor dignitaries and locals of good standing and influence. The room was awash with bright, distracting colours. She had no doubt that the Reverend Mother would find a way to disparage the expensive clothing of the guests. Over dinner, Sigrid would probably have to listen to a lecture about unnecessary displays of wealth distracting from the glory of the Shepherd.

Finally, the echo of footsteps on the tiled floor announced the imminent arrival of the Reverend Mother. The gossip faded away and all eyes turned towards the double doors. The footsteps were slow, and they reminded Sigrid of a funeral procession. Interspersed with them was a repetitive tapping sound and the scrape of feet.

In spite of everything, when the Reverend Mother finally came into view, Sigrid felt a stab of pity for the old woman.

Hunched over her crozier, gripping it tightly with gnarled hands, Britak moved towards the throne room at a painfully slow pace. Her right foot scraped across the floor, suggesting a stroke, but there was no sign of a lapse on her wrinkled face. Her skin was thin, slightly yellow, and the back of her hands were covered with brown spots. Sigrid's father had been much the same at the end, shrivelling up inside his clothes. The Reverend Mother's plain white robe hung off her body, as if she were a scarecrow.

Walking a step behind Britak was the old woman's personal assistant. Sallie wasn't helping the Reverend Mother to walk, but she was poised to catch her if she fell. Four burly priests in sparkling white robes followed in their wake. They were grim-faced and judgmental, staring at the crowd in way that made many look away in shame or embarrassment.

With one final tap, shuffle and step, the Reverend Mother reached the centre of the throne room. Sigrid's pity for the old woman melted away as their eyes met. While Britak's body might be failing, the intense fury of her glare showed that her mind had been unaffected. She had travelled all of this way for a specific reason. Nothing was going to stop her uniting the Five Kingdoms under the banner of the Shepherd.

"The Shepherd's blessings be upon your house, your children and all of your family," declared the Reverend Mother, making the symbol of the crook with one clawed hand. A few people in the crowd murmured a brief response, but it was muted. The four priests glared at the crowd with obvious disappointment while the Raven watched them intently. Violence seemed imminent.

"Thank you, Reverend Mother," said Sigrid. Last time she had cleared the room of chairs so that everyone had been forced to stand. Today she remained on the throne and didn't get up to curtsey. Sigrid was certain the slight wouldn't go unnoticed. "And thank you for making what must have been a difficult journey for someone of your considerable age."

Britak sneered, showing her yellowing teeth. "I have endured physical hardship in his service my entire life. It's good for the soul. Cleansing. Today is no different."

"Would you like some time to freshen up from your journey?" asked Sigrid. "Or would you prefer we immediately discuss the reason for your visit?"

All attempts, subtle and clandestine, to find out why the Reverend Mother had risked making the arduous journey, had been unsuccessful. More than anything, that made Sigrid incredibly nervous.

Britak's smile was feral. "Now would be a good time, your Majesty," she said, managing to make Sigrid's title sound like an insult.

"Very well," said Sigrid, getting ready to dismiss the crowd. The Raven came to attention at their posts, and the audience gathered themselves to leave.

"But perhaps, we could conclude this audience with a brief prayer of thanks to the Shepherd," said the Reverend Mother. Her eyes slid across to Malina and then back.

The conniving old bitch.

Whatever Sigrid said, it would cause a problem. If she refused to accept the blessing, then the rumours about her being a heathen would spread. Wild tales of her consorting with godless Choate, and their disturbing rituals, wouldn't sound far-fetched with one standing beside her. Even worse, the stories would be carried across the city by the hundred witnesses she'd invited to the palace.

If she agreed to the prayer, Britak's next comment would be about non-believers in their midst. Either she would have to publicly distance herself from Malina, potentially creating a rift between Algany and the Choate, or admit to being friends, which would lead back to the rumours.

"I would welcome a prayer to the Shepherd," said Malina, surprising everyone in the room. "Would you do the honours, or would you prefer I lead the assembly?" she asked.

The Reverend Mother looked horrified at being directly addressed by the Choate before she found her voice. "And what would you know of the Shepherd?"

Malina cocked her head to one side. "Among my people you would call me a priest. I can quote the whole Book, if you like?"

"What nonsense is this?" said Britak, playing to the crowd.

"*When mankind trembled in the night, the Shepherd brought fire and with it light,*" quoted Malina. "*But the twelve pillars were what the tribes cherished, as without them, they would all have perished.*"

"Blessed be the Shepherd," said Sigrid, and most of the room echoed her a moment later.

"That is not from the Book!" scoffed the Reverend Mother, but it was too late. The words had been simpler than those typically quoted, but everyone recognised them. Many were now looking at Malina in a different way.

"It sounded like it to me," said Sigrid, "but I don't think this is the right time or place for a theological discussion."

Before the Reverend Mother had a chance to respond, Sigrid signalled to the guards. The Raven opened the doors and gestured for the crowd to disperse. Seeing the bottled fury on Britak's face, they were happy to leave.

The old woman remained immobile in the centre of the room. Everyone was forced to walk around her, but no one wanted to get too close, creating a pool of space.

After a few minutes the room was empty of all spectators. The ambassadors were the last to leave. Malina went with them until only Sigrid, Lukas, the Reverend Mother, and her slow-witted assistant, Sallie, remained. The Raven and Britak's priests waited outside in the corridor.

"Shall we?" said Sigrid, gesturing towards the side door.

Moving even slower than when she arrived, the Reverend Mother trailed after Sigrid down the corridor to her negotiation room. As she'd done in the past, a simple repast had been laid out for her frugal visitor. It was the kind of fare Sigrid would expect to find at a modest roadside tavern. Bread, butter, boiled eggs, cheese, water and a limited selection of local fruit. There was still a formal meal to endure tonight, but Sigrid considered cancelling it.

While Britak made herself comfortable, Sigrid filled a plate and waited for the old woman to get to the reason for her visit. The attempt to embarrass and humiliate Sigrid in public had been an added bonus. For two years, Britak been trying to paint Sigrid as a heathen, in order to start a holy war, and so far it hadn't worked. That meant the old woman had something else up her sleeve, and this visit was the opening move.

Sallie filled two plates with food, then took a chair to the corner of the room where she began to stuff her face. The Reverend Mother stared at her food for a moment, as if lost in thought or praying, but Sigrid knew it was just another delay tactic. She wanted to stretch out the silence between them and try to make Sigrid uncomfortable in her own palace. It was not going to work. She refused to be intimidated by the old crone.

"Are you not hungry, Reverend Mother?"

Britak slowly raised her head and stared at her surroundings with a total lack of recognition. The confusion on her face was startling. It aged her even more and made Sigrid think of her father, whose mind had wandered towards the end of his life.

Ignoring her food, Sallie got up from her corner and whispered something in the Reverend Mother's ear. Steel returned to the old woman's gaze. She seized the edge of the table so tightly her knuckles turned white. Sigrid didn't know if she was trying to steady herself or supress her rage.

"Algany has lost its way," said Britak, firmly in control of her faculties again. Sallie drifted back to her corner where she continued to graze on bread and cheese. "In order for it to be welcomed back into the fold, you must lead by example and publicly repent your sins."

"And what sins would those be?"

"Don't play games with me, girl," said Britak, dropping all formalities. "You're consorting with godless heathens, and even worse, I am told one of them is living in the palace. The hubris of that savage, pretending to be a priest of the Shepherd. Did you think I wouldn't find out that you'd made her an ambassador?"

Sigrid shrugged. "It's not something I really thought about. I don't factor you into my thinking."

"You threw my missionaries out of the country," said the old woman, as if Sigrid hadn't spoken. "They were selfless heroes, dedicated to helping others. You may not care about your immortal soul, but such reckless ambivalence towards your people is unforgivable. Only the Shepherd can save them."

"The people of Algany are free to worship whichever god they choose," said Sigrid, struggling to hold on to her temper.

"There is only one God," said Britak. "Do you really think imps and spirits in the trees are real? I didn't think you were that gullible, child."

"I'm not a child and this isn't a theocracy."

"More's the pity," said the Reverend Mother. "Will you agree to publicly repent?"

Sigrid counted to ten in her head before answering. "No."

Britak pushed herself up from the table. With an oversized robe hanging off her skeletal body, she more resembled a herald of death than a priest dedicated to life. "Then you will rue this day for the rest of your life," promised the Reverend Mother.

"This is a bad idea," said Malina. They were standing together in the corridor outside the royal chapel. Normally it was reserved for Sigrid and her family, but the Reverend Mother had made an unusually polite request to pray there instead of at the convent where she was staying. After giving it some thought, Sigrid realised it would have been petty to refuse. Besides, Britak was due to leave in the morning and return to the Holy City. Sigrid still wasn't sure why the old woman had made the long and difficult journey. If there was a plan in motion, neither Sigrid nor any of her people could see what it was. This was her last opportunity to find out and, perhaps, salvage her diplomatic relationship with the Reverend Mother and the Holy City. King Roebus might sit on the throne, but Sigrid had no illusions about him being in charge.

"She's not going to have changed her mind overnight."

"I know, but it's worth a try," said Sigrid. "What do I have to lose?"

The inside of the chapel was cool and still. Dust motes shimmered in the air and coloured bars of light shone through the stained-glass windows. Each one had a pictogram depicting one of the twelve pillars.

Sigrid was surprised to see that the Reverend Mother was alone. Her escort had not been in the corridor and even Sallie was nowhere to be seen. The old woman was sat on the front pew with her head bowed, but she raised it as Sigrid entered the chapel.

"I've always liked them," said Britak, gesturing at the windows. "The design is simple enough that even a child can understand. Sometimes, we make things a lot more complicated than they need to be."

She didn't know what the old woman was really talking about, but Sigrid was certain it wasn't coloured glass.

"Come, sit down child," said Britak, patting the pew beside her. "It will stop me straining my neck."

Sigrid took a seat and waited for another tirade, but the old woman seemed a lot calmer.

"I had hoped we could talk before I left the city."

"At least we agree on something," said Sigrid.

The old woman smiled and looked towards the hooded idol of the Shepherd. No artist had ever attempted to show his facial features. Sigrid understood the reasons why, but had always thought it peculiar that someone would pray to a faceless god, unable to depict compassion, love or kindness.

"My eyesight might be failing, but I can see that you're afraid," said the Reverend Mother.

"There's no one here but you and me. So, for once, let's not play games," suggested Sigrid. She waited until Britak nodded before she continued. "I know about the training camps. I know that you're building an army. If you invade Algany, under any religious pretence, the other kingdoms will not just stand idly by. Thousands could die in a pointless conflict. I want to find a peaceful solution to our disagreement."

"You must think that I'm evil. That I relish the thought of war, and the suffering of others. My entire life has been dedicated to helping people and saving lives." The Reverend Mother stared up at the Shepherd. "I've fed the hungry, cured the sick and sheltered the poor. I was certain that if I led by example, and showed people the right way to live, they would follow. That they would care for one another. That the rich would help those less fortunate. After fifty years of service, do you know what I've discovered?"

"No."

The look of peace evaporated as a sneer curled Britak's lip. "People are stupid, greedy and selfish. Showing and asking them to do something isn't enough. They need to be told."

"By using force?"

"Sometimes it's necessary. Polite requests often fall on deaf ears, but we all remember the first time we were smacked for misbehaving. A lot of people grow old, they don't grow up."

"Not everyone is like that," argued Sigrid.

"You're right, but enough people are, and that makes a difference to those with less. Time is running out for me, but I will live long enough to see the start of a new age in the Five Kingdoms."

"What have you done?" said Sigrid.

"The training camps are just the beginning," said the Reverend Mother. "Once I return to the Holy City, the real work will begin in earnest. Every nation will be cleansed by the church. Initially, it may lead to a great deal of suffering and some deaths, but in the end, people will be happier."

"How will any of that make them happier?"

"Free will is distracting. It creates chaos and inequality. Those who survive the purge will be thankful. It will be glorious!"

Sigrid stared at the old woman in horror. "You're mad."

"Embrace the future, child. Repent and you may yet survive."

Sigrid walked out of the chapel as the Reverend Mother cackled with glee.

Malina was waiting for her in the corridor. "What's wrong? What did she say?" Sigrid told her everything in a rush, but her mind was thinking about the future. Armies of zealots sweeping across the Five Kingdoms. Fanatics bringing the glory of the Shepherd to the masses at the point of a blood-drenched sword. Kinnan would resist and fight back against such indoctrination, but she knew the King of Hundar had strong ties to the Reverend Mother. What if his armies converged on Algany, as well as those from the Holy City? Would anyone come to their aid?

"What if there are soldiers already on their way here?" said Sigrid, wondering if this whole visit was just a distraction.

"Don't you have spies in the Holy City? Wouldn't they have noticed such a large gathering?"

"You're right. I'm not thinking clearly." Sigrid took a deep breath to settle her mind. She'd been pacing up and down without realising, but now stopped. "Every day that she's alive, it brings us one step closer to war."

"Do you want me to kill her?" asked Malina, producing a knife from up her sleeve.

"Don't tempt me."

"If she died, what would happen? Would the war be averted?" said the Choate.

"There would be a delay and an investigation into her death. Then a funeral and a vote to choose her successor, but I'm not sure it would stop the war."

"But it might."

Sigrid shrugged. "Maybe, but you can't kill her."

"Why not?"

"It would make her into a martyr."

And suddenly it all made sense.

"What is it?" asked Malina.

"This whole thing is a sham. That's why she's without her guards, or even her assistant. That way they can tell everyone their version of the truth. If she's murdered here, in Algany, it will be the spark that starts the war. It's just the excuse King Roebus and her successor would need."

"She's mad."

"Perhaps," said Sigrid. "But she's also desperate and dying."

Sigrid gestured at the two Raven who were lurking out of earshot further.

"Your Majesty?" said Hanno.

"The Reverend Mother isn't well. I need you to watch her, and make sure she doesn't try to take her own life."

Hanno raised an eyebrow and said nothing before immediately heading into the chapel. It was likely that the war would still happen, but this way it wouldn't be the result of something she'd done. If Britak died here, Sigrid didn't want anyone to blame her. At best she'd thwarted the Reverend Mother's immediate plans. Sigrid would have liked to believe that she'd averted it completely, but she didn't believe in miracles.

The door to the chapel opened and Hanno emerged, his face deathly pale.

"What's wrong?" asked Sigrid.

"The Reverend Mother is dead."

CHAPTER 15

Staring down at the grisly tableau, made from animal body parts, Odd felt a prickle of fear run down his spine. Whatever was out there, it wasn't afraid of anything. It was the dominant predator in the forest, and it was showing exactly what it was capable of. It didn't have to hide its true nature as it had no fear of reprisal. Odd envied its freedom.

He couldn't tear his eyes away from the tower of skulls. Whatever had done this was intelligent enough to understand how to create fear in others. In the creature's mind, killing them would be easy. It could rip them apart, as quickly as it had dispatched the beasts littering the clearing. It wanted something else from them. The thrill of the hunt. It wanted to make them scared, and for its excitement to build in anticipation of a kill.

He'd never seen anything so brutal and fascinating.

"Do you know what did this?" Yarra asked Willow, searching the ground for clues.

"Perhaps," said Willow. She was looking in the clearing and finally squatted down beside something. It was a large footprint, roughly twice as long as Willow's hand. There were a few more prints heading away, but she didn't try to follow the trail. "Orcus," she muttered, apparently lost in thought.

"Willow?" asked Kell, gripping her by the shoulder.

"I'm still here," she said, smiling at the king. It was a peculiar response, until Odd remembered that her mind had begun to wander. "Before my people lived here, there were the Orcus.

The Ogg. The Yogren. We never went to war with any of them, and yet they died out until only a handful remained. They were as elusive to my people as we are to yours. They lived in the quiet places, high in mountains and deep in the forest. I have not seen any since the Malice took hold. I thought they were all dead."

"How dangerous is it?" asked Yarra.

Odd didn't need to hear the answer because he already knew. He could feel it. Even now, if he closed his eyes, he had a vague awareness of the Yogren's presence. The malevolence radiating from the monstrous being was immense. Its rage was like a furnace in his mind. It relished the idea of hunting them for sport.

"Like everything else, I suspect the Yogren have been affected by the Malice," said the Alfár. "They were not a war-like people, but they must have been tainted."

"We keep going," said Kell. "This doesn't change anything."

Odd knew he was lying but didn't say it. Everything was different. But then again, what choice did they have? They couldn't turn back and, even if they tried, the Yogren would come after them.

"Odd?" asked Yarra. "What is it?"

"Is your mother talking to you again?" asked Kell.

Odd realised he'd been staring and shook off his reverie. "No, she's not here. It's the Yogren. I can feel it."

The others looked askance at him. To prove his point, Odd turned slightly to the right of where they were standing and pointed. Willow traced his finger and stared into the forest.

"It's out there," she confirmed, surprising them all. "I also feel a connection."

Odd wondered if they could both sense it because of the Malice, or because he'd fed on one of Willow's people.

"Then we'll use that to our advantage," said Kell, but he didn't sound hopeful. "I'm not going to get any more sleep tonight, so we may as well keep going."

* * *

For the rest of the night they walked in a daze. By the time the sun rose, they were exhausted and dehydrated. More and more, Odd had to pull on his energy reserves to keep walking. Simply putting one foot in front of the other became a challenge. He didn't risk drawing too much energy, or else he'd look refreshed and the others would notice. Looking at their haggard faces, he had no idea how they were managing.

They didn't see a single beast all morning. They were deep in the blighted forest, and yet they were utterly alone. The only sounds beneath the trees were the constant buzzing of insects and the crunch of their boots.

The Yogren was still out there. Odd could feel it, trailing behind them. He guessed it wanted to study them. To find out what kind of creatures they were and how they coped with their fear. Despite its obvious power, it was proceeding with caution. It intended to deal with them, but on its terms and only when it was ready.

They stopped at what Odd thought was midday, and ate another meal out of habit. If they rationed their food, they probably had enough to get them through the Tangle. But now was when they needed their energy the most. They should have been eating and drinking more, to prepare themselves for the fight. The Yogren had all of the advantages.

"We should try and get some sleep," said the king.

While Kell couldn't sense the Yogren, he clearly understood enough to know this was just foreplay. The monster would tease and torment them. Maybe try a few feints to keep them on edge, until they were ready to snap. Only then would it actually come after them, when their fight or flight mentality was all that remained. A cornered animal always fought that much harder when it had everything to lose.

Odd wondered which of them it would target first. Who was the weakest of their pack?

"I'll take first watch," said Odd. The others were too tired to disagree and quickly lay down to rest. Kell and Yarra fell asleep quickly, but it took Willow a long time before she passed out.

"You know they're not going to make it," said his mother. This time the apparition resembled a young, carefree version of her. It was one he hadn't seen since he was a small boy. Before the hunger had surfaced in him, the worry lines in her forehead had been less prominent. There were also no bags under her eyes, and she wasn't absently grinding her teeth. Over the years, living with the fear that they would be discovered had taken a toll on her.

"I know," said Odd, talking quietly.

On his left, something moved through the trees. Odd was surprised to see a simian fetch, flitting from branch to branch. It was in a hurry, which made Odd draw his sword and lay it flat across his knees.

"Then you know what you have to do," said his mother. Odd took a deep breath and stared at the apparition. "What? What is it?" she asked.

"You're not her."

"Not this again," she said, rolling her eyes.

"I don't know why it sent me a vision of her, but it doesn't matter. I won't do anything you ask."

"Do you know where the soldiers took me after I was dragged away?"

"You know that I don't. I never saw my mother again. I was told that she was beheaded and then burned."

"They were terrified of me," said his mother, smiling at the memory. "They thought that because I'd ripped out a few throats with my teeth, I was a cannibal. Idiots."

A gentle wind stirred the trees, but Odd thought he heard something off to his left. The faint thump of heavy feet.

"They dumped me in a cell and chained me to a wall, like an animal. I was there for two or three days. After a while, it was difficult to measure the passage of time. A trial was conducted, in my absence of course, and I was found guilty of murder.

"Eventually, they came for me in my cell. There were four

heavily armed soldiers and a greasy weasel of a man. He gave me one last chance to repent." His mother's mocking laughter was a little unsettling. It sounded just as he remembered. Laughing at their ignorance. Laughing at their fear.

She grinned and tucked loose strands of her hair behind both ears. It was a familiar mannerism he'd seen a thousand times. The Malice was digging deep into his mind.

"He wanted me to tell him what I'd done with the bodies. To give the families closure."

"Did you?" said Odd.

His mother snorted in derision. "Don't be absurd. As if I could remember where I'd dumped them all. Do you know how many I fed on over the years? I'm not even sure of the number. Three hundred. Five hundred. Who can say?" she said with a shrug. "They had to die so that I could live. Predator and prey. That's what it always comes down to."

Odd gave his mother a withering look. "Let me guess. This is where you point out that I'm not prey, but my friends are."

"You don't need me to tell you what you already know."

"Then why are you here?" he asked.

His mother bit her lip. It wasn't something he'd seen before. "To tell you that it's stronger than you."

"You want me to run?"

"Of course I do. I want you to live."

She said something else, but Odd tuned out the sound of her voice. There had to be a reason the Malice had chosen a vision of his mother. Normally he was decisive. If he constantly second-guessed himself, especially now in such a dangerous situation, it could be lethal. He had to ignore what the apparition wanted and listen to his instincts.

"Are you listening to me?" she shouted.

"I know what I have to do," said Odd, ending the conversation. She wanted to say something else, but Yarra woke up with a start, clawing at the air as if being attacked. "It's all right," he said, trying to soothe her. When Odd looked for the apparition of his mother she'd disappeared.

Yarra tried to go back to sleep again, but claimed she was too on-edge. Less than an hour later, the others were also awake.

"Anything?" asked Kell as he rubbed his eyes.

"No, but it's out there," said Odd, looking toward the trees.

When darkness began to fall, they'd been walking for most of the afternoon without a break. They still hadn't seen or even heard any other beasts, which worried them all.

"My head is killing me," said Yarra, rubbing her temples.

Kell stumbled and had to prop himself up against a tree.

"Are you all right?" asked Odd.

"Just a bit dizzy. I just need a little rest."

"Chew some of this," said Willow, passing around some more willow bark. It eased the pain, but their nerves were raw. "There will be a full moon tonight," said the Alfár. "We should find a good place to make camp."

In this part of the Tangle, the ground was fairly dry and mercifully free of crawling vines. The trees were more evenly spaced and the gaps in the canopy were wider. As the moon rose overhead, shadows in the forest receded until there was nowhere to hide.

"We should eat a hot meal," said Willow.

"Are you sure?" asked Kell.

"It already knows where we are. There's no point trying to hide from it," said Odd, gathering some fallen branches.

"I'm so hungry," said Yarra. "Is there anything here we can eat?" she said, gesturing at the forest.

"We could eat some of the beasts, if we can catch them," said the Alfár. "But the risk is great. The poison will work faster."

All of them decided it was better to stretch out their remaining supplies for as long as possible.

"How much further until we leave the Tangle?" asked the king.

The Alfár winced at the question. It was not something Odd had seen her do before. Kell also seemed surprised at such an obvious display of emotion.

"What's wrong?" he asked.

"I can't remember," admitted Willow.

She had warned them this would happen when the Malice inevitably affected her memory. So far, there had only been the slight fugue at the stream, but this was more worrying.

"It's fine," said Kell. "We'll just keep going north. The edge of the Tangle can't be far away now."

They set up camp in a hollow, surrounded by the thick roots of blighted trees on three sides. The wood burned easily, but the smell was appalling, and they all kept their distance until the meat was hot. Black, greasy smoke gave way to green flames, as the poison was expelled from the wood. It was only when the fire had burned down that it became bearable, although an unpleasant aroma lingered.

After eating, they dozed by the fire while Willow kept watch. In the distance, Odd heard a faint rumbling sound that roused him and the others. At first, he thought it was thunder, but peering at the sky he saw that it was clear. A second later, Willow stood up and, turning in a full circle, she pointed off to their right.

Kell and Yarra struggled to their feet and drew their swords. At the first sign of movement, Odd thought it was the Yogren, but then he noticed that it was several shapes.

A stampede.

A huge number of fetch, lizards, and creatures they'd not seen before, were running for their lives. Branches were torn off, creatures were trampled underfoot and their bodies were smashed apart.

There was no time to run. They were caught in a trap of the Yogren's making. Either it had intended to soften them up with the stampede and then attack, or it was curious about how they would react.

"Put out the fire," said Yarra, kicking dirt over the glowing coals. Kell joined in, while Odd tried to calculate which of the beasts would reach them first. The full moon showed that the agile deer-like beasts were ahead of the others. A dozen had been running straight for the camp, but at the sight of Odd and the others they split apart, veering away from them.

Next came the fetch. Some fled through the trees overhead, and the rest ran on the ground towards them.

Odd took a deep breath then let it out slowly before he trickled energy into his muscles. When a fetch leapt at his face, Odd dropped to a knee and disembowelled it with the point of his sword. Its innards splatted on the ground, but the creature's fear was so great, it kept running for a few steps before collapsing.

Something slammed into Odd's hip, another fetch leapt onto his shoulders from on high, and a third tried to bite his leg. Whirling around, he dropped his sword in favour of his dagger, and began to stab and fling the creatures away. Sour blood splashed across his face and he spat to clear the taste.

No sooner had he flung one fetch away, two more took its place. One tried to bite his shoulder then hissed in pain as its teeth broke on the scale armour. Odd stabbed it twice in the head and it fell away. Grabbing the other by its neck, he whipped it down hard against his leg, batting another beast away. Using the dead creature like a club, he bludgeoned several others until it began to come apart in his hand.

Yarra was shouting as she fought, cursing the beasts, telling them to stay back. She'd been a soldier her entire life. Taught to fight people who would listen to reason, or at least appreciate when they were losing the fight. Whatever instincts the fetch and other creatures possessed, they had been overridden by their terror.

Kell fought methodically in silence, teeth gritted, face scrunched up into a mask of concentration. He was too stiff and often swung too hard, but he still managed to cut a bloody swath through the beasts. Beside him fought Willow, swinging her heavy, two-headed weapon with ease, braining and slicing anything that came too close.

When a tight knot of beasts knocked Kell to the ground, the Alfár protectively stood in front of him. Once he was back on his feet, they fought beside one another again. The king was bruised and a little battered, but otherwise unhurt.

Odd thought the flow of bodies would slow to a trickle in no time, but they just kept coming. He hadn't thought there were so many beasts in the Tangle until now. The Yogren must have corralled them from far and wide.

As more beasts dashed and dodged past the camp, everything was torn apart. Their packs were ripped open, any remaining food was trampled, and their belongings were scattered about, along with a few glowing embers. Odd quickly stamped them out before they had a chance to set anything on fire.

The press of bodies swelled until it became impossible to fight against. Covering their heads with their arms, they hunkered down in a group for protection, as the stampede trampled over them. The others cried out as they waited for it to be over, but Odd refused to give the Yogren the satisfaction of knowing that it had caused him any pain.

Slowly the rumbling faded, the flow of bodies eased and then mercifully stopped. A few stragglers ran past, bleating and crying out, but they swerved to avoid the camp.

Odd's limbs were heavy, bruised and splattered with blood. Some of it was his, but most belonged to the dead beasts littering their camp. The others were equally raw and bruised. Kell stumbled to a knee and Yarra sat down heavily on the ground, breathing hard.

The air became quiet and then absolutely still.

Instinct made Odd look to his left. Standing not far away from their camp was the Yogren. Its expression was difficult to read, but he thought it was disappointed to see that everyone was still alive. But then it smiled, showing off big square teeth, before loping off again, back into the Tangle.

They had been battered and bruised, hammered by bodies, teeth and horns. It was softening them up, tenderising the meat, before the kill. This was only the beginning. Odd knew that if he didn't do something, the others would not survive.

The words of his mother's apparition came back to him.

He knew what he had to do.

CHAPTER 16

Kell could barely stand upright. Despite the protection from his armour, his ribs were bruised and possibly cracked. The top of his left arm was no longer numb, but his fingers were still tingling. He had cuts and scrapes all over his arms, and a gash across his scalp that was shallow, but bleeding badly. Bruises were forming all over, and he could see the others were in an equally bad way.

But until they left the Tangle there would be no relief.

The camp had been ripped apart, their belongings scattered, and it took more than an hour to gather everything together. Kell's pack had been torn and trampled, one of the straps was broken, and a hole was punched in his water flask. It had been more than half empty and now only a few swallows remained in the bottom. Any remaining food had been ground into the dirt. The only small blessing was that some of Willow's medical supplies had survived.

They applied bandages and a few stinky salves to the worst of their wounds, but there was nothing for the pain. There were leaves to brew tea, but they had no water to spare, and chewing them wasn't effective.

Kell sat perfectly still, breathing hard through his teeth, as Yarra stitched together his scalp. To keep his mind off the needle, Kell watched the others. Willow had been injured as badly as everyone else. Fresh bruises were forming on her arms and face. There were streaks of dark blue down her right arm from a nasty bite on her wrist. It had been wrapped, but they had nothing to wash away the dried blood.

"Nearly there," said Yarra, while he hissed like an angry cat.

Odd was limping on his left side and holding his ribs, huffing slightly as he retrieved a few items. One of their packs could not be salvaged, so Odd was converting one of the tents they'd been given. Kell had begun to lose track of days, but it felt as if months had passed since they'd left Algany. Thinking on it, he guessed it was probably about two weeks, although he couldn't be sure. He wondered how long that would be to his family back home.

"Done," said Yarra, tying off the last stitch.

Kell's jaw ached from clenching it so tightly that he had to massage it before it would relax. "Thank you."

Yarra had a black eye and cuts all over her head. Three of her earrings had been ripped out and she'd removed the others for safety.

"So, what do we do now?" she asked.

It was a good question. It was late at night, but the idea of sleep seemed impossible. He didn't think they were at risk from any of the smaller creatures, as they had all been chased away. However, there was still the serious threat of the Yogren. Kell couldn't sense it like the others, but he was confident that it was nearby. It was probably watching to see how they coped with the stampede.

"We keep going," said Kell, because they didn't have another choice.

"We need a plan to deal with it," said Yarra.

"You're the strategist," he pointed out, getting to his feet with a grunt of effort. "Come up with something."

Kell left Yarra to think about their situation while he checked on the others.

"Are you all right?" asked Kell, sitting down beside Willow.

Her expression was strangely whimsical, which he found disconcerting. The Malice was affecting more than her concentration. Kell had to tap Willow on the leg to get her to focus on the present.

"I feel it," she murmured.

"The Yogren?"

"No. The pull of memory. The past. That which I missed, or avoided because I was afraid."

"We all have regrets," said Kell, thinking of the time he'd wasted keeping Sigrid at arm's length. The death of their first child should have brought them together, but instead it had driven them even further apart.

"Years ago, when you returned from the Frozen North, you were alone on the farm." Willow said it as a statement, but he sensed she wanted confirmation.

"Yes. I was on my own for ten years."

"Did you ever want a... wife?" she asked, stumbling over the unfamiliar word.

"Of course. Even a mate would have done," said Kell, thinking of the many nights he'd spent alone. At one point, he'd even reached out to an old friend, Mona, but then she'd been murdered by bandits. The pain had faded over the years, but the regret was still there. His life could have turned out very differently if they'd been married.

"Why do you ask?" asked Kell.

Willow bit her bottom lip. It was a very human mannerism and looked out of place on her face. "I spent many cycles, many of your years, in the Five Kingdoms. Several human lifetimes. Always searching for a cure, and I was always by myself."

"You were lonely."

Willow's eyes became distant and she sighed, another human mannerism. "Most of the time, your people were scared and they kept their distance. Sometimes, I would visit a town in Kinnan for food and to hear the news. There I met a young man called Juanne."

The Alfár fell silent, but she was staring at nothing. Her eyes were blank and almost lifeless. Kell nudged her and Willow came back to the present.

"The first time I met Juanne, he was an apprentice hunter. Unlike the rest of his people, he showed no fear when he saw me. The next time I visited, many years had passed, and he was a grown man. He was strong and well-liked by many, but he was alone. The way he looked at me…" Willow trailed off and Kell turned away as her feelings were so close to the surface, he could see what she was thinking about.

"We need to keep moving," said Kell, changing the subject, but Willow hadn't finished with her story.

"The next time I visited, he asked me to his house late at night, when the others were asleep. He knew they wouldn't understand."

"Maybe we should get a few hours' sleep first. What do you think?" asked Kell.

The question flew past the Alfár without her noticing. Her mind was firmly locked in the past with its regrets.

"I had been alone for a long time, and I was lonely," said Willow. "One part of me wanted to go to him. Another part said that I should give up on finding a cure and leave the Five Kingdoms. It was an impossible decision to make."

It wasn't his place to ask what had happened. Kell also knew that if Willow's mind hadn't been affected by the Malice, she wouldn't have told him this story. He didn't think she would be embarrassed, but he wasn't comfortable knowing something so personal. He hadn't earned it. She hadn't chosen to tell him this on purpose.

A heavy silence fell. Kell let it settle and avoided making eye contact. Instead, he watched Odd as he had finished making a new pack and was sorting through his belongings.

"Are you well?" asked Willow.

"Bruised and sore," Kell replied. Her eyes were clear and she seemed slightly puzzled.

"What were we talking about?" asked the Alfár.

"If we should we keep going, or sleep for a while."

"I do not think the Yogren will attack tonight. We should sleep, if we can," said Willow. Their previous conversation had apparently been forgotten.

"If we can," agreed Kell, unsure if it was possible.

His body hurt whether he was moving or standing still. Part of Kell was tempted to take off his armour, but in the end, he decided against it. Nothing had punctured the scalemail, and the only thing he'd find underneath was more bruises. Besides, he wasn't sure that he would be willing to put the armour back on once it came off.

"So, what do we do about the Yogren?" he asked the others as they gathered together. He looked at each of them, hoping for an idea, but no one had any answers.

With dawn still hours away, they decided to try and get some sleep. Odd offered to take first watch in case the Yogren attacked. However unlikely that seemed, no one argued, as they didn't like the idea of sleeping without someone standing guard.

Despite the fresh stiches, the bruises and the deep-set pain in his body, Kell managed to get some rest. He drifted in and out sleep for hours, waking often, his head full of unpleasant images.

Odd was still watching the forest when Kell woke fully a few hours after dawn. The Raven had apparently stayed up all night. Bruises had formed on Odd's face, and Kell knew that his own body must be a patchwork of painful swellings too.

Odd was so perfectly still that, at first, Kell wasn't sure if he was alive. Then he cocked his head to one side like a bird. Or an Alfár. Kell left the others to their rest and sat down beside Odd on a fallen tree.

"Is it out there?" he whispered.

"It's there." Odd sounded confident. Sensing Kell's doubt he closed his eyes and pointed off to the right. "It's not focused on us at the moment, but it did come to the edge of the clearing in the night."

Fear clenched Kell's stomach tight and a prickling ran down his spine.

"Why didn't you wake us?"

"We weren't in any danger."

"Then what did it want?"

Odd smiled. "It's never seen a human before. It was curious about its prey."

"Prey?"

"That's all we are to it. Something to play with and, perhaps, eat."

Kell wasn't sure what was more disturbing. The idea that the Yogren saw them potentially as food, or that Odd understood it so well.

"So, you two stared at each other for a while and then it just... went away?"

Odd shrugged. "More or less."

Kell had always known that Odd was a little strange, but it hadn't bothered him until now. The prickle of fear returned and, this time, it wasn't because of the Yogren.

With growling bellies, they drank what little water remained, then resumed their march through the forest. It was already warm beneath the trees and Kell knew the temperature would continue to rise throughout the day. The walk loosened some of the stiff muscles in his legs and hips, but he still had to clench his teeth against the pain.

When evening came and the worst of the heat faded, his mouth and throat were parched and his stomach ached. They were all bone-weary, hungry and desperate for water, but they still hadn't cleared the Tangle. They decided to press on rather than rest, in the hope that once they were out of the forest, their situation would improve. The waning moon rose high, providing them with enough light to navigate around obstacles.

"Do you think we'll be able to find some food once we leave the forest?" asked Kell.

Willow stared at him with a puzzled expression. She'd heard the question but was unwilling – or, more worryingly, unable – to answer. It seemed as if every day her memories were becoming more jumbled. Sometimes he saw the Alfár staring at their surroundings with astonishment, as if she were seeing it all for the first time.

Leaving the question unanswered, Kell focused on putting one foot in front of the other. So he was surprised when Odd stopped him with a hand on the shoulder.

Looking up from his feet, Kell saw that dawn was approaching. More importantly, they had finally reached the edge of the Tangle. But directly in front of them, hanging from the branch of a tree, were four of the deer-like beasts. Kell guessed they had been put there by the Yogren as a warning. It knew exactly where they were heading, and somehow, it had not only managed to outpace them, but left them a surprise without anyone noticing.

"Look," said Yarra, focusing on what lay beyond the trees. Kell joined her and together they stared down into the valley at a vast city, unlike anything he'd seen before.

Yantou-vash had been built by necessity and slowly cobbled together over many years. The desolate city in front of them had little in common with it, except that it was also outlandish. It had been designed by a people whose values and principles were significantly different to humans. The result was difficult to understand.

To Kell's eye, more than half of the city was a forest. It was overgrown, but in the past it must have been an integrated part of the layout as the trees sat in uniform rows. He could see a large field, or arena, that was now awash with wild flowers and several small lakes. Many buildings resembled ziggurats with huge flat walls, small windows and tiered layers with hundreds of stone steps. The pyramidic structures had been made from a sand-coloured stone and he had no ideas about their purpose.

Dotted around the city were small structures that were walled off from the rest. Squat towers sat at all four corners of the enclosures, and within were several small buildings and an open area. He didn't know if they had been homes, small freehold farms, or something else entirely. The rising sun reflected on few surfaces. Most of the buildings were made from the same sand-coloured stone, which he guessed was by design to absorb heat.

There were many other peculiar structures he couldn't identify. One section of the city had dozens of circular towers that were several floors high, with conical roofs. In another was a huge ring-shaped building. At first, he thought the roof had been destroyed, or fallen down with age, but it appeared to have been left open on purpose. It could have been an arena. Despite its peculiarity, the city was beautiful and vast in scale. It dwarfed anything in the Five Kingdoms. It was also, quite obviously, abandoned.

A strange heaving sound drew his attention away from the city. The others stared at Willow as she keened, her chest heaving, hands clenched in impotent rage. It took Kell a moment to realise she was crying.

"Willow," he said, gently touching her arm.

"This was my home. The city of Laruk. Now, it is called the Boneyard." She raised one arm, pointing at the sweeping meadows that lay between them and the edge of the city below. Dull brown grass coated the land like a uniform blanket, its colour broken up by countless tiny, orange flowers.

"At the beginning, when the Malice came, we planted one for each of my people that died. Eventually we had to stop. There were too many to count."

Thousands and thousands of flowers ringed the city. It was an immense display of remembrance, of death, and perhaps the futility of fighting against the Malice.

Willow turned away from the dead city. Much to Kell's surprise, she took down the animals from the tree and began to skin them.

"What are you doing?" asked Kell.

"The Yogren meant it as a warning or a threat. I will make it a gift," said the Alfár.

"You want us to eat them?" said Yarra.

"We have no choice. I think they will taste like venison," said Willow.

Kell's stomach growled. It had been a long time since he'd eaten a proper meal and it seemed unlikely they would find any supplies in the city.

"Are you sure?" said Yarra.

"The Malice is already in us. It was inevitable that we would eat something from the land. Even the supplies we were given by Nyandar were a little tainted." A change had come over Willow. The sight of her abandoned home had renewed her determination. She intended to survive.

Yarra didn't press the matter, but she was obviously still reluctant to eat. However, once the beasts had been butchered and hung over a spit, Kell saw her mouth-watering at the smell of roasting meat. Fat sizzled in the fire, and soon all of them were drooling at the promise of a good meal.

The meat tasted slightly sour, as if it had been marinated in lemons, but after a few bites, Kell didn't care. They all ate their fill and packed away the rest, not knowing where their next meal would come from.

As they readied themselves to head down to the Boneyard, Odd approached Kell.

"I'm not going with you."

"What do you mean?" said Kell.

"The Yogren is cunning, and it can move faster than us.

It's strong, healthy and it knows this territory. If we go into
the city, it will hunt us there as well. Up to now, it has been
taunting us. Soon it will tire of that and change its strategy.
It will become more aggressive. I will stay here and buy you
some time to escape."

Kell had never seen him so earnest. "We need you for
protection. I need you."

"They are enough," said Odd, gesturing at the other two,
"and you are fairly competent with a blade. You will survive."

"You can't win against that thing," said Yarra.

Odd's smile was unsettling because of its rarity. "You're as
bad as me at talking to people."

"I could order you to come with us," said Kell.

"You could, but it would not change my mind. This is the
best way for me to serve."

He seemed so determined that Kell wasn't sure how to
respond. Willow stared at Odd with an unreadable expression.
For a little while, she'd become opaque again.

"It is stronger and faster than you," said the Alfár. "It will
test your limits."

"I am ready," said Odd, dropping his pack to the ground. He
sat down, laid his sword across his knees, and waited.

Kell wanted to offer his thanks, for all that Odd had done
for him and for making this sacrifice, but he couldn't find the
words.

Odd didn't like physical displays of affection, but Yarra
rested a hand on his shoulder and whispered something in his
ear. Before he could say anything in return she walked away,
wiping her face.

Without a backward glance they set off for the city, leaving
Odd alone on the edge of the Tangle to face the Yogren.

CHAPTER 17

Hours passed in silence as Odd sat waiting for the Yogren to appear. Midday came and went, and it didn't emerge from the forest. After a while, he thought it had gone around him in pursuit of the others, but then he sensed it moving.

Just as he had hoped, the Yogren was intrigued. It didn't understand why Odd was waiting. It showed caution, which he took as a good sign. The longer it stayed in the Tangle, the safer his friends were.

He guessed that the Yogren had not encountered humans before, so it didn't know what to make of him and the others. That was why it had been testing them in the Tangle, first with grisly trophies and then with a stampede. It wanted to see how they would react. After tormenting them, it probably thought all humans were the same.

A feral grin crossed Odd's face. It was in for a rude awakening. There was no one else like him.

"You're free of the others," said the spectre of his mother. She was sitting nearby, dressed in loose trousers and a shirt with the sleeves rolled up to her elbows. The skin on the back of her hands and forearms was flawless, without any blemishes or scars. Her face had a few lines around the eyes and mouth, giving her the approximation of someone in their forties. It was the only concession she'd made in order to go unnoticed.

"You can finally be your true self," she said. "You don't need to pretend anymore."

Odd closed his eyes and reached down into the well of energy inside. With no one around, he drew heavily on that which he'd taken from the Alfár, letting the power regenerate the bones, muscles and skin of his body. He didn't need a mirror to know that the bruises had disappeared, the torn muscles had been repaired, and his cracked bones made whole. He was pain free and felt like his old self again.

The Yogren was moving. It was inching closer and yet, it seemed to be waiting for something.

"It doesn't want to come out," she said, echoing his thoughts.

"The forest is familiar hunting ground," said Odd. "It likes to use the shadows. It doesn't like change."

"You should even the odds. Force it out of the woods."

Odd grunted in agreement, picked up his pack, and carefully made his way down the slope towards the city. The others would be far away by now and were out of danger from the Yogren.

"What do you hope to achieve by this?" asked his mother, walking beside him.

He found it a little puzzling that the mirage didn't already know, since it was a part of him. "To keep the others safe."

"You've never cared about anyone before. What makes them so special?"

"I don't know," admitted Odd. "But when I'm around them, I don't feel so lonely."

After giving it some thought, it was the only thing he'd been able to come up with to explain his actions. He genuinely wanted them to succeed in their quest. That meant he had to delay the Yogren for as long as possible. Even if it meant sacrificing his own life, although he wasn't sure it would come to that.

As Odd started walking across the huge field of orange wildflowers, a peculiar peace settled on him. Churches of the Shepherd always felt like dusty old halls to him, echoing with the sound of shuffling feet. There was no supernatural presence, no guardian spirit. On the other hand, he'd always found graveyards calming.

"They are not your friends," said his mother.

"Perhaps," he conceded.

"They wouldn't do the same thing for you. Sacrifice their lives."

"Who said I'm sacrificing myself for them?" asked Odd.

"You can't win," said his mother.

"That's very supportive of you."

"Let me finish. I meant, not like this," she said, gesturing at his body. "If you insist on doing this, you need to make yourself better, so you're more evenly matched."

"We'll see," said Odd.

The Boneyard, once known as the city of Laruk, was a remarkable place. Not just because of the incredible architecture, but the scale of it was astonishing. If Odd had started walking at dawn, it would have taken him most of a day to walk from one end of the city to the other.

Unlike any city he'd visited in the Five Kingdoms, it had a layout that wasn't easy to understand. There were clusters of buildings that were different from one another. No obvious rows of shops and what he thought had been homes were scattered around almost haphazardly. The Alfár saw the world differently to humans. They had their own way of thinking, and without a guide, he wouldn't be able to decipher the city. Nevertheless, after a few hours of exploring, Odd was able to navigate through the streets without getting lost.

He stashed his pack and armour, taking only his sword and knife with him. Anything that could make a noise or rattle was torn off or tied down.

Time had stripped the desolate city of anything soft that would muffle sound. All that remained was dust and stone, dry scrub, overgrown trees and rampaging weeds. The inside of every building he explored was cool, empty of any furniture, and the walls were bare. In such an environment, the sound of scuffed boots or the scrape of metal would carry far. Odd wanted a chance to observe the Yogren without it knowing he was watching.

Eventually, he sensed it leaving the Tangle as it approached the city limits. Odd moved towards it at an oblique angle until he found a good spot. He was three storeys up from the ground, with multiple ways out, just in case it came after him.

A short time later, he heard the Yogren coming down the street. It was moving with great caution but loudly sniffed the air as it went.

Finally, the creature came into view and Odd had his first good look.

It was bigger than he'd expected, broad across the shoulders, but it also had a round belly. He didn't think it was fat, more its natural shape. Its skin was the colour of wet clay, and the shaggy brown hide he'd glimpsed in the forest was its clothing, made from the fur of some animal. It covered the Yogren's torso and hips, but left its arms and legs bare. Its limbs were wide, hard with muscle, and bristling with coarse black hair.

As he studied its face, Odd saw why it had been sniffing the air so much. It had a wide, flat nose and probably a powerful sense of smell. Its sloping forehead and deep-set green eyes gave it a brutish appearance. Even with its mouth closed, two of its bottom teeth protruded. Bald, with small ears for such a large creature, the Yogren looked slightly comical until you studied its eyes. It wasn't a bumbling simpleton, or a primal creature. It was a predator. Its dominance of every other beast in the Tangle had proven that.

It was quite a distance away from where Odd was hiding when it stopped suddenly in the middle of the street. Its eyes began to roam the buildings, searching for something. He froze, thinking that somehow it had seen or smelled him. There was no wind and he should have been too far away.

They both waited in silence, frozen in place. Odd kept his breathing slow and even, ignoring the primal urge in the back of his mind that was telling him to run. Finally, the Yogren carried on down the street. It had been a bluff. It didn't know where he was.

As it passed below his hiding place, Odd heard it muttering in its own coarse language. It was talking to itself or, perhaps, the imaginary ghost of its mother.

When he was certain of its location, Odd scraped his dagger along the wall of the nearest building. The rasping sound was louder than anticipated, but it served its purpose. Odd heard a grunt of surprise, but didn't wait to see if the Yogren was following. It had much longer legs, so he needed a good head start to maintain the distance between them.

The heavy thumping of its boots on the road told him it had taken the bait. Skipping over a low wall, Odd sheathed his dagger and then leapt at the next wall, digging his fingertips into the top before pulling himself up. From there he had a good vantage point of the whole street. At the far end, the Yogren lumbered into view, saw him standing and cried out a primal challenge. Odd dropped down the other side of the wall and ran as fast as he could, zig-zagging left and right, doing his best to keep the Yogren focused on him. As long as it was chasing him, it wouldn't be thinking about the others.

There was a roar and what sounded like the breaking of stone behind him. Either the creature had fallen off the wall, or just smashed through it. Odd kept going, passing through buildings, sometimes going up to the roof before leaping to the next one, pushing the limit of his strength and endurance.

At first, he thought the Yogren was slipping back, but several times he saw it from his eye corner and forced his legs to go faster.

For almost an hour, it relentlessly pursued him, never

slowing down or losing his scent. Odd ran into another building and this time stopped outside the back door. He scrambled up to the flat roof and then positioned himself above the door. With a little time before it arrived, he focused on slowing his breathing. Once it was under control, he drew his dagger and waited, silent and still, perched like a murderous gargoyle.

He heard the Yogren approaching, sniffing the air as it ran into the building behind him and then straight out the back door. It was moving so quickly Odd almost missed his chance. By channelling energy into his muscles, he made the jump and landed on its back. Wrapping one arm around its throat and his legs across its broad back, he tried to hold on as it skidded to a halt.

It howled in surprise as Odd stabbed downwards with his dagger, aiming for its neck. The Yogren shifted about and the blade bit into the flesh of its shoulder.

It had almost no effect.

The Yogren's grey hide was so tough the steel barely penetrated. Instead, Odd switched to slicing, which proved more effective. He managed a long slash down its shoulder before he was spun about and had to focus on holding on. Blood, as black as pitch, leaked from the shallow wound.

Instead of trying to reach behind and pull him off its back, the Yogren rammed Odd into the wall, driving the breath from his body. He tried to cut it again, but it slammed him once more, hard enough to see stars. His grip around its throat eased, long enough for it to grab his arm and pull him bodily over its shoulder. Odd landed hard on the ground and nearly blacked out before he was yanked off the floor by his arm.

Dangling him in the air from one wrist, the Yogren lifted Odd up to eye level so that it could inspect him. He swung at it with the dagger, but the creature swatted it aside, sending the blade skittering away down the street. Odd felt its eyes boring into him as it turned him this way and that, studying him.

As he began to lose the feeling in his hand, Odd felt like a child who had been lifted into the air by an adult that didn't know their own strength. The Yogren took a deep breath, inhaling his scent, and then it grinned before dropping him to the ground.

It chuffed something at him in its own language. The words were unintelligible, but the message was clear.

Run, little rabbit.

The Yogren watched as Odd rubbed his wrist and then retrieved his dagger. The hunt had been far too easy. The creature had been hoping for a challenge and he'd barely made it bleed. A steady trickle of blood ran from its shoulder, but the Yogren didn't care. Odd had been sure the ambush would work.

It would take a lot more to stop it than he had thought.

As a child, before the hunger had developed, Odd had played games with other children. This hunt across Laruk felt like the worst version of hide and seek. It had his scent and, the next time they met, he knew the Yogren would not be so gentle.

Until that moment, he hadn't really believed what his mother had said. Odd had been confident that despite its size and power, he would be able to beat it. Nothing in his life had ever been stronger or tougher than him, not even the Alfár. The fight had been vicious, but he'd still emerged victorious. Despite all of his gifts, the Yogren had beaten him with ease.

Odd reached the end of the street, and just before he turned the corner, he looked back. The Yogren hadn't moved, but it was still watching him intently. If it were human, he would have expected a smirk, or a little wave. It merely stared at him with hungry eyes.

His intention had been to sacrifice himself for the others, but only as a last resort. Now Odd began to wonder if buying them time to escape was the best he could hope for.

Odd methodically ate the remaining meat in his pack, barely tasting it, but he needed the energy to fuel his body. The hunger could only do so much.

The sun was beginning to set. Strange shadows began to stretch and multiply in the streets below. The cracked and pitted surface of the waning moon provided him with enough light to navigate to one of the ziggurats. By the time he'd climbed up the giant staircase, his legs were burning, but the view was worth it.

At the top of the pyramid was a narrow entrance, and positioned directly in front was a stone bench. The interior would be as empty as the rest of the city, so instead of exploring, Odd sat down to think.

Something flickered on his right-hand side but he didn't react.

"I told you. It's too strong," said his mother.

"I'm not sure I can beat it." It felt strange, saying the words out loud. Freeing, somehow, as if his surrender had lifted an immense weight off his chest. He could breathe easier and even managed a smile.

"You should run. Save yourself. The others are far away, but you could catch up." She sounded desperate. As if she genuinely cared about his wellbeing.

"If you were truly my mother, then you'd know why I can't run."

She sighed and looked out at the city. "Because you haven't run from a fight in your entire life."

"Exactly."

A comfortable silence settled between them. It didn't matter anymore if she was really his mother or not. Odd was becoming used to her presence.

"You can win, but the cost would be high," she said.

"Then I'll pay it."

"You might still die."

She reached out and laid a hand on top of his. For a brief moment Odd was surprised to feel pressure and warmth from her touch. The Malice was deep inside his brain now, playing tricks on his senses.

He understood that the only way to beat the Yogren was to remake himself.

"I've never made such a drastic change before, only small alterations."

"I know."

"Did you ever do something like that?" he asked.

"Once," she said. "Do you remember living with a friend of mine when you were seven?"

Odd vaguely remembered another house and sharing a room with another boy for a while, but not the reason.

"It took me weeks to find myself. After that, I couldn't take the risk and had to be more careful."

It was uncanny how much the phantom resembled his mother. Every tiny mannerism was perfect. It was almost good enough to make him believe. Odd was glad that he wasn't totally alone, even if it wasn't real.

"How did you find your way back?" he asked.

His mother smiled. "By thinking about you. I couldn't bear the thought of you growing up by yourself."

"I'm glad you came back. Even if it was only for a few more years."

"I wish it could have been longer," said his mother.

Odd took off all of his clothes and neatly folded them on the bench, placing his sword and dagger beside them. The temperate had fallen a little, and a cool breeze caressed his body. In the pale light of the moon, he noticed the patch of grey skin on his leg had spread down to his knee and up towards his crotch. There was another smaller blemish on his other leg as well. The Malice was spreading.

Closing his eyes, Odd reached down into the well of energy inside and began to draw heavily on it. Once this was done there might not be enough to change back. He would be stuck for the rest of his life. That was assuming he survived his battle with the Yogren.

"Show me your true face," said his mother.

It was a simple request and yet also the most difficult of his life. All he had to do was change his appearance to resemble what he saw every time he looked in the mirror.

The muscles across his back rippled and then began to bunch together, bulking out, stretching the skin to its limit. At the same time, his jaw began to lengthen and expand. Bones cracked and stretched, and a scream of pain erupted from his throat. It echoed off empty stone buildings and he knew the sound might draw the Yogren towards him. It was a risk he would have to take.

His internal organs began to shift, something new blossomed inside his swollen stomach and his knees cracked apart. With a wail of agony, he fell to the ground, back arched, head down. His shoulders swelled, becoming thick and heavy. His feet became longer and narrower, ending in claws to match his hands which were now tapered.

Odd's vision of the city was blurred from the pain, but when his pupils changed shape, the pale shadows peeled back revealing their secrets. And still the changes came. He felt something shifting inside his skull as it cracked and then reformed. The pain was so intense he passed out momentarily, but when he awoke, it still wasn't over. The bones in his legs reset and he cried out again as the muscles in his joints were rebuilt, one after the other.

Slowly the pain ebbed away. Odd stood up on new and unsteady legs, staring out at the city as if for the first time. His eyes picked out details he hadn't noticed before. The lack of chisel marks or obvious joins on the buildings indicated skills far beyond any human endeavour. He noticed patterns, as groups of structures were repeated as part of a much larger design, but he still couldn't comprehend their purpose.

The empty city was cold and abandoned. The only life within its limits came from the overgrown gardens and parks, which called to him. He wanted to feel the grit of soil between his toes, smell the green of nature and lose himself in the wild.

Throughout the torturous process, he'd kept the image of his true self firm in his mind to guide the transformation. Now, he tried to hold onto the reason for enduring the change.

The Yogren.

Once it was dead, he could go wherever he wanted. Be whatever he wanted. Perhaps he would become the alpha predator in the Tangle and claim it as his domain. But only once the Yogren was dead.

With a snarl, Odd dropped to all fours, raced down the staircase towards the city, and began to hunt for his prey.

CHAPTER 18

As she studied the faces of her friends around the table, Sigrid realised that all of them had lost hope of preventing a war across the Five Kingdoms.

The months following the apparent assassination of the Reverend Mother had been rife with speculation, conspiracy theories and slander about Sigrid. Her ongoing feud with the Reverend Mother was well known and no-one would believe she had not been involved. Attempts to direct the blame elsewhere, towards a foreign power trying to sow dissent, fell on deaf ears. No matter how many times she said it, few people were willing to believe that Britak had taken her own life.

According to the church, suicide was a grave sin. For most people, it was ridiculous to suggest that after a lifetime of service, the leader of the church would do something so heinous and damning. It went against a lifetime of work and sacrifice. To make matters worse, several witnesses, including some of her own people, placed Sigrid in the chapel with the Reverend Mother.

The Reverend Mother's priests and assistant had played up her age and frailty. They'd also painted the old woman as a saint who only wanted the best for people. According to their version of the story, Britak had gone to the chapel to make a last plea to save Sigrid's soul. Looking at it objectively, Sigrid could see why people would think she'd murdered the old woman.

To make matters worse, the day before she had died, many had witnessed their disagreement in court. It was also a well-known fact that over the last few years, theirs had been a fraught and combative relationship. Trying to convince them she didn't have a grudge against the Reverend Mother was impossible and pointless. Everyone knew she didn't like the old woman, but few people had thought Sigrid would actually kill her.

What galled her most was, if she had intended to kill the Reverend Mother, why would she do it in such a crude fashion? It surprised Sigrid that so many people were willing to believe she would be so obvious. Their opinion of her was very different from what she'd hoped to project to the world.

Those closest to Sigrid knew the truth about what had happened, but that did little to ease her mind. Algany was rife with rumours. The murder of the Reverend Mother was the main topic of conversation in every tavern across the nation. Talk of war had been rumbling along for months, and now it was finally coming to a head.

It had taken almost two months for the church to decide that Sister Reyna would become the new Reverend Mother. During that time, soldiers in Hundar had begun to gather, and ships full of missionaries ferried across the Narrow Sea into the Five Kingdoms. The old Reverend Mother had set up training camps in the lands beyond Corvan, and now a sizeable army was gathering in the Holy City.

"Has there been any word from King Roebus?" asked Sigrid as she sat down.

"A few short missives," said Lukas. He looked exhausted. There were deep bags under his eyes and his skin was grey. "He's claiming to be a neutral party. That he just wants to maintain the peace."

"That chinless idiot is a puppet for the church," said Natia. "He has been for years. These days, he's led around by his cock. I wouldn't be surprised if his young wife belongs to the Reverend Mother."

"It's very possible," agreed Sigrid. "What about King Elias of Hundar?" Elias was devout and had been an ally of the late Britak for a long time.

"He's thrown his full support behind the Holy City and wants to see you put on trial for murder," said Lukas.

"That won't happen," said Malina. "No one will get anywhere near you. I promise."

Sigrid squeezed her hand in thanks. The Choate warrior had offered to bring in an army of her own to support Algany in the war. The King of Hundar might be able to keep the northern army of Kinnan out of the war, but they would be hard pressed if they suddenly found themselves facing two enemies at the same time.

"There must be something we can do," said Sigrid, hoping that someone had some inspiration.

Hundreds, if not thousands, of soldiers would die in a pointless war if she did nothing. At this point, it didn't really matter if she had killed Reverend Mother Britak or not. The Holy City and the church were just using it as an excuse to cleanse Algany of heathens, starting with the queen. If left unopposed, alongside their letters, children across the country would be taught from an early age about the Shepherd. In time, churches would begin to fill up again and the church would become as rich as it had in the past. And with wealth came power, control, and the ability to direct the future of Algany.

Sigrid knew the old woman's ambition had been to have all Five Kingdoms united under the Shepherd's crook, but right now she had to worry about her own people. Ahead of them, she worried about her son and her friends.

"Is there any other news?" asked Sigrid, hoping for a distraction.

Lukas nodded grimly. "More bad news, I'm afraid. There

have been three more formal requests for you to declare that the king is dead."

Kell had been gone for over three years. At the start, she had been confident that, somehow, he would find a way to send her a message. Even if it was just a few words, to let her know that he was still alive. There had to be a way, even in the distant lands of the Alfár.

As the weeks turned into months, Sigrid had begun to wonder if Kell was ever going to come home. The darkest parts of her mind told her that he had run away, and that had been his plan from the start. She pictured him enjoying a new life with a new family. The bitter voice, the one that whispered to her in the middle of the night, said that he was already dead.

"There's been no word?" she asked, out of rote. She had a few remaining embers of hope that he would return, but they too had almost been snuffed out.

"Nothing," said Lukas, refusing to make eye contact.

Natia paused in her endless carving and put the blade and piece of wood aside. "It's time."

"We are blood. You will never be alone," said Malina.

Sigrid took a deep breath before giving her answer. "Very well. Thank you all for being so patient. I know I should have done this some time ago."

"We all hoped that he would come back," said Natia.

"You have read the truth about his journey to the Frozen North. You know what he endured," said Malina. "If he was still alive, he would have found a way by now."

"What happens with the throne?" asked Sigrid.

"Legally, it passes to your son, as the heir," said Lukas. "In reality, things will continue as normal until he comes of age."

"Assuming any of us live that long," said Sigrid.

"This is a bad idea," said Malina.

"I have no choice," said Sigrid.

The two of them were sat atop their horses, riding towards the enemy, under a flag of truce.

"There must be another way," said Malina.

Despite their peaceful mission, the Choate warrior was dressed in her leathers and armed to the teeth. They were outnumbered several hundred to one, but Sigrid knew that if she asked, Malina would attempt to fight their way out. For her, fighting was as natural as breathing, and any form of surrender felt alien.

The front ranks of the missionaries grudgingly stepped aside, letting them pass to the rear of the camp, where their leaders waited outside a command tent. Sigrid noted the camp was still in the process of being set up. The army had started its slow march from the Holy City, towards the heart of Algany, but had not made it very far. Soldiers could only walk so many miles each day, especially when they relied heavily on so many others to keep them alive. The supply wagons probably stretched along the west road all the way back to the walls of Lorzi.

Six people were waiting for Sigrid outside the command tent. She didn't recognise any of the figures, but the plain-faced woman dressed in white and yellow robes could only be Reverend Mother Reyna. She had a no-nonsense look, was solidly built and had grey, wavy hair. The others were all soldiers, and Sigrid guessed they were her generals.

As they dismounted from their horses, half a dozen soldiers armed with swords ran forward.

"Put them away, you idiots," snapped the Reverend Mother, freezing the soldiers in their tracks.

"But the savage is armed," one of them said.

Reyna gave him a withering glare then turned to one of her generals, a tall man with a bushy grey moustache. "I thought you said they were professionals?"

"That won't be necessary," he said, waving the soldiers back.

"Come, child," said the Reverend Mother, ignoring everyone except Sigrid. "Your bodyguard can come as well."

"But she will need to surrender her weapons," added the general.

Reyna grunted but didn't comment. She went into the tent without waiting to see what happened. Much to Sigrid's relief, Malina gave up her weapons without an argument.

Inside the tent, the air was cool and, despite the situation, Sigrid felt a lot more comfortable with less people watching.

"Please sit," said the Reverend Mother, gesturing at a couple of chairs which had been padded with brightly coloured cushions. She fetched two mugs, of what turned out to be water, and offered one to Sigrid. When she hesitated to take a drink, Reyna rolled her eyes and sipped from both mugs before Sigrid accepted.

"So, tell me, why are you here?" asked Reyna.

Sigrid took a moment to gather her thoughts. The Reverend Mother was younger than she'd anticipated, but she had a bullish attitude that was familiar.

"You sound just like your predecessor," said Sigrid. "She was also direct, and when she said jump, people did as they were told."

"True enough, but you should know I don't have her skill with words. She loved to fence, but I don't have the patience. So, let us speak plainly."

"Aren't you worried about being alone with us?" asked Sigrid.

The Reverend Mother's smile didn't reach her eyes. "Should I be worried? Is your pet savage going to try and kill me?"

"Call me a savage one more time and I'll snap your neck like a twig," promised Malina.

"I like you, girl," said Reyna, turning to Malina. "You've got plenty of grit. No brains, though."

Sigrid put a hand on Malina's arm before it went any further. "I came here to see if we could find a way to avoid the approaching bloodbath."

"You should have thought of that before you killed Britak."

"I didn't kill her," said Sigrid.

"At this point, it doesn't matter. All of the little soldiers outside are desperate to stick their swords into something."

"Is there anything I can do?"

The Reverend Mother took a deep breath and sat back in her chair. "Admit your guilt, beg forgiveness and publicly confess to being a godless heathen."

"Is that all?" scoffed Sigrid.

"No," said Reyna, pursing her lips. "You will allow missionaries to return to Algany and continue their good work."

"I will not have thugs roaming the streets of my towns and cities, breaking skulls for imagined sins."

"I agree," said the Reverend Mother, which came as a surprise. "My predecessor and I differ in a few significant ways. She believed the stick was the best way to motivate someone. I prefer the carrot. I think wars are a waste of time and people."

"With that attitude, I'm surprised they chose you as her successor."

The Reverend Mother's smile became sly. "When you're known for being straight talking, they rarely look for subtlety. I merely ignored certain facts, when asked. It's too late now. The rest of the church can't do anything about it."

"What about my son?" asked Sigrid.

"What about him?"

"He is the rightful heir to the throne."

"I agree," said Reyna. "That has nothing to do with me. If you want him to be educated about the Shepherd, then I would be happy to send a tutor. Otherwise, his upbringing is your business."

It all sounded so reasonable; however, it was still an enormous gamble. Even if Sigrid publicly claimed responsibility for the murder of Britak, there was no guarantee the war would end before it properly began. So far, there had been a few skirmishes between scouts, and a handful dead on either side, but nothing more. If nothing was done, they were days away from a full-scale conflict, where hundreds would die in the first hour.

If Sigrid agreed to the Reverend Mother's terms, it could prevent all those deaths. The only thing it would cost was her life.

One life to save many.

"I agree to your terms," said Sigrid.

"No," said Malina, grabbing her arm. "You can't. Don't do this."

"I must," said Sigrid.

They had been arguing about this for days. It was the last thing she wanted, to leave her son alone after he'd already lost his father, but she had to think of others before herself. If she did nothing, and put her life ahead of everyone else's, how many children would become orphans? How many soldiers would die in a pointless war?

Sigrid expected gloating, but once again she was surprised by the new Reverend Mother. "You are far braver than I am, child. I'll give you some time alone while I break the bad news to the soldiers outside."

A short time later, two armed guards appeared at the entrance of the tent with the Reverend Mother. One of them was carrying a set of irons and heavy chains.

"It's time," said Reyna.

"Protect my son. Keep him safe," said Sigrid.

"On my life, I swear it," said Malina, squeezing her hands. "Blood of my blood."

Taking a deep breath, Sigrid stood up and let them clamp the irons around her wrists. Holding her head up high, she marched out of the tent towards the prison cart.

After being stripped and having her head shaved, Sigrid was dumped in a rancid cell, pending the outcome of her trial.

At the start, she had counted the days, scoring a mark on

the cell wall with a pebble. Even though she slept on a cold stone floor every night, wrapped in a moth-eaten blanket, Sigrid had been confident that it wasn't the end. But when the tally on the wall reached thirty, she stopped counting. At that point, it became apparent that her imprisonment would never end, and she would die in her cell.

Time had lost all meaning.

Despite being permanently hungry and thirsty, it was the monotony that she found the most difficult. There was nothing to do or see. No distractions and no conversation.

In the first week, her jailor, a lecherous man called Bailey, had taken great pleasure in tormenting her. Every day he would taunt her with news of her trial, inadvertently providing her with information about the outside world. Up to that moment, she hadn't been sure there would even be a trial.

Part of her hadn't trusted the new Reverend Mother and Sigrid thought this was all part of an elaborate ruse. The most cynical part of her mind told her that, despite the public humiliation of being carted through the streets of the Holy City in chains and being forced to admit her guilt, the war had still happened. At least her sacrifice had achieved something. The war effort had stalled, probably pending her trial, and the legal difficulties of executing a monarch.

Bailey had been confident she would be swinging from a rope in no time. He took great pleasure in eating most of her food, before tipping a few scraps into her cell. If nothing else, the grotesque man provided a distraction from the endless silence.

With so much time to reflect, Sigrid realised her greatest sin was pride. She had believed that because of her station, she deserved better treatment than others. At first, she'd been confident that someone would appear at her cell door, savagely punish Bailey for his horrible behaviour, and apologise for the treatment she'd endured. When that didn't happen, she wondered if she'd simply been forgotten by everyone.

Eventually, Sigrid realised she was no different from anyone else. Her position, heritage and good deeds in the past made no difference. In here, she was a criminal and nothing more.

Bailey's gloating about her imminent death continued for another week, but eventually he tired of making promises he couldn't keep. After that, his remarks became aggressive and more personal. He promised to give her a full plate of food in return for a favour. In this place there were no soft edges. Sound carried along the corridors, and she'd heard another prisoner paying Bailey in kind for their food. Every time Sigrid refused, he cursed her.

With only a little food and water, she began to sleep more and lose track of time. Sometimes she slept through the whole day. Other times, she would wake with the dawn. But every day, it was always the same. Nothing and then more nothing.

After two – or maybe it was three – more weeks when the weight had continued to drop off her body, Bailey stopped asking for sex. Maybe he no longer found her attractive. Looking down at her withered limbs, Sigrid barely recognised herself. All of the fat in her body had been consumed to keep her alive, and she now resembled a living scarecrow. Her hair was slowly growing back, but without water it was filthy and constantly itched with lice. Everything in the cell stank and, after a while, Sigrid wasn't sure if the smell of rot was her own body or something else.

She barely had the strength to stand and eventually couldn't even manage that. Staying awake became a struggle and she continually drifted in and out of consciousness. Whatever food was dumped in her cell she ate without question, but it was never much, and it barely sustained her.

The rage had come and gone, passing through her like a summer wind that had briefly warmed her skin. Next came regret. She regretted that her son would grow up without a mother, but at least he would be surrounded by people that loved him. Marik would never be alone or come to harm.

Malina and others would give their lives before they let that happen. She managed a few tears, but her body was so starved of moisture, she couldn't cry for long. She regretted not telling her son that she loved him more often or finding a way to reconcile with Kell sooner. Over time, her regrets faded too, and she was left with only an overriding sense of guilt.

Finally, when Sigrid allowed herself to accept that which she could not control, she experienced a sense of peace. Perhaps it was because of starvation, or because her mind needed company so badly, but Sigrid began to hallucinate. Her father was the first to visit. He sat with her in the cell but never said anything. He just smiled and held her hand. Soon she would be reunited with him and her mother. She hoped that whatever came next was peaceful and quiet. The moans and cries of other prisoners grated on her ears.

One day, when the sun was low in the sky, Bailey came to her door.

"Still alive?" he asked.

Sigrid didn't have the energy to reply but managed to turn her head. Even though he had all of the power, and she was close to death, he couldn't meet her gaze for long. He was a coward and an opportunist. It didn't take him long to shuffle away, cursing her for imagined slights. It wouldn't be long until she was free of him and this place. The end would come as a blessing. Sigrid closed her eyes, and with the sun on her face, drifted off into the darkness.

Later, when it was dark and cool, she heard a faint scratching sound. Fearing rats and the idea of them gnawing on her flesh, she struggled to wake. Her eyes were gummed shut and she barely had enough strength to turn her head, but there was someone at her cell door. Of course. Only now, when she couldn't defend herself, would he come into her cell.

In the gloom, she watched as the door crept open and a shadowy figure shuffled in. They moved slowly with heavy steps, showing caution in case she was faking her immobility. As if she could. Sigrid tried to laugh, but all that emerged was a faint wheezing sound.

"Shhhh," said a woman's voice. It sounded familiar, but she couldn't be sure. All of this was probably nothing more than a figment of her imagination. Lately, Kell had been visiting her during the day.

Something heavy thumped down on the floor beside her, and it took Sigrid a moment to realise it was a naked woman. Before she was able to process what that meant, the shadowy figure crouched down in front of her.

"You're not real. It's another hallucination," she croaked.

"I'm real," said Malina, touching Sigrid on the cheek. Her skin felt warm. None of the others had been warm. They hadn't cried, either. "Drink this, slowly," said the Choate, holding a flask to her lips.

At first, Sigrid thought it was water, but the liquid smelled spicy and quickly began to burn her throat. It wasn't alcohol, but something else as her skin began to tingle, coming alive for the first time in days. The warmth spread throughout her body, and she felt more alert. The fog that had descended on her mind, clouding her thoughts, began to lift.

"Why are you crying?" asked Sigrid.

"Later. Here, put these on," said Malina, passing her some plain clothes. Sigrid didn't have the energy to dress herself. The Choate had to help her out of the ragged dress they'd left her in. The new clothes were far too baggy, but at least they were clean. Malina dressed the dead woman in Sigrid's cast-off dress and then propped her up against the wall.

"Who is she?"

"Ask me tomorrow," said Malina, helping Sigrid to stand. Her legs wobbled and she would have collapsed if the warrior hadn't picked her up.

"Wait, tell me what's happening?" she asked, gripping Malina's shoulders with both hands.

"I'm taking you away from here, but the cost is high. You have to die," she said, gesturing at the dead body.

Sigrid had lost her husband, her son and her country. Now she was being asked to give up her name and everything that came with it.

"Take me out of here," she pleaded.

"I'm sorry," said Malina, gently picking her up and draping her over one shoulder. Sigrid would like to have walked from the jail, but she knew it was impossible. She had no strength or pride, so she grimly held on tight to Malina's clothes. "Try not to make any sounds."

Clamping her jaw shut, Sigrid watched the world upside down as the cell, and then the jail, receded into the distance. They passed over several rooftops, down a ladder, through gardens and eventually over a wall.

She tried not to complain as she was bounced around, or when the warrior's shoulder jabbed her in the stomach. Closing her eyes made it worse, so she tried to focus them on something in the distance.

The air smelled fresh and clean. Even late at night, the streets of the Holy City were full of enticing smells which made her stomach growl in response. Her body was desperate for sustenance. Whatever Malina had given her was already wearing off. Her lethargy was returning, but Sigrid fought it, determined to remain conscious.

At some point though, she must have blacked out, because when she opened her eyes she was being laid down in the back of a cart. Malina got in with her and the driver clucked their tongue. Looking past the back of the cart, Sigrid saw the walls of Lorzi. They were outside the city.

She was free, and the only thing it had cost her was everything.

CHAPTER 19

Kell did his best not to slow down while gawking at the city, but with so much to see, it was difficult. Willow had no such problems and was determined to reach the far side of Laruk as soon as possible. She marched along, stretching out her legs, and the distance between them began to increase.

"You need to slow down a little," he shouted, wincing at having to raise his voice. With some reluctance, Willow fell back to walk beside him and Yarra.

As soon as they'd entered the city, Kell felt uncomfortable speaking too loudly. It felt as if they were walking through a giant mausoleum. He'd instinctively whispered out of respect and fear of disturbing the dead.

"We shouldn't have left him," said Kell. It was suicide for Odd to face the Yogren alone. If they had worked together, they could have come up with a plan to defeat it.

"You could not have stopped him," said Willow. She was continuing to surprise him. Joining in with conversations, without being asked a direct question, was another effect of the Malice. She probably wasn't even aware of the change.

"It was his decision," said Yarra, keeping her voice low.

"Why are you both whispering?" asked Willow. "The city is empty. There is no one here. Not even the dead linger."

They marched past a two-storey building that was shaped like a fat teardrop with a pointed stone roof. It had slit windows and a narrow doorway at the front. Kell paused to glance inside, but he couldn't see anything to help him determine its purpose. Willow noticed where he was looking but didn't volunteer an answer which, although it didn't satisfy his curiosity, was actually a relief. Perhaps the changes to her personality weren't as significant as he'd feared.

"Is your house nearby?" asked Kell, remembering that Willow had lived in the city.

The Alfár shook her head. "It would take a long time to find, but even if we went, there is nothing to see inside. Only dust and empty rooms. The whole city is full of nothing but memories."

"Still, it would be nice to see it," said Kell, thinking of his childhood home.

"We need to keep moving," said Yarra. "Odd bought us some time to get away from that creature. We should honour his sacrifice."

"Do you think there's even a chance that he will win?" asked Kell.

Yarra considered it and then shook her head.

"He cannot win," said Willow. "The Yogren controlled all other beasts in the Tangle through fear. Odd is strong and skilled, but against such a powerful creature, even he will fall."

"You're right," said Kell, wishing it weren't true. Even seeing it at a distance had been terrifying.

Another rogue emotion was flourishing in his mind. Something out of place that wasn't natural. He was suddenly filled with curiosity, and a desperate urge to explore the city and unravel its secrets. The sensation was so strong he had to force himself to stare ahead, ignoring the wondrous and weird sights on either side.

It was another distraction. A delay to keep him in one place. The Malice wasn't aware, but it kept generating various emotions that were designed to put him at risk.

From what Kell had seen, the disease had altered every creature in the world, often remaking them into something new. Some reverted to their base needs and were stripped of all higher thinking. Others, like the martok, became primordial versions akin to their ancestors. If the Malice stripped away all of the noise and distractions, all of the worries and chatter that filled his mind, what would he become?

"Did you say something?" said Yarra, and Kell realised he'd been talking to himself.

"How are the voices?" he asked, knowing he wasn't the only one that was struggling.

She stared at the buildings, perhaps searching for a distraction, but he knew they were empty. "The whispering is getting louder. I can hear individual voices now."

The city wasn't haunted, but Yarra's ghosts seemed determined to keep her anchored in the past. They all needed something to keep their minds occupied, but the city gave them nothing.

The Yogren was still coming for them.

Kell couldn't maintain the same level of fear all day, and after a few hours of walking, it faded into the background. He was still concerned about the Yogren, but he didn't think it was breathing down their necks just yet. The growling in his stomach was a mild distraction, but he knew that over time it would only become worse. Food was going to be a constant problem. The remaining meat was enough for two small meals if rationed, but they still had no water. Their flasks were empty and Kell was starting to feel light-headed. In addition, his limbs kept cramping uncontrollably and he found himself drifting, chasing strange ideas in his mind for no reason. They could manage for a few more days with little or no food, but without water they were in serious trouble.

Late in the afternoon, Willow took them down a side street when she spotted something in the distance. Despite her insistence that the city was empty, he was still reluctant to shatter the quiet. He had the same feeling when he entered a church dedicated to the Shepherd. Even if he didn't believe, he knew that it was a special place for others. The building had soaked up so many strong emotions over decades, it created an inherent atmosphere of reverence.

Before entering Laruk, they had crossed the enormous pasture dedicated to the dead. Walking over a mass grave had been eerie. By comparison, the city wasn't as unsettling, but the uneasy feeling in his gut seemed to be getting worse. Kell wondered if the Malice was playing tricks again.

"We shouldn't be here," said Yarra, echoing his feeling about the city.

"If we press on after nightfall, we might be able to clear it."

"I'd prefer to sleep elsewhere tonight," said Yarra, and he agreed. His dreams were already troubled.

"Here," said Willow, directing them to a group of buildings surrounded by a six-foot enclosure. Given its age, Kell was surprised to find the stone wall intact. It showed no signs of decay, but the gate had rotted away long ago. They entered the compound to find what resembled a small farm holding.

Ignoring the main building, the Alfár went straight towards one of the smaller structures. It had a low door, but once inside the roof was high enough for them to stand upright. Inside was a waist-high stone circle that had been covered with a thick stone cap. Willow gently eased it to one side, as if it weighed little, revealing a well. Kell held his breath as she dipped her flask below the surface.

To his enormous relief, it came up dripping wet.

Wasting no time, they all drank their fill from the well until their bellies were swollen. The water was stale and icy cold, but it tasted delicious. With plenty of water available, they used some to wash the dirt, sweat and dried blood from their skin, cleaning their wounds before binding them from Willow's dwindling supply of bandages and unguents.

"We should keep going," said Yarra as she filled her flask.

"We would not reach the end of the city until late into the night," said Willow. She looked sad and wistful, nostalgic for a city and way of life that no longer existed. Kell guessed that it must have been over a hundred years since Willow had been in Laruk. It was so long ago, it probably felt as if another person had lived here.

"We'll stay," said Kell.

He could see Yarra wanted to argue, and part of him hoped that she would object. Instead, she just fell in line and meekly followed his orders.

It was an unusual homecoming for Willow. It made Kell wonder about the kind of reception he would receive if they ever made it back to Algany. Right now, his family seemed so far away, and every mile they travelled took him further from them. Every morning when he woke up, and every night when he lay down, Kell thought about his family. He wondered what they were doing and how often they thought about him. Time moved differently here, and he often wondered how long he'd actually been away from the Five Kingdoms. And most of all, he wondered if he would ever see their faces again.

He still felt guilty about leaving Sigrid. He had no way to send her a message, and with every day that passed, Kell knew she would begin to doubt if he was still alive.

His son wasn't old enough to notice if he was gone for a few months. At least, that was what he hoped. Even so, he would still be missing so many special moments. So many little changes that they'd celebrated with their daughter. It didn't matter that every other baby did the same things. It was *their* baby, and it was miraculous.

For most of Kell's life, he had grown up without a father. Whatever happened with Sigrid and their relationship, he promised he would be there for his son. He would not be an absent father. Nothing short of death would stop that from happening.

* * *

After eating a small meal, which did little to satisfy their hunger, they settled down to get some sleep.

Kell had been dozing for some time when he awoke with a start, his dreams full of disturbing images. Reluctant to go straight back to sleep, in case the same nightmare returned, Kell searched for a distraction.

Yarra was asleep, head resting on her pack, but Willow's blanket was empty.

Racing outside with his sword, Kell was surprised to see her standing a short distance away, staring up at the sky. The fractured moon was almost gone, and heavy shadows clung to the buildings, painting them in shades of black and grey. Without any birds, insects or bats, the silence was eerie.

"Willow, what are you doing?" he asked coming up behind her.

"Just thinking," she said, her eyes on the horizon.

"What about?"

Willow's smile was unnerving, because he recognised the underlying emotions. The mask normally worn by the Alfár was continuing to crack. "What is that saying you have? Listening to your heart and not your head."

"Something like that," said Kell, getting increasingly worried.

"I should have listened to my heart that night and come to your home. No one would have known. Can you forgive me, Juanne?"

"Willow, it's me, Kell," he said, moving to stand in front of her. The Alfár's eyes lost their distant sheen. "Kell?"

"Yes. Do you know where you are?"

Willow glanced at their surroundings and then nodded. Her legs folded up and she sat down heavily on the ground, holding her head in both hands.

"Are you all right?" he asked, not sure what to do.

"It's getting worse," said Willow. "I do not hear voices or see the dead, but the present recedes and the past looms large. I am becoming unstuck in time."

"What can I do to help?"

"By your standards, I am ancient," said the Alfár. "By that of my own people, I am of middling age. For the first time in my life, I am afraid. Not just for myself, but for all of my people. I am afraid that this is all that will remain," she said, gesturing at the empty city.

"I understand," said Kell. "I thought the Five Kingdoms were going to become an icy wasteland. I was terrified."

"Yes. That is one fear I have, but there is also another. Something closer, between you and I," said Willow. "I have no wish to die, but if it comes, then so be it. You have a new wife and a small child. So much of your life still lies ahead. In many ways, it has barely begun."

Kell couldn't remember the last time she'd talked so much. "You're afraid for me?"

"I am afraid that I have damned you and the others, by asking you to come here."

"It's not over yet," he said, trying to cling on to some shred of hope.

"That's because you don't know what lies ahead." Willow grabbed him by the shoulder and pulled him close. Her face was tortured with guilt and grief. "I hope that you can forgive me," she pleaded.

"It's Kell," he said, thinking she had slipped into the past again.

"I know," said Willow, "and I'm sorry for bringing you here."

The scale of Laruk turned out to be more deceptive than any of them had realised. By midday they still hadn't reached the edge of the city. Kell had almost grown accustomed to the unusual buildings and the vast silence that filled every structure. He remained uncomfortable though, hearing only their footsteps and the occasional gust of wind. The monotony began to wear on them all. After a while, he became desperate for something to change.

Although the city seemed to stretch on forever, rising up in the distance above the buildings was a low mountain range. The black, uneven peaks gave Kell something new to focus on. With every hour, they inched closer.

Willow continued to drift in and out of the present and Yarra still muttered to her ghosts. For Kell's part, the emotional outbursts became more difficult to hide. At one point, early in the afternoon, he began to weep uncontrollably at the thought of never seeing his wife and son again.

He had no way of knowing how long it had been for them since he'd left the Five Kingdoms. The pessimistic voice in his head told him it had been years. That they would have forgotten all about him and moved on with their lives. That Sigrid had found a new husband, and that Marik now called someone else father. Kell had become a remnant. Just a vague memory from the past that people rarely spoke about.

At first, the tears ran silently down his face, but as his stomach began to clench with fear and regret for all that he would miss, a cry erupted from his throat. The others heard but didn't ask. Both of them were struggling with their own demons.

Finally, after hours of walking, they reached the far side of the city. The broken peaks of the mountain range beyond were ancient, their sides uneven and scattered with gravel and massive slabs of volcanic rock. Peculiar craters littered the mountainside. In the afternoon sun, some of the rocks reflected the light, like polished glass. Other sections gave the illusion of movement or flowing water, where the molten lava had erupted and then frozen over time.

Despite the late hour, they kept walking, crossing a valley of scrub and tumbled rocks. When they reached the edge of the lava field at the base of the first mountain, Kell bent down to inspect the pitted surface. It was black as pitch and razor sharp. The lightest touch cut the skin on his fingers. It would slice through the leather of their boots with little difficulty.

"How do we pass through the mountains?" asked Yarra, realising the problem.

"There are several paths. Let's try this way," said Willow, gesturing off to their left. Her uncertainty made Kell exchange a worried look with Yarra.

They clung to the edge of the scrubland and combed the mountainside for a path. Trying to scramble across razor sharp rocks in the dark would be a death sentence. They would need to stop soon.

The gnawing pain in his stomach was worse than ever. Kell did his best to ignore it, but no matter how much water he drank, it didn't help. He was worried they wouldn't find a way through before nightfall, when Willow pointed towards something in the distance.

"There," she said.

Kell couldn't make it out until they were practically on top of it. Someone had cut an avenue into the rock face, wide enough for a cart, with room to spare on either side. The dusty track followed the natural curve of the mountain before looping back on itself over and over until it disappeared out of sight.

"Who is that?" said Yarra, pointing suddenly at something further up the path.

Kell followed her finger, but he couldn't see anything besides lifeless rocks.

"What can you see?" he asked, scouring the mountainside. Willow's eyesight was sharper than theirs, but she was equally puzzled.

"There's nothing there," said the Alfár.

"She's there. Right there!" said Yarra, gesturing wildly. "Don't you see her?"

"Yarra. There's no one there," said Kell.

She glanced at him as if he was mad, but when she looked again, her arm wavered. "There was a woman. I swear, I saw her."

"You were hallucinating."

"It was so real," she said, rubbing her forehead.

"There are caves along the path. We should go as far as we can," said Willow.

Kell's boots rang on the stone with peculiar echoes, as if the ground beneath his feet was hollow. Unsure if it was real or imagined, he didn't mention it to the others.

As darkness fell, they were on the second curve up the side of the mountain, feeling along with one hand touching the rock face. As Willow had said, there were a few shallow caves created along the way, and they made camp in one for the night. It was empty and cold inside, but as a light rain began to fall, Kell was glad for the shelter.

They huddled together beneath their blankets for warmth, but the cold and hunger meant none of them slept very well.

For two days they slowly trekked through the mountains, their pace erratic, as each struggled with their own malady and ongoing pangs of hunger. By the end of the second day their flasks were empty. On the morning of the third day, dehydrated again, half-starved and slightly delirious, Kell saw something peculiar in the distance.

"Is that real?" he croaked.

Yarra had been staring at her feet, afraid of tripping, but now she looked ahead. "I think so," she said. "Do you see a wall?"

"I see it," said Kell, relieved that it wasn't just in his imagination.

"The Choke," said Willow, gesturing at something.

Ahead of them, a new range of mountains rose higher than those they'd crossed. These were steep, jagged peaks that stretched into the distance to their left and right, creating a natural impenetrable barrier that he'd mistaken for a wall. Squinting at where Willow was pointing, he saw a narrow opening.

"Can you see a figure?" asked Yarra. Now, whenever she saw someone, her first instinct was to ask if it was real.

"I see it," said Kell.

"There's someone ahead on the road," said Willow.

All of them found a burst of energy from somewhere and picked up the pace. As the figure started to walk towards them, a wild thought popped into Kell's mind.

"Is that Ravvi?" he asked, wondering if they'd finally caught up with him. Perhaps Ravvi had given up or had a change of heart. After all that they'd struggled through together, he couldn't begin to imagine how someone could endure it by themself.

Hope swelled in Kell's chest as he realised what it could mean. If they'd found Ravvi, it was over. They could turn around. He could go home and see his family.

"It's not Ravvi," said Willow.

Kell stumbled and would have fallen if the Alfár hadn't caught him by the elbow.

"Are you sure?" he asked, hoping she was wrong. Several times she'd called him Juanne, so it was possible she'd made a mistake.

"I'm sure," said Willow.

"Then, who is it?"

"I don't know," said the Alfár. "I don't recognise him."

A short time later they came face to face with the stranger.

With discoloured grey skin on his face, arms and neck, the Alfár had more visible signs of the infection than any Kell had seen before. He was also badly scarred, missing an ear and two fingers on his left hand. His armour was dented, his clothes filthy and his cheeks gaunt. But his eyes were sharp and he carried a sword in his right hand. The stranger spared a curious glance for him and Yarra, but he addressed Willow.

They briefly conversed in their own burbling tongue before he sheathed his sword and gestured for them to follow.

"What did he say?" asked Kell.

"Welcome to the war," said Willow.

CHAPTER 20

Odd relished the feeling of his body as he raced through the streets of Laruk on all fours. The power coursing through his muscles as they contracted and expanded was addictive, driving him forward on his hands and feet. He was several streets away from the ziggurat before he reluctantly slowed down and made a note of his surroundings.

Standing upright, he studied the city with fresh eyes, noting many small details he'd previously missed. He had assumed that the sand-coloured stone, which dominated the city, had been quarried elsewhere and brought here. Now, he wasn't so sure. Most of the buildings were in good condition, but from his elevated position atop the ziggurat, he'd spotted a couple in the midst of being repaired.

Odd approached one structure that had a hole in one wall and the roof. Sat beside it on the ground were several large uneven chunks of what he thought were stone. They were pale yellow, like fool's gold, and for some reason had not been quarried into blocks. He tapped one with his foot and was surprised when it echoed, as if hollow. It felt like stone, but it smelled different to his sensitive nose. Odd couldn't be certain, but he thought it was bone.

The city hadn't been built. It had been grown.

Sunrise was a few hours away and he hadn't slept for a while. Part of him wanted to keep searching for the Yogren, but he also knew it was better to get some rest while he had a chance. Once the hunt began, he wasn't sure it would end until one of them was dead.

After scaling one of the large conical buildings on the outside, Odd curled up in the highest room on the top floor. A gentle wind blew through the open windows, filling the space with odours from across the city. Even in his sleep, Odd's mind processed them, discarding that which was commonplace as he searched for his enemy.

Something bitter wafted past his nose. Odd opened his mouth and inhaled deeply, letting the sour scent move across the glands in his nose and mouth to identify it. The city smelled of dust, pollen from the weeds and ash from an unknown source. There was also water nearby. He didn't know where, but if needed, Odd was confident he could find it by following his nose. This was something else. Something that didn't belong.

Sweat. Salt. And somewhere in the distance, he could hear the muttering of a deep voice. The Yogren.

Odd had been asleep for almost a full day, and dawn was close. He could smell a change in the air. It was cool outside, but the temperature would soon begin to climb. The trees and plants were waking up, stretching towards the sky, ready for the light.

After descending the tower, Odd stalked his prey, following his nose until the stink of it became stronger. Moving silently along the streets, he heard it approaching up ahead. Odd scaled a building, digging his claws into the outside to gain a better vantage point.

In the pre-dawn light, he studied the Yogren, watching how it moved and searched for him. The creature was methodical, careful and patient. Testing the limits of its senses, Odd drifted close and then withdrew to a safe distance to observe how it reacted. It only smelt him once, although it was initially confused, as his scent had undoubtedly changed.

He had thought about ambushing the Yogren and finishing it with one swift cut to the throat, but its skin was too tough for that. It was also remarkably strong and, when necessary, could move very fast. But it lacked subtlety and grace. The last time it had chased him, the Yogren would go through an obstacle instead of going over or around. Odd intended to use that to his advantage.

Odd thought that the only way to kill it would be to rip it open while it was otherwise impaired, or with severe blunt force trauma. After studying it for a couple of hours, he decided it was time to test his theory.

Moving ahead of its current position, he waited for it in the middle of a wide street. The sun rose behind him, warming his back while shining directly into the eyes of his enemy. When the Yogren came around the corner, it actually recoiled in surprise, taking a step backwards. Its eyes widened and it said something unintelligible, no doubt startled by the changes to his appearance.

They stared at each other in silence, reassessing one another. Shadows moved and stretched across the paved street. Odd grinned at the Yogren and readied himself to attack. Bunching the muscles tight in his legs, he dropped to all fours and ran towards his enemy, rapidly picking up speed as he went. It didn't hesitate and raced to meet him, lumbering along as it bellowed a war cry.

Odd skidded beneath its grasping hands and lashed out, scoring a set of shallow cuts across its calves. As the Yogren began to turn around, Odd hit it as hard as he could in the lower back. The force of the blow travelled up Odd's arm until he felt a stab of pain in his shoulder. It felt as if he'd punched a wall. The impact had little to no effect on the Yogren. It grunted in discomfort but didn't slow down at all.

It swung wildly at Odd, but he managed to avoid its clumsy blows while testing its body for weak spots. He scored half a dozen more cuts on its legs and arms, but all of them were shallow. Every time he managed to strike it somewhere in the torso, the Yogren barely reacted. Beneath its skin, it had layers of muscle and cartilage that acted like armour, protecting its vital organs. Disembowelling the creature was going to be a lot harder than he'd initially thought, maybe impossible. He required a change of tactics.

When it tried to hit him again, Odd instinctively moved to the right, but the Yogren had been feinting. With a cry of success, it grabbed Odd by the arm and flung him across the street. Spinning in mid-air, Odd twisted his body around, landed on the wall on all fours and then sprang back towards the Yogren. It was running towards him and didn't have time to move aside. It raised its arms to protect its face, but Odd barrelled into it, knocking the thing backwards.

The Yogren slammed into the ground with Odd on top. He began to slash wildly at its arms with his claws, gouging chunks of flesh, spraying black blood everywhere.

Once its shock wore off, the Yogren rolled over and threw Odd to one side. It was huffing through its mouth, slightly out of breath from the fall, but seemed otherwise unhurt. Before the creature could regain its footing, Odd charged towards it.

It was on its knees when Odd rammed the Yogren's shoulder, spinning it around. The impact hurt Odd almost as much as the creature, because it was so dense. Standing upright, it was almost an immovable object, but on its back it was clumsy and off balance, like a turtle. From a short distance away, Odd watched it roll to one side and then struggle to push itself up to its hands and knees. While it was distracted, he dashed behind the creature, but it heard him coming. When it grabbed him by the arm with an iron grip, Odd bit down on its wrist as hard as he could, relying on the crushing pressure of his jaw rather than his teeth. His sharp canines penetrated its skin, and the sour taste of its blood filled his mouth.

Howling in pain, the Yogren tried to shake him off. Odd let go and skittered away, rolling over and over before coming upright. He spat its blood on the street and waited.

The Yogren was watching him as it clambered to its feet. There was something else in its eyes now. Not fear, not yet, but it was apprehensive and reassessing its first impression of him. Odd wiped the last of its blood from his mouth, grinned and ran forward again.

The air was driven from Odd's body as the Yogren slammed him into a wall by his shoulders. Its thick hands circled his neck, trying to choke the life from him. Ignoring that for a moment, Odd bunched up his legs and then drove both knees hard against its chest. His second blow connected with its chin. The Yogren's head rocked backwards and it dropped him to the street. Such a hit to any other creature would have snapped its neck, but the Yogren was merely dazed.

As he tried to catch his breath, Odd shuffled down the street, resting one arm against a building to stay upright. They had been fighting across the city non-stop for a long time. He was bruised, battered and his left shoulder had popped out of its socket. It had shifted back almost immediately, but the blinding pain had been so intense, he'd nearly blacked out. He needed a little time to rest, heal and re-think.

A quick look over his shoulder showed the Yogren was where it had been left. Much to Odd's surprise, it wasn't following him. It took two steps backward and sat down on the ground, breathing heavily. It glared at him, but then intentionally turned its head away. It also needed a break.

Odd had never encountered anything like it before. Whether the creature had always been that way, or if it was because of the Malice, the Yogren was extremely resilient. Odd had cut it dozens of times, enough that it should have bled to death, and yet it was still able to fight. The wounds hadn't closed up, but they clotted so quickly that the bleeding had been minimal.

As he rounded the corner of a building, Odd found his mother waiting for him on the next street.

"You have to push it harder," she said. "Don't give it time to rest and heal. It will easily recover from those wounds."

"I need to rest."

"You can make yourself better in the blink of an eye. That creature will need hours to fully recover."

He knew she was right. Odd didn't know how much energy he had left in reserve. The longer the fight went on, the tougher it would become, and more energy would be needed. But his choices were limited. Reaching down into the well inside, he flooded his body with its healing power. The damage to his shoulders faded, the muscles knitted back together, the aches receded, and his body became whole.

The look of surprise on the Yogren's face when he came back around the corner was priceless. The creature was upright but was obviously still recovering. For the first time since they'd been fighting, and perhaps the first time in its life, the Yogren experienced a moment of fear.

Odd came off the ground and slammed his knees into its face. It stumbled back a few steps but didn't fall down. While it was dazed, Odd went after the tendons in the back of one of its legs, sinking his claws in as deep as they would go before clenching his fists.

The roar of pain was unlike anything he'd heard before. The Yogren lashed out, clipping him on the shoulder with a fist. Odd was driven into the ground and, before he could recover, its foot caught him in the torso, sending him flying down the street. Trailing blood, the Yogren came after him full of rage, but now it couldn't support its full weight and was forced to limp.

Grinning with savage glee, he laughed at the Yogren, which drove it into a frenzy. When it reached for him, Odd slashed at its hands, catching it across the wrists and fingers. It hissed in pain and pulled back, snarling at Odd in its grisly language. Maybe it was telling him to stand still, or maybe it just wanted him to die.

"You first," said Odd.

When he went after it this time, the Yogren waited,

arms outstretched, daring Odd to attack. In his haste, and overconfidence, Odd misjudged the length of its arms and its speed. As he tried to get behind the Yogren, it grabbed him by the shoulders and lifted him off the ground. Its arms closed around his torso and its hands locked together in the small of his back. Then, it began to squeeze.

As the air was driven from Odd's body, he tried to slash it across the face and throat, but it kept its head tilted down. The wounds he inflicted on the top of its skull bled freely, but they were superficial.

Odd started gasping for air. His legs kicked at the Yogren's thighs, but he had no real power. Black spots danced in front of his eyes, so he fed more energy into his body, preventing it from crushing his spine. But his lungs were starved of oxygen and no amount of energy would change that. He had to get free.

Odd clubbed both sides of the creature's head at the same time, aiming for the Yogren's ears. It bellowed in pain and slightly relaxed, but not enough for him to wiggle free. He struck its head again, but the damage was minimal and made no difference. It was simply ignoring the pain.

Odd's view of the world began to fade in and out. His vision blurred and his attacks became more frantic. He jabbed at its head with his claws, shearing off parts of its scalp, but he couldn't penetrate its skull. He would have cried out in pain, but he didn't have the air in his lungs. Something shifted in his back and he heard an audible crack as the Yogren flexed its forearms.

In desperation, Odd leaned back, pressed a palm against its forehead and tried to shove the creature away from him. The Yogren had a strong neck, but the agony gave Odd a burst of strength, and with both hands he managed to force its head back a little. The tendons in its neck were taut, and the muscles in its arms were bulging as it used all of its strength to hold on to him.

With his free hand, Odd managed to jab his finger into one

of the creature's eye sockets. Screaming, it shoved him away, and stumbled backwards. It tripped over its own feet and knocked the breath from its lungs.

Odd lay on the street, testing the limits of his body and found that he could barely move anything below his hips. His legs were still attached, but when he told them to get up, they only twitched. The Yogren was howling, one hand pressed against its face. He couldn't tell if it had been blinded, but at least it was severely hurt. The wound wasn't lethal, though, and eventually it would recover. If Odd couldn't even stand up, the fight was already over.

Once more, Odd reached down into the well inside, wondering if there would be enough energy to heal himself. If not, the creature would stomp on his skull and smash it like an egg.

With one eye on the Yogren, Odd watched as his legs began to jerk and spasm. The nerves in his spine were slowly repairing themselves. The pain was intense, like needles jabbing him over and over. It felt as if his lower back had been cut open and someone was sewing it back together.

The Yogren's cries hadn't stopped, but they were becoming more concentrated as it came to terms with the agony in its head.

Odd's healing wasn't finished, but he was running out of time. He tested his legs again and thankfully they moved on command. The fibres around his spine were slowly weaving together. He felt the vertebrae in his lower back realign, as they regrew and repaired the damage. The process could not be rushed, no matter how much energy he used. If he tried to stand before it was finished, he would be crippled for life.

His mouth stretched wide in a silent scream as a few bone fragments detached from his spine and pushed their way to the surface. The skin split and they fell onto the street, raining down like loose teeth.

Finally, the feeling crept back into his calves and then his feet. Odd tried to wiggle his toes and was relieved when he saw them move.

The Yogren was already on its hands and knees, but then its left leg gave out and it fell over again.

Odd's healing was done, but he still couldn't stand. Feeling was only just creeping back into his extremities. He made it to a sitting position and then up to all fours.

The Yogren was also struggling and used a wall for support. By the time both of them were on their feet, neither was ready to resume their fight.

The hate in the Yogren's remaining eye was clear. The other was a mess of blood and damaged tissue. Its face and scalp were streaked with blood, and it was covered with dozens of vicious cuts. Finally, it seemed, the number of wounds it had sustained were taking their toll. It wasn't very steady on its feet and, despite its anger, Odd could see it had little remaining stamina.

The Yogren said something short and then repeated the phrase. Odd didn't know what it was trying to tell him. It said it a third time and made a cutting motion with one hand.

It was done. It didn't want to fight him anymore.

The Yogren probably wanted to return to the Tangle, where it could rule over the other beasts, pretending it was dominant. It was telling him it wanted to live. It wanted to surrender.

Part of Odd was tempted to let it go. The problem was, in time, the Yogren would recover from its wounds and then there would be nothing to stop it from coming after them again. And if they ever came back this way, assuming there was a return journey, it would be waiting for them.

As the tingling in his feet faded, Odd forced himself to stand upright. The Yogren watched him carefully, waiting for a response. He knew that it was afraid of him, but it hadn't been defeated. It would be a mistake to assume that it was on the verge of collapse. The creature would fight him, as hard as it could, to its final breath.

For the first time since Odd had seen the Yogren, he wondered what it had been like before the Malice. Willow had said they were peaceful and lived in isolation. Was this violent, calculating version a primordial ancestor, or had the disease created something new?

"No," said Odd, firmly shaking his head. "This isn't over."

It didn't understand the words, but Odd's meaning was clear. Its shoulders slumped briefly and then, much to his surprise, the Yogren ran.

Odd was so startled that it took him a moment to realise it was trying to escape. By the time he'd set off in pursuit, it was already halfway down the street.

The savage thrill of the hunt made Odd's heart pound and he began to salivate. He growled and called after the Yogren, harrying it along like any other prey. By constantly reminding it that he wasn't far behind, its fear remained elevated, just as it had done to them in the Tangle.

On the empty streets Odd was faster, and he began to close the distance between them. Sensing that Odd wasn't far behind, the creature ducked sideways into a building, as its wide shoulders scraped against the doorframe.

Odd relentlessly pursued it through buildings, across rooftops and over walls on a strangled route across the city. He had its scent firmly in his nose and it could not escape.

In a panic, the Yogren ran into one building only to find there wasn't another way out. With nowhere else to go, it had to squeeze up the stairs, skin being scraped off on the walls either side. Odd sped up, nipping at its heels. It growled and ran faster, leaving more skin and hair behind. Up and up they went, until there was nowhere else to go. It disappeared around a final corner and Odd slowed, suddenly suspicious, sensing a trap.

He paused before the threshold, noting the colour of the sky and the time. It was already late in the afternoon. They had been fighting for most of the day. His own reserves were low, and he was afraid to see if there was any energy left in the well.

A careful search revealed that the rooms at the top of the building were empty. It had gone through the door to the outside. The primal part of Odd's brain urged him to chase down his prey and finish the hunt. His instincts begged caution.

Moving slowly, he ducked his head outside, scanned the area and then pulled back. But the Yogren's hands swung into the doorway and grabbed Odd by the arm. With a surge of strength, it yanked him outside.

Odd skidded across the ground, using his claws to scrabble for purchase as he raced towards the edge of the small veranda. There must have been a barrier at some point, but it had rotted away long ago, leaving a ledge with no protection and a long drop to the street below.

The Yogren's fear was real, but its attempt to escape had been a ploy. It came at him in a rush, arms spread so he couldn't go around, trying to force him backwards off the ledge. Odd bunched up his muscles and launched himself into the air. As it ran forward, they collided, stopping each other in mid-stride. When he tried to rip its throat out, the creature took a step backwards, but its damaged leg collapsed. With a cry of surprise, it fell back against the wall before hitting the floor. As Odd clambered on top and tried to claw out its remaining eye, the Yogren panicked. It lashed out with both arms, catching him on the side of the head.

The world tilted sideways. Odd's vision blurred and he found himself staring up at the sky, chest heaving with black spots dancing in front of his eyes. With one foot, the Yogren tried to shove him off the roof, but Odd reached out, clamping both hands around its ankle and pulled.

With a yelp of surprise, the Yogren began to slide across the ground, heading towards the edge of the terrace. Its fingers scrambled about for something to grip, but to no avail. Its fear turned into terror, and with one final surge of strength, Odd pulled it off the roof.

The air whipped past his ears in a loud whistle as they fell together. It was so heavy, the Yogren plummeted down to the street with him riding on top.

The creature managed a brief scream and then Odd's world turned black.

CHAPTER 21

At times, the whispering was so bad that it was difficult for Yarra to hear other people speak. The dead demanded that she listen to them. They wanted her to ignore the living and repent her sins. The number of voices had increased, and sometimes, when they all spoke at once, it created a susurration, like the murmuring of the tide. The words blurred together and lost all meaning. At other times, a single voice would start shouting above the din, until she couldn't hear anyone else. The volume was so great, it often caught her by surprise and even made her wince.

She did her best to ignore her ghosts while the others struggled with their own problems. Kell's emotional outbursts were becoming more frequent and difficult for him to control. One minute, he could be laughing so hard that he was bent over double; the next, his whole body was racked with sobs. In contrast, Willow was becoming even more distracted and quiet. She often stared into the distance, into the past, and from time to time would even stop walking. They had to nudge her to keep moving, jab her in the arm or even slap her cheek to return her to the present. Her grip on reality was slipping as the Malice took hold.

None of it was helped by the fact that all of them were starving, and so thirsty it had become difficult to speak.

As they followed the strange Alfár towards his camp, Yarra's eyes began to pick out details. Zig-zagging staircases had been hewn out of the huge wall, revealing five different levels before reaching the battlements at the very top. On the ground there was a single opening, wide enough for a cart, but on the upper levels there were only narrow doorways, making them easier to defend. There was a single gate in the wall, but it was sealed with huge blocks of stone piled almost to the top, creating a dense barrier. Even if the gate was torn apart, there would be no way to pass through without first moving tonnes of rock.

The wall was made of a jet-black stone, but she saw veins of purple running through it, which sparkled in the light. At multiple points along the wall, there were fist-sized weep holes, and beneath each a streak of pale green, as if something had leaked from inside.

She didn't have a chance to see anything else as they were immediately taken within. They entered a large room with uneven walls that looked as if it had been carved by hand. Their Alfár guide, who had introduced himself as Bewligg, led them down a narrow corridor past many doorways, all of which were covered with a thick curtain so she couldn't see inside. The air smelled dusty and dry, and there was a mild hint of something sour like rot.

Yarra smelled the food before she saw it, as her mouth began to water. The corridor had a gentle downwards slope and up ahead it opened into a huge cave, four or five times as tall as an Alfár. The air was much cooler, and as she stared at the ceiling with its network of ribs, Yarra thought it resembled the innards of some huge beast.

Kell paused on the threshold, and she walked into his back, banging her nose. As he stepped to one side, Yarra looked past his shoulder and her mouth fell open. All thoughts of food were briefly forgotten as she stared at the massive gathering of Alfár.

Sat around the edges of the cave, on tiered rows carved out of the living rock, were hundreds of Alfár. The cave was roughly circular, and there were at least a dozen rows descending towards the centre. Everything was roughly-hewn and uneven, scarred and chipped with edges that had been worn smooth by countless feet. At the bottom of the cave was a huge kitchen, where at least a dozen Alfár were serving food to a huge snaking line of warriors waiting for their meal. Several vast black cauldrons were full to the brim of some kind of stew, which bubbled away, filling the air with tantalising smells. Her stomach growled and she heard similar noises coming from the others.

As they followed Willow to one side of the cave, they received a lot of curious looks but nothing more, which came as a big surprise. Yarra had thought they were the first humans to have visited the Alfár's homeland, but now she began to wonder.

All of the Alfár in Yantou-vash had been infected with the Malice, but none of them had been severely affected. Every single occupant in the cave must have been exposed for a long time. All of them had discoloured skin and calcified veins on their face and arms, but the disfigurement went far beyond what she had seen before. Although unusual in appearance, when compared to humans, Yarra thought the Alfár were graceful and beautiful. These warriors were like crudely fashioned copies, from someone who had never seen a real Alfár.

"What happened to them?" asked Kell.

"This is but a glimpse of what the Malice does to my people," said Willow.

Like the stonework in the cave, their facial features were crudely made, with blocky noses, thick foreheads, oversized ears, deep-sunken eyes and misshapen heads. Some had jaws too wide for the rest of their faces, and others had heads too small for their broad shoulders. One Alfár had a face that more closely resembled melted wax, but they had not been the victim of burns. Yarra noticed several had unusually asymmetrical faces, as if they had been made by combining two different people.

The cruelty of the disease was unparalleled. It seemed to have no end in its creative ways to inflict pain. Yarra could see all of them were suffering from the changes, but were doing their best to hide their discomfort.

Most startling was that some of the Alfár had human-looking eyes, with white sclera surrounding the yellow. It made them look out of place among their own people, even those with severe disfigurements.

Bewligg returned with bowls of stew and chunks of bread on a tray which he passed around. Yarra thought the suffering of the Alfár would have squashed her appetite, but once she saw the food in front of her, she tucked in with relish.

"Eat slowly," warned Bewligg. He spoke the common tongue, but with a heavy accent. "Your body will not want it."

It had been days since they'd eaten a decent meal. She took his advice, taking small mouthfuls and pausing often to let her body get used to the food. Once they'd finished eating, groups of Alfár filed out of the cave and more took their place. The cave only had room for so many bodies, and she guessed those coming in had been on the battlements.

At one point during the meal, Yarra thought she was going to be sick as her stomach began to clench. Eventually it faded, and they all managed to finish their food without complaint. She wanted to know more about what was going on, but as Kell had not asked, she didn't think it was her place to take the lead. Instead, she studied those around her. Did the Malice also haunt them with their failures?

To make room for others, Bewligg led them back out of the cave to a small chamber on the first level. Like everything else, it had been carved by hand. Six shelves for sleeping had been cut into the walls, each one lined with a thin blanket. It made Yarra think of the old crypts she'd seen in Kinnan.

Yarra was convinced the voices would keep her awake for hours, but for some reason they had fallen quiet, murmuring in the back of her mind. Perhaps it was this strange place, or the idea of sleeping in a room that may have once stored the dead. Whatever the reason, as soon as she laid down, sleep claimed her, and for a time, she was free of the sins from her past.

For two days Yarra drifted in and out of consciousness. Even when her eyes were open, she didn't feel wholly awake. The combination of utter exhaustion from their journey, and a lack of food and water finally caught up to her. Her body desperately needed rest and nourishment.

She drifted along in a daze, taking care of the essential needs of her body, feeding it every few hours before immediately going back to sleep. The others were in a similar condition, and whenever she woke, they were asleep or resting fitfully.

It would have been a peaceful respite if not for the screams and sounds of battle. On the third day, she woke early to the sound of whispering voices. When she sat up in bed, Yarra was relieved to find Kell talking quietly with Willow.

"We didn't mean to wake you," he said.

"No, it's fine. I thought the voices had returned," she said, pulling on her boots. "I'd rather it was you than the ghosts in my head."

In the distance, the Alfár screamed, and there was a crashing sound from above that shook the room.

"What's happening?" asked Yarra.

"Those you have seen are suffering greatly because of the Malice, but they are not the worst affected," said Willow.

"Then who?" asked Kell, although he clearly didn't want to know.

"It is difficult to describe. Once they were Alfár, but now, they are nothing. Abominations. Madness. Chaos made flesh." This time, when Willow's eyes became distant, it was clear she was still with them. Even so, Kell anchored her in the present by gripping one of her hands.

"When the rest of us fled in order to survive, those who stayed behind to argue were slowly driven insane. The worst were brought here, to the Choke, and sent through the black gate, never to return. Over time, more and more were forced to take the Long Walk. We thought they had all died, but somehow they survived and were changed again by the Malice.

"One night, long ago, something crept back into Laruk. It slaughtered a dozen people before it was destroyed. My people have been fighting them ever since. Holding them at bay."

"Show us," said Kell, strapping on his sword.

Once they were armed and dressed, Willow led them up the stairs to the battlements. The endless black wall stretched into the distance on either side, before it became one with the mountains, creating an impenetrable barrier. Whatever monsters there were to the north, they could not travel south of the wall, except at the Choke where the land was flat. Snaking into distance, away from the black gate below them, was a narrow trail. Spread out across the open ground, north of the Choke, was a horde of creatures that Yarra knew would haunt her nightmares.

They were barely recognisable as the Alfár. Much like the tainted fetch of the Tangle, they had been remade. With twisted limbs ending in claws, jaws full of sharp teeth, and bony protrusions breaking through the skin, there was no rhyme or reason to the brutal changes.

Several Alfár had been merged with one or more others, so that some had three or four arms. There were some that more closely resembled huge spiders, with six arms and two powerful back legs. Most of them had red eyes, two or three or ten of them. Some had no eyes, and yet, they were not blind. Some even had two heads that bickered with one another. After a while she stopped trying to catalogue the differences, as there were too many. The only thing that united them was their determination to kill, and their desire to make it over the wall, so that they could kill some more. They lived for no other purpose.

Dressed in rags, they carried an array of weapons made of steel, wood, random lumps of metal and even sharpened stones.

Hundreds of Alfár along the battlements were doing their best to repel the horde of invaders. The monstrous creatures skittered up the wall using ladders, chains and grappling hooks, and sometimes their own arms and legs to propel them upwards. Like a crawling swarm of ants, they surged towards the thin line of defenders who struggled to hold them back. This was not only because there were so many creatures, but also their own disarray.

There was no coordination and no obvious strategy, as fights quickly changed into a rolling melee that surged along the wall, this way and that. Those fighting in formation would break apart, ignoring those around them. It was almost as if they had forgotten about their allies. It was a jumbled mess that suggested a lack of instruction and leadership.

Yarra watched one Alfár repel an invader, only to turn her back on two more creeping up the same ladder. The monsters stabbed the Alfár through the back and then hurled her body off the wall. The corpse whistled past them and landed with a sodden thump, spraying blue blood everywhere. Defenders were dying for no reason, and soon the wall was slick with their blood and that of the monsters. The reason for the weep holes became apparent, as the blood drained off the battlements and trickled out of the wall.

A group of Alfár near them were about to be overwhelmed. A spider creature, and two similar monsters, had breached the wall and were creating room for others to climb over the battlements.

"We must help them," said Kell.

"Stay close," said Willow, hefting her two-headed weapon.

Screaming like an animal, the Alfár ran towards the nearest monster, with Kell and Yarra a step behind. While they engaged the first monster, she dragged one of the defenders out of the way.

The Alfár was bleeding from a wound in his shoulder, but it didn't look fatal. When he was safe, she briefly watched the skirmish, then carefully timed her swing. It severed one of the spider's legs at the ankle, causing it to topple towards the battlements. Willow seized it by the head and hurled it bodily from the wall, where it struck several other creatures coming up a ladder.

Kell was hacking away at another beast, growling and spitting, his face sprayed with blood, all technique forgotten in favour of savagery. Once the twisted monster was dead, he and a defender lifted it up and then waited, before throwing it over. Yarra heard the collision, then more screams, as other attackers fell to their death.

The defenders around them rallied, and together, they butchered the remaining spider-creatures before tossing them into the oncoming horde. It was a small victory, but the fight was far from over.

Hours later, barely able to stand, Yarra watched as the enemy withdrew. For creatures with little apparent compassion, it was surprising when they made an effort to take the dead with them.

"Do they bury them?" she gasped, gesturing at the corpses being carried or dragged away.

Bewligg shook his head. "They need them. For food."

Yarra had seen enough. She sat down on the wall with her back resting against the battlements. Her shoulders burned and her lungs felt as if they were on fire. Kell and Willow were still upright, but exhaustion was etched into their weary features. They had all pushed themselves too hard too soon. Resting for a couple of days had helped, but now they had depleted their energy reserves.

"Let me help you," said Bewligg, offering a hand. He pulled Yarra to her feet and together, she and the others, shuffled down the stairs in search of food. The wounded were taken away to be cared for. The dead were left where they had fallen.

"What happens to them?" asked Yarra, gesturing at the bodies.

"Once the living have been treated, we will care for them," promised Bewligg.

"Do you bury your dead?"

"We used to, but now they are burned, so they can't be dug up," he said, gesturing at the creatures beyond the wall. Swallowing bile, Yarra focused on not tripping over her feet as she descended to the ground level. Her knees were unsteady, and several times she would have toppled over, if not for Bewligg's steadying hand.

Drenched in blood, her boots squelching with every step, Yarra made her way down to the cave to wait in line for food. Too tired to stand, she and Kell sat on the floor with the others, until there was enough space for them inside.

They ate in silence, just two more weary soldiers who barely warranted a glance from the Alfár. But she and Kell had saved lives. That was more than enough for everyone else to accept them.

When fighting, there had been too much noise to hear or worry about the ghosts in her mind. Now that it was quiet, the volume of the voices began to rise.

"So, what do we do now?" asked Yarra, desperate for a distraction.

Kell turned to Willow who had finished eating, but she seemed lost in thought.

He nudged the Alfár and she came back to them. "Has there been any sign of Ravvi?" he asked.

Willow shook her head. "No one was looking for him. In all of this, who would notice one more Alfár?"

"Did he make it over the wall?" asked Kell.

"No one knows. He may be dead, but we cannot take the risk. We must continue north," said Willow.

"How do we get past the horde?" asked Yarra.

"I was about to ask you that question," said Kell. "You've seen the defences and how the Alfár fight. How do we do it?"

Yarra didn't even need to think about it. She'd been mulling it over all day.

"We need to come up with a strategy, so that we can slip through unnoticed. The problem is, the defenders are as disorganised and chaotic as the enemy. Orders sent along the wall don't always reach the intended recipient. Squads break apart for no reason and start wandering off. There's no cohesion when they fight. They're sometimes dying because of the effect the Malice has had on their thinking."

"It is difficult for me to stay rooted in the present," said Willow. "All of them are suffering far worse."

"Then we need to keep the plan really simple," said Yarra. "And we just have to hope they follow it long enough for us to get through."

If they were caught by the horde, they would be torn to pieces. Then all of this would have been for nothing.

The following morning, Yarra walked the length of the wall with Bewligg, talking to defenders and gauging their level of concentration. All of the Alfár had minor wounds, but a few with more severe injuries still wanted to fight. Normally they were adept at concealing emotion and discomfort, but the Malice was stripping away their self-control, making them easier to read. She made a mental note of who she thought would be capable, and who would be a liability. It was impossible to remember their real names, as most of them were long strings of sounds and she had no feel for the language. Instead, she assigned nicknames, picking out distinguishing features to help her remember.

Once she'd completed her circuit, she asked for a meeting with Kell, Willow and the leaders of the Alfár. They gathered out in the open in front of the wall, as all chambers were

occupied with sleeping bodies. The enemy often attacked in
the morning, but on occasion had been known to wait until
later in the day. There seemed to be no way to predict what
triggered such a change. Today the enemy had decided not to
attack early, so everyone was using the time to catch up on
their sleep.

In addition to Bewligg, there were three other Alfár, whose
abbreviated names were Adami, Krizan and Mihok. All of
them were weary, with minor wounds, and they had the air of
veteran warriors or generals. She had seen how the other Alfár
deferred to them, even giving up a seat so they could sit down
to eat. They commanded great respect, but they were also
victims of the disease and their struggle to focus was apparent.

Yarra briefly outlined her plan to create a distraction, so
that the others could slip through unnoticed when the horde
attacked. Only Krizan didn't speak the common tongue, but
she understood enough to listen and then quiz Bewligg.

"So, do you think it will work?" asked Yarra.

Adami had said little so far, but now he grunted and nodded.
"It is worth trying."

Krizan spoke briefly with the others and then bobbed her
head in agreement.

Yarra thought Mihok had not been listening, or her mind
had drifted as she was staring at nothing. Instead, she said
something to her fellow Alfár, and then stared hard at Yarra.

"Why should we do this for you?" asked Mihok.

"You know why," said Willow.

Mihok shook her head. "Ravvi's errand is a foolish one. The
blood ritual will not work, and nothing will change. You know
that after all of this time, there is no cure. All we are doing is
delaying the inevitable. You should stay here and help us, not
go after him."

"One person will make little difference," argued Willow.

"It depends on the person. A clear mind is worth much to
us," said Adami.

They began speaking in their own language, leaving Kell and Yarra on the outside. Despite not knowing the words, she began to understand the flow of the conversation. The others were trying to make a bargain, and Willow was refusing to compromise.

"I will stay," said Yarra, ending the discussion. She tried not to flinch, but it was difficult under the scrutiny of so many Alfár. "It was my plan; and besides, you will need another to get them back over the wall on the return journey."

"Are you sure?" asked Kell. "What about the voices?"

"They're still there, but they don't bother me as they once did. I can do this. I can help the Alfár fight against the horde."

The veterans were assuaged and quickly dispersed, leaving her alone with Willow and Kell.

"You can still change your mind," said Willow. Yarra was touched by the gesture, but her decision was made. On that fateful day, back in the throne room, out of all the members of the Raven, Willow had chosen her and Odd. There had to be a reason, or at least, she wanted there to be.

"I'm sure," said Yarra. Few people were given a second chance to make up for their mistakes. If this was hers, then this time, she was determined to do it right.

CHAPTER 22

After Malina carried her out of the Holy City of Lorzi, Sigrid drifted in and out of consciousness. She remembered being loaded onto a covered cart and wrapped up in blankets. She was surrounded by crates on all sides which smelled strongly of spices. If someone glanced in the back of the cart, she was hidden from view. Dappled sunlight played across the canvas above her head. She was reminded of lying beneath a tree as a child, staring up at the sun between the branches.

A deep sense of peace filled her. Sigrid wondered if this was what it felt like to be dying.

"You're safe. Rest," said Malina.

Sigrid let herself sink down into sleep, where she drifted for hours. The next time she woke, the cart was in motion and a different Choate warrior was sitting by her side. He was a mature man with broad shoulders and large hands. He had intricate tattoos on his weathered face, but the designs had faded with age and were partly concealed by wrinkles. His grey mane of hair and beard were streaked with white, and when she moved, he awoke, revealing clear blue eyes.

"Ah, good. You're awake."

Sigrid tried to speak, but her throat was so dry she couldn't even manage a croak. Cradling her head, he brought a flask to her lips and she took a few tentative sips. The water was cool, and the rocking of the cart was soothing, but she fought the urge to fall back asleep.

"Who?" she whispered, still struggling to speak.

"I am Dos Mohan, War General for the Choate people," he said, giving her a seated bow with one hand placed over his heart. "I am also Kell's uncle."

The name was familiar, but her tired mind could not join the dots. Looking closely at his face, there were a few similarities, particularly around the eyes and nose. Sigrid cleared her throat a few times before she could speak.

"Where are we?"

"I would guess somewhere in northern Algany." His expression turned grave and he gently took her hand. "I am sorry, but we cannot take you back to Thune. The world now thinks that you are dead. The war has been averted and your son now sits on the throne. Malina has stayed in the city to protect him, and Natia is still by his side. I swear that he will be safe."

Tears leaked from her eyes at the image of her son being told that she was dead. She pictured him running around the palace, surrounded by adults. He would be asked to make decisions about the fate of the nation, without being able to understand the consequences.

"Where are we going?"

"To my homeland," he said.

"Can I ever go home?" asked Sigrid.

Dos Mohan sighed and squeezed her hand. "Focus on getting well. That is the first step."

Sigrid turned her face away and sobbed in silence. Piece by piece, she shed her dreams of a new beginning with Kell, where they had lived together as a family. He was dead and her son was now beyond her reach. She had no money, no power and even her name would be anathema. It was a new beginning, but not one she would have wished on her worst enemy.

The journey to the Choate homeland passed in a daze. She drifted in and out of consciousness, but every time she woke up, Mohan was there with a friendly smile, a kind word and some broth. After what she guessed was a couple of days, some of the crates were unloaded from the cart, allowing a breeze to circulate. The fresh air smelled so good that she wanted to be outside, but Sigrid didn't even have the strength to sit up without support.

The next time she woke, it was dark and she was floating through the air. Mohan had wrapped her up in a blanket and she was being carried somewhere. She sensed other people nearby, and caught glimpses of lights, but all of it was a blur.

"Let me carry her, War General," said someone.

"I'm not so old that I need your help," snapped Mohan and the people fell back. Sigrid saw several Choate with tattooed faces watching her from a distance, and then she was carried inside a building and gently laid on a bed. The room was dark and it smelled of dried flowers and herbs. Glancing at the rafters she saw bunches of green plants drying in the warm air.

"Rest, child," said Mohan. She instinctively felt safe in his presence. Sleep called to her, but she fought it a while longer and lingered on the threshold.

"She's all skin and bone," said a woman's voice.

"Then you'll just have to fatten her up," said Mohan, a smile in his voice.

There was a long, awkward silence and then the woman spoke again.

"She may not recover. Her body could be too frail."

Mohan sighed again. "Then we will try our best, my love, and pray to Govhenna."

Sigrid felt a cool hand on her forehead, but she didn't react. "Her spirit is strong," said the woman.

"She survived for months in a cell with almost no food or water. She will make it. She must."

"Once again, I find myself looking after your kin."

"There shouldn't be any need for murder this time," said Mohan.

"A shame," sniffed the woman.

She leaned down beside Sigrid so that she could see her face. The woman was of a similar age to Mohan, but her tattoos were limited to the right side of her face. A series of intricate whirls and loops decorated her cheek and jaw.

"Girl, my name Grellka. I will do my best to keep you alive. Remember that, in the days ahead, when you come to hate me."

It was difficult to judge the passage of time, but for weeks Sigrid did nothing but sleep, eat and stretch her muscles. Every day Grellka took care of her, washing her, feeding her broth and moving her arms and legs. And every day, Sigrid cursed and swore at the Choate for the pain she had to endure.

Her body had wasted away so badly that even stretching her muscles was agony. Grellka was relentless, and she accepted all of Sigrid's insults in silence with a slightly mocking smile on her face. The Choate thought she was weak. After a while Sigrid stopped her cursing, gritted her teeth and worked twice as hard. Even when Grellka wasn't around, she forced herself to stretch. Day by day, her strength began to return, but it was still a challenge to stand up by herself.

One morning, Grellka appeared at the door to Sigrid's room with a wooden staff which she dropped on the floor. She returned with a steaming tray of food which she set down on the far side of the room. Sigrid noticed it was something other than broth for the first time since her arrival.

"If you want to eat today, you have to get up and walk," said Grellka. "Enough lying around, feeling sorry for yourself, girl."

Before Sigrid could reply the Choate turned and left the room.

Doing her best to ignore the pain, Sigrid swung her legs out of bed. When she tried to put weight on them, she nearly blacked out. Clenching her jaw, she gripped the staff with both hands, noting they were like bird's claws. It seemed to take an age, but eventually she unfolded her body to its full height. Blood rushed to her head, and she swayed on her feet. Closing her eyes, she waited for it to the pass then began to shuffle across the room, one painful step at a time. When she reached the far side of the room, she was sweating and ready to collapse. She slid to the floor and began stuffing food in her mouth with both hands.

A little later, Grellka appeared at the door and offered a rare smile. "Good. Come, you need some fresh air."

Eager to see more of the Choate's territory than just her room, Sigrid struggled to her feet. Grellka waited until Sigrid was upright before offering her arm for support. She was a hard woman, but not unkind. She'd suffered through Sigrid's tirades of abuse, and never once had she replied in anger.

"Thank you," said Sigrid, as she rested part of her weight on the older woman.

"You have heart," said Grellka, briefly touching Sigrid's cheek. "You remind me of my second daughter."

Given their sedate pace, Sigrid had plenty of time to look at the rest of the house. For a senior figure in Choate society, she was surprised that it was fairly modest, with only three bedrooms, all on the ground level. It was extremely clean and tidy, and the tiled floors gleamed from being polished.

When they stepped outside, Sigrid was partially blinded by her first glimpse of direct sunlight in months. Black spots danced in front of her eyes; she felt dizzy and would have fallen if not for Grellka. Once it passed, she stared at the nameless Choate city with surprise. As far as she was aware, Sigrid was the only outsider to have been inside their territory.

"What were you expecting?" asked Grellka. "Mud huts and burning horse shit to stay warm?"

"No. I mean, I don't know. It's always been such a mystery," said Sigrid.

The first thing she noticed was that the city was so colourful. Almost every building was decorated with tiles, creating intricate mosaics depicting landscapes full of wild animals, portraits of important figures and even special phrases. Every minaret gleamed in the sunlight and, from where she was standing, Sigrid could see two large plazas crammed with market stalls. Hundreds of people were bustling about, buying and selling food, laughing, drinking, eating and talking. And every single one of them was a tattooed Choate.

They were all fairly similar in build and height, with only the occasional tall person's head sticking up above the crowd. If she closed her eyes, the bustle of the market was so familiar she could have been at home in Algany.

Even in the palace, if the wind was right, sounds from the nearest market would reach her bedroom. Tears stung her eyes as she thought about all that had been taken from her. She wondered what her son had felt when he'd been given the news. Did Marik cry himself to sleep? Who did he turn to when he had a nightmare? Darker thoughts crept in around the edges. Had he even noticed that she was gone?

"Let's take a short walk," said Grellka, squeezing her arm. Most of the homes she could see were of a similar size, and all of them were built with only a ground floor. The only structures with more than one storey were shops and what looked like churches.

It took them a long time, but when they reached the end of the street, Sigrid saw a tearoom with tables outside. She collapsed into a chair, while Grellka went inside to get them something to drink.

A few other tables were occupied by very old Choate men and women, who smiled or waved when their eyes met. Young people bustled about the streets, leading animals to the market, carrying on with their friends, while children ran screaming after each other, caught up in their secret games. Every single person she saw, except for the young children, had tattoos. She guessed it was a part of a rite of passage when they became an adult.

Another stark difference from any city in the Five Kingdoms was the lack of soldiers. Some Choate were armed, but not many, and she saw no enforcers on the street. When a disturbance broke out in the market between two hot-headed young men over a woman, a mature woman stepped in to mediate. Moments earlier, she had been browsing a stall, so was not obviously involved. Sigrid was too far away to hear what was said, but an apology was given, and the argument ended before it devolved into violence.

Grellka returned to the table with two glasses of tea and a plate of pastries. She saw where Sigrid was looking and grunted. "Young men and their big balls. Always out to prove something."

"A stranger intervened and they listened to her."

"We teach our children to respect their elders. If they had not done as she asked, their parents would have heard about it. Then it would have been much worse. The young men may seethe and disagree, but violence was averted. We have other ways to settle scores that fester," said Grellka.

Sigrid thought that sounded rather ominous, so she didn't push it.

"You don't have people to enforce the peace? Soldiers or something like that?"

"Of course, but it's different here. Eat," said the Choate, pushing the pastries towards her. Grellka picked up one and gobbled it down before sipping her tea. Sigrid took a bite, savouring the sticky sweetness and the rich flavours. The tea was a little weak, so she left it to steep in the glass.

Grellka seemed content to sit in silence and listen to the city, but Sigrid was on edge. The older woman had her eyes closed, but she opened one and peered at Sigrid.

"Ask your questions, girl. I won't be offended."

"How long have I been here?"

"Almost three months," said Grellka. "You've now been dead for five."

"Do you have any news about my son? Or my husband?"

"We've heard nothing about Kell, but your boy is fine. I received news from Malina a few days back. She tells me he is growing like a weed. Natia dotes on him and he is guarded, day and night, by the Raven. No one will ever harm him. This, I swear."

The tightness around her heart eased, but it was replaced with another form of pain. "I miss him so much," she said, biting her lip to hold back the tears.

Grellka didn't try to placate her with platitudes. She said nothing for a while, waiting for Sigrid to regain control. "Longing is a hard pain. It does not diminish with time. We lost our second son when he was ten years old. There was an accident." Grellka scratched at her cheek and then ate another pastry. Her eyes did not fill with tears, but Sigrid sensed she was buying time. "I still see his face in my dreams."

"I need to go home," said Sigrid.

"You can barely walk. Besides, you're dead."

"Then I'll sneak in. No one needs to know I'm there, but I have to see my son. He needs me. Grellka, please, I can't live here for the rest of my life."

The older woman took a deep breath and nodded. "I know, and I promise, we will talk about this again, but only when you are well. You came very close to death. That is not something you can just ignore."

Sigrid knew she wasn't a prisoner, but she still felt trapped. Deep down, she knew that Grellka was right. Her body was still in very bad condition, and she tired easily. Her mind wasn't sharp, and she couldn't walk down the street without leaning on someone. Before she could be of any use to her son, or her country, Sigrid had to rebuild herself. The thought of delaying a reunion with Marik, for any reason, hurt so badly she couldn't put it into words. But at least he was safe and surrounded by friendly faces.

Her sacrifice, it seemed, had also paid off. War had been averted. The new Reverend Mother had proven as good as her word. Thousands of lives had been spared in exchange for hers.

So, if the old Sigrid was dead, who was she? It wasn't a question she could answer, but she was determined to find out.

"What must I do?" asked Sigrid.

"Prove to me that you're ready," said Grellka.

This time, despite the sun on her face, Sigrid felt a shiver down her back.

CHAPTER 23

Since coming to Willow's homeland, the sky had been clear or cloudy, but it had always been dry. As the black, stinking rain fell from a slate-coloured sky, Kell wished the good weather had lasted a while longer.

It was still early in the morning, and so far the horde of abominations had not shown up. Their lack of routine spoke of the chaos running rampant through their ranks. Kell had been told they had no leaders, only an urge to kill and maim. Their only aim was to get over the wall and kill everything. The one thing holding them back, protecting the many complacent Alfár in Yantou-vash, were the ragged and disorganised defenders. They were not insane or twisted, like the horde, but they were still struggling. Every day, many of them died because they were distracted.

Despite the poisoned rain, which burned Kell's nostrils and stank of rot, the wall at the Choke was washed clean by the storm. Rain relentlessly slashed down at an angle, like rods of iron, scouring the black stone. Any remaining blood was wiped clean, but the memory of all of those who had died on the previous day remained fresh in Kell's mind.

A healthy Alfár was a powerful force to be reckoned with. Their strength and stamina were unparalleled by human standards, but every single person here was not at their best.

A few defenders kept watch on top of the wall, covered head to toe in waxed cloaks with a hood, but the rest were elsewhere, sleeping, eating or healing in the infirmary, preparing themselves for what was to come.

Kell stared up at the rain and hoped that it would soon end. There was little wind, and the ominous clouds were barely moving. The storm was going to be with them for a while, so he went back inside to join the others. Yarra, Bewligg and the other three leaders had gathered to discuss the specifics of how they were going to get him and Willow past the horde.

"Any sign of the enemy?" asked Bewligg as Kell came into the room, which was much like the others, a carved-out hollow with rough walls and a dusty floor. There were no cushions or blankets for comfort, only cold stone benches to sit on. He had always thought of Willow as tough and enduring. These Alfár made her look delicate by comparison. Their faces and bodies were all hard edges, their bones more pronounced.

"It's all quiet," said Kell, preferring to lean against the wall rather than sit down. After a while, he always had to get up and move around as his arse went numb.

"You should use this," said Mihok, tossing Willow a small pouch.

She opened it and peered inside, sniffed once and then raised an eyebrow. "Mousco powder?"

"Yes."

"What is it?" asked Kell.

"It will make the flames of any fire turn bright blue. It burns hot and high," explained Willow.

"Upon your return, throw it on a fire, and we will see it from the wall," said Yarra. "That will be our signal to create another distraction to get you back on this side."

They were all thinking it, but no one had said it out loud. As much as he appreciated Yarra planning their return, he wasn't sure they would be coming back. First, he and Willow had to get past the enemy without being detected. Then they had to put enough distance between them, so that the abominations didn't follow. Yarra's plan was risky, but all of the Alfár leaders had agreed that it was the best strategy.

When talk moved on to defending the Choke after he and Willow were gone, Kell slipped out of the room. He didn't have anything to add to the conversation, and even worse, he was starting to experience a strong feeling of euphoria. Everyone would worry about his well-being if he suddenly burst out laughing in the middle of a strategy session, where Alfár were going to die.

When he got back to the room he shared with the others, Kell realised Willow had followed him.

"Are you all right?" she asked.

"I'm still struggling with controlling my emotions," he said, fighting against a smile. Slapping a hand across his mouth, Kell pulled his lips down, holding back a grin that was out of place. He thought of his family, of his son Marik, hoping that heartache would temper the unnatural mirth, but it had no effect. Being out of control was harder to deal with than he'd expected.

"I understand," said Willow. For once her expression was fairly neutral, but he could see she was also fighting to maintain a semblance of normality. Today, she was having a good day. Her mind was in the present, but it could drift off at any moment.

There were also the other changes to her behaviour. Her affectations, and even her movements, were becoming more human every day. Instead of simply sitting down like normal, Willow bent her knees and folded down to one side. It was something he'd seen women in dresses do many times, but she always wore trousers.

"I think you should go home," said Willow.

The surge of relief was so strong Kell didn't know if it was the Malice or a genuine emotion. "I can't turn back now."

"You've done more than enough. I can finish the last part of this journey alone."

"Why now?" asked Kell. "Why not before we reached the Tangle?"

Willow didn't answer and he waited, hoping that the silence would make her uncomfortable enough to answer. That too had changed as the Alfár showed no sign of unease at the unanswered questions.

"There's something you're not telling me." When she didn't respond again, he took her silence as confirmation of his growing suspicion. One part of his mind was screaming at him to accept her offer and just go home. The rest of him knew something else was going on. "I've come this far, Willow. Don't shut me out now."

"I have lied to you," said Willow, hanging her head in shame. "I did not want you to be disappointed in me."

"Whatever it is, you can tell me." At this point Kell didn't think there was much that would surprise him. "We are still friends," he added.

"Very well," said Willow, lifting her eyes to meet his. He was slightly alarmed to notice the sclera in one of her eyes had changed colour from black to grey. "This is as far north as I have ever travelled. I do not know what lies beyond the Choke."

Up to now she had been leading them, confident of their route and the dangers that lay ahead. Kell had happily relinquished control, as he didn't enjoy the responsibility that came with leadership. With her mind failing, he knew what she was asking him to do.

"I will lead us," he said.

"Are you certain?" asked Willow.

"Whatever happens, I will see it through to the end," said Kell.

Later that day, as the rain was mercifully starting to tail off, the horde arrived in a furious mood. Something had riled them up, or perhaps they had just woken up madder than usual, but they stormed the walls with vicious intent.

Kell watched as Yarra, supported by the four Alfár veterans, coordinated the defence. Squads had been formed, orders given and then repeated over and over, until it felt as if she were teaching children, but they needed to be reminded. A dozen others had been carefully chosen whose minds were sharper than most. Their only role was to keep their brethren focused, and make sure they didn't drift away or become distracted. The four veterans and Yarra served as a second layer, who would nudge the others back in line. Such drastic measures wouldn't normally be necessary, but it showed how much damage the Malice had caused the defenders.

Kell and Willow were positioned a short distance back from the fight, waiting for their signal. After that came the really terrifying part. They had to go over the wall by themselves and then attempt to outrun the horde, before it noticed the two of them were there. The harness chafed around his hips and shoulders, but Kell did his best to ignore the discomfort. It would be the only thing stopping him from falling to his death when they went over.

"Here they come!" shouted Yarra. "Ready yourselves!"

Her words were echoed along the wall by the veterans in the Alfár's own language. The defenders drew their weapons, pressed their shields together to form a solid line, and waited. Next came the awful moment of tense silence before the fight. The air was full of pent-up aggression, the stink of sweat, fear, rot from the rain, and the reek of corruption from the horde.

The storm passed and as weak sunlight broke through the clouds, a scream of defiance erupted from the Alfár. The ululating cry was repeated over and over, until Kell's ears rang with the sound. He had to cover them with his hands as the noise became so shrill it caused a stabbing pain in his head.

It quickly came to an end and the sound was replaced with the familiar ring of steel. The horde slammed into the defenders and the melee began. Bodies went sailing over the wall, but a few defenders also tumbled backwards, crying out as they fell. The unluckiest clipped the stairs with their bodies, before landing in a tangled heap of broken bones at the bottom.

Willow was desperate to join the fight. The knuckles on both of her hands were white from the strain. At the moment, she was focused, and Kell had to keep her with him, at least for now.

"We can't stay," he reminded her.

Willow didn't reply, but she handed him her weapon so that he could secure it to her back. He tightened the leather straps that held it in place and checked her harness.

The battle was progressing. Defenders were still fighting well in groups, but already the enemy had managed to breach the wall in one place. Bewligg and another Alfár hacked away at an abomination that was a mass of legs and arms, while two others forced it towards the battlements. With a savage swipe, Bewligg partially severed the creature's head from its shoulders. Before it had even finished screaming, the others shoved it off the wall where it crashed into more creatures climbing up.

"Get ready!" shouted Yarra as she ran past their position.

The defenders began to move away from the west of the wall, leaving an opening in their defences on purpose. It took a while, but eventually the horde saw an opportunity and the message began to spread. Kell double, and then triple-checked that the rope was securely tied to him, reassuring himself that it would hold his weight.

The air was ripe with the stench of open bodies. Blue blood was being splashed about liberally, and the crash of bodies had become a constant din. The screams and grunts of the Alfár merged into one giant voice, denoting death and misery.

A six-legged abomination burst over the battlements and landed on the wall. It was massive, two or three times the height of the others. It was surrounded on both sides by

Alfár, but it didn't seem intimidated. With a spear in each of its four arms, it attempted to keep the defenders at bay, while more of its kind made it over the wall.

"Let's go!" said Willow, tapping him on the shoulder. Kell had been staring at the battle. He wrenched his gaze away, leaving the fate of the monster to the defenders.

When they reached the battlements, Willow peered over the wall. Kell was pleased to see the majority of the horde had headed towards the breach. There were some stragglers lurking at the back, but most were engaged. It wasn't what they had hoped for, but it was the best opportunity they would get.

Two pairs of Alfár gripped the ropes, while he and Willow dangled their feet over the edge into space. Staring down at the ground far below, Kell's stomach leapt into his throat. He really didn't want to do this, but he needed to move. Every moment he hesitated was costing lives. The thought of more blood on his hands gave him the push he needed. Kell tipped forward, gritting his teeth to stop himself screaming, and began to run down the wall.

Despite moving at a steady pace, the ground seemed to rush up at an incredible speed. Glancing to his left he saw Willow was a step ahead of him, bounding down the wall on her long legs. When they were close to the bottom, Kell felt the harness begin to bite into his hips. He walked the last few steps and then lay down on the ground. The slack eased and he was able to stand upright and unhook the rope. As soon as it was clear, it was whipped away, speeding up the wall faster than he'd walked down.

"Watch out!" shouted Willow, shoving him to one side.

Her axe came around in a whistling arc, biting into the chest of an abomination that had been lurking. It flew backwards through the air and landed heavily on its back. Before it had a chance to call out, Willow flipped her weapon and caved in its head with her mace. Black brains splattered across the ground, ending its life.

Scrambling to his feet, Kell tugged at the harness while he ran away from the enemy. The land north of the Choke was much the same as south of the wall: broken, rocky ground, no sign of any plant life, and no insects or animals. Just desolate unyielding rocks and the stink of decay.

Someone shouted out behind him, but he didn't turn to see if they were being followed. Keeping his eyes focused on the ground, Kell watched for trip hazards. The rocky channel was fairly narrow. At some points the walls of the pitted cliffs were close enough to touch on both sides. A short distance ahead, it opened up into a small canyon that was littered with a vast array of bones. Some of them he could identify, and others were the twisted, malformed remains of the horde.

Every scrap of meat and festering skin had been stripped clean. Left behind were hundreds of cracked bones, each one decorated with teeth marks. Gaping jaws from creatures that had once been Alfár stared at him on all sides as they raced past. It was a stark warning of what would happen if they didn't escape.

"I don't want to be eaten," muttered Kell, using it as a mantra to make him run faster.

The scrape and bellow of something told him they were being pursued by one or more of the horde. It was inevitable that the monsters would catch up, so they needed to find a defensible spot. At the far side of the canyon the path narrowed again, until it looked as if only one of them could pass through at once. Even then, it would be a squeeze for Willow. It was perfect. All they needed to do was get there before they were hamstrung and ripped apart.

A pain was forming in Kell's side, and he began to wheeze. It felt as if one of the abominations was breathing right down his neck. He could hear it talking in a mangled language while he zig-zagged around large boulders strewn across the path.

It was gaining on them. The chattering was getting louder, and it was starting to sound excited.

"Just a little further," said Willow, slightly out of breath. She unhooked her pack and hurled it into the narrow gap ahead of them, freeing up both hands for her weapon. Kell dropped his to the ground and kicked it forward, while drawing his sword.

When he turned around, he saw three of the horde racing towards them. The one in the lead had two heads, four legs and four arms, while the others were merely malformed Alfár. There was no time to plan. He and Willow stood shoulder to shoulder as it launched itself towards them through the air.

Willow's axe bit into the first creature's shoulder. The force and weight of its body was enough to drive her back a few steps. Kell swung with both hands and his blade sliced off an arm. One of the heads snapped at him, while its other hands grabbed at his clothes, pulling him forward. Willow's mace came down again with deadly force, smashing one of its heads apart. Kell stabbed the other head in the throat and it stumbled backwards, screeching in a high-pitched voice.

There was no time to celebrate. The other two were almost upon them. Willow kicked the dying monster to one side, then braced herself for the next wave.

Much to Kell's surprise and horror, the two creatures ignored them in favour of attacking their dying ally. Before it had even stopped moving, they were hunched over it, ripping off chunks of meat with their claws, smearing their faces with blood. The creatures had forgotten about them in favour of a large meal.

Turning his back on the grisly scene, Kell picked up his pack and jogged on down the path, heading deeper into the unknown territory beyond the Choke.

The two of them kept running. Kell caught glimpses of caves, and primitive stone shelters, on either side of the path. The rest of the horde seemed to live outside, as the area was littered with random belongings in haphazard piles. He noticed collections of clothing, weapons, trinkets and shiny bits of metal and glass. There was a huge pile of boots, a stack of skulls, a chair made of bones, and even some bizarre sculptures or totems. The abominations had once been Alfár, and a creative part of their mind was clearly intent on turning imagination into reality.

The scale of the camp was vast. There could easily be a thousand in the horde. It was a stark reminder that the defenders were outnumbered at least two to one.

The fear creeping down his spine kept Kell running long after he would normally have stopped. The burning in his side steadily grew worse until he was forced to slow to a walk. Willow was less out of breath, but she matched his pace.

"I can't hear anyone following us," she said, cupping a hand to one ear.

The only thing Kell could hear was the thumping of his heart. The landscape around them was utterly lifeless.

Beyond the camp, they encountered multiple forks in the path, but kept heading in a northerly direction, ignoring any branching routes. The ground beneath his boots changed from broken rock and bone, to something softer like damp moss. A yellow and green substance had grown over everything, creating the false impression of a colourful meadow. With every step, they sank a little, but looking behind him, Kell noticed the ground immediately recovered and there were no signs of their passage.

He didn't dare touch the colourful mould, as the smell was fetid and made him gag. They both tied a damp piece of cloth across their face to try and mask the smell, but it only helped a little.

The emaciated corpse of one of the abominations lay face down amidst the mould. The fungus had partially grown over its body, and all that it left behind was a green-streaked skeleton.

Running through the mould were thick black cords, like

malignant tree roots. They reminded him of the calcified veins he'd seen on the faces of the Alfár. They were getting close to the source of the Malice.

After a little while, the main path was crisscrossed with dozens of twisting tracks. The spongey ground became uneven with bulbous lumps, which they did their best to avoid touching. Twisting around the outcrops like black ropes, the disease had created gnarled imitations of trees, with tiny feelers that twitched in the breeze. Kell kept his distance from them as well. He didn't know if they were alive or not, but he didn't want to find out.

As they trudged along through the blighted landscape, Kell felt the last embers of hope flicker and die. He'd done his best to believe that somehow they would find a way out of this. After two quests to the Frozen North, he'd thought himself ready for a final adventure in Willow's homeland. He was not a hero of legend. Nor an unstoppable force of nature that always came home in glory. Experience, and the loss of friends, had taught him that the hard way. But deep down, some stubborn part of him had remained optimistic about their chances.

Now, with only Willow for company, who was not at her best, Kell realised he was never going home. He would never again see his wife and son.

CHAPTER 24

It was the pain that told Odd he wasn't dead.

When he tried to move his jaw, something stabbed him in the side of his face and he blacked out.

The next time Odd woke up, he drifted in the void, not moving, just listening to the world. The sun felt good, beating down on his back, warming his skin. He was lying face down on a hard surface. Beyond that, and the catalogue of horrific pains throughout his body, he didn't know what had happened. The memories were there, but he couldn't quite reach them. They were concealed behind a wall of fog. He had vague recollections of recent events, but he didn't push.

The silence was deafening. He couldn't hear any other living creature, which he took as a good sign. It meant he was less likely to be killed by someone else, or eaten by a predator that mistook him for carrion.

Cracking open his eyes, he waited for the light to become manageable. Something big and dark was blocking much of his view. It took an eternity, but Odd managed to turn his head to the right, giving him a better perspective of the obstruction. It slowly came into focus and Odd eventually recognised the brown and grey lump.

The Yogren was staring at him.

His memories of recent events came crashing back. A cry of surprise surged up his throat, but it quickly died when the creature failed to blink. Its one remaining eye stayed open, staring at nothing. The other was a ruined black socket and the Yogren's head was misshapen from the fall. Odd was partially lying in a cooling pool of its blood.

He tried wiggling his toes, but nothing happened, and then he noticed he couldn't feel his legs at all. Looking down he saw they were still there, but all feeling in his body ended at his navel.

The fingers on his left hand were mangled, bent backwards and at peculiar angles. His right hand had swollen, almost three times its normal size. The skin on his fingers was so tight, they resembled sausages that were about to burst. Blood trickled from his one corner of his mouth, and the air rattled in and out of his lungs in a wheeze. Somehow his heartbeat was a steady, even rhythm.

Reaching down into the well inside, Odd was surprised to find there was still some energy. It wasn't much, but perhaps it was enough. He didn't want to die lying in the middle of the road like a stray dog that had been run down.

Focusing on his hands, Odd trickled power into his arms, watching as the swollen tissue was gradually reduced. His fingers cracked and popped as they shifted back into joint. He didn't try to heal them completely, just enough for them to be useful again. One of his lungs had been punctured by several ribs. He didn't risk repairing the bones, but instead eased them away from his damaged lung. With that done, he patched the holes and his breathing became stronger and more even.

One of his shoulders had popped out of joint. Putting pressure on his arm he snapped the shoulder back into its socket and promptly blacked out.

When he woke up, the sun had moved across the sky and part of his face was now in shade. The contrast created interesting sensations across his skin, but the cold was seeping into his bones. He was afraid he wouldn't be able to warm up again and needed to move.

On hands and elbows, Odd dragged his body away from the

Yogren's corpse which had begun to smell. Following the sun, Odd dragged his legs towards a building and propped himself up against the wall. As he sat there, he noticed his left foot was bent almost completely backwards and a bone was poking through the skin on his right shin. More worrying than the injuries was that he still couldn't feel his legs or hips.

With the remaining sun on his face, he drifted in and out of consciousness, summoning the courage to do what came next. Just before he passed out, Odd saw someone walking down the street towards him. He recognised the figure but didn't try to speak as his jaw was still broken. Just before he fell into the dark, Odd smiled at his mother as she squatted down beside him.

"Wake up."

Odd came awake with a start and tried to scream, which sent spikes of pain lancing through his head. Black spots danced in front of his eyes, but eventually they cleared. The sun had moved and once again he was in shadow. His skin, which he noticed was mostly grey and mottled, was covered in goosebumps. The veins on the back of his hands had turned black, and more were creeping up his stomach and down his legs.

He should have been freezing cold, and yet sweat was pouring down his face.

"Your wounds are infected," said his mother, glancing across the street at the Yogren. "At least it's dead."

Odd grunted and his mother rolled her eyes.

"You need to heal your jaw," she said. When he hesitated, she knelt down directly in front of him. "I know your reserves are low, but if you don't do it, I can't understand you."

Taking a deep breath, Odd closed his eyes and grasped for more energy. He was scared to find out how much was left. What if he tried to repair his legs and nothing happened? Perhaps it was better not to know.

Focusing on his jaw, he let the power wash through his head. The broken pieces in his jaw began to fuse together, while stones and chips of bone were forced out through the skin. The wounds bled a little but then healed, leaving behind pink scars. Normally he would have kept going, until the skin was perfect, but he didn't take the risk. With one final pop, his jaw snapped back into place and his head was pain free.

"Why are you still here?" he asked.

His mother looked at him askance. "I'm here to help you. Don't you know that by now?"

"I'm dying."

"No, you're not. You need to heal your body. Go back to who you were before the hunt."

"There's not enough power. Just let me die," he said, waving a hand to dismiss her.

"That's not you. That's the Malice. It's infected your mind and is telling you to give up. Just look at your body," she said, gesturing at the discoloured skin and calcified veins.

"Leave me alone."

"I cannot. I will not," she shouted. "The Malice is killing you, and you're letting it win. You have never been beaten by anything in your life," she said, pointing at the Yogren's corpse.

"The Malice is too powerful."

"Son," she said, resting a cool hand against his forehead. "You need to travel deep inside and cut out the poison. You are stronger than it."

Just the thought of another battle was tiring, but the idea of giving up was not an option. Odd had never surrendered to anything in his life. He'd controlled the hunger for years, far longer than his mother. He would not be beaten by this. Nevertheless, none of that stopped him from being a little scared.

"Will you stay with me?" he asked.

"I'll never leave you."

Odd closed his eyes and began to drift, down and down,

passing through layers of consciousness, into a place of pure thought. The world around him disappeared. The agony of his tortured body became a distant thing and his sense of time faded away.

When he opened his eyes, Odd was back home in Thune. Madam Ovette pottering around downstairs, muttering to herself. Outside on the street, he could hear the murmuring of people's voices and the sound of wagons rumbling by. He noticed he was naked, but with no one around, he didn't care.

Everything looked and sounded real, and yet he couldn't smell anything. Normally, from dawn until dusk, he could smell fresh bread from the bakery behind his building. The stink of horses and animals always wafted in through his window as they moved down the street. The mass of people passing by brought with them the faint aroma of sweat. But in this place, there was nothing.

"Where am I?" he said.

His mother appeared in the corner of his room, sat on a chair.

"Look," she said, gesturing at his full-length mirror. He kept it polished to a high sheen, but this version was pitted and dull. When Odd looked down at himself, he saw a healthy body without scars or blemishes. The image in the mirror, however, showed a half-dead thing. It was emaciated with grey skin, black veins and cavernous black eyes in a narrow face. It barely had a nose, and its mouth was full of sharp teeth. With long claws and elongated legs, there was little about it that was human.

"What is it?" he asked.

"It's what you will become if you surrender," said his mother. "You stand at the threshold, but the hunger won't let you die. Instead, it will merge with the Malice, fill your body with poison, and remake you into something horrific. The two will combine and create a predator, far worse than the Yogren. Something savage and without mercy."

There was little about himself that Odd recognised in the reflection. He was merely a shell from which the new creature would be created, by blending two primal forces. It was not his dark half, or even the true face of the hunger, but something worse. He had changed his body in order to defeat the Yogren, but that transformation paled in comparison to the thing in the mirror.

"Even now, the darkness is creeping through your body, twisting your flesh," said his mother.

In this place, Odd wasn't aware of his real body and couldn't hear a heartbeat. There was no way of tracking the progress of the Malice, and he didn't know how much time remained before he was engulfed. Running a hand down the edge of the mirror, he couldn't feel the grain of the wood against his fingers. It was all an elaborate illusion.

"What do I need to do?" he asked.

"Fight it!"

"How?" asked Odd.

"Get angry," said his mother, crossing the room. "Aren't you angry that it's killing you?"

"No. Just tired." He felt utterly drained and exhausted. All he wanted to do was sleep. A part of him knew that, if he fell asleep in this place, it would be the end.

"Stay awake! Don't let it win," she said, grabbing Odd by the shoulders, but he couldn't even feel that. She slapped him across the face but there was no pain.

He was trying to stay awake, but everything was so difficult. Talking became an effort. Even blinking his eyes seemed to take an eternity.

"Do you remember the day they took me?"

"Of course," he muttered, barely able to open his jaw. The images from that day were burned into his memory. Blood on her teeth. Wild laughter at the horror on their faces. "You killed some soldiers. More came to our home and you were dragged away as you laughed."

"But do you know why they came for me?" she asked.

Darkness was creeping in around the edges of his vision.

"It's because I gave up. I couldn't shoulder the hunger any longer," she said.

Somewhere deep inside, sparks of rage began to swirl about and his vision cleared. "What did you do?" asked Odd.

"I killed some strangers on a busy street. I didn't even take their essence. I wanted it to be over. I did it, knowing that they would come for me."

The rage began to build. Odd became aware of his body, even though it was at a distance. The fire that was kindling inside his heart began to spread. Warmth trickled into his arms, and then more slowly down his body. His mother's words banked the flames higher.

"I did it, knowing that you would be left alone. I couldn't live with the hunger anymore. Every waking moment, my thoughts were consumed by it. In the early days, I sated it once every full moon. I could forget about it for weeks, but after a while it came back stronger and more insistent. Over the years, I was feeding more and more often."

Lances of pain shot down his spine, and somewhere Odd felt his body contorting in agony. Intense heat, real or imagined, surged through his hips and down his legs. It felt as if his skin was on fire. Pinpricks of pain stabbed one leg and then the other. His feet twitched and jumped.

As the pain spread, his mother's confession continued. "I told myself that you would be better off with someone else. That my sister could look after you far better than me. But the truth is, I was a coward. I gave in to the hunger, because I was weak and selfish."

Thoughts of falling asleep evaporated. Odd focused on feeding the fire. Stoking it with his rage at all that he had lost.

His aunt had not taken care of him. After only a few days, she'd sent him to an orphanage. He'd been forced to survive, on his own, while shouldering the burden of the hunger alone.

He smelled burning hair, felt the grind and pop of bones and, in the distance, heard someone screaming. Odd's nerves were on fire, but now he could feel his whole body, right down to his toes. The pain became so severe it stopped hurting. He was vaguely aware of pressure, but nothing else.

"I gave up on you. It's not your fault," said his mother.

"Are you really here?" asked Odd.

"Does it matter?" she asked, cocking her head to one side. "Don't let the Malice consume you. You never let the hunger take control. Don't give up now."

Fighting against the lethargy that was telling him to surrender, Odd came awake, shouting in defiance.

At first, he thought he was still asleep, because his skin was glowing with an inner white light. It radiated out from his chest in waves, spreading across his whole body, and where it touched his skin, the grey mottling of the Malice receded. The black veins broke apart and the disease was cleansed from his blood.

Without knowing it, while unconscious, Odd had been channelling energy from the well inside him. The worst parts of reversing the changes were already done. His legs and arms looked normal and his ribs had been repaired, but the disease was still there. It manifested as a nagging insistent voice, telling him to give up. That he couldn't win and wasn't strong enough. This wasn't doubt; the Malice was still inside his mind.

Throwing caution to the wind, Odd reached even deeper inside. He'd always used the energy sparingly, keeping the flow to a steady trickle. Now it became a torrent, washing over him like the tide, sweeping away that which didn't belong as it healed him, inside and out. Every part of him was bathed in it, again and again, repairing organs, removing scar tissue and driving it from the dark corners of his mind.

In the blink of an eye, the light disappeared.

Moving tentatively, Odd tried to wiggle his toes and was pleased when they responded. In fact, he could feel his whole body again. Cautiously, he tried to stand and found he had no difficulty getting upright. A cool wind blew down the street, covering his naked body in goosebumps. With one hand touching a wall, just in case he started to feel weak, Odd retraced his steps across the city to the ziggurat.

It felt as if his body was waking up after a long sleep. His muscles were slightly lethargic, but after a short time they warmed up and he felt steady on his feet.

His clothes and pack were exactly where he'd left them. It felt like a lifetime ago. Once he was dressed, Odd felt more like his old self, but there was something different. He couldn't put his finger on it, but there was a distinct absence. Looking around for his mother, he was surprised not to see her. At first, he had questioned whether or not she was real but, after a while, realised it didn't matter. He had enjoyed their conversations, especially as he didn't have to monitor what he said. It had been liberating. If she was truly gone, he would miss that.

As he watched the sun slowly move across the sky, Odd tried to work out what was bothering him. It took a long time, but eventually he realised the well inside was empty. By healing himself, he'd expended every drop of borrowed energy. His skin showed no signs of infection from the Malice, and it had cost him everything. But there was something else as well.

Turning his senses inwards, he searched every single part of his body and mind. Far down, in a quiet and dark corner, he found what remained of the hunger. After feeding, it was normally dormant, like a sated bear asleep in its den, but this felt different. It wasn't waiting for another feed; it was silent. Instead of a sleeping animal, only the desiccated skeleton of the hunger remained. And yet, his instincts told him it wasn't really dead. All it would take was one drop of borrowed energy, from a dying soul, and it would come back with renewed vigour.

Never before, in his entire life, had the well been completely empty. By scouring the Malice away, he had completely remade his body and been reborn. Odd had proven he was stronger than the Malice, and now, he had beaten the hunger too.

Its absence made him feel lonely. Even when he'd been an orphan with no friends or family, he'd had the hunger. It had been his constant companion and ally, keeping him alive, but now it was gone. When he tried to channel some energy to increase his speed or strength, nothing happened. The hunger didn't flare to life, demanding sustenance.

He was whole, and now he was just like everyone else.

CHAPTER 25

As she stared at the violent horde racing towards her, Yarra felt a rush of excitement.

"Ready!" she yelled, signalling the four veterans who had become her commanders. They all waved back and then nudged, or yelled, at the soldiers under their command. The order was passed down the wall, left and right, and the Alfár began to shout and draw weapons, preparing themselves for battle.

Everyone was tired before the fighting had even started. They had been doing this for a long time, but today they were excited. Yarra had brought different tactics and a new approach, which proved a welcome change to the previous monotony.

The wave of abominations reached the bottom of the wall and began to scramble up. Hooks attached to long chains sailed towards the battlements. Crudely fashioned metal ladders followed, held at the base by several larger creatures.

Yarra wished she had some archers, boiling oil or anything flammable. She'd considered having rocks hauled up to the top of the wall, but realised it wasn't worth the effort. That meant relying on different tactics to defeat the enemy.

"Wait!" shouted Yarra.

The temptation to immediately cut the chains and push the ladders away was strong among the defenders. They'd done it in the past, wasting time and energy. Several Alfár had started to move towards the wall, but her order, relayed by others, brought them up short. Right now, it would do little or no damage, and Yarra wanted to hurt them badly.

Screeching in wordless tones, the monsters were a living manifestation of the Malice. A brutal and efficient poison that didn't just kill everything in its path, but remade it into something ugly. At least with death there was a definitive end. She didn't feel pity for the enemy, and intended to kill every single one of them, but she didn't hate them.

The noise from the churning bodies rose in volume. There were dozens of them on the ladders, and many almost at the top of the chains. When the first mangled claw appeared on top of the battlement, she raised her sword.

"Now!" shouted Yarra, bringing her blade down on the nearest monster. It screeched and tumbled backwards, clipped three more of its kind on the way, before all of them fell to their deaths.

All along the wall, the Alfár slashed and hacked at the enemy. Dozens of bodies fell, and more were dragged with them on the way down. Yarra stepped back to study the flow of battle. The Alfár were doing well, severing limbs and choosing their targets with precision, rather than wading into a savage melee. When one of the enemies managed to breach the wall, a group of five Alfár instinctively moved to intercept. The trouble was, once the monster on the battlements was dead, the squad wouldn't return to their original position without guidance, leaving a gap for others to exploit. She gestured at Bewligg, who saw where she was pointing, and went to investigate.

Just as they had planned, Krizan and a squad of eleven she had been holding back temporarily filled the breach. Two six-legged creatures were just scrambling up over the battlements when the dozen defenders arrived. Krizan was less distracted than most, and proved to be a savage fighter. Wielding a sword in one hand and a dagger in the other, she slashed and stabbed, gutting one beast before spinning around to deal with the next. The rest of her squad smashed the injured creature to a pulp with their maces, while she drove the other monster backwards. In a panic, it tripped over its own legs and landed on the battlements on its back.

Krizan shouted something in her own language, and three Alfár helped her throw it off the wall. The weight of the monster was immense, and it snagged several others as it fell. Yarra heard the impact and the resulting shrieks from the dying from below.

Her plan was working. They were keeping the enemy at bay, with few or no mistakes. Every time there was a breach, someone moved to stop them getting a real toe hold, and once they were done, one of the other veterans ushered them back to their original position.

As the fighting continued, Yarra noticed some errors creeping in. All of the Alfár were inhumanly strong, but so were the enemy. This led to some moments where the defenders would test their strength, pushing and shoving in a melee, instead of relying on their skill. When four defenders started a ruckus, she ran towards them, gesturing for Adami to help. By the time she reached them, the brawl had already grown to twenty bodies. Some defenders had shields and they formed a hasty wall, but instead of stabbing between the shields, the second row just piled in, shoving from behind. The front row couldn't use their weapons, which trapped them between their own kind and the enemy.

The combined weight of the soldiers forced the monsters backwards. The defenders cheered and then redoubled their efforts, ignoring their weapons. On either side though, the defenders had left gaps, and several monsters made it unopposed to the top of the wall. They immediately began attacking the flanks of the defenders, who were tangled up, unable to defend themselves. The horde surged over them, clawing and bludgeoning the defenders, whose piercing cries tore at Yarra's ears.

Screaming like a madwoman, Yarra waded into the crush, swinging her sword. Her blade caught one monster across the throat as it turned, almost severing its head. Before it was dead, she stabbed a second and then a third. Next to her, Adami was yanking bodies out of the scrum, then sending them back to their posts.

By the time she and Adami had managed to disperse the melee, almost a dozen Alfár were either dead or dying. It was a pointless waste of lives and should not have happened, but they'd been carried away in the moment.

Despite her best efforts, defenders overextended themselves and were sent off balance, falling into the claws and blades of the enemy. In newly trained soldiers it was to be expected, but all of the Alfár were experienced fighters.

Time and again, Yarra did her best to help the defenders, calling on the other veterans, but no matter how fast they moved, the soldiers kept dying for stupid reasons. She had carefully planned this strategy with the others, and yet they were dying because of her. It was happening all over again.

After hours of savage fighting, the horde finally withdrew, dragging the injured and dead with them. Any Alfár that had fallen over the wall were also carried away to suffer a final indignity after death. Much to her chagrin, the defenders cheered as if they had won a great victory.

Yarra slumped to the ground as exhaustion washed over her, not caring that she sat in a pool of congealing blood. Swirls of blue from the Alfár mixed together with black ichor from the enemy, creating peculiar patterns. Somewhere in the distance, she heard a distinctive trickle as blood drained off the wall through the weep holes.

The horde didn't attack again that day, but just in case, Yarra made sure the wall was manned at all times. They had not yet attacked at night but she didn't want the Alfár to become complacent. Squads of defenders were put on a rota, so they only had to be on watch for a few hours.

After getting something to eat, Yarra reluctantly convened a meeting with the veterans. She couldn't hide from the truth about what had happened. The accusing voices in her mind had been quiet during the battle, but now they resurfaced. All of them blamed her. She had wasted lives. There was more blood on her hands.

The four commanders were talking amongst themselves when she entered the room, but it quickly trailed off, which she took as a bad sign.

"Welcome, sit," said Bewligg, gesturing at the floor beside him. There were no chairs or cushions, just a thin colourful rug that had faded over time. Now, much like the Alfár, it was threadbare, frayed and showing considerable signs of wear. Part of the design was visible, and Yarra could see peculiar animals she didn't recognise. Long ago it might have decorated a home in the city of Laruk. Now, it was all the comfort they had against the cold stone floor.

"It was my fault. I was arrogant and your people died," said Yarra, unable to look them in the eye. "I'm sorry."

Krizan frowned and said something in their language, which Adami then answered.

"She is confused and so am I," said Adami. "We wanted to thank you for your efforts today."

"Why? The plan didn't work," said Yarra.

"Our plans never work," said Bewligg. "Not for a long time. You have seen our people. Every one of them is badly infected. This far north, we are closer to the source of the poison. Our minds drift, even when fighting, and it becomes difficult."

Mihok grunted. "Death becomes a vague notion. A thing, half-remembered, so they have no fear."

"You did well. Less of our people died today than in a long time," said Adami, scratching at a patch of infected skin on his forearm. She noticed the grey mottling had spread towards his wrist.

"But a lot of them still died," said Yarra, struggling to understand why they weren't angry.

"You do not understand," said Bewligg. "When we first came to the Choke, we were as you are now. We had passion, focus and great plans."

"And now?" she asked.

"Now, we are more realistic," said Mihok.

The others chuckled, but she didn't see what was funny. "What does that mean?"

Krizan hissed something and Adami translated. "She says it means a good day is when we are not overrun," said Adami. "A good day is when our people are not dragged from the wall to be eaten, like animals. A good day is when we hold back the darkness."

"Is that enough?" asked Yarra.

"It is more than enough for us," said Bewligg. "We know we cannot win this fight."

"Then why do it if you can't win?" she said.

A peculiar silence settled on the room. At first, she thought it was because they didn't have an answer, but each Alfár had a slightly different expression. After spending a few days among them, Yarra was getting used to their different personalities and how they expressed themselves.

Willow had started off reserved, but during the course of their journey she had begun to open up, as the Malice stripped away her self-control. The Alfár at the Choke were raw, had almost no filters, and were more human than she had expected. Despite all of that, it was still difficult for them to discuss some issues with outsiders.

"Because it has to be done. If we don't fight, who will?" said Bewligg. "A victory today still means something. We beat them. Tomorrow, we start again."

"If we do nothing," said Mihok. "Our people, far to the south, will suffer. To them, this fight is just a rumour. If we stop, every one of them will be killed. We hold back the tide."

"Every day that we win, it is one more day for a cure to be found," said Adami.

Yarra didn't have the heart to tell them that the people in Yantou-vash had all but given up on finding a cure. It was only Ravvi and Willow who had broken ranks, and they had been seen as rebels for daring to travel to the Five Kingdoms.

"We fight," hissed Krizan, grinding out her words in a heavy accent. "For life."

"And now Willow has gone north," said Bewligg, gesturing at the land beyond the wall. "She is our best hope."

"What will you do?" asked Adami.

They needed her. Apart from the voices, which she could ignore most of the time, she was still in control of herself. All of the Alfár were suffering far worse, physically and mentally, and yet they had chosen to stay and fight. Even though it wasn't a fight that they could win.

As a soldier, it was a difficult idea for her to come to terms with. To knowingly enter a fight where the best-case scenario was a draw.

"I will fight," said Yarra.

She had to stay. Not only to give them a chance, but also because she had faith in Willow and Kell. If there was even a small possibility that their mission could succeed, then she had to buy them time.

Yarra would stay, to save lives, because it needed to be done.

CHAPTER 26

"Fieruz is watching you again," said Darya. "He wants you."

Sigrid said nothing. She was too busy gritting her teeth against the pain as she stretched. Her whole body was covered in a layer of sweat. It was something that had become an everyday occurrence, and not one she'd been used to before coming to the Choate homeland.

The morning after she'd visited the tearoom with Grellka, Darya had shown up on the doorstep. Although she was a few years younger than Sigrid, Darya was already a skilled warrior. As a young girl, Sigrid had shadowed her father and eavesdropped on court politics. Darya had spent her time playing with wooden swords and shields. When Sigrid had progressed to dabbling with trade and diplomacy, Darya had moved on to steel blades.

They made for an odd but perfect couple. Sigrid had more knowledge and experience of the world, so was happy to answer endless questions about the Five Kingdoms. Darya knew seven ways to kill with just her thumb and demonstrated her skills with an almost child-like glee.

She'd loved Darya from the first day.

Darya grinned and leaned her weight harder against Sigrid's calves, forcing her knees even further back towards her face, almost bending her in two. This daily ritual – or torture, as she often thought of it – was one of the reasons she could now walk unaided. Regular meals and going for short walks had not been enough. After being so close to death, she'd been forced to rehabilitate her whole body. Exercising every single muscle had been a long, arduous and painful experience.

Sigrid knew that Fieruz was interested in her, but she did nothing to encourage it. A relationship of any sort was the last thing on her mind. Besides, she still thought of herself as married to Kell.

"Maybe he wants you," said Sigrid.

"Maybe he wants both of us," said Darya with a grin. Their faces were not far apart and Darya leaned closer, puckering her lips for a kiss. There was a sudden crash and, looking over, Sigrid saw that Fieruz had walked into a wall. Surreptitiously rubbing his bruised nose, the warrior hurried away as the two women laughed.

Once they had finished stretching, they moved on to sparring with weapons. Today it was a sword and buckler. In Algany, Sigrid had never held a sword before and wouldn't have known a kitchen knife from a skinning knife. Now that she was over a year into her new life with the Choate people, she was competent with a wide variety of weapons. However, Sigrid understood that she still had a great deal to learn. She'd moved past the stage where she was in danger of cutting off her own foot, but she was far from what any Choate warrior would call skilled. Most of the time she relied on luck, waiting for her opponent to make a mistake, while she desperately fended them off.

In the beginning, her training had been slow, because her body had still been waking up, but since then she'd made up for lost time. Every day, she pushed herself as hard as she could and never complained.

Officially, she'd been dead for almost two years. At times, it was hard to believe and the pain of what she'd lost was too much to bear. Late at night, when no one else was around, Sigrid would sometimes sob into her pillow. Grellka never mentioned it, but Sigrid was sure the older woman had overheard her more than once.

Most of the Choate thought Sigrid had adapted to her new life and would stay with them forever. A handful, including Grellka and Dos Mohan, understood it was inevitable that she would return to Algany and her son, even if it cost her life.

Every few months, she received news from home about Marik, but the information in the letters was never enough. Malina always included some anecdote about how he had changed in the interim, but there would be so much she wouldn't notice because for her, it was an everyday thing. As nice as it was to know he was doing well, it still hurt that she was not seeing it for herself.

In some ways it was worse, knowing how much she was missing. Her own son didn't even know that she was alive. The fewer people that knew, the better, and asking a child to keep such a big secret was impossible. Somehow, she would find a way to make it up to him.

The harder she trained, the sooner she would be ready to go home. Nothing would stop her from seeing her son.

"What's the latest news?" asked Sigrid, gesturing that she was ready.

"More of the same," said Darya, dropping into a defensive stance. Sigrid mirrored her and the two of them began to circle one another. "The roads are unsafe, and every day more merchants are being robbed. Apparently, the fat King of the Seithland is very angry. He loves nothing more than gold."

The new Reverend Mother was a complex woman. Despite being straight talking and fairly unpopular among her peers, she was far more subtle than Sigrid had realised. The Choate had people everywhere and, although they couldn't prove it, they believed the Reverend Mother was working with the King of Hundar to disrupt travel. Worry about the safety of the roads had infected many cities across the Five Kingdoms.

In response to the disruption, the price of transporting goods rose, as they needed protection. In turn, people had sought comfort and reassurance, and where better than the church?

Part of Sigrid didn't want to believe this had been the Reverend Mother's plan all along, but credible sources told her it was likely. Britak had been desperate because her time had been short, and she'd concentrated on quick results. Her successor wasn't in a rush, and her plan was focused on the long term.

"We need to work on your footwork," said Darya. "Ready?"

Pushing thoughts of Algany and the Reverend Mother from her mind, Sigrid focused on her opponent. "Ready."

They ran through a series of drills, with one attacking and the other defending before switching around. After an hour, they began to spar, and Sigrid was pleased when she scored points almost half of the time. The Choate had no concept of letting her win because of who she had been. Sigrid's title and rank in Algany meant nothing to them. Nor did they believe in going easy on someone, which made every touch she won worth something.

"Let's take a break," said Darya, stepping back. "You're getting better. One day, you'll be ready to take the Trial of Rustam."

Sigrid had stopped asking when that would be. The Trial was something that all Choate had to endure to prove they were an adult. Darya was twenty-four but had only completed the challenge five years ago. Most completed it at seventeen or eighteen years old. Although Dos Mohan was the War General, it was his wife, Grellka, who was responsible for Sigrid's fate. Hers was a special case and, on this occasion, he had no authority.

"I hope so," said Sigrid, thinking back to her son. She wondered how much he had grown, how he was developing, and if he was starting to look more like her or Kell.

They switched to training with spears and then, later in the day, changed again to unarmed combat. By the time they finished it was verging on evening and Sigrid was bone-tired. She also felt a little sick, as they'd started training too soon after eating lunch. All she wanted was to get some sleep. Some days though, when Sigrid got back to the house, she was given chores by Grellka. She hoped this wasn't one of those days.

Darya walked with her, chatting amiably about a young woman she was interested in courting. Rituals for unpaired Choate were quite different from what Sigrid was used to, but she knew that Darya would have to speak with the woman's mother. Once she had expressed an interest, it was then up to the mother to decide if Darya was suitable. Of course, as in every other culture, young people snuck away all the time for secret trysts before declaring an interest. In that regard, it wasn't too dissimilar from what happened at home.

"Is she serious about you?" asked Sigrid.

"Of course. But we haven't had a chance to..." Darya trailed off suddenly and Sigrid looked around in alarm.

Half a dozen warriors had gathered outside Grellka's house. Standing at the front of the group was Grellka and behind her, Dos Mohan. As Sigrid and Darya approached the house, the conversation dried up.

"What's wrong? What's happening?" asked Sigrid, directing her questions at Grellka.

The older woman said nothing, but Sigrid noticed that she was armed. It was the first time she had seen Grellka carrying a blade. In fact, all of the warriors were holding an assortment of blades and maces.

"Has war broken out?" asked Darya, rather excitedly.

Grellka tutted. "No. Nothing like that. Run along girl, this is serious business."

"She stays," said Sigrid, holding Darya's hand. She was the only close friend she had, and whatever was about to happen, Sigrid didn't want to face it alone.

"Very well," said Grellka, looking grave. "Sigrid, the time has come. Today you will face the Trial of Rustam."

A dozen excuses ran through her head. That she was already exhausted after a long day of training. That she felt sick and needed to sit down. That she was desperate for a drink of water and some sleep. Grellka seemed to be waiting for her to say something along those lines. When Sigrid remained silent, she grinned before turning serious again.

"I am ready," said Sigrid.

Standing behind his wife, Dos Mohan was beaming with pride.

"Come," said Grellka, taking her other hand. "It is time for you to enter the arena."

Sigrid spat and wiped sweat from her eyes in time to see another opponent coming towards her. She couldn't remember all of their names. She was too tired, desperate for some water, and her body was screaming at her to stop. But she held up her arms, ignored the burning in her shoulders, and waited.

She'd knocked three opponents to the dusty ground and they'd retreated out of the fight. The arena could hold almost five thousand in tiered seats, but today only a hundred had gathered. Despite the late hour, the sun was still baking. Sweat trickled down the middle of her back between her shoulder blades. More was beading in her hairline, threatening to drip in her eyes again. With an angry shake of her head, she flicked it away.

After besting three opponents, the fourth Choate warrior came forward more cautiously. He wasn't taking any risks. He was taller than her, but she didn't watch his hands. Instead, she kept a close eye on his face. Everything she needed to know was right there. When the attack came, she was already moving to react, bringing up her sword, planning her parry and the riposte that followed.

Their wooden blades clacked together as she drove him backwards. Orange sunlight glared in her eyes between the slats of the wooden seats, threatening to blind her. When he stepped back a third time she didn't follow, letting him move out of her reach. She circled to the right, putting the sun behind her.

That had been his plan all along. She'd quickly learned that a fight was more than just two people hitting each other with weapons. It was about emotion. It was about using the environment against your opponent. And it was about finding a weakness and then exploiting it.

He said something. A taunt perhaps, but Sigrid didn't have the energy to waste on banter. For him, this was just an exercise. Afterwards, he would go on with his life and nothing would have changed. For her, it meant everything. As a child in Choate society, Sigrid had no power, no station and no voice. As an adult, she would be able to make her own decisions, even if it displeased Grellka, her host and surrogate mother.

Her opponent spat and then quickly came forward, eager for this to be over. She wanted that too, but Sigrid didn't know how many more she had to face. There was only one rule. Survive.

When the warrior feinted to one side and then changed direction, she saw an opening but was too tired to exploit it. Instead, she stepped back out of reach, conserving her energy, looking for another opportunity. He could see that she was tired, but he wasn't making light of this. The Trial was something that everyone had to endure.

The distraction almost cost her. The warrior was moving again, his blade whistling towards her head. Sigrid parried and made a half-hearted attempt at a counter, but he was already moving forward, reducing the space between them. If he came any closer their blades would be useless. As she tried to step back, he stepped forward, jabbing at her with the point of his sword. Sigrid made a clumsy parry, barely keeping it away from her body. Her arms refused to respond anymore. They were throbbing and her shoulders felt as if they were on fire.

When he stepped forward again, she tried to shove him

backwards with her forearm. Instead, Sigrid's elbow was driven into his stomach and the air whooshed from his lungs. He stumbled and then fell to one knee. Sigrid tapped him on the chest with the point of her blade.

"It's over," said Dos Mohan, just as he had for the previous three. Sigrid went to help her opponent, but he waved her back. Then she realised he was pointing behind her.

"You're not finished," gasped the warrior as he tried to catch his breath.

Turning around to face the crowd, which had swelled in number, Sigrid saw another warrior coming towards her with a practice blade. Her heart sank. Two more Choate rushed forward to help the injured warrior off the field.

Sigrid's new opponent was a woman she recognised and had spoken to many times. It was Gar Brielle. The youngest daughter of Grellka and Dos Mohan. No emotion showed on the warrior's face. Whatever feelings she had were buried deep. Sigrid knew their familial connection meant nothing. Brielle would treat her like any other opponent.

When she was in the centre of the ring Sigrid waited, sword held ready. She tried to slow down her breathing but was having difficulty. The sun was so bright, and she was starting to feel light-headed.

"Begin!" shouted Dos Mohan.

Brielle came forward, swinging her blade in tight arcs that drove Sigrid back. She retreated carefully, trying not to trip over her own feet. When they reached the edge of the arena, Brielle changed tactics and started jabbing at her. Sigrid did her best to block, but the Choate was relentless. Sigrid's timing was poor, and Brielle's blade clipped her fingers, but she refused to let go. Thoughts of her son and returning home made her hold on.

Taking a deep breath, Sigrid screamed in defiance, startling her opponent, but only for a moment. It gave her a chance to go on the offensive, but every attack was easily blocked, and the ripostes came thick and fast.

It was over before she knew it. Sigrid felt something clip her across the ribs, but she didn't stop.

"The Trial is over!" someone shouted.

Moving on instinct she raised her blade to attack. Muscle memory had taken over. Brielle blocked it with ease and then stepped back, lowering her sword.

"Stop. It's done," she said, offering Sigrid a faint smile.

"What? No. I can still fight. It can't be over." The sun was so bright. She had to keep going. She didn't have a choice.

"It's over," said Grellka, coming up beside her.

To have lost so much and fought so hard only for it to be over. Sigrid was ready to cry. "What happens now? Can I try again?" she asked.

The details about of the Trial of Rustam were kept secret from children. The only thing she had been told was it involved stamina and a fight in the arena.

"You won," said Grellka pulling her close. "You passed the Trial."

The last bit of willpower keeping Sigrid upright evaporated and her knees gave out. She would have fallen if Grellka hadn't been holding her so tightly. Tears filled Sigrid's eyes and she took a moment to gather herself. Only when she could stand unaided did the older woman let go.

"But I didn't beat Brielle," said Sigrid. "I thought I had to beat them all."

"The Trial is a little different for everyone," said Grellka. "But the purpose is the same. To be Choate is to fight because you have to, not because you want to kill."

"Today you are reborn," said Dos Mohan, as he approached. "My daughter."

Sigrid tried to hold back the tears, but when she saw others getting emotional she let them flow. Brielle and Darya hugged her tightly.

A moment ago, she'd been teetering on the point of exhaustion, but now she was full of a new, raw energy. One that gave power to her tired limbs. That fired her lethargic mind and focused her like never before. Dos Mohan exchanged a knowing look with Grellka. They'd seen the shift in her and understood what it meant. Sigrid was going home to her son.

"Hold still," said Grellka.

Sigrid was about to reply, but instead she said nothing. Darya excitedly gripped her right hand, while Sigrid did her best not to stare at the large bald man with the needle in his hand.

She couldn't return home as Sigrid, Queen of Algany. That person was dead. The only way to go home was to be invisible in plain sight. She had passed the Trial of Rustam and was now regarded as an adult in Choate society. That meant being tattooed with the symbols of her family and their ancestors. As she had no blood relatives, Grellka and Dos Mohan had welcomed her into their family. For the first time, Sigrid studied the tattoos on Darya's face, if only to distract her from what was about to happen.

Darya had a swirling design across her left cheek and the bridge of her nose. The rest of the design ran down the left side of her face and neck. When she had first arrived, Sigrid had stared at everyone, startled and amazed at their tattoos. Now she barely gave them a second glance because most had them. It was those without who stood out.

As the needle pierced into the skin of her right cheek, Sigrid bit her lip so she didn't scream. Darya gripped her hand and Sigrid squeezed back, trying not to move or make a sound. Over and over the artist filled the needle with fresh blue ink, often wiping blood away from her face. Soon his cloth was completely red so he picked up another from the pile, leaving the first to soak in a bowl. She watched as her blood slowly turned the water red. After a while, her face felt five times its normal size and the pain had spread down her neck into her shoulders.

"Relax," whispered Darya. "You're tensing your shoulders and it's making it worse."

She was right. Sigrid had been holding herself so still that she'd forced her body into a strange position. The artist took a moment to let her catch her breath before continuing.

It seemed to go on forever. After a while Sigrid felt a bit light-headed and sick. Finally, the artist wiped her face one last time and sat back, critically studying his work. He grunted in satisfaction, gathered his tools and left the room. From now on, everyone would look at her differently. When a group of people gathered, she could offer an opinion and they would listen to her as an equal.

Grellka saw the artist to the door while Darya fetched a mirror.

"Are you ready, girl?" asked Grellka.

Sigrid had not seen her reflection in nearly two years. She had no idea what she would look like anymore. A lump had formed in her throat. Unable to speak, she just nodded.

Darya turned the mirror around and Sigrid stared at the stranger.

It had taken a long time for her hair to regrow and, after nearly two years, it was just below her ears. It was a lot shorter than she was used to, but that was the smallest of changes about her appearance. The tattoos on her face accentuated the angles of her cheekbones, which were sharper than she remembered. The ridges between her eyebrows were more pronounced, and her eyes had changed colour slightly. Perhaps it was all that she had experienced, or maybe it was just her imagination. Dressed like a Choate warrior, carrying a blade, she knew most people from her old life wouldn't give her a second glance.

"I barely recognise myself," said Sigrid.

"That's what you want, isn't it?" asked Grellka.

"Yes. It is."

"So, what will you do now that you are an adult?"

The words were easy to find this time. "Travel to Algany."

"I'm coming with you," said Darya. "Don't try and stop me."

Grellka frowned but didn't argue. She had no authority over Darya. It would be up to her family and the war leaders to decide. After spending so much time together, Sigrid was pleased, as she couldn't imagine doing it by herself.

"And what do you intend to do when you get to Algany?" asked the Choate.

"Protect the people. Serve," said Sigrid.

"You make me very proud, daughter," said Grellka.

It was time to go home.

CHAPTER 27

With his eyes on the ground to avoid falling into one of the swampy pools of water, Kell immediately noticed when the land around him changed. Before the swamp, there had been barren tundra with standing pools of fetid water. And before that, spongey fields of toxic mould that choked with every breath.

What lay ahead was thousands and thousands of razor-sharp growths, like a sea of swords embedded in the ground with their blades pointing towards the sky. At first glance, the white shards looked smooth, but looking closer, Kell saw the surface of some were pitted. One false step and he would be impaled on dozens of spikes. At the least, the air was clean. It was arid and had a slightly floral aroma like drying lavender, but it was breathable.

This far to the north, where the poison was deeply entrenched in the land, almost nothing could survive. The grey and black monotony of the festering landscape was broken up only by mould and colourful toxic mushrooms.

During the day, they trudged through the barren, rotting world. At night they slept on rocks that they carefully scraped clean. Despite taking precautions, their clothes were marked with green, purple and yellow smears. Fungus spores drifted through the air, painting them in lurid colours, like brightly dressed bards.

If the empty landscape had been their only problem, Kell

would have been less worried. Despite being two days from the Choke, they were still being followed by something. At first, he thought it was one of the horde, but twice he'd caught a brief glimpse, and that was enough to see that it was something different. It had the right number of limbs to be an Alfár, but there was something wrong with its shape and how it moved. He didn't know if it was a twisted remnant, or something else entirely. It preyed on his mind continuously.

The horde were desperate, shambolic and driven by want. The thing tracking them was cautious and patient. Biding its time and waiting for the right moment to strike. Not once had it occurred to Kell that it was friendly. In this tainted land, there were no allies and there was nothing that offered comfort.

On top of those worries, Willow was becoming more and more distracted. She needed more guidance, more urging to stay in the present, and with hazardous footing, it made the journey slow and more difficult. His own emotional state was also becoming an increasing struggle. Bouts of maniacal laughter or heart-wrenching sobs would wash over him, coming out of nowhere, and yet the emotional weight would be crippling. His heart would be breaking at thoughts of never seeing his family, and a moment later they would be gone. Then mirth, like nothing he'd ever felt before, would fill him until his sides ached and his eyes ran with tears of joy.

Every day was mentally and physically exhausting, and although he tried to keep watch at night, it became impossible. Willow would forget to take her turn and lie down to sleep. When Kell tried, he would quickly doze off and wake up sat on a rock outside their tent. He often woke with a start, expecting their patient enemy to be looming over him, but it never attacked. It seemed to be waiting for something, although Kell didn't know what.

"Willow, you need to stay close," said Kell, warning the Alfár.

She was staring off into the distance at something. From the look in her eyes, he knew it was a memory. Willow didn't react until he touched her on the arm and then squeezed her hand, connecting her to the present.

"Kell," she said, smiling down at him. "Where are we?"

She must have been drifting worse than he'd realised.

"Do you know what this is?" he asked, pointing at the land ahead. "Do you recognise it?"

"It's familiar," she said, which he knew was a lie. She'd never been this far north before. The distinction between the present and the past were becoming more opaque.

"You need to be careful. Place your feet exactly where I do," he warned her.

"I'm not a child, Juanne," she muttered. Kell didn't react, but he feared they were running out of time. They were close to their destination, and yet he didn't know if she would remember why they had made this journey in the first place.

Taking Willow by the hand, as if she were indeed a child, Kell led her towards the field of spikes. She went with him willingly, half in a daze, not fully aware of her surroundings or the danger they posed.

If Ravvi had travelled this way, there was no indication of the path he'd taken. However, there were narrow tracks running through the spikes where the ground was worn smooth. The stone shards started at knee height, but soon rose above Kell's head, making it impossible to see where he was going. When he accidentally brushed his arm up against one, it easily cut through his shirt. Several times his back scraped against one of the blades without realising and the scalemail screeched in response.

It felt as if he were back in the maze of the Ice Lich. More than once the trail they were following came to a dead-end, forcing him to squeeze around Willow so he could take the lead again. Despite his best efforts, it didn't take long before they were both covered with dozens of shallow cuts on their arms and legs. The leather of his boots had been torn open in several places, and Kell could feel the air stirring around his feet.

"Do you remember the maze in the castle?" said Kell, trying to jog Willow's memory, but she didn't respond. "It kept changing shape, and eventually you'd had enough. I'd never seen you so angry before. You smashed through the first wall like it was made of paper."

"Of course, I remember," said Willow, squeezing his hand. "Do you know we're being followed?"

Kell paused and carefully turned around to face Willow, mindful of keeping his elbows close to his body.

"Do you know what it is?" he asked.

Willow glanced behind them, peering through the sea of shards, but even she wasn't tall enough to see over them. "No, but I have an idea how we can find out."

It took them a long time to make any real progress through the spikes. There were multiple branching pathways, several of which often seemed to be heading in the same direction. After the twentieth dead end, Kell thought there must be only one way through, but he soon came to realise that the randomness of the place had not been planned.

"I don't think this was built," said Kell, gesturing at the stone spears around them. "I think it was grown."

"Of course. I thought you knew," said Willow, as if it was obvious. "It was all grown. We built our homes and cities on top of the dead."

"What does that mean?" he asked, but she didn't answer.

Willow stopped and pointed at something to their left. They had been looking for the perfect place for an ambush. At another narrow crossroads, there were two paths that led in a roughly northerly direction, and one that headed west. It quickly ended around a corner, and there was just enough space for the two of them to hide. It was a tight squeeze, but having spent so much time with Willow over the last few months, it didn't bother him. With no water to bathe, Kell knew he smelled bad, but Willow either didn't notice or didn't care. Much that he'd previously worried about was falling away.

At the crossroads there wasn't much room to swing a sword. Instead, Kell held his dagger in one hand and focused on breathing quietly. Willow stood perfectly still, her flesh almost becoming stone. It reminded him of the first day they'd met outside the tavern in Algany. He'd been so terrified of saying or doing the wrong thing, in case she interpreted it badly and tried to kill or eat him. He'd never seen anything so strange as the Alfár, and now she was his closest friend.

As if she could hear what he was thinking, Willow looked down and shared in his smile. In the distance, Kell heard the scraping of feet against stone. Whatever was tracking them was close. Kell heard it shuffling about with an unsteady gait. It didn't seem to be in a hurry. And then he heard it talking. The words were mumbled and lilting, in what he recognised was the Alfár's language. Willow's brow furrowed, but she didn't lower her weapon. It probably meant nothing. Perhaps one of the horde had managed to regain some semblance of language.

Finally, a figure came into view and Kell readied himself for a fight. He noticed a few details, the ragged clothes, the long hair, the stink and the spatter of fungus, but he didn't have time to think about what it meant. Kell took a deep breath, bunched up his muscles and rocked back on his feet. Just as he was about to launch himself forward, Willow put a hand on his chest, holding him back. Lowering her weapon, she walked towards the newcomer. Kell followed in her wake, ready for a fight to the death.

Willow said a word and the figure stopped, its back towards them. She repeated herself and something changed in the stranger's posture. The curved shoulders and bent back straightened. The twitching subsided and slowly it craned its neck around to stare at them. Kell swallowed the lump in his throat and tried not to scream.

"Kell," said Willow, dropping her weapon. "This is my kinsman, Ravvi."

Ravvi was insane.

From the moment Kell looked in his pale, yellow eyes, it was all he could see. The absolute madness. Physically, he wasn't so different from Willow, and yet there was a gulf between them. There was a terrible absence inside. As if a piece of his soul had been taken away.

Ravvi was gaunt, filthy, dressed in rancid, stained rags and had no shoes on his feet. His hair was matted and streaked with colourful stains from the fungus. A putrid and sweet smell hung about him, like rotting fruit. His wet clothes were coming apart, but he didn't have enough self-awareness to notice. His skin was mottled, and beneath the surface, his veins were black. The Malice had taken a heavy toll.

Willow put down her weapon and tried to guide Ravvi to a flat piece of ground where they could sit. Ravvi flinched when first being touched, but then went where he was told as if he had no will.

"What happened to him?" asked Kell.

Willow spoke slowly and carefully to Ravvi in their own language, trying to coax some answers out of him. At first Ravvi said nothing, merely studied his feet and then the sky, as if searching for something. When Willow produced some food, Ravvi's eyes widened and his nose began to twitch. He stuffed the bread in his mouth, tearing it apart and swallowing it without properly chewing. Gnawing on it like an animal, he ate it within moments and then looked towards Willow like a dog begging its master for another treat.

Willow tried asking him questions again, and this time Ravvi replied, slowly and with difficulty. After a few sips of water, the rasp faded from his voice.

The extent of Ravvi's infection was something to behold. He

was no longer an Alfár, but neither was he one of the horde. He had become something in between, barely grasping on to the remnants of his sanity.

Slowly, Willow coaxed answers from her kinsman, but he quickly grew tired of speaking and lay down to rest. In a few moments he was deeply asleep, uncaring or unaware of any dangers around them.

"Everything happened as we thought," she said, staring down at Ravvi with pity. "In desperation, he took something from the Five Kingdoms and came home, hoping that it would cure this place and our people of the Malice." Willow wiped her eyes.

"Then we're too late," said Kell. "We failed."

"No. He hasn't gone any further north," said Willow. "Without someone to keep him focused, he lost his way. He's been wandering for days. Ravvi barely knows his own name, never mind anything else. There's so little of him left."

The Malice had taken so much from the Alfár. Their homeland and the glorious cities. Their children and the future. Their health and now their minds. It was all-consuming.

Willow reached into Ravvi's shirt and withdrew an item wrapped in cloth. It was the only clean thing about his whole body. Once she'd unwrapped it, Kell stared at a small glass container, stoppered with a cork. Inside was a gold-coloured fluid that shimmered and reflected the sunlight. The sight of it made Kell's mouth dry up and a prickle of fear ran down his spine.

"What is it?" he finally managed to ask.

"What he hoped would cure the land and save our people." Willow tilted the vial one way and then the other, watching the liquid move. "It's Govhenna's blood."

After all that they'd done to defeat the Ice Lich, who had been draining the Shepherd of energy, he understood Willow's disgust. It showed Ravvi's level of desperation to consider such a solution. Although until Kell had spent hundreds of years searching for a way to save his people, without hope, it was not his place to judge Ravvi.

"So what do we do now?" asked Kell.

"I don't know," said Willow.

They made camp at another crossroads, where there was space to stretch out. Ravvi came with them, happily being led along like a child. While they set up the tent, Kell caught Willow staring at her kinsman. Perhaps she was contemplating her future.

They shared their food with Ravvi, who vigorously ate everything he was given. It must have been days since his last meal. Kell didn't even want to think about what he had been eating before their arrival. As a people, the Alfár were not particularly hefty, but in comparison to her kinsman, Willow looked overweight. The hollows of Ravvi's cheeks were so pronounced it made the bones stick out, like the stone forest that surrounded them.

Despite the offer of the tent, Ravvi fell asleep outside before night had fallen. Willow was lost in thought, contemplating what came next, so Kell left her sitting beside Ravvi and went to bed. With so much on his mind, Kell thought he would lay awake for hours. But exhaustion dragged him down into the dark that was mercifully free of nightmares.

Something was pulling at his body. Someone was in the tent with him, and it took him a moment to realise that it was Willow. At first, he thought she must be settling down to sleep, but then he felt her hands on his chest.

"Willow? What is it?" he asked, sitting up on one elbow.

"I don't want to fight it anymore," she said.

"I know. It's exhausting," he said. Struggling against the Malice felt like a battle they'd been waging for years.

"Don't speak," said Willow. "Let me talk."

The doorway to the tent was open. Kell was surprised to see moonlight playing across the naked flesh of her chest and hips. Willow was always warm, so often slept in little clothing, but this was different. She'd let down her hair and was looking at him in a way he'd never seen before. She was breathing deeply and when he tried to speak, she placed a warm hand against his lips.

"I don't care what people will say. Loneliness is like a disease. It eats away inside. No one should be alone forever." Her lips brushed against his neck and a jolt of energy ran down his spine.

"Willow," he said, trying to ease her away, but she was incredibly strong.

"Lie with me, Juanne," she said in a husky voice.

"I'm not Juanne. I'm Kell," he said. Willow's lips pressed against his and Kell slowly drew back. "I'm Kell. Kell Kressia."

Willow moved towards him again, but then hesitated. "Who?"

"Kell. We travelled to the Frozen North. We defeated the Ice Lich. You were afraid the Malice had infected the Five Kingdoms." At the sound of his voice, some of the heat faded from her eyes.

"Kell?"

"Yes. It's me."

Recognition filled her eyes, and with a deep sigh, Willow sat up, wrapping her arms around her knees. He expected her to be embarrassed, or try to cover up her nakedness, but she didn't seem concerned, except that there was a terrible sadness in her eyes.

They sat together for a long time in contemplative silence.

"I was alive in the era of your grandfather," she said finally, holding Kell in place with her eyes. "Can you imagine all that I've seen from then to this moment? And after all that time, not being with Juanne is what haunts me. I didn't take the risk, because it meant being vulnerable, and that felt like surrender."

Kell knew he should say something. Offer her some comfort, but he had similar regrets about the time he'd wasted being apart from Sigrid.

"It's not too late for you," said Willow, reading his thoughts.

"I hope not," said Kell.

"If we do nothing, there is no hope for my people. This world and everyone living here are already doomed," said Willow. With the relentless march of the Malice, and no children left, they both knew what would inevitably happen. "We have come so far. I think we should take a risk."

"What do you mean?" he asked.

Willow pulled out the vial of Govhenna's blood. Even in the dark it glowed, full of energy and power. Full of potential.

"I thought you said it could make things worse."

Willow's laugh was bitter. "I've spent so long in the Five Kingdoms that a part of me had forgotten how bad it was here. Everything is already corrupted. After everything that we've seen to reach here, I don't think it can be made any worse. Do you?"

Given all that he'd experienced, Kell couldn't disagree. "So, what will happen if you use it?"

"Maybe nothing."

"Or?"

"Or, it heals the land."

"And if it doesn't?"

"Then, I will accept that all hope is lost for my people."

"Then we will go north," said Kell. "And finish this, together."

CHAPTER 28

When Odd arrived at the Choke it was late in the day, but the heat of the afternoon sun was still intense. He expected to find the battlements abandoned, with the Alfár resting indoors, but the fight was still underway. Either the enemy were determined to breach the wall, no matter the cost, or they weren't affected by the weather.

As he approached the stairs, a few Alfár about gave him curious glances, but none stopped to question why he was there. They weren't surprised to see a human, which gave him hope that his friends had made it this far.

Injured Alfár were being escorted down the stairs and taken indoors, presumably to a hospital. At the top of the wall the battle was raging. The enemy were a horde of misshapen monsters with too many limbs, mangled bodies and snarling faces. The defenders were all Alfár, but each of them was showing severe signs of infection. He could see Yarra in their midst, directing individuals who helped bully and shove squads back into formation, to prevent the line being breached.

Odd drew his sword and took a deep breath, preparing to draw energy to bolster his strength and increase his speed. He let it go in a rush, remembering that there was nothing in the well anymore. That part of his old life was over. Now, he was as mortal as everyone else.

Seeing a squad getting into trouble as a six-legged creature started to dominate, he ran to assist, hacking off one of its legs with an overhand swing. The force of the blow travelled up both of his arms to his shoulders. The sharp pain that followed was astonishing. The monster hadn't seen him coming, but now it lashed out. Odd tried to move out of the way but found that he was too slow. It clipped him on the chest, and he stumbled back a couple of steps. Thankfully, he wasn't seriously injured, as the scalemail absorbed the brunt of the blow. Even so, Odd felt there would likely be a bruise across his ribs in the morning. It was going to take time to adjust to the limits of his body. Clearly there was much about his new life that would be more difficult.

His intervention gave the rest of the squad time to recover. Working together, they hacked the creature apart and hurled the remnants over the wall.

The horde were frenzied in their attack, as if they sensed victory was near. Despite the Alfár having the upper ground, they didn't have the numbers and were spread thin. The pace of the battle never waned, suggesting that it was always like this.

Odd became lost in time as the tide of the battle flowed over him. His only focus was the next breath, the next enemy, the next swing of his sword. Before long, his lungs ached, his shoulders burned and he was bruised all over. Sweat poured from his brow, and at every moment to stay alive was a struggle. There was no relief as he rolled from one fight into the next.

He'd never felt more alive in his life.

Death was so close. Odd could almost see the place where the others went, just before the end. He caught glimpses of it in the eyes of Alfár that fell around him. And throughout the fight, as he maimed and murdered, the hunger remained silent.

Even when one dying Alfár fell against him, dragging him from the fight, he didn't feel the familiar urge. Odd lowered the warrior to the ground and attempted to stop the bleeding. With so much noise and so many bodies around him, it would have been easy to take the remaining energy. Instead, he helped the warrior descend two flights of stairs, before someone else took him off Odd's hands.

Something about the battle had changed and the ragged defenders let out a cheer. It was over. The enemy had turned and fled. The remaining monsters on the wall were quickly dispatched, and the fighting stopped.

"Odd?" said a familiar voice. Turning around, he saw Yarra staring at him in shock. Much to his surprise she rushed forward and embraced him. "How are you alive?"

"It's a long story," he said. "It looks as if you're in charge here. How did that happen?"

"It's another long story," said Yarra, but her mirth was soon quashed as more injured Alfár were carried past them off the wall. "Come, we'll talk downstairs."

Odd was so exhausted that if he sat down, he would fall asleep, so he was glad to keep walking. Below the wall was a labyrinth of tunnels and large subterranean spaces. Yarra led him with confidence through the cool and airy corridors to a small room. Her few belongings were piled in one corner, or they sat in nooks that had been carved into the wall. There was just enough room for a cot and little else.

They sat together on the cot, studying each other. Odd noticed the guilt that usually hung around her shoulders had been lifted. But in its place was something else. Duty to others, and a reawakened spark of leadership. He'd seen how the Alfár had responded to her. Yarra might be an outsider, but after only a few days she commanded their respect.

"You look tired," said Yarra.

"I was fighting in the battle."

"I know, but that's not it." She bit her lip as she tried to make sense of what she was seeing. She might not have been able to understand the change in him, but it was clear that she could sense it. "I've never seen you look so exhausted. Even in the Tangle. Even when we went for days with little or no sleep."

Odd shrugged. "The fight with the Yogren changed me." It was the truth and as vague an explanation as he was willing to give her. "Why did they cheer?" he asked.

"Cheer?"

"When the fighting ended, the Alfár cheered, as if they'd won the war. But the horde wasn't wiped out. I heard them retreating."

"Ah, that," said Yarra wiping her sword clean on a piece of cloth. "The Malice has deeply affected the mind of every Alfár. Most days, some of them are lucky if they can remember their own name, never mind that they've been fighting for months, maybe even years."

"Every day is a new battle."

Yarra shrugged. "It's horrible and tragic, but it stops them worrying. They don't remember the friends they've lost, or the horrors they've witnessed. Every day they live is a victory against the darkness."

Odd grunted. "You've changed too."

Even though they had only been apart for a few days, the differences were noticeable. Yarra had grown into the leader she'd always been destined to become.

"I have," said Yarra.

"And the voices? Do you still hear them?"

"I do, but they don't bother me as much. Besides, I know it's not guilt that keeps them around. It's the Malice."

Odd had been wondering about that as well. There had been no sign of his mother since he'd healed himself. He still wasn't sure if she had been a product of the Malice infecting his brain, or something else. Somehow, she had known things that he didn't. It was possible all of it was buried deep in his mind, and yet part of him doubted that. She'd been a witness at events where he'd been absent. Or perhaps she was a figment of his imagination, telling him exactly what he wanted to hear, so that he felt better about the choices he'd made. Whether real or imaginary, Odd still missed her company.

"Are you all right?" asked Yarra.

"Sorry, I'm just tired. I think I'm still recovering from the fight with the Yogren."

"I'll show you where to get some food and a place to sleep. We'll talk later."

After a filling meal of hearty stew and slightly stale bread, Odd lay down to sleep in a large room with a dozen Alfár. Despite only having a blanket for a bed, Odd drifted off almost immediately, smiling to himself.

Early next morning, sore and ravenous, Odd took his breakfast up to the top of the wall. Sitting on the battlements, with his legs dangling over the edge, he stared out at the blighted land. He could smell the old blood and knew that only yesterday, where he was sitting, Alfár had died. The future was bleak, and today the horde would come again, desperate to kill everything in its path. In spite of all that, Odd found himself smiling because he was free. Free to make his own decisions and mistakes.

Alone with his thoughts for the first time in months, he watched the sun rise and thought about the future.

A while later, Yarra sat down next to him with a steaming mug of tea.

"How long has it been since Kell went over the wall?" he asked.

"Three, no four days," said Yarra. "I'm starting to lose track."

"The Malice?"

"No, just tired," she said. Her wry smile faded quickly. "Every day we lose people, and yet the enemy never seems to tire. I'd worry about our supplies, if not for the fact that every morning we have less people to feed."

A heavy silence settled over them, and for a time, they were both lost in thought.

"How long do you think you can hold out?" asked Odd.

Yarra shrugged. "It's difficult to say. There's so much that changes every day. Squads who were reliable suddenly fall apart for no reason, so I have to move people around. Wounded soldiers return to the wall before they're ready but insist they can fight. The Alfár know how to follow orders, but sometimes they just forget or start going rogue. With every battle, I'm fighting against more than just the horde."

"Do you think the Alfár in Yantou-vash know what's happening here?"

Yarra's laugh was harsh and bitter. "They have no idea. For them, the Malice is a distant thing. A mild discomfort that causes a rash and sore joints. Here, we fight it every single day. The horde are a living manifestation of the disease at its worst."

"When we first arrived in this place, it felt to me as if the others had already given up."

"They're just biding their time. Waiting for it to be over. Whether it's futile or not, at least the Alfár here are trying to fight it," said Yarra.

"So, what do we do now?" asked Odd.

"You're asking me?"

"You're the one in charge," he said. Odd expected her to dodge the question, but instead she mulled it over before answering.

"We fight and we wait."

"And then?" he asked.

"We hope that Kell and Willow find a way to cure the disease, or at least stop the spread."

"That sounds like a good plan to me," said Odd.

The day that followed was full of brutality, suffering and fugues that cost the lives of the many defenders. Being of sound mind compared to most of the Alfár, Odd found himself placed in the role of senior officer, coordinating the battle alongside several veterans. The Alfár accepted him without question, following his orders as if they came from one of their own.

He'd expected some resistance for being a newcomer or prejudice for not being an Alfár. Once again, he was reminded of the many differences between their people. Part of him wished he'd met the Alfár during their golden age. When they lived in huge cities and were masters of their domain. Looking at the ragged figures that surrounded him, Odd wondered if any of them remembered that time.

Yarra watched over the whole battle, controlling the flow of the defenders, often wading into a fight herself to prevent a disaster.

Several times Odd saved lives, because he was aware of peripheral danger that eluded the Alfár. After several hours of shouting, his voice was hoarse, and his armour and clothes were soaked in black ichor from the horde and blood from the Alfár. His lungs burned with every breath, and a lingering pain on his left side had spread upwards to his collar.

When there was a lull in the fight, he took a step back to catch his breath before he collapsed. Every moment of personal agony was a new experience that he relished for its originality. Never before he had felt weak, inept and often overwhelmed during a battle. Thankfully, he was not on the front line in a squad. If that had happened, he would have been killed very quickly. The power of the Alfár had never been more apparent. Odd witnessed inhuman feats of strength that he would have been able to replicate in the past, but were now beyond him.

In less than a day, Odd became aware of the limits of his body and gradually adapted to his new status quo. Before, he'd relied on his speed and, sometimes, his superior strength to overpower an enemy. Now, the years of training and endless drills paid off, as muscle memory took over. When a squad faltered due to injury or another reason, he directed others or stepped in himself, moving with instinct.

Even with the Alfár veterans and him coordinating the fight

under Yarra's guidance, many defenders still died. Many of them could have been avoided, but the officers couldn't be everywhere all of the time.

Never before had he been so aware of the ebb and flow of the battle. As a member of the Raven, he'd rarely led others and had spent most of his time protecting the royal family. For the first time in many years, Odd felt like a soldier again. At some point during the fighting, he realised it was something that he'd missed.

For hours at a time, death was only a heartbeat away. One badly timed slash, or clumsy thrust, and he would be ripped apart. The enemy had no skill, no plans and no common sense. But they had brutality, superior numbers and an insatiable will to destroy.

Odd wondered how much of their minds remained intact. Were they simply empty shells for the disease, driven to kill only because it wanted to spread the infection? Or was there a remnant of a mind within each monster that still had independent thoughts? After stabbing the tenth monster to death, he realised it was the former. There was nothing in their eyes. No compassion, no mercy, no emotions of any kind. When one of their brethren died, they didn't react. They were all nameless and anonymous to one another. In some ways it made killing them easier, but Odd also found that he pitied their emptiness. Once, they had been Alfár, but now they were nothing.

For no reason that he could see, when the battle was going badly for the defenders, one of the monsters decided to flee. One became two, and then ten and soon the horde were in full retreat. Leaning heavily on the battlements, Odd watched them run, scrambling over one another to escape.

That night Odd expected to fall asleep with ease, but despite being exhausted, he lay awake with his mind turning in lazy circles. Hoping that some cool night air would help, he went to the top of the wall.

He'd been told that the horde had never attacked late at night, but the Alfár continued to keep watch regardless, which he thought was sensible. A few of them roamed about, walking up and down to stay warm in the chilly air. They acknowledged his presence but left him alone, which he appreciated.

Odd could see his breath frosting in front of his face and feel the cold in his chest. Taking slow, deep breaths, he waited for his mind to tire and catch up with his body.

The wound on his left arm ached, the stitches pulling when he clenched his fists. It wasn't the first time he'd been injured, and yet this was different. Normally he would have sped up the healing process and removed the sting of pain. Now he was just like everyone else. He had to wait for it to heal at its own pace.

"You know that you're going to die here, right?" said a familiar voice.

Turning his head, Odd wasn't surprised to see his mother standing beside him on the wall. Resting her hands on the battlements, she leaned out and peered down at the ground. They stood together in companionable silence for a while, listening to the night. It had a peculiar, stilted quality. It lacked the familiar sounds of nocturnal animals and insects. Despite being a charnel house earlier in the day, the air at the top of the wall smelled reasonably fresh. A southerly wind brought with it a faint stink of rot and decay, but it was something that Odd had grown used to since arriving.

Wet patches of blood had dried, leaving behind dark stains on the stones. Odd picked at one on the battlements with a fingernail, revealing a smear of dark blue beneath the black ichor. The rocks had soaked up layer upon layer of blood. If he analysed them like the rings of a tree, could he interpret the battle's history?

"Doesn't it bother you? Knowing that you're going to die," said his mother.

"Everyone dies."

"Yes, but you don't have to. At least not here."

Odd shrugged. "I could die here, doing something worthy, or I could die many years from now, fat and old in my bed."

"Many years," stressed his mother. "It could be a long time from now. I'm not sure what the limit is, but I think it could be the span of several lifetimes."

"It's all in the past. Now, I'm just like everyone else."

His mother snorted in derision. "No, you're not. You're anything but normal."

One of the Alfár on sentry duty walked past, and Odd waited until she had passed out of earshot before speaking.

"Why are you here, mother?"

"The same reason as last time. To protect you."

"You can't save me."

"I can if you listen," she insisted, moving a few steps closer. "Walk away from this place. Go home to the Five Kingdoms."

"I can't. They need me."

"They're already dead. We both know it. What you're doing here isn't something that matters. All they're doing is delaying the inevitable."

"It matters. Besides, we need to wait for Kell and Willow to return."

"They're probably dead," she said.

"Perhaps," Odd conceded. "But at least they tried."

Odd's mother frowned at him. "What does that mean?"

"It means I have no desire to die a hundred years from now and have accomplished nothing of worth. If we're successful, we will change the fate of the Alfár people."

"And if you fail, you'll all die. Together."

"That's right. For it to be precious, life has to end. If I live forever and do nothing, then what was the point?"

"You want to die?"

"No, I don't. For the first time in many years, I want to live. There's so much I can feel, now that I'm not a slave to the hunger." Odd was already thinking up a list of things he wanted to try if he ever made it home.

"Make no mistake, this is the end," said his mother.

"Then I'm at peace with that," said Odd.

From her glare it was obvious there was a lot more she wanted to say. Instead, his mother remained silent. Together, they stared out at the decaying remnants of the Alfár's world.

"What a miserable place," said his mother.

She grumbled some more but didn't disappear as she had done in the past. Despite her complaints, Odd was glad for the company. He'd lived alone for all of his adult life, but after being close to other people for months, he had grown used to it.

Part of him would always need a little solitude, but it gave him hope that, if he ever made it to the Five Kingdoms, then perhaps he could find someone with whom to share his life.

CHAPTER 29

The merchant train comprised of four wagons laden with barrels of spices and bolts of silk. Sat beside each driver was a mercenary, armed with a loaded crossbow. In addition, each carried a sword and was dressed in leather armour.

Sigrid was hiding in a copse of trees a short distance from the road, watching the wagons' slow progress, waiting for the inevitable. Darya was beside her on the ground, dozing in the sunshine. She was also supposed to be keeping watch, but it had been a long day, and nothing had happened. Sigrid let her sleep, knowing that she would be ready for a fight if it came to that.

As the first wagon came abreast of where she was hiding, Sigrid started to turn away. The thunder of hooves made her turn back as more than a dozen riders came up the road. The riders were dressed in an assortment of armour, and all of them were brandishing weapons. They circled the wagons, forcing the drivers to slow and then stop.

Sigrid nudged Darya in the ribs, and she came awake, wincing at the bright sunlight. She was about to complain, when Sigrid put a finger to her lips and jerked her head towards the road. The Choate sat up, scanned the road and immediately slipped away through the trees.

Some of the robbers had shields, and the rest were hiding behind their horses for protection from crossbows. The guards might be able kill four of them, but once fired, there wouldn't be enough time to reload before being overrun. No one wanted to take a bolt in the throat, and none of the guards had an itchy trigger finger.

It was a stalemate.

The leader of the robbers was trying to negotiate with the driver of the first wagon. Sigrid caught snatches of their conversation, but she could see from the tense postures that it wasn't going well.

Taking a deep breath, she stood up and casually walked out of the trees towards the road. At first, no one noticed her, as they were focused on getting ready to kill each other. Eventually one of the robbers spotted her sauntering along and, placing a finger between his teeth, he whistled. The high-pitched sound ended all conversation, and the combined attention of both groups turned its focus on her.

"What do you want, Choate?" asked the lead robber, a bald man with a nasty scar across one cheek.

"I want you to surrender."

Scarface stared at her for a moment and then began to laugh. His friends joined in and some of the tension eased. The caravan guards were still nervous, but their weapons never wavered.

"Girl, we outnumber you a dozen to one. Get out of here, before you start to annoy me," said Scarface.

"This is your only warning," said Sigrid.

"Kill her," said the robber, turning back to the caravan driver.

Raising one hand, Sigrid pointed a finger at the robber on the left, a gangly man with a long nose. He'd taken a couple of steps towards her but now he stopped, waiting for something to happen.

"What are–" was all he managed to say before an arrow went through his throat. As he choked to death, walking around like a headless chicken, the other robbers didn't panic. They all turned outwards, putting their horses' bodies between them and the new threat. Each robber looked towards Scarface, waiting for additional orders. They were far too calm and organised to be anything but professional soldiers.

Thirty Choate emerged from the surrounding area with a dozen archers among them. The robbers still had four crossbows pointed at their backs from the wagons. They were now severely outnumbered and trapped between two groups of enemies.

"You," said Sigrid, walking towards Scarface, "tell your people to put down their weapons and surrender. They won't be harmed."

"Why should I trust you?" he asked, nervously licking his lips. His eyes kept darting around, looking for a way out.

"You don't really have a choice."

They both knew it and yet he still hesitated.

"Do I need to make another example?" said Sigrid, raising a finger again. This time she pointed it at Scarface's chest. "Do as I say before you start to annoy me."

He was trapped with nowhere to go. With a sneer, he threw down his sword then ordered everyone else to follow suit. The Choate moved in and carefully checked them for additional weapons before tying them up. Once they were secure, Gar Brielle approached the leader of the caravan to discuss the situation.

"Next time, you can be the bait," said Sigrid as she approached Darya.

"That's fair. You've done it two days in a row."

As the two youngest warriors under Brielle's command, they took turns. Sigrid knew that she hadn't been in any real danger, but facing off against so many warriors by herself still made her nervous. They had been doing this for a few weeks, and so far, had captured five groups of soldiers. Despite being trapped, a sixth group had chosen to fight to the death, rather than surrender. It had been a slaughter.

Choate across the Five Kingdoms had been capturing and killing Hundarian soldiers for over a year. There was only so many times that the King of Hundar could declare them rebels who had been expelled from the army.

Sigrid had been hearing rumours that war was on the horizon. Now that she was no longer the Queen of Algany, she wasn't involved with conversations at that level. She only knew what Gar Brielle shared with her and the others. Part of her missed being involved, but much to her surprise, she also felt relief. Being responsible for an entire nation took a heavy toll. The only thing she was now responsible for was looking after her own weapons and armour. She could never again be queen of Algany but, with a bit of luck, one day she could become a mother again.

"It's happening," said Brielle, coming towards her and Darya. "We're going to war!"

The journey through the streets of Thune, Sigrid's home city, was the most nerve-wracking experience of her life. She wanted to scream and cry at the same time. She wanted to call out to people she recognised and ask after their families. She wanted to point out the changes to the city she'd noticed after being away for so long. But she kept her mouth shut and said nothing.

Sigrid, the Queen of Algany, was dead. She had murdered the former Reverend Mother, and while some were happy with what she had done to protect her country, many were disappointed and angry. She had been an aspirational figure, but in the end had turned out to be just like everyone else. That had always been the case, but some couldn't cope with the notion that their idols were flawed individuals.

When people in the street looked at Sigrid, there was no recognition in their eyes. They saw only the tattoos and that she was one of the Choate. It was a blessing, but Sigrid was also somewhat disappointed. She had not been erased from history and would only be remembered as a divisive character in Algany.

Darya leaned over in the saddle and briefly squeezed Sigrid's hand, knowing this was difficult for her. Keeping her jaw clenched stopped Sigrid from screaming, but it did nothing to prevent tears welling up. It was not the homecoming she had dreamed of, but regardless of the circumstances, it was good to be back in Algany.

For a long time, the Choate had been viewed with suspicion and even fear. Although the war between them and the Five Kingdoms was a distant memory, grudges had been passed down from one generation to the next. However, a change was slowly coming and attitudes were shifting.

In some ways, the climate of fear artificially created by the Reverend Mother and the King of Hundar had backfired. While the churches were seeing a surge in visitors, the standing of the Choate had also risen among the people. The church loudly denounced them as godless heathens, but for the most part, the priests were ignored. After all, it was the Choate who had been keeping the roads safe for nearly two years.

And so, the boy-King of Algany had asked for a representative from the Choate to visit the palace, in order for them to discuss going to war against the Holy City. Dos Mohan had sent one of his daughters, Gar Brielle. Sigrid's only official purpose for being here was to protect her leader. Unofficially, she was hoping for a chance to meet old friends and, hopefully, see her son. She had been waiting for this moment for almost two years. Excitement made her heart race, and she took deep breaths to settle her nerves.

At the palace gates they were asked to surrender their weapons and were then searched by the royal guards. Gar Brielle, Darya, Sigrid and Vashan, second in command, were permitted inside the palace. The rest of Brielle's dozen would wait in the palace grounds.

Once inside the building, Sigrid did her best not to react while Darya gawped at the size of the building. As she stared at the paintings of her ancestors on the walls, Sigrid felt a peculiar detachment from her bloodline.

The royal guards escorted them to a waiting room where they were met by two members of the Raven. They were carefully searched again for weapons, showing that the heightened sense of caution had not dissipated since Sigrid had last walked the halls. None of the Raven recognised her, for which she was grateful. Brielle even heaved a sigh of relief when they left the room. She quirked her eyebrows at Sigrid, but then her face settled back into its usual neutral expression.

A short time later, four members of the Raven escorted them to what had once been her negotiation room. They had expected this to be a formal meeting, taking place in the throne room with all appropriate pomp and ceremony. She and Brielle had discussed court decorum in great deal, with her briefing the Choate on what to expect. Neither of them had prepared for this sort of a meeting.

When they entered the negotiation room, Sigrid thought it looked smaller than she remembered. Waiting for them was Lukas, the King's Steward, Gar Malina, who had managed to hold on to her role as ambassador in Algany, and a swarthy woman from Seithland. She was dressed in a bright red shirt decorated with a dozen different coloured threads, indicating the wealth and history of her family. Already seated at the table was General Talleish, a severe man from Kinnan.

Another familiar figure stood off to one side, and Sigrid had to bite the inside of her mouth to stop herself from reacting. Natia had barely changed, but despite all that Sigrid had been through, the former Raven immediately recognised her. Most surprising was seeing Natia in a Raven uniform again. A smile tugged at the corners of Natia's mouth and then it was gone.

"Perhaps your guards would like a tour of the palace," suggested Lukas.

After Brielle had given them permission, Sigrid followed Darya and Natia out of the room. Malina briefly touched Sigrid's hand as she passed, but otherwise didn't react. Behind her, Sigrid heard Lukas introducing the woman from

Seithland as the King's personal advisor. The war council against the Holy City had gained a new ally from the west.

Natia led them down a short corridor to a different room, ushering them inside before closing the door. Sigrid barely saw the inside of the room before she was hugging Natia. Pent up sobs she'd been holding back burst from her mouth and, for a time, she cried without any sound. The older woman held her tightly until it faded, and Sigrid remembered they were not alone.

"Natia, this is my dear friend, Darya. If not for her, I wouldn't be here," said Sigrid, wiping at her eyes.

"A pleasure. Please, sit," said Natia. Four comfortable seats had been placed around the room and the walls were lined with bookshelves. A long time ago, she had used this room when she needed some privacy to read. At the back of the room, she spotted an assortment of toys scattered across the floor.

"He sometimes plays in here," said Natia, noticing where she was looking.

"You're back in uniform," said Sigrid.

"Lukas thought it was appropriate, given what will happen."

"What do you mean?" asked Darya.

"There will be some negotiation, but the outcome of the meeting will be the same. The army of Algany, with support from Seithland and the Choate living here in the south, will move on the Holy City to detain the Reverend Mother for her part in what has happened. The running total is nearly a thousand dead on the roads. If you want, the Seith can tell the cost in money down to the nearest apple."

"And the King of Hundar?" asked Sigrid.

"Forces from Kinnan and the Choate homeland will move on the Hundarian capital, Pynar, seeking the King's surrender. Once the Holy City is secure, we will march north, splitting the Hundarian forces in two, creating a war on two fronts."

"It sounds simple enough," said Darya.

Natia grunted. "Sadly, it won't be that easy. Kinnan is awash with hundreds of missionaries. Supposedly, they are there to bring the glory of the Shepherd to the people. In reality, it's a second army spread out across the countryside. Enough about that, tell me about you?" she said, turning to Sigrid.

She started telling Natia everything, from the moment she'd been arrested, but then had to start over when Malina came into the room. After shedding more tears, Sigrid told them the whole story. Natia touched the tattoos on her cheek and shook her head.

"I knew it was you, but still, you look so different. And it's not just these," said Natia tracing the design with one finger.

"Can I see him?" asked Sigrid.

Natia and Malina exchanged a look before the Raven nodded slowly.

"He can't know it's you. Not yet," she said.

Sigrid understood. The political situation was delicate enough without revealing that she was alive. The new alliance could crumble if the truth leaked out, and the ramifications would be far-reaching.

"Come. I'll take you," said Natia. "It can be part of the tour."

Sigrid feigned interest as Natia led her and Darya on a tour of the palace and its grounds. More interesting were the changes she noticed, such as heightened security in the building. Some were obvious, such as an increased number of palace guards patrolling the corridors, and others more subtle. They passed through three open doorways, but the beautifully crafted iron doors had heavy locks. They looked delicate, but she was confident they would be difficult to breach once secured.

Now that she was dead, and Kell had been declared dead after being missing for so many years, every precaution was being taken to protect their son. It gave her some comfort to know that he was safe, but it also saddened her that it had ever been necessary. No child, no matter their station, should grow up in a prison. The palace resembled one, with its barred doorways and armed guards in every corridor.

"He's just around the corner," said Natia, pausing at the next door. "You must be quiet," she warned.

Sigrid nodded, unable to speak past the lump in her throat.

On the other side of the door was the largest walled garden inside the palace. It was the main herb and vegetable garden used by the kitchens. A narrow winding path circled an area which was awash with a sea of leafy green plants and fruit trees. Benches sat beneath the largest trees, where she had often read in the shade.

Natia led them down the path and then paused at the first bend. A short distance ahead, Marik was sat on a bench beside one of his tutors. Today it was Tesha, a mature man who had worked in the kitchens for years before retiring. The gardeners knew their jobs well, but even they listened to Tesha when it came to growing fruit and vegetables.

"Now, watch closely," Tesha was saying. He had a dried-out flower head in his hands, which he shook onto a cloth on his lap. Dozens of tiny black seeds spilled out. "Fetch me one of those pots, there's a good lad."

Marik obliged, bringing over a small clay pot filled with earth. They made a small depression in the soil, dropped in a few seeds and then covered it up. After watering the pot, they set it in the sunlight. Marik stared at the garden with such innocent joy, Sigrid felt tears running down her cheeks. She desperately wanted to run over and pick him up. To smell his hair, hold him tight against her chest and never let go.

"He's grown so much," said Sigrid, surprised at how hoarse she sounded. Darya rested a hand on her shoulder and gave it a squeeze. Sigrid was so grateful that Darya had made the journey with her to Algany.

Marik's dark hair was getting long and would soon need a

cut. It was starting to make him itch and he kept blowing it out of his eyes. Natia smiled at him like a proud aunt. Sigrid was beyond thankful that she had been with her son since the beginning. At least there had been a few constants in his life. Theirs was an unusual family and, in some ways, it had been from the start, but at least Marik had never been alone.

"How much does he know?" asked Sigrid.

"Only that his father went on a long journey and never came home," said Natia.

"What about me?"

"He knows the truth about your sacrifice," said the Raven. "But we also had to tell him that you died at the hands of bad people. We told him that you were a hero of Algany."

"There must be less favourable rumours," said Sigrid.

Natia sighed. "We do our best to shield him, but he's probably heard some gossip in the palace."

The past couldn't be erased. Dwelling on what could have been, or what she should have done differently, wouldn't change anything. But the future was yet to be written and, while Sigrid was no longer a queen, she was determined to play a part in what was to come.

"I'm going to the Holy City and I'm going to drag the Reverend Mother off her pedestal. Then everyone will know who she really is and what she's done."

"We'll do it together," said Darya.

"And then?" asked Natia.

"Then I will come home to my son and try to build a new life."

"You could stay here, where it's safe," said Natia. "It would be easy to add a new face to the Choate ambassador's staff. Once the war is over, we'll find a way to unpick the rest."

"I can't," said Sigrid.

"Why? Because of your pride? Your thirst for revenge? The boy needs his mother."

"He does, but this is about more than me," said Sigrid. "And as much as it pains me to say, it's about more than just him too. If I don't do this, I will never be able to rest."

"You might die in battle."

"I won't."

"You don't know that," said Natia.

"Then if I do, Marik will be no worse off and you can keep telling him that I died a hero. Natia, I can't sit idly by and do nothing, while others fight on my behalf. This is my fight as much as theirs. I will see it through to the end."

"I will keep her safe," said Darya.

"We all will," said Gar Brielle, coming into the garden. Behind her were Malina and Lukas.

Sigrid cast one final look at her son, trying to fix the image of him in her mind, and then turned away. Swallowing her tears, she readied herself for war.

CHAPTER 30

The following morning when Kell woke up, Willow had already left their tent. He emerged to find her standing over the corpse of Ravvi. His eyes were closed and she had folded his hands together on his chest. In some ways, Kell wasn't surprised. Ravvi had been courting death for such a long time, Kell was amazed he'd managed to hold on until now. It was admirable that he'd journeyed this far north by himself, and been able to hold on to a shred of his sanity.

The ground was too hard to bury him, but they didn't want to leave him uncovered. The stone shards were incredibly sharp, but they proved no match for Willow's mace, which shattered them like glass. When they had enough pieces, they erected a small cairn over the body. It wasn't much, but it was all they had. Willow said no prayers for her kinsman, but once they'd finished, she sat for a while in quiet contemplation. Kell sat with her, and his thoughts inevitably turned bleak. He'd been carrying a tiny glimmer of hope for a reunion with his family, but it had winked out. Only now did he realise how lucky he'd been, and how much he'd lost. Never again would see his wife or hold his son, Marik.

Struggling against a growing sense of despair, which wasn't from the Malice, Kell led Willow out of the stone forest onto a featureless plain. It was almost perfectly flat, but in the distance beyond the horizon, was a massive white cliff.

Willow started talking and didn't stop all morning. Her

clarity faded and she rambled on about many different topics. Kell mostly tuned her out, but when she started talking about this place, he listened intently. Somewhere in the depths of her mind was a story about one of her ancestors. He had come this far north, hoping to be the first to map the entire continent. The tales of his adventures had been passed down to her as a child, but over the years she'd forgotten them, burying the memories deep in her mind.

Beyond the plain was something she called the chimney, and after that, at the end of the world, the Crown. Apparently, it was a vast sloping crater that could only be accessed via the chimney, the only break in the sheer cliff. In the Crown, they would find the source of the poison.

In the afternoon, they reached the base of the cliff and Kell peered towards the top. At first glance, the surface resembled pale rock, but up close it was slightly yellow from age. Even in the sun it was cool to the touch and had a slightly grainy feel.

"His family told him not to go, but he wouldn't listen. He was a rebel," said Willow. She was talking about her ancestor again. "Perhaps that's where it comes from. My restless spirit. Others seem content to wait for the inevitable, but I cannot."

Staring up the chimney, Kell was amazed at the smoothness of the walls. There were no cracks, hand or footholds, and when he tapped it with the point of his sword it didn't chip or flake. As he was pondering how to get to the top, Willow came to stand beside him. After strapping her weapon to her back, she approached the chimney.

"What are you doing?" asked Kell.

Spreading out her arms and legs wide, like a spider, Willow began to skirt up the chimney. Moving slowly at first, she built up speed and quickly scaled the chute before disappearing over the top.

"Well, that was unexpected," said Kell.

Willow's face appeared over the top. "You need to see this. Get up here."

"Easy for you to say," he muttered, sheathing his sword. Part of him was tempted to leave the armour behind, but in such a dangerous place he couldn't risk it.

"What are you waiting for?" asked Willow.

Grumbling to himself, Kell tried to imitate what the Alfár had done but, with his entire bodyweight focused on his fingers and toes, he couldn't support himself. Approaching it sideways on, Kell pressed his back against one side and his feet against the other. When he felt comfortable with the position, he slowly began to shuffle up the chimney. Progress was much slower than Willow and he paused often to rest, but felt in no danger of falling. Much to Kell's relief, his boots didn't slip on the surface, and he slowly inched towards the top.

"Here," said Willow, offering a hand when he was nearly there. With considerable ease she lifted Kell over the lip. For a brief moment he was dangling over the edge, and when he peered down, his stomach flipped over. As Willow lowered him onto solid ground, Kell heaved a sigh of relief.

They were standing on the edge of an almost perfectly round crater that had gentle sloping sides. In the centre was a gaping hole that yawned with menace. Without being told, Kell knew they would have to go down there.

The ground was made of the same muted yellow stone and spread out across it was a huge network of what resembled black vines and twitching tree roots. And all of them originated from the hole in the centre.

It was the source of the Malice.

The logical part of Kell's mind told him the disease wasn't alive, not in the same way as animals and people, with independent thoughts, but the rest of him wasn't convinced. The sprawling threads left greasy black residue in their wake. As he watched, they pulsed and stretched a little further towards the edge of the Crown.

Willow had another lucid moment as she glared with hatred

at the poisoned vines. It was the source of so much misery in her world.

"We must try to destroy it," she insisted. "No matter the cost."

The Alfár's mind wandered again and she stared into the distance, lost in thought. Sheer force of will had brought her back and he could see the struggle on her face to stay in control.

"We need to..." was all Willow said before she drifted off.

Kell was being emotionally battered at the same time, and his head began to pound as he was pulled one way and then the other. A surge of euphoria made him want to shout with joy, but with the next heartbeat, he was ready to throw himself off the cliff from the misery rising up.

His chest ached for his family – he would never see them again. His stomach churned and the hairs on the back of his neck prickled – he was terrified of what lay before them. His instincts told him to run away as fast as he could – his legs refused to move. Kell went into a fugue and his awareness of the entire world faded.

At some point, Kell came back and realised he was kneeling on the ground, laughing hysterically. Biting the inside of his mouth chased away the unnatural emotions. With blood on his teeth, while the wild laughter bubbled up again, he managed to stand.

A short distance away his pack and sword lay where he'd dropped them without realising. Willow was aimlessly wandering about the Crown, talking to herself. Kell's face was wet with tears and the muscles in his legs ached as if he'd been sprinting. He had no idea how much time had passed. If he didn't do something soon, he might become overwhelmed again, and there was no way to know how long the next episode would last. He could end up like Ravvi, permanently lost in thought with only brief moments of clarity.

Focusing on the pain in his mouth, Kell picked up his sword and dragged Willow towards the centre of the Crown. He had no idea if there would be anything to fight down there, but he felt naked without a weapon. The closer they moved to the centre, the more difficult it became to avoid stepping on the black threads. Eventually Kell had to risk it, or else cut a swathe through the tangle.

His feet sank a little into the surface of the roots, leaving an oily residue on his boots. Thankfully it did nothing in response to their presence, which gave him hope that it was more a plant than something with a conscious mind.

When his foot slipped on a wide appendage, Willow grabbed him by the arm, keeping him upright.

"I'm here," she said. For the time being, her eyes were clear. "Lead on."

They slipped and shuffled towards the middle and finally made it to the mouth of the chasm. Inside it was pitch black with a strong cloying smell, which he associated with rot, wafting up.

"Do it," said Kell, biting his mouth again to stay focused. "Use Govhenna's blood."

Willow shook her head. "We have to go down there," she said, confirming his fear.

With no ropes, they had to hold onto the black roots. Willow went first, swinging her legs over the chasm and then shimmying down. Kell watched closely, but she quickly disappeared from view. There was no way to know how deep it went.

"Kell, come down," said Willow. Her voice was slightly muffled but she didn't sound too far away. "There's light down here."

Although the surface was slimy, Kell could squeeze the vines tight enough to support his weight. Gritting his teeth against the stench and the rising heat, he swung his legs into the hole and tried to control his descent. Almost immediately, his hands began to slide, so he locked his legs around it as well. Hanging in mid-air, he felt himself slip a little and knew that if he didn't move, he would begin to fall. Moving faster than was probably safe, he shimmied down, hand over hand.

The small window of light above his head contracted. The deeper he went, the thicker the vines became. They pressed against him on all sides, coating his clothes and then his skin with greasy residue.

The light faded and then he was in the dark. The roots bunched together above his head and soon it made no difference if his eyes were open or closed. Trusting that Willow wouldn't steer him wrong, he kept going and was surprised when his feet struck the ground.

He fell over and sat there, letting his eyes adjust to the light that was now available. They were sat together in a kind of a room, but the walls were made of the same black, living tissue. This close to the source, the roots stretched and contracted like a muscle, and when Kell touched one, he felt a pulse. Dotted around on the walls were small yellow growths, like the early buds of a flower. Each gave off a faint yellow light, which was the only reason he could see. Even so, the shadows were heavy and he didn't want to know what was lurking in the corners.

"Why are we here, Juanne?" asked Willow. Her pale yellow eyes seemed to glow and the shadows gave her face a menacing quality.

Powerful emotions began to surge through Kell in time with his heartbeat, which had synced with the throbbing in the walls. It was taking over. Willow began to talk to herself again, mixing up memories of the past and present. She talked about events in the Five Kingdoms that had happened long before he was born. Sometimes he was Juanne. Other times she called him by different names he didn't recognise.

Taking a deep breath, Kell tried to stay in control of his emotions. He felt there was something just beneath his skin that was trying to break through. Something had burrowed deep inside his body that desperately wanted out. He needed a release. Before he could change his mind, Kell jabbed his dagger into the meat of his leg. The white agony blotted out everything. All thoughts and emotions were washed away.

Ignoring Willow for the time being, he explored their surroundings. The floor was made of a peculiar spongey material that was slightly porous but solid. The pulsing walls had some give, and when he leaned against one section, it bent outwards but didn't break. Taking the dagger from his leg Kell jabbed it into the wall. Expecting a scream or another complaint, he was surprised when nothing happened. The material was slightly rubbery, but with a bit of sawing, he ripped a hole in the black curtain.

Beyond was another space filled with fat, writhing tentacles, like a nest of snakes piled on top of one another. Some were wider than his body and these were stationary. Others were crawling, exploring and filling up the area. There was just enough room for him to squeeze through from one section to the other. The air was humid, and beneath his clothes he began to sweat. The smell was overpowering and breathing through his nose made little difference.

"Where are you, Kell?" shouted Willow.

Kell retrieved Willow from where he'd left her and pulled her through. Together they began to explore. It was like being in another maze. The places where the roots had piled up into thick knots created a solid wall with no way through. They were forced to backtrack and try and find a way around.

This far into the heart, the yellow spores were more frequent providing them with plenty of light. The wound in Kell's leg was throbbing and he focused on that, not the emotions flooding his mind. When it was necessary, he hammered a fist against the injury, breaking the skin, making it bleed again.

Willow gripped his hand, and when she began to drift off, or started talking to herself, he squeezed it as tight as he could. Sometimes the pain brought her back. Other times, she remained locked in the past, talking to ghosts.

Kell had no idea how much time they'd spent roaming about in the gloom. At one point, despite the pain, he had to stop and laugh. His sides ached and he was bent over double, laughing at nothing, when Willow tapped him on the shoulder.

"Are you alright?" she asked.

"I can't keep this up for long."

"I think we're close. Look," she said, pointing at something behind him.

It resembled an oval doorframe. The black sprawling vines had swarmed around and through it, but somehow it remained in one piece. It was made of the same white stone as the Crown, but long-term exposure to the black slime had stained it an unpleasant grey.

"Time to find out if it's really alive," said Kell, drawing his sword.

Willow hefted her axe and together they began to attack the thick black vines creeping through the doorway. Kell's sword barely made a dent and the Alfár's axe left only a small mark on the surface. A faint trickle of black ichor dripped from the wound like a small cut.

"It's as tough as old tree roots," said Kell.

"This close to the source, these must be the oldest parts of the infection."

Kell was already sweating from the heat. Swinging a sword made it ten times worse. At first, they only managed to chip away small bits of the black roots, but once they'd broken through the hard shell, it was more compliant underneath.

After a while, both of them were covered with black ichor and the stink of decay was horrific. Thankfully, the severed parts of the vines remained inert and didn't crawl about. Even so, that didn't stop Kell from being nervous about them. Several times he turned around to check they weren't moving when his back was turned. The Malice was feeding his paranoia.

After chopping and sawing at the roots for what felt like hours, there was enough space for them to squeeze through. Beyond the doorframe was a peculiar domed space. It was twenty paces across and all around the edge were other doorways like the one they'd hacked their way through. Suspended in the centre of the room, at head height, was a roughly spherical, large black growth. It was from there that all of the roots originated.

It was the source of the Malice.

The surface was mottled with black and grey veins, and it had dozens of the yellow growths. Unlike the rest of the disease, the core was convulsing like a massive heart.

Willow stared at it in horror. Her eyes were unfocused but Kell could see that she was still in the present.

"What is it?" asked Kell.

"I don't know," said Willow. "No one knows where it came from."

Willow retrieved the glass vial from inside her armour where she'd kept it safe. Govhenna's blood shone in the dim light.

Taking out a knife, she stabbed the heart over and over, until the wound was large enough for her fist. The blood that emerged from it was black and viscous.

"Uh, the smell," said Kell. It already smelled putrid, but this had released something much worse. It felt as if it were burning the inside of his nose. It stank so badly Kell started to cough and then retch.

"Are you all right?" asked the Alfár.

"Just do it," he gasped, waving her forward. They needed to get out before he choked to death.

Wincing at the smell, Willow pulled out the cork from the vial with her teeth. In one swift movement she shoved her hand inside the heart. The gaping wound closed about her hand then drew her forward, until her whole arm was submerged up to her shoulder.

"It burns," she hissed, gritting her teeth against the pain.

Kell saw the muscles strain in her neck and arms as she tried to get free. Kell used his weight, and working together they slowly extracted Willow's arm from the heart. It burst out with a loud pop and they fell backgrounds to the ground.

The skin on Willow's arm was red from where it had been burned. It had only been exposed to the heart for a short time, and yet the damage was severe. Much longer and it could have melted the flesh from her arm.

Kell stared at the heart of the Malice, expecting a reaction, but it continued to pulse as normal.

"So, now what happens?" he asked.

"We wait and hope that this works," said Willow. "We've done all we can for my people. It's time to go home."

CHAPTER 31

Yarra collapsed with her back against the wall as the enemy withdrew. She sat with her head between her knees, trying to slow her breathing, while she waited for the black spots to clear.

"Yarra?" someone said.

"I'm fine. Just give me a moment," she said without raising her head. Slowly the world swung back into focus, the black dancing motes faded and eventually disappeared. The pounding in her temples started to recede, and gradually she came back to herself.

Today had been a close call. Several times their defences had crumbled, and they'd teetered on the edge of defeat. If it hadn't been for some heroic interventions, which had cost precious lives, it would have been over.

The horde was no less ferocious in their attacks, but the defenders were worn down and many were on the verge of collapse. Yarra had never fought alongside soldiers as tough as the Alfár. Their strength and endurance far surpassed the limit of any human, but even they had a breaking point.

The Alfár's numbers had also dwindled so much that every death was significant. The advantage of higher ground was only useful if they had enough people to cover the length of the wall. Every time someone was taken off, due to injury or death, it became harder to manage. They had reached their limit.

Yarra rested the back of her head against the wall, but kept her eyes closed. For a little while, she wasn't needed by anyone. She didn't have anything to do except sit and rest.

"Any sign of Kell?" said Odd, off to her left.

"Nothing," said Bewligg.

It had been six or seven days since Kell gone over the wall with Willow. No, it was six. Six days. Despite Yarra's best efforts, she was starting to lose track. If they had successfully made it past the enemy, which some doubted, no one knew what fresh horrors awaited them. Kell and Willow could be lying dead in a ditch, or they could already have been eaten by the ravenous horde. Just thinking it felt treasonous, but at times the darkness inside won. And it wasn't just the voices that told Yarra they were dead. It had become second nature to blot them out. A part of her truly believed it was already over.

"Come on," said Odd, resting a hand on her shoulder. "Let's get you something to eat."

She nodded and accepted his hand up. Odd leaned back, using his full body weight to lift her. Previously he would have done it with just one arm. Ever since he'd appeared at the Choke, he'd been a different man. For one thing, he smiled. That was probably the most peculiar and obvious change.

In Algany, he'd practically been a mute and had rarely shown emotion. Now, he smiled, laughed and made attempts at humour which were, occasionally, amusing. It was even more surprising when Odd actually made an effort to lighten the mood. Despite the dire circumstances, it was as if a great weight had been lifted off his shoulders. Odd pretended that nothing had changed, but it was obvious to her that it had.

She'd casually asked him about it a couple of times, but he'd been vague with his answers. Whatever had happened in the past didn't really matter, because she needed him. His mind was clear, he was a skilled soldier and he could rationally command others in the heat of battle.

"How many did we lose?" she asked.

"We can discuss it later," said Odd.

"No," she said, pushing past him. Not far away Bewligg was knelt down beside an Alfár on the wall. She was covered in blood and black ichor. Her mottled skin was unusually pale. The warrior was sat in a growing pool of rich blue blood, but Yarra couldn't see the wound.

Bewligg held the Alfár's hand and was talking softly in their native language. Her eyes were open and she was blinking very slowly. One of her eyes looked human, with a green iris on a white sclera. The infection was deep in her body to have made such a drastic change. Yarra watched as the Alfár's breathing slowed, slowed and then stopped. At least she hadn't died alone. These days, that was all any of them could wish for.

"There's nothing you can do," said Odd. "Come away."

At the moment, the dead were being walled up inside the deepest cavern. Part of her was afraid that when they were overrun, the horde would dig them up in search of food.

The Alfár were getting worse every day, and even some of her most stalwart veterans were starting to have bouts of forgetfulness. Without a miracle, none of them were going to survive for much longer. If Kell and Willow were still alive, it was up to them to deliver.

Yarra and Odd sat with the others in contemplative silence as they ate. Her mind sought out fresh ideas to defend the Choke. Some trick that would give them an advantage and buy a little more time. Perhaps there was something in the stores she could use. The horde didn't seem susceptible to heat or cold, but unlike the Alfár, they had poor night vision. It was the only explanation she'd been able to come up with to explain why they hadn't attacked in the dark. Perhaps there was a way for her to use that against them.

The Alfár were relying on her to keep them alive. The situation was desperate, but it had been like that before they had arrived. Putting that aside was difficult, but she tried to look at it logically. There had to be something.

When Odd left the room to stretch his legs, she didn't react. She knew exactly where he was going. It was the same place he went every night before going to sleep.

Back to the top of the wall, where he'd talk to the ghost of his dead mother.

CHAPTER 32

"We need to buy them more time," said Odd.

"If they're even still alive," said his mother, keeping pace with him on the stairs.

The few Alfár on patrol were so used to his presence they showed no surprise when he reached the top of the wall. Leaning on the battlements, he peered down at the ground below. There was still enough light in the sky to see a few scattered limbs and severed heads at the base. It was all that remained of the dead. Everything else had already been dragged away for food.

"I have to believe they are, otherwise, what is all of this for?" asked Odd, gesturing at his surroundings. "It's the best chance they have. Without Kell and Willow, without some hope, they're already dead."

"You've given enough," said his mother. "You don't have to do this."

"I've spent a great deal of time thinking about the past."

"It wasn't your fault," she said. "You were trying to survive, in the only way that you knew."

"True," said Odd, "but I still took a great deal from others."

"You didn't have a choice."

Odd knew that was a lie, but he didn't want to argue.

"I've been trying to work out how many people I hunted over the years, but I can't remember. I don't even remember all of their faces."

"So what? Neither do I."

"Did you ever dream about them?" he asked.

Odd's mother stared off into the distance, far beyond the wall. She was silent for a long time before speaking. "Sometimes, late at night, I would see their faces. In the dream, they would gather around my bed. Row upon row of people, stretching into the distance. They'd start pawing at me and then rip off my clothes, my flesh. Tear me apart, drink my blood and gobble me up."

"Mine just stare at me," admitted Odd.

"One used to haunt me when I was awake," said his mother.

"What?"

She shook her head. "A long time ago, before you were born, I killed a boy. He must have been twelve or thirteen. At the time I was only a few years older, but we were friends. We went somewhere quiet together and he never came back. For years, I'd see him, standing in the shadows. He never said anything. He just stared at me."

"This is something that only I can do," said Odd. "The others will die without me."

"You know that this won't make up for it," she said. "It won't even the scales."

"I know," he admitted, "but it's a start."

He found Yarra standing in front of the gate with Bewligg, staring at the massive pile of boulders and rocks.

"We can't risk it," the Alfár was saying. "If you take them away, the horde could breach the gate."

"They don't have any kind of a ram," she argued. "They might not get through."

"Might?"

"Just think of the damage we could do," said Yarra. "Will you at least speak with the others about it?"

"I will," said the veteran, leaving them to talk alone.

"I'm just trying to buy us some more time," she explained.

"I know," said Odd.

"Did you need something?"

"I wanted to offer you another choice."

"I don't understand," said Yarra.

"I can buy you some extra time. To give Kell and Willow a chance," said Odd. Yarra stared at him in confusion, but there was also a sense of knowing in her eyes. She didn't fully understand but, more than once on the journey, she'd seen what he could do and hadn't been able to explain it. His speed. His strength. How he'd survived against the Yogren.

At this point, Odd would have told her everything, but to her credit Yarra didn't ask. Instead, she took a moment to process what he was saying. There was still a little light in the sky and a gentle wind blew away the stench of death and drying blood.

"How much time?" she asked.

"Enough," he conceded, gesturing for her to go ahead of him up the stairs.

Together they climbed to the top of the wall. It was peculiar, that they were both called back to this place. All day they fought for survival in a charnel house of horrors, surrounded by vicious monsters. And yet when the battle was done, both of them would walk the wall. It provided a peculiar form of solace.

"What will it cost?" asked Yarra.

"Everything. I won't be coming back," said Odd. "Not this time."

"I understand."

"It's your decision. Or, if the others agree, we could haul up the boulders and try that instead."

He knew what she was thinking. She could try it his way, and if it worked, then it gave her what she needed. But if it didn't, she still had another option. His choice would only cost her one life, and there was little risk to the others. The alternative weakened the gate and, potentially, put everyone at greater risk.

It was cold and calculated, but as a leader her goal was to protect as many lives as possible for as long as she could.

"I'm sorry," said Yarra, resting a hand on his shoulder.

"For what?"

"For being so standoffish with you in Algany. For listening to rumours and letting other people put me off."

"It's in the past. It doesn't matter," said Odd.

"It does matter," she insisted. "Because now is the only time we have."

They stood together in silence for a long time, watching the unfamiliar sun slowly crawl down towards the horizon. Odd wondered if the Alfár had a name for it, or the fractured moon.

"Can you imagine what this place was like before the Malice?" she asked. "I've been having vivid dreams about walking through the city of Laruk like a ghost. Thousands of Alfár are just going about their lives around me. It was amazing."

"I wonder if it will ever be like that again," said Odd.

"I hope so. I have to believe that it will," said Yarra.

"Me too."

The sun dipped behind the horizon and night quickly fell. Torches were lit along the wall and a small portion of the darkness was driven back once more.

"Do it," said Yarra.

Odd wasn't angry. He didn't blame her for making the decision. It was the logical thing to do. Given the circumstances, it was also the only real choice.

"I'll need your help talking to the others," he said. Odd knew they wouldn't like it and wouldn't understand, but they'd accept it, because the alternative was worse. And all that it would cost them, was the life of someone they barely knew.

It took some time to arrange, and a lot of fast talking from Yarra to explain what she wanted. Their first reaction from the veterans was one that Odd had expected; horror, revulsion and shock. Eventually, they agreed to her terms.

Bewligg and the others stared at Odd with a mix of fear and apprehension. They were noticing him for the first time. They'd also realised there was something more beneath his placid façade. The veterans whispered in their native tongue, and even though he couldn't understand, Odd knew what they were saying. They were afraid and sickened that it had come to this. But they were desperate people and, in dire circumstances, the line they were unwilling to cross had moved.

The corridors in the area were cleared of all people and a path was left open with no obstructions to the stairs. Temporary barricades needed to be created, to block off the side passageways, so that there was only one way out. Odd had no way to know what frame of mind he would be in afterwards. He wasn't even sure if he would be self-aware. It was better that every precaution was taken.

At first, some of the Alfár were reluctant to help, but even though they had not been told the full story, they realised something was very wrong. Even those with addled minds picked up on the mood of the others. Thereafter, everyone did as they were told in a sombre silence.

Those Alfár who would eventually recover from their injuries walked, or were carried, to a new temporary hospital. Odd stayed away from the preparations as much as possible, but word travelled fast as he saw several Alfár looking at him with suspicion and fear. It was possible rumours had sprouted up, but deep down he knew the truth. They weren't staring because of anything they'd been told. It was because of what they felt.

Yarra, for all of her abilities, was a normal human. Odd was not. His true nature was reasserting itself, and while the Alfár didn't understand, they could feel it. At times, Willow had been suspicious and wary. She'd sensed that something was amiss.

"Ignore them," said his mother. "They're ignorant."

"They're afraid of me," said Odd. "And they should be."

With some reluctance, Yarra approached him once the preparations were complete. He'd told her the basics and, admirably, she was doing her best to hide her revulsion. She had made the decision, and now she would have to live with the consequences.

"They're ready," she said, swallowing hard. "Odd, I just wanted to..." Yarra trailed off, unable or unwilling to offer thanks for what he was about to do.

Before she could say anything else, he passed across his sword. He'd already stripped out of his armour. Dawn was near, and despite the chill in the air, he had taken off his boots as well. Wielding only a small dagger, Odd gave her one last smile and then set off down the hallway. Following the twisting path, he descended to a part of the caves he'd not explored before.

The hospital was quiet. The air, unusually still and heavy. This deep underground light came from torches set at intervals down both sides of the room. Normally they were muted, because the Alfár had sensitive eyesight, but today they had been uncovered, providing him with a clear view of the room. The hospital had a row of beds on either side of a central aisle. There was enough room for at least a hundred, if not more. Today, only a dozen beds were occupied.

As Odd stood on the threshold, the ragged sound of breathing reached his ears. Some of the injured Alfár were wheezing because of their damaged lungs, but some of it was due to fear. The twelve here had wounds that were so severe they would not recover. Time and again, Odd had seen first-hand that the Alfár were a tough and enduring race, but they were not immortal.

For those who remained in the hospital, death was close. They had not been told what was about to happen. Perhaps they thought he was the final spectre, come to collect at last.

Odd sat down at the bedside of the first Alfár. He was missing his left hand, his left leg ended at the knee, and there was severe damage to his torso. The bandages wrapped around his ribs were already soaked through with fresh blood. Odd had seen it happen on the wall. One of the horde had shredded the Alfár with razor sharp claws. Amazingly, the warrior's face was untouched by damage, but it was still ravaged by the brutalities of the Malice. One eye was white with a blue iris and the other was yellow on black.

"Is this the end?" wheezed the Alfár. His breath rattled in his throat. He was delirious with pain. Odd had no idea what the Alfár was seeing, but he seemed to have accepted that Odd was a harbinger.

"It is," said Odd, giving the warrior some time to mentally prepare.

The hunger did not cry out. It did not demand that he feed it, and yet it was still there, deep inside. Denying it didn't change the truth. It was an intrinsic part of him, as much as his heart or his hands. He could never get rid of it.

Odd didn't have to use the dagger or wait very long. He felt the moment approaching. The silence in the room swelled and became heavy, so very heavy. A prickle ran down the back of Odd's neck, telling him they were not alone. From his eye corner, his mother sat down on the empty bed beside him. Tears ran from her eyes, sobs hitched in her throat and she wept.

The warrior's eyes grew wider and he stared at something in the distance.

"I love you," said his mother.

"I know," said Odd.

Leaning over the dying warrior, Odd took a deep breath and then placed his mouth over the Alfár's. As the light faded from the dying man's eyes Odd inhaled deeply, taking energy into himself. It coursed down his throat, into his stomach and then exploded throughout his body. His fingers and toes tingled. His hair stood up and his eyesight sharpened, driving away the lingering shadows. Every part of his body came alive like never before.

His senses were amplified ten, twenty, a hundred times. On and on it went, flowing into him, breathing new life into his once normal body. His fear and worry evaporated. Lingering doubts vanished and Odd understood his purpose like never before. He knew what he was.

And then it was over.

He leaned back from the dead Alfár, closed the warrior's eyes and took a moment to adjust. This time there was no pain or discomfort. Only the glorious bliss of what had been taken.

His mother continued to weep. Her tears splashed against the floor as he stood up from the bed.

One down. Eleven more to go.

CHAPTER 33

The gap-toothed missionary leered at Sigrid, so she smashed the pommel of her sword into his face, breaking his nose. It did little to improve his looks, but the splash of blood made a pretty pattern across his white robe. As he started to snarl, she side-stepped a clumsy attack and thrust the point of her sword into his stomach.

He started to choke and splutter as blood ran from the corners of his mouth. With a sharp twist she ripped her blade to one side, slicing through his guts. Putting a foot against his hip, Sigrid yanked her blade free and moved on.

The Choate were cutting through the missionaries like a scythe through a field of dry wheat. The zealot army had the numbers, made up from people across the Five Kingdoms and the lands beyond Corvan, but they had no skill. They were rabid and righteous, and the soldiers of Algany and the Choate warriors were experienced fighters. Nevertheless, Sigrid was aware of her own limits. A year of practise didn't put her on par with them, many of whom were keeping a close eye on her.

When three zealots came towards her, Darya stepped up beside her on the left and Gar Brielle on the right. Facing three Choate warriors gave the missionaries pause, but belief drove them forward. With two quick movements, Brielle had sliced her opponent apart, opening up his chest and throat. Darya severed her opponent's arm then stabbed her dagger into the woman's head.

The last missionary came on, undeterred by the death of her compatriots. She was clumsy but strong, using brute strength to drive Sigrid back with a barrage of heavy blows. Sigrid gave ground, letting the woman tire herself out, then when an opening came she parried and stabbed the woman in her throat. Her head rocked back and she stared at the sky, puzzled by what had happened. The zealot dropped to her knees, said something through a mouthful of blood and collapsed onto her face.

There was a brief lull in the battle, giving Sigrid a chance to catch her breath and study her surroundings. Even though the two armies were fighting together against the missionaries, they stayed apart from one another on the battlefield. The Alganese army was guided by its generals, and the Choate by its war leaders. It felt peculiar, to be fighting among the Choate and not with the soldiers from Algany. But when her countrymen looked at Sigrid, they didn't see one of their own. They only saw the tattoos. It still hurt, but not as much as before. Perhaps in time, she would get used to it. There was no going back to her old life or who she used to be. She could only move forward and hope to build something new.

Reverend Mother Reyna had been efficient in controlling the minds of her followers. Their belief was absolute. The Choate were tattooed heathens, and the people of Algany needed saving from themselves, after being led astray. It was that simple. But the missionaries were being cut down, their units killed or routed.

Someone in their ranks obviously had some knowledge of warfare, as they had attempted to flank the invading army. But the heavily armoured Alganese cavalry came thundering in from the east, smashing into rank upon rank of missionaries who wore no armour and carried no lances or pikes. Apparently, the only defence they needed was their shield of righteousness.

Most often, the final expression Sigrid saw on the faces of dying missionaries was one of surprise. They couldn't understand why they had failed when their cause was the right one. Groups of missionaries would fight to the last man or woman, rather than surrender, never questioning the lies they'd been told. Their destiny was to bring the glory of the Shepherd to the Five Kingdoms. In their final moments, Sigrid wondered how many of them realised the truth.

"They're retreating," said Gar Brielle, wiping her sword clean on her latest victim. The missionary wasn't quite dead. One of his arms flapped about, searching for something. Solace. Forgiveness. Companionship. Anything, so that he didn't die alone.

Sigrid stared at him without mercy. She wondered when that had changed as well. Forgiveness and compassion used to come easily. When she came face to face with her son, would he even recognise her?

The zealots began to flee, first in small groups and then all of them dropped their weapons and ran for their lives. The panic spread and the broken remains of the righteous army fled back the way they'd come.

"Are we not going to follow them?" asked Sigrid.

"We will," said Brielle, "but first we must take care of the wounded."

Sigrid was so eager for revenge, she'd forgotten about everyone else. It had been a long time since she'd been in charge of others. She'd grown comfortable with having no responsibilities.

A light drizzle began to fall across the battlefield. She couldn't remember the last time she'd been this far east in Algany. At a slow march, it would take the combined armies less than a day to reach the Holy City. Then she would get vengeance on Reverend Mother Reyna and her puppet, the idiot king.

Turning her face towards the sky, Sigrid relished the feeling of the rain against her flushed skin. It was a good first step, but there was still a long way to go. Her mind kept shying away from what would happen after the war. Without an enemy to fight, she would be forced to stand still and look inwards. Sigrid didn't really know who she was anymore and was terrified to find out.

When the combined army arrived at the Holy City, they were surprised to find the gates standing open. They had been expecting a siege, against the remnants of the zealots and whatever soldiers King Roebus could summon. Sigrid had been told by Gar Brielle to temper her rage, as it could be weeks before they seized the Reverend Mother. It seemed too good to be true, so Sigrid kept a firm grip on her emotions.

Fearing that it was some kind of a trap, every precaution was taken. Scouts were sent to infiltrate the city, to gather information on the enemy's forces, while a camp was established outside. Trenches were dug, temporary fortifications were built and hundreds of tents assembled. As night fell, the scouts returned and slowly word began to filter through the ranks.

Brielle joined Darya, Sigrid and three other warriors at their campfire. Sigrid felt a nervous flutter of excitement in her chest, but she kept her mouth shut in case it wasn't good news.

"What's happened?" asked Darya, as Brielle made herself comfortable.

"I've been told that the people of Lorzi have been unhappy for some time. When the army left to engage with us, only a few soldiers remained behind. The people rebelled and took control. Our leaders are talking to the rebel leaders now. The zealots who fled the battlefield are in hiding. The people were happy to surrender to Algany."

Sigrid noticed that Brielle hadn't said the Choate. The tribespeople were not seen as a legitimate power in the Five Kingdoms. Not yet, at least.

"Where are the King and the Reverend Mother?" asked Sigrid.

"King Roebus is surrounded by guards and has locked

himself in the palace. We'll start digging him out tomorrow. The Reverend Mother could be in one of a hundred places. It's going to take some time to check all the churches and rectories."

"She's in the cathedral," said Sigrid. The conniving hag wouldn't be anywhere else. It was her seat of power and she would believe that holy ground would protect her. "She's there."

Brielle gave her a look but didn't disagree in front of the others. "In the morning, we start combing the streets for those who fled the battlefield. Get some rest. We start early."

Sigrid took her advice and immediately went to bed. She tossed and turned for a long time before eventually falling asleep. In the morning, she was sandy-eyed, but full of nervous energy about what lay ahead. Although she hadn't asked for any special treatment, she knew it wasn't a coincidence when she was assigned to search the cathedral. Fifty Choate warriors and fifty soldiers from Algany were being sent to locate and detain the Reverend Mother. She was to be unharmed, so that she could stand trial for her crimes. As much as Sigrid wanted to kill her, she was more determined to see the priest torn down in front of others.

As they walked through the streets of Lorzi, most of the local people stayed indoors. Sigrid saw anxious faces peering out through windows as she marched past with the other Choate. The locals had welcomed them into the city, but they were still an invading force. It was understandable that people were nervous. Now all they had to do was prove that they were as good as their word, unlike the Reverend Mother.

Long before they reached the cathedral, Sigrid caught sight of the towering blue dome. It was taller than every other building in the city, and the white walls gleamed even in weak sunlight. It was supposed to be a beacon of hope that welcomed all with open arms. After having read the full account of what had happened in the Frozen North, she wondered if the Shepherd had ever set foot in Lorzi. It was probably yet another lie, like so many others, that the church had told to further its goal of domination.

"Are you alright?" asked Darya.

"I'm fine."

"You're grinding your teeth," she said.

Sigrid relaxed her jaw and tried to stay calm, but it was a struggle. As she expected, the main doors of the cathedral were barred and all of the side doors had been barricaded with something on the inside. A dozen soldiers went to fetch a ram and the rest secured the building, guarding all doors so that no one could escape.

"We could just smash the windows and smoke them out," suggested Darya, pointing at the colourful stained glass. Whatever her feelings about the church and the Reverend Mother, the magnificent windows were at least four hundred years old, and Sigrid didn't want to destroy them.

Thankfully Brielle shook her head. She understood the importance of causing as little damage as possible in the city. The image of Choate being bloodthirsty savages was still prevalent in the minds of many. It was bias that had been passed down from one generation to the next, and Brielle was determined to dispel the myth.

A short time later, the soldiers returned with the battering ram. Working in teams, they began to pound the double doors. At first, they barely moved, and after peering in through a window, Sigrid saw many of the wooden pews had been cleared away. They were probably stacked up behind the doors, adding weight to the bar.

Despite the defences, the repetitive motion of the ram began to have an effect. First the doors splintered, and then the beam inside began to crack. The relentless hammering began to give Sigrid a headache. She rubbed her temples and tried to dispel it. She wanted a clear head for what came next.

When there was a narrow gap, one of the soldiers tried to

reach through the doors and shove the obstacles aside. He was rewarded with a sword in the face from the zealots inside. They had been the ones to spill blood on holy ground, and it would not be forgotten. The hammering resumed, Sigrid drew her sword and kept her buckler raised in case of archers.

"Ready," said Brielle, drawing her weapon.

The opening widened until they could see inside the nave. Peering over the top of the other warriors, Sigrid could see that chairs, pews and other pieces of furniture had indeed been stacked to create a barrier. Hunkered down behind it were several missionaries. Those by the main doors ran for cover, joining the others. She spotted a few trying to escape via another door, but they wouldn't get far. Every exit was being guarded.

Twice more they swung the ram, crashing the angled head into the doors. On the last swing the damage was so severe one of the huge doors fell off its hinges. Those at the front pushed it inwards, flattening some of the furniture inside. The weight of the massive door smashed chairs and cupboards into kindling, clearing a path into the cathedral.

"Shields!" shouted Brielle. The first three lines of Choate warriors had larger shields which they locked together, creating a solid barrier. After them came the Alganese warriors, with shields and plate mail. Behind them was Sigrid and other Choate warriors with only bucklers for protection. It chafed a little, being so far back, but she was the least experienced and the situation was volatile. Darya would never admit it, but Sigrid was certain that her friend been tasked with keeping her safe.

The zealots were rowdy and disorganised. Someone was shouting orders, but over a dozen left the safety of their barrier to attack.

It was a bloodbath.

The missionaries broke upon the shield wall, most dying immediately from stab wounds. The second row of Choate

shoved their swords through gaps and the righteous screams of
anger gave way to cries of pain. As pools of red began to spread
across the tiled floor, Sigrid felt a twinge of regret. Whatever
she thought about the Shepherd and the Reverend Mother,
this place was important to a lot of people. She had a feeling
that their sacrilege would not go unnoticed, and that there
would be a price to pay.

Once the first dozen zealots were dead, the shield wall
moved forward, step by step. Rocks and the occasional arrow
bounced off the wall with no effect. When they reached the
barrier, Alganese soldiers flanked it to the left, while Sigrid and
the other Choate warriors went to the right.

After bottling up her emotions for so long, it felt good to
scream at the enemy. Sigrid barely stayed in control as she
bellowed at the zealots, startling them with her voice as much
as her ferocity. When a woman tried to jab her with a spear,
Sigrid mercilessly brushed it aside and stabbed the woman
twice in the chest. Another zealot raised an axe and she hacked
off her arm, then sliced her across the stomach, spilling innards
on the floor. Unsatisfied, Sigrid kicked the woman aside and
slashed at another opponent, catching a man across his face.
He cried out and fell to the floor, clutching at his cheek as
blood welled from between his fingers. Sigrid raised her sword
and would have killed him if Darya hadn't caught her arm.

"Leave him," she said. When Sigrid saw the look of terror on
the man's face, she lowered her arm. Her heart was pounding
and her arms were shaking with pent-up anger. The real target
of her rage wasn't here.

The fight was over. With the vicious deaths of their friends,
the missionaries spirits were broken. Many chose to surrender,
throwing down their weapons rather than be cut down.

Kneeling down beside the injured man, Sigrid saw him
flinch. Reflected in his eyes she saw herself as he did. A
tattooed savage who had desecrated holy ground. It was time
to use that to her advantage.

"Tell me where she is or I'll cut out your eyes," said Sigrid.

With one trembling hand he pointed at one of the doors.

"Take six and go," said Brielle. The Alganese commander was too busy rounding up survivors to notice.

Even though it wasn't her place, Sigrid led the warriors through the door and down a narrow corridor lined with doors. They checked every room carefully and, in several, found zealots hiding or waiting to attack. At the sight of the Choate, some immediately surrendered and some had to be disarmed, but each time she held on to her rage.

Sigrid expected the final door at the end of the corridor to be locked, but when she turned the handle, it opened. Inside was a small, private chapel, with only two pews and small idol of the Shepherd. Reverend Mother Reyna was sat facing the door when they filed into the room. She wasn't surprised to see them and wore a smug little smile, as if somehow she'd still won. Perhaps she had. After all, they'd proven her point. They were vicious heathens who weren't afraid to kill people on holy ground.

When Sigrid stared the Reverend Mother in the eye, she hoped for something. A flash of recognition. A moment of surprise, or perhaps regret for all that she'd done. The only thing in Reyna's eyes, though, was arrogance that she was in the right. Sigrid had changed so much that the Reverend Mother had no idea who she was.

"Tie her up," said Sigrid. After all that she had endured, all that she had sacrificed, Sigrid expected to feel something in her moment of victory. Satisfaction that justice had finally been served, but her rage had drained away, leaving her feeling hollow and tired. Nothing could make up for what she had lost, and it would not restore the years of her life that had been taken.

Sigrid sheathed her sword and leaned against the wall, while the others secured the prisoner.

"The Shepherd will not forgive you for this," said the Reverend Mother.

The others ignored her, but Sigrid felt moved to say something. "And what will your punishment be?" she asked. "For all of the murder and mayhem you've orchestrated in his name. You will be judged and found lacking as a priest and a leader. You are nothing."

As she started to answer, Sigrid shoved a cloth in the old woman's mouth. As Reyna tried to spit it out, Sigrid tied it around her head, securing it in place. Even with her hands tied, the Reverend Mother was a threat. Her tongue was a far more dangerous weapon than any sword. They would have to be careful about who guarded her.

Darya was looking at Sigrid expectantly, waiting for her to say something more to the Reverend Mother. With a tired shake of her head, Sigrid dismissed the old woman.

"Take her away," she said, sitting down on one of the pews.

Staring out at Algany, from the walls of the Holy City, Sigrid felt a strange pang of loneliness. She had friends, and hopefully, one day, would be reunited with her son, but in the dark hours of night, she would always be alone. It had been that way for years. Perhaps she should have had some fun with Fieruz when she had the chance. It would have been exciting and maybe it would have helped her to feel alive. She missed waking up in bed, reaching out and finding someone else there. Someone warm and solid.

King Roebus was in a prison cell, along with the Reverend Mother. The Holy City was secure and they were awaiting the arrival of their allies from the north. Word had been sent to forces in Kinnan and the rest of the Choate.

They had been in the city for almost two weeks and so far there had been no word. Tomorrow they were marching north into Hundar to engage the enemy. They should have heard something by now. What if their allies had been defeated? What if the Hundarians had proven to be more formidable than anticipated? What if they lost the war to Hundar and the zealots? What would happen to the Five Kingdoms then? What if they won the war but she died during the battle? Did the Reverend Mother know something she didn't? Is that why she'd been smiling?

"Any sign?" asked Darya, joining her on the wall.

"No," said Sigrid.

"Are you all right?" asked Darya, sensing something was amiss. Sigrid hugged her friend tight and fought back a wave of tears. "What's wrong?"

"I didn't think it would be like this," said Sigrid.

"This isn't the end," promised the Choate. "They'll come."

Although she was worried about the pending war, Sigrid was more concerned about her own fate. The moment had come and gone. Now, when she looked to the future and tried to make plans, there was nothing. All of her dreams were nothing more than that. She would never again be Queen of Algany. She might be able to meet her son, but the notion of being his mother again was far-fetched. An unranked Choate, living in the palace, spending all of her time with the young king. It was an absurd notion. Politics, opinion and the outcome of the war would dictate where she went and what she could do. After the war, if Algany and the Choate people weren't on good terms, she might not even be allowed back into Thune. It wasn't up to her anymore. The power that she had shed so easily, what she thought she didn't miss, was now what she craved more than anything.

Sigrid didn't realise she'd been crying until she saw the wet patches on Darya's shoulder. After wiping her face, Sigrid shared her concerns about the future.

"Do you remember when you first started your training?" asked Darya.

"Of course. I didn't know how to stand or even hold a sword, never mind fight with a blade."

"But you took it one step at a time. Dos Mohan always

says he makes the plans, but we are the ones who win the battles. Tomorrow, the only thing you need to worry about, is marching north. The rest will come in time, and we'll face each challenge together."

Darya was right. Unravelling it all by herself seemed impossible. She didn't need to, and it wasn't her responsibility. Sigrid was just a soldier, and as such, she would try to think like one. It wouldn't be an easy adjustment, but if she focused on the task at hand, the rest would come in time.

CHAPTER 34

As the sun reached its zenith, Yarra made her way to the top of the wall with weary steps. The remaining Alfár were in position on the battlements, ready for another day of fighting. So far, not one of them had raised their weapon. The horde had attacked shortly after first light, but none of them had even made it to the bottom of the wall.

Over time, the Malice had turned healthy Alfár into primal monsters. But the thing fighting the horde was something much worse. It was a fiend, crafted from nightmares. It was a massive beast, bulging with muscle, covered in razor sharp spines, and armed with vicious claws. Its face was elongated, with a row of dagger-like teeth, and it relished in the destruction of others like nothing she'd ever seen before.

Yarra had to call it a fiend, because it wasn't her friend. Not anymore. Just as the Alfár of old had been erased by the Malice, so too had Odd by his transformation. There was nothing recognisably human about him anymore.

The veterans had been outraged and appalled by her request. Now, as they watched the fiend lift one of the horde above its head, then rip it apart with its claws, she could feel their self-loathing. They had allowed this to happen. It didn't matter that Odd was cutting a swathe through the enemy. They had willingly let a dozen of their people be murdered. Some might argue that, in time, they would have died from their injuries, but that didn't matter.

Perhaps they could convince themselves that the Malice was responsible. That if not for their own infection, which impacted their thoughts, they would never have agreed to her request.

Krizan said something harsh in her own language and then spat over the wall. The other veterans nodded and added their own curses. No matter the outcome, Yarra wasn't sure they would ever forgive themselves.

Howling with glee, the fiend waded into the horde, throwing bodies left and right. A dozen surged over it, only for half of their number to fall away, screaming in pain, quills buried in their bodies. The injured monsters writhed on the ground. Yarra didn't know what substance was on the spines, but she guessed some kind of poison. While the fiend ripped apart some of the horde with its teeth and claws, it stomped on those underfoot, crushing their skulls.

The horde didn't feel anything about the death of their allies. They never reacted or showed concern. The only reason they retreated every day was that somewhere, buried deep in what remained of their minds, was the primal instinct of fight or flight. Eventually, the butchery of many would trigger this response and they ran, to live and fight another day.

As Yarra watched the thing cut into their ranks, she wondered what the horde could be thinking. It must have come as quite a shock, to be faced with something just as savage and even more brutal than themselves.

It wasn't long before the first rout.

In their dozens they ran, scrambling over one another in an attempt to escape. The dead and dying were left behind, which was another first. Even as they attempted to flee, spines chased them, catching a dozen or more in the back and legs, dropping them to the ground where they writhed in agony until they died from the poison.

"What have we done?" said Bewligg.

"We have damned ourselves," said Adami.

Yarra knew they detested her for making the request, but there was plenty of hate to go around.

The horde ran and kept on running. Soon, the only living thing beyond the Choke was the fiend. The dying monsters were quickly dispatched, black ichor splattering everywhere as their bodies were torn asunder. The fiend seemed to relish the ripping of meat and the crack of bones breaking underfoot.

Soon it was alone, surrounded by carnage.

Yarra wasn't sure what she was expecting. Anger. A grisly feast perhaps. Maybe it would turn its rage upon them instead. Climb the wall and tear every defender apart. Instead, the fiend stood amidst the broken bodies and it began to sway, rocking back and forth. It bobbed its head and shuffled about, never staying still. There was something oddly hypnotic about its movements.

"What's it doing?" asked Mihok, staring down at the thing.

"It's getting ready for another fight," said Bewligg. "Keeping itself warm."

The horde had been defeated, but they were not gone. Only a small portion of their number was dead. They would be back. It was only a matter of when.

As the others discussed the fiend, Yarra was reminded of something she'd seen as a child when visiting relatives in Hundar. Her father's family had bred and raised hunting dogs. They were highly social animals that lived in a pack. During one visit, she'd gone to the pen and found only one hound. It was a huge, fluffy thing whose head came up to her waist. The others had been sold on and it had been left alone for a long time. Eventually, the dog had become deeply distressed and it began to sway and bob its head. Loneliness was eating away at it, and without the company of others, its mind slowly began to unravel.

Staring down at the monster, that had once been her friend, Yarra felt only pity for a creature that was suffering inside.

* * *

Three more times the horde attacked and each time the fiend repelled them. They tried swarming over it, beating it with numbers, but its spines poisoned them by the dozen. It ripped them limb from limb with brute force, until the ground was awash with black ichor and a mound of broken bodies. Some of the Alfár cheered whenever the horde fled. They didn't know where the fiend had come from and they didn't care. They didn't know about the sacrifices that had been made.

But the fiend was not without its limits. Odd had told Yarra that a time would come when what had been taken from the dying Alfár would run out.

Any wounds that the fiend sustained were minor and they regenerated. In addition, the spines regrew with unnatural speed, so that every time the horde attacked it had a full complement. Eventually, its regeneration would slow and its strength would fade. She hoped that it happened after Kell and Willow reached their destination. The monster hadn't changed the course of the war, it had merely delayed the inevitable.

As night fell, the enemy withdrew. The fiend sat down amidst the dead bodies and promptly went to sleep. Yarra was about to leave the wall and go in search of something to eat, when she saw a light flare in the distance. The flame burned yellow, red and then turned blue. It glowed so bright she was forced to shield her eyes until it had died down. At this distance, it was difficult for her to see who it was. She had no idea if it was another enemy, or if her friends had returned. Bewligg was standing beside her, staring at the torch in surprise.

"Can you see who it is?" she asked.

He squinted against the light and grunted in surprise. "They both made it."

Yarra knew what his first question would be, because she was thinking the same thing. How were they supposed to get them past the fiend?

They couldn't risk opening the gate. It would take hours to

clear away the boulders, and it would leave them vulnerable. The only way up was the way they had gone down, via a rope.

"We should kill it," said Bewligg.

"Do you even think that's possible?" said Yarra, gesturing at the countless dead it had thrown around like toys. What if they tried to kill it and failed? She really didn't want to make it angry. There was no doubt in Yarra's mind that it could climb the wall and kill every single one of them. So far, it hadn't shown that it was aware of them, and Yarra wanted to keep it that way.

"Besides," she reasoned, "why would we kill our best weapon?"

"Then what do we do?" asked Bewligg.

"Send me down on a rope."

At first Bewligg smiled, thinking it was a joke, but then he realised she was serious. "It will kill you the moment your feet touch the ground."

"He won't hurt me."

"That is not your friend," said Bewligg. "You know that he is gone."

"We cannot risk losing you," said Adami, coming up the stairs.

"You managed well enough without me," said Yarra.

That wasn't strictly true, but at this point losing her really wouldn't make that much of a difference. Even with her help, they were still failing. All she'd done was slow down the pace.

"If it attacks, there may not be enough time to pull you back up," warned Bewligg.

If it chose to attack her, there was nothing anyone could do, but there wasn't another choice. It was better that she faced the problem head on.

After lighting a blue fire on the battlements, they secured three ropes to the top of the wall. Overhead, the moon hung fat and low in the sky. It provided just enough light for her to see the outline of obstacles littering the terrain below. The horrors were painted with a silver sheen, turning everything into shades of grey and white. The shadowy corners became black pits of nothing. Sitting perfectly still amidst the silent bodies, as if it had been turned to stone, was the fiend.

It hadn't moved in over an hour, but as Yarra dangled over the side, she was certain that it shifted on its haunches. Some predators barely moved, preferring to wait for their prey to come to them.

Swallowing the lump in her throat, Yarra took up the strain and slowly began to walk down the wall. She had rarely seen the Alfár look afraid, but all of them were visibly concerned about her safety. They thought she was walking into a trap. Yarra's instincts screamed at her to stay away, but it was too late to turn back.

When her feet touched the ground, she kept facing the wall, waiting for the inevitable. Taking a deep breath, she prepared herself for the feeling of its teeth sinking into her throat. When nothing happened, Yarra slowly turned around, being careful not to make any sudden movements.

The fiend was staring at her.

It was still in the same position, but now it was looking directly at her. Yarra hadn't seen it up close and, although some of it was concealed by shadows, the worst part was the eyes. Despite all the quills, claws, and teeth making up its monstrous visage, its eyes were human.

The lump in her throat swelled, until it felt as if she'd swallowed an egg. Sweat trickled down the sides of her face, and as the terror mounted, a huge weight settled on her chest. Yarra began to wheeze and had to focus on controlling her quivering bladder. For what seemed like an age, it just watched her. The rising of her chest. The nervous movement of her eyes. The anxious flicking of her fingers.

Long before she heard anything the fiend turned away, staring at something in the distance. Slowly, two figures emerged from the gloom. When they caught sight of Yarra and the fiend, they froze. She could just make out that it was Willow and Kell. They stared at the monster and then noticed the many broken bodies around it. The smell was grotesque. A mix of stagnant rot, sweet decay and the bitter stench of poisoned blood.

Yarra broke the stalemate. She took one shaky step forward, her feet crunching loudly on the stony ground. The fiend's ears twitched, but it didn't turn its head. Taking that as a good sign, or at least indifference, she stepped forward again and then again, until she was level with its profile. Standing on all fours, it was as tall as her. If it reared up on its back legs, it would be at least twice her height.

When she went to take another step, it growled, so deep in its throat that she felt the vibration in her bones. She pulled back her foot and it stopped. Long strings of drool ran from between its teeth, pooling on the ground beneath.

A heavy silence settled across the valley.

Yarra was close enough to the others that she could see their faces. They wanted to ask her what was happening, but also understood the fragility of the situation. Their questions would have to wait. One wrong move and the fiend would kill them all. Its eyes moved slowly, passing over Kell and Willow. If there was any recognition, she didn't see it. Perhaps somewhere, buried deep in its brain, the fiend knew who they were, but the thread holding it back was tenuous and could break at any moment.

Slowly raising one hand, Yarra gestured for them to approach. At first, they didn't move. Kell was terrified, but Willow looked desperately sad. Somehow, she knew what had happened.

Keeping his hands empty and by his sides, Kell walked in a straight line towards Yarra. His eyes never strayed from the fiend. Its nose twitched as he approached, but she didn't know if it remembered his scent or was smelling his fear. When he reached her side, Yarra sent him on towards the wall.

As he began to secure himself with the rope, Willow came forward. The fiend tracked the Alfár with its eyes. Its whole body was tense, muscles twitching. Yarra sensed it was on the verge of violence. Sweat trickled down her face. Her nerves were on fire, and the hair on the back of her neck started to lift.

When she was beside the thing, Willow paused and turned towards it. Yarra made a grab for her arm, but the Alfár shook her off. Slowly, as if the muscles in its neck didn't work very well, or perhaps there was an internal struggle, the fiend turned and stared at Willow. When their eyes met, Yarra felt a wave of something pass through her. Nausea and fear and regret. It lasted only a moment and then it was gone. Willow attached herself to the third rope and prepared for the climb.

Yarra wanted to say something. To offer thanks, to say how sorry she was, but she had no idea if the fiend would even understand. Instead, afraid for her life, she said nothing and retreated.

With her feet on the wall, she began the climb alongside the others. The ropes were hauled up so fast, it was all she could do to hold on. There was a subtle shift in the air. A high-pitched whine began from somewhere below. Slowly, the noise swelled, becoming louder and louder. She heard the crunch of stone and the grinding of something being broken.

Soon Yarra was running on the wall to keep up, then hands were hauling her over the battlements. She sat beside the others for a moment, trying to catch her breath.

At the bottom, the fiend was going berserk.

It was savaging the dead bodies in an appalling frenzy. Shaking them in its jaws, like a dog worrying a bone. Biting through limbs and hurling them aside. Tearing off heads and smashing them into the ground, over and over, until the skulls broke apart. It didn't take long before every single body had been reduced to lumps of meat and splintered bones.

With nothing else to attack, the fiend howled, and Yarra

felt her throat tighten at the awful noise. It was full of despair, loneliness and savage pain, so visceral it made her want to cry.

Over a bowl of stew and warm bread, Yarra exchanged stories with her friends. Kell and Willow told her and the veterans what they had seen north of the Choke. Everyone listened in rapt silence as they described the maze of bone spikes, their encounter with Ravvi, the crown and what they had discovered within.

"Was it alive?" asked Yarra.

"Not like us, but we destroyed it," said Kell. He exchanged a look with Willow, but Yarra couldn't read the message that passed between them. Willow seemed distracted, and Yarra noticed a new patch of discoloured skin down one side of her face. Being so close to the source of the poison must have been unbearable. There was a strange hunch to Kell's shoulders, and his face was thinner and more worn out than she remembered.

"So, is it over?" said Yarra.

Willow finally looked up from her food and said something in her own language. It wasn't good news, as Bewligg and the other veterans scowled or spat on the floor.

Yarra glanced at Kell but he just shrugged.

"What's happening?" said Yarra, looking around the circle for an answer. Krizan grated something short and the others laughed, but it was a dry bitter sound. "What did she say?" she asked.

"She said that it's time for you to go home," said Bewligg.

Yarra knew it was a lie. "What did she really say?"

"The heart of the poison is gone. Destroyed," said Willow. "But it's already too late. You've seen much of this world. The poison is buried deep in everything. There are no insects or birds. It cannot spread any further, but the damage has already been done. This land is dead and so are its people."

"You're just giving up?" said Yarra. Looking at the others she saw defeat on every face. "All of you?"

"We were too late," said Kell. "I hoped that if we destroyed the Malice, something could be saved, but everything here has been tainted. Every plant and drop of water."

"One day, the land may recover," said Bewligg. "But by then, my people will have been dead for a long time."

Yarra understood what they were saying, but she refused to give in. "So, you're all just going to lie down and let the horde kill you?"

"No. Never," said Adami with a feral grin. "We will fight, and keep the others safe, so that they may live in peace, for long as they can. We can do that much for them."

"Every day is a victory," said Krizon, struggling with each word. She placed her hand on Yarra's shoulder and said something in her own language.

"She says you've done enough. More than anyone could ask," translated Bewligg.

"We're all grateful," said Mihok.

"It's time for you to go home," said Willow. "Both of you."

"No," said Kell. "Come with us."

"This is my place," said Willow.

"One more soldier will not make a difference," said Adami. "You should go back. Tell the others in Yantou-vash what has happened."

Willow stubbornly shook her head and an argument followed. It went on for some time but it was apparent Willow was outnumbered and eventually she conceded to their request.

"It is settled," said Adami, making a cutting motion with one hand. "In the morning, she will leave with you."

"I'm not going," said Yarra.

"Why not?" asked the veteran.

"You're wrong, Adami. One more soldier can make a difference. Without me, you would have already been overrun. I can help you hold back the horde."

She knew what they were thinking. That if she stayed,

eventually the effects of the Malice would incapacitate her. Her mind would drift free and the whispering voices would become overwhelming. It was inevitable, but if she stayed at the Choke she could save lives. Those on the wall, but also those back in Yantou-vash.

"Why?" asked Kell.

Yarra had been thinking about that for a long time. Ever since she'd decided to stay when Kell and Willow had gone north.

"Few of us get a choice about how or where we die. It just happens."

Her father had died a bitter old man in his bed. He'd been so angry about having never accomplished his ambitions. By contrast, Yarra's mother had died far too young from a wasting disease and she'd been equally frustrated. The experience had shaped the lives of both Yarra and her sister. It was the main reason she was so organised and desperate to control every aspect of her life. Some people said time was a thief. It flew by too quickly, but at least she could see it happening. Death was far worse. It rarely announced its presence and it stole much that could never be recaptured.

"If I stay, then my death will have meaning. Here, I can do more good in one day than in ten years as a member of the Raven."

"Are you sure?" asked Kell.

Yarra reached inside her armour and handed him a letter for her family. She'd written it partly for them, but also for herself, as a way of letting go and saying goodbye.

"I'm sure," she said. "It's time for you to go home."

"You should come with me," said Kell, gripping Willow's hand. "To Algany."

"I cannot leave my people," said the Alfár. "Even if the rest have given up."

"Not just you, I mean everyone in Yantou-vash," said Kell. "Without the taint of the Malice, it would be a fresh start for your people."

"Where would we live?"

"There are many wild, undiscovered places beyond Corvan. I cannot say that life will be easy, but your people are resilient. Having seen this place, and all that they've survived, I'm sure they could make it work."

Willow shook her head sadly. "It is a nice idea, but Ravvi and I were seen as rebels for using Govhenna's doorway. They will not listen to me."

"Then we will talk to them together," said Kell. "Tell them about the Choke, and make them understand all that has been sacrificed for their freedom. If they stay in Yantou-vash and do nothing, then all of that would be meaningless."

"It will not be easy," said Willow.

"What is the alternative?" he asked. "You said it yourself. You are a dying people. There are no more children. This generation is the last."

"Even if we travel through the doorway, that may not change."

Kell gripped Willow's hand. "I know, but right now, everyone in Yantou-vash is on borrowed time. They're not really living. They're just waiting to die. Wouldn't they rather live free, in a world with clean water, fresh air and the possibility of hope?"

"I think they would," said Willow, but then she sighed. "I admit, for the first time in many years, I am worried."

"But excited, too?"

"A little," she admitted.

"I promise, you will not be alone," promised Kell. "As the King of Algany, I can make sure your people have everything they need to start their new life."

Finally, they were going back to the Five Kingdoms, together.

CHAPTER 35

The army of Algany, with support from the Choate, had captured Lorzi without much of a fight. The south was secure and so all eyes had turned north, towards Hundar. Their King, Elias, had been the Reverend Mother's closest ally and co-conspirator in destabilising the Five Kingdoms. With Choate forces closing in on Pynar from the west, warriors from Kinnan in the north, and Algany from the south, Sigrid had expected it to be a short and decisive war. Despite her best efforts to think only about today, it still irritated that she was one of the last to find out what was going on.

Gar Brielle gathered Sigrid and the others in her unit together to brief them. They had been marching north through Algany for five days and were now at the border with Hundar. The combined forces had been waiting for three days for any news, and finally it had arrived. Rumours had been flying around the camp for hours and Sigrid had listened to all of them.

"It's not good news," said Gar Brielle, wasting no time with preamble. "The war has reached a stalemate."

"How?" asked Sigrid.

They should have crossed the border days ago. They should have joined forced with more Choate from the west and have engaged the enemy. They should be laying siege to the capital city, or fighting them in the surrounding countryside.

"We should have crushed them by now," said Darya, echoing Sigrid's thoughts.

"The reason we took the west of Algany and the Holy City so easily, is that the bulk of the missionaries retreated to Hundar. King Elias knew the south was lost, so he sacrificed the Reverend Mother to consolidate his forces."

It was brutal, but it also made sense from a strategic standpoint. It was much easier to fight on your own terrain and let the enemy come to you. King Elias would have had plenty of time to bolster his defences, set traps, gather supplies and turn his people against outsiders. If they marched north into Hundar and started killing, it would play into people's perceptions of the Choate as bloodthirsty savages. It wouldn't matter that they had joined forces with the army from Algany. Whatever the outcome, survivors would forever tarnish the tribespeople and the prejudice against them would remain.

"What does that mean?" asked Darya.

Brielle sighed. "It means even when we join forces with the rest of our people, we're going to be outnumbered."

"What about the army from Kinnan?" asked Sigrid. "The King in the north pledged his support."

"I don't know," said Brielle with a shrug. She wasn't much further up the chain of command than Sigrid, and would only know what her superiors wanted to share. "They're not here yet, or maybe they're not coming. All I know is, we're on our own."

"So, what will we do?" asked Darya.

Brielle gave her a feral grin. "What we do best. We'll fight and show them what it means to be Choate." Her smile included Sigrid, for which she was eternally grateful. Until that moment, she hadn't really felt as if she belonged.

The Choate were not savages, but they had a reputation of being fierce warriors. The Choate had not gone to war in the Five Kingdoms for over two hundred years. King Elias and his forces were about to find out that their reputation was well earned.

* * *

Sigrid's lungs were burning. She was struggling to breathe and stand upright. A white-clad missionary carrying a mace, stepped out in front of her. Upon seeing her blood-splattered face, he dropped his weapon and ran in the opposite direction.

Never before had she realised that widespread battles had ebbs and flows. The worst of the fighting had moved away for the moment, but she knew it would soon roll back around in her direction.

Darya passed her a water flask, and she drank deeply. Cupping a hand, she poured a little onto her palm, before splashing it across her face. The water ran red and brown off her chin. Slowly, her breathing eased and she could stand up straight without a burning pain in her side.

To the west, rolling down the hillside like a deadly wave, cavalry from Algany smashed into the exposed Hundarian flank. Even from where she was standing, Sigrid heard the impact when the two forces collided, and the accompanying screams of pain. Bodies were smashed apart and trampled underfoot by the horses, while the riders stabbed and slashed at the enemy. Rank upon rank of warriors went down, and all that was left behind was a sea of broken bodies. Feeble hands reached towards the sky, pleading for help, but there was none to be had.

The northern forces had marched out to meet them. If all else failed, they could still retreat to the relative safety of Pynar, but from the way the battle was going, Sigrid didn't think that would happen.

The Hundarian forces were organised, but thankfully the missionaries were not. The Hundarians were using them as fodder, sending rank upon rank of the zealots to be cut down. Some of them attacked in a frenzy, spitting and foaming at the mouth, while they ranted about sin. Others were silent, focused on working together, but their units soon fell apart when they met an organised and trained force.

While the missionaries had suffered heavy losses compared to the Choate, if the forces from Kinnan didn't show up, Sigrid was worried about what might happen.

"Here they come again," said Darya, giving herself a shake.

Sigrid raised her shield, readied herself and stepped into line with the rest of her unit. She guessed the missionary group in front of her numbered at least a two or three hundred, almost twice the number in her unit.

"Shields!" shouted Brielle.

This time, Sigrid was in the second row. They were far from the heart of the fighting, but nowhere on the battlefield was safe. The only way they could have ensured she survived was if she had stayed back in the Holy City, but her friends understood that was not an option.

Sigrid interlocked her shield with the front row, braced her legs in a wide stance and readied her sword. The third row locked their shields in place together, obscuring her view of the sky, placing her in a cocoon, surrounding her on all sides with warm bodies. She heard someone firing up the enemy with a few choice phrases about sinners, and then the zealots charged.

"Brace!" someone yelled, so loudly it made her ears ring. Barely a heartbeat later, she felt the zealots crash into the shield wall. The weight of the enemy sent everyone back a step, but then they dug their heels into the mud and shoved back. The front rank spit and screamed, grabbing at the shields, trying to rip them away, while those behind flailed about with their weapons.

Brielle waited until the third rank had pushed forward, and all of the zealots were squashed together with nowhere to go.

"Now!" came the command.

Sigrid and everyone in the second row thrust their swords between the shields, stabbing the zealots over and over. Blood sprayed everywhere, dripping to the ground, and the wailing cries of dying men and women filled her ears.

Driving her arm back and forward, Sigrid felt the warm rush of blood over her hand. Without armour and nowhere to pull back, the front rank of the enemy was decimated.

"Advance!"

Bracing against the weight, the Choate moved forward a step and everyone followed behind. Sigrid could barely look down, but she felt the dead and dying beneath her feet. Locked into place, she stepped on something soft that groaned and sent her off balance. She leaned against her neighbours and adjusted her weight, until she was steady on her feet again. Desperate hands clutched at her legs. Her foot sank into a puddle of blood, but she ignored it.

Moving together, they advanced another step and then another, and another, climbing over the bodies. Sigrid's arm began to tire as she stabbed the enemy over and over, cutting down more and more zealots. Caught between their own people and the Choate shields, they died by the dozen.

Brielle was a little way back from the shield-wall, keeping an eye on the action. Sigrid heard her curse and wondered what was happening. She drove her sword forward and heard a scream, but when she tried to pull back it caught on something. Her fingers were already slick with blood and her grip was slipping. A dying woman smashed her head into Sigrid's shield so hard it shattered her nose. Dead or unconscious, she dropped to the ground and everyone stepped over her. Sigrid felt a snap and heard an unpleasant grinding sound. Her sword came loose so quickly, she nearly dropped it in surprise.

"Get ready to break!" came the command.

The screams of the injured behind them added to the noise of the battle, making it difficult to hear, but the order was repeated again and again.

"Break!"

With relief Sigrid pulled back her shield then stepped out of the ruck. She rested the point of her sword on the ground as she tried to slow her breathing. The enemy had broken ranks and were running for their lives. A few surrendered and were taken prisoner. The injured and dead were left where they'd fallen, a feast for the crows.

"Look!" said Darya, pointing over Sigrid's shoulder.

In the distance, she saw another army forming into ranks, organised units of soldiers from Hundar. Archers, cavalry and foot soldiers. All of them were untouched by the battle with pristine uniforms. Glancing at the sky, Sigrid realised it was barely past midday. She thought they had been fighting for hours, but it had only been about an hour.

Despite the numbers, the battle had been going well for the southern army. The Hundarians had held back almost all of their trained forces, and now they were ready to play. Sigrid didn't doubt the skill of the soldiers from Algany, or the ferocity of the Choate, but without support from Kinnan, they would be crushed. The odds had been tough to begin with, but now they were stacked against them.

The zealots and Hundarian forces had been routed, but now they began to cheer when they saw their allies. Their confidence swelled and the mood of the battle began to turn. With a slow and methodical pace, the Hundarian army advanced.

People started shouting orders, and slowly word spread through the Choate ranks. There was no time to withdraw to higher ground, or construct any kind of defences. Their only choice was to dig in.

Sigrid had imagined her own death a hundred times, but not once had it been on the battlefield. After nearly starving to death in the cells beneath the Holy City, she was glad to be on her feet with a full belly. At least she was free.

Staring at the pale blue sky, she took a deep breath and held it. She had cheated death once and narrowly escaped. It seemed as if today, her debt was finally due.

Darya was starting to panic, and some of the other less-experienced warriors were nervous. Gar Brielle was doing her best to keep them calm, but Sigrid could see she was anxious as well. She glanced at Sigrid and raised an eyebrow. Sigrid shook her head. She wouldn't leave now. If she was the same as everyone else and no longer the Queen of Algany, then her rightful place was here.

"It will be fine," said Sigrid, pressing her forehead against Darya's. "Whatever happens, I will be with you."

"I should be the one trying to keep you calm."

"But I'm older and smarter," said Sigrid, making her friend laugh. "Plus, I'm much prettier."

"You wish," said Darya. There was little time, but Sigrid and a few others did their best to lift spirits. The Hundarian army continued to march forward. The time for jokes and bolstering morale dwindled and then came to a swift end.

"Shields!" someone yelled. The command was repeated over and over, as the enemy's archers came into range. She was too far away to hear the bows, but Sigrid watched as hundreds of arrows were fired high into the air. The sky turned black, and a moment later deadly rain began to fall, punching through shields, spearing legs and arms, impaling skulls. Sigrid was crouched down beside Darya with their shields locked together for protection. Even so, she felt something strike the leather hard enough to jar her left arm. She dropped her sword in favour of steadying her shield with both hands. All around them, arrows continued to fall and Choate began to scream. Someone next to them had an arrow go through her leg. Tumbling backwards she cried out, but her agony was cut short when two more arrows went through her chest.

Blood trickled from the warrior's mouth in a continuous flow for several heartbeats before it stopped, but her eyes stayed open. Death wasn't majestic or pretty. There was no poetry or grace. It was painful, unpleasant, smelly and a struggle to the bitter end.

Another arrow bounced off their shields and then Sigrid found she was lying on her back, staring at the sky. It took her a while to realise what had happened. There was a white-hot pain in her shoulder. Turning her head, she saw the shaft of an arrow sticking out of her flesh. All around her, the dead and the dying littered the ground. The sun was extinguished as Darya covered her with a shield then dragged her into a sitting position.

"On your feet!" she screamed. Sigrid did her best to comply, but her legs wouldn't work. Her strength was ebbing away. Looking down she saw no blood on her armour, so she didn't understand why she was suddenly so weak. Darya snapped the arrow and pain shot through her chest. Sigrid's right arm was starting to go numb and now there was blood, oozing from the wound.

"Walk," shouted Darya, over the wailing of the injured.

Leaning on her friend, Sigrid managed to get to her feet and together they retreated.

Gar Brielle was rallying her unit, pulling back the wounded able to walk, and sadly leaving the rest where they had fallen. A third were dead, and despite their shields, many others were wounded. In the distance, the archers had stepped back and now the foot soldiers were coming forward. The cavalry would be held in reserve, to be used as and when they were needed.

As the Hundarian army advanced, Sigrid realised this was the end. Her only regret was that she wouldn't get to spend time with Marik. She desperately wanted to see him grow up and become a man, a great king.

Sigrid had forgotten her sword and now felt naked without it. It wouldn't have mattered anyway. She couldn't hold a weapon and didn't know how to fight with her left hand. At least she could still wield a dagger. She wouldn't surrender. Death would find her long before that happened.

The sound of the Hundarians' feet began to shake the ground. As the foot soldiers came forward, Sigrid saw a group of officers on the edge of the valley, coordinating the attack. They had erected a command tent and were probably sipping wine, enjoying the spectacle like it was a sport.

Anger rushed through her limbs, giving her strength, firing her blood. She stood up without support and readied herself. Sigrid was determined to kill at least one Hundarian before she died. It wouldn't change anything. It wouldn't tip the balance of the war, but it was better than nothing. She didn't want to think about what would happen if Hundar was victorious. She expected war, in one form or another, would continue across the Five Kingdoms for years. This was the world in which her son would become a man.

"Are you all right?" asked Darya.

"I'm fine," said Sigrid, lying through her teeth. "Why?"

"You're shaking."

The rage simmering underneath the surface was rising up.

The space between the two armies contracted so slowly it was painful. Sigrid couldn't raise her right arm, but she held a dagger in her left. Beside her, Darya had sword and shield. Looking both ways down the line, all she could see was determined faces. If this was the end, then they would make it one that the bards would sing about.

The Choate began to shout their defiance at the enemy, screaming for blood, screaming for life, expelling their rage. Sigrid added her voice to the clamour, spitting curses and boiling down all of her hate into one sound.

Above the clamour of marching feet, she heard the thunder of hooves. The Hundarian cavalry was probably going to flank them and start cutting into them from the rear. She knew that the Choate wouldn't run. They would fight to the last.

The enemy soldiers came closer, shields locked tight, spears and pikes held at the ready.

Time slowed to a crawl. A bead of sweat slowly inched its way down her nose, then dripped off the end. It sailed down, down and finally splashed on the damp ground.

As it struck the wet grass, the soldier in front of her sprouted an arrow in the middle of his forehead. With one foot raised, he balanced briefly and was frozen in place. The colour drained from his face and then he toppled forward onto the ground. The thundering of horses grew louder and the ground trembled. More of the Hundarians were punctured by arrows and another volley tore into their front ranks. The first cracks appeared in the discipline of the well-coordinated army.

Far in the distance, beyond the Hundarians on the battlefield, Sigrid caught sight of the enemy's command tent. It had been trampled and torn apart. Bodies littered the ground around it, as row upon row of warriors marched over their remains.

The army of Kinnan had arrived.

With the arrival of their allies, the battle wasn't yet finished.

Caught between two enemy forces, with no one to direct them from the top, commanders further down the chain began to coordinate their own forces. The army started to break apart into smaller units, but chaos was now running rampant.

"Advance!" came the command, shouted from one Choate officer to the next.

Finding her voice again, Sigrid shouted at the enemy, driving fear into the hearts of those who, only moments earlier, had been certain of victory. The smugness on their faces evaporated as the Choate came towards them.

Darya handed Sigrid an axe, which she took in her left hand. Her right hand hung useless by her side, so she tucked it into her belt. Just doing that nearly made Sigrid black out, but she shook it off and stayed in rank.

The swell of voices rose all around her, rolling back and forth down the line, overlapping until the cacophony was deafening. The warriors from Kinnan slammed into the Hundarians, and then the Choate were attacking them as well.

Raising her axe on high, Sigrid brought it down on the shoulder of the woman in front. The blade split her collarbone, blood spurted out of her neck and she toppled over sideways.

On her left, Darya was mercilessly hacking away at the enemy with desperation. On her right, Gar Brielle danced between soldiers, her movements sharp and precise. Lines of red appeared like magic across the skin of the Hundarians she faced.

Every time Sigrid swung her axe, it felt as if someone was driving a blade into her right shoulder. The pain kept her sharp, but she knew it wouldn't last. Eventually, her stamina would run out.

The lines broke apart. A fractured melee developed across the battlefield, with small groups fighting one another. Horses rode past with no riders. Groups of cavalry pursued each other. Sigrid saw one Hundarian horseman about to attack a group of Choate from the rear. Grabbing his foot, she dragged him off his horse and smashed his head apart before he knew what was happening.

The air was full of screams. Men cried out for their mother. Women screamed for the Shepherd to save them. The dead stared and the living huffed and groaned, cutting each other apart.

When a shadow fell across Sigrid, she thought the sun was going down. Surely that was impossible? Had they been fighting for that long? Turning her head, she saw a tall figure standing beside Gar Brielle. It took her a moment to recognise the figure as an Alfár. Her skin was a pale grey-blue. Her yellow on black eyes were so startling and strange. Staring at the Alfár's face, Sigrid knew that this wasn't Willow.

Looking behind her, Sigrid saw another army. Rank upon rank of Alfár, armed with swords, spears and those peculiar two-headed weapons she'd seen Willow carrying. They were an outlandish and imposing force that was hundreds, perhaps thousands strong. And still more were coming over the rise. Turning back to the battle, Sigrid saw one of the Hundarians rush towards the tall Alfár with a spear. Casually, she plucked the weapon from the soldier's hand like an adult snatching a toy away from a child. The Alfár's backhand caught the Hundarian across the side of the head and he fell, his neck bent at a peculiar angle.

The Alfár stared up at the sky, took a deep breath and tracked the movement of a crow. At the prospect of a feast, a murder was gathering above. A smile tugged at the corners of the Alfár's mouth. Then she turned away from the fight and went back to her own people. Following her gaze, Sigrid was surprised to see a shorter figure walking among their ranks. He stood out because he was so different in height from the others.

It was impossible.

It had been eight years, and yet he had hardly aged a day. Leaner from his journey, and whatever he had endured, but otherwise it was the same man. She couldn't believe it, but it was him, in the flesh.

Kell had returned.

His eyes passed over the Choate and didn't pause when they came to her. Sigrid didn't blame him. She had changed so much in their years apart.

The Hundarians had seen the new army, and now they were outnumbered ten to one. Their momentum had come to an abrupt halt. Their chain of command was gone, and at the sight of an army of Alfár, their spirit was broken.

With a blood-soaked axe in one hand, Sigrid turned away from the enemy and slowly approached the Alfár. She felt Darya shadowing her and was pleased that she didn't have to do this alone. He was so busy surveying the battlefield, Kell didn't notice her approaching until she was almost in front of him.

Beside him was Willow, her face blank and expressionless. If she recognised Sigrid, there was no outward sign. When Kell focused his attention on Sigrid, his mouth fell open in surprise. He looked her up and down, noting the many changes, before realising that she was injured.

"I'm fine," said Sigrid, finding her voice.

Kell pulled her into his arms and Sigrid hugged him tightly with one arm.

"Our son, is he alive? Is he well?" he asked.

"He's safe. And well," said Sigrid.

The war was over. They were going home.

EPILOGUE

Excerpt from an Alganian history of the Five Kingdoms by the scribe Aldous Souri

And on the day of his twentieth birthday, King Marik of Algany welcomed a new ambassador from a distant land into the palace of Thune and, indeed, into the Five Kingdoms. The king was dressed resplendently, in a red cloak edged with white fur that fluttered behind him like a pennant when he strode majestically through the hallways. He was a handsome young man in his prime, of good health and noble character.

Behind him, as always, came two members of the Raven. They were the best warriors in Algany and, in this humble scribe's opinion, the best in the Five Kingdoms. Their armour was polished. Their weapons shone and they marched in rigid unison, ever watchful for danger. Either one of them would be happy, at a moment's notice, to give their life for the noble king.

Once he had sat down on the throne, the king's official advisors took up their positions behind him. On his left, was the tattooed Choate woman known only as Anya. Her expression was grim, her demeanour threatening and her savagery was well known. She had a fearsome temper and, though she spoke like a person familiar with court, it was obvious that her heart remained Choate.

Days after the Holy War had ended, she arrived in the palace at Thune to take up her official post as strategic advisor to the king. And in all of that time, right up to this very day, she has not left the king's side. Not once is there any record of her returning to her homeland to be among her own people. Though she is not of Algany, her dedication to the king has been exemplary, as she has supported him in all endeavours.

And, forever on his right was the boy's father, Kell Kressia, two-time saviour of the Five Kingdoms, who many had started calling the Eternal King. One cannot argue that, during the period where he was absent for many years, he barely aged. However, since his return during the final days of the Holy War, his hair has turned grey in places. But far be it for me, a humble scribe, to point out an obvious flaw in such a colourful and popular sobriquet.

Some believe him to be a three-time saviour, claiming that he ended the war with the timely arrival of the Alfár army. However, closer inspection of historical events will show that it was the arrival of the army from Kinnan that saved the brave and resilient soldiers of Algany. It was they who had held the line until that moment. They had some assistance from a handful of Choate warriors, but it was the staunch soldiers of Algany who changed the course of history.

Surrounded by his most trusted advisors and family, protected by the legendary Raven, King Marik gestured for the doors to the throne room to be opened.

Into the room came one of the Alfár, walking with an odd, loping gait, more like a wolf than a person. Even now, I find my skin covered in goose bumps as I describe her peculiar body and uncanny visage. The elongated limbs and dusty blue-grey skin. The strange angles of her face, and the penetrating yellow eyes on a sea of infinite black. Those eyes watch me from the shadows in my dreams, and yes, in my nightmares. They harbour great knowledge and great evil, too. Or perhaps, as some have suggested, it is simply my imagination that they intend us harm. However, there is no denying that the Alfár are strange creatures and not like us.

With the war over, and their own distant home reduced to a poisoned wasteland, they left the Five Kingdoms, crossed the Narrow Sea, and travelled into the east. Into the lands beyond Corvan, to the primal places that no one has ever seen. Somewhere, far from the Five Kingdoms, they found a new home and built a new city. There are stories of wonder from merchants who claim to have made the arduous journey. However, having studied the descriptions, I believe them to be nothing more than the idle fancy of people seeking attention. To create such majestic wonders and feats of architecture, as has been described, would be impossible.

The king, graceful as ever, welcomed the new ambassador to Algany, the heart of the Five Kingdoms. The ambassador answered politely enough, but it was not their words that disturbed me and all who were present. It was the Alfár's voice. It had a peculiar resonance, as if two people were speaking at once, and underneath there was a faint hum, like the rumbling of bees. Both are crude comparisons and not wholly accurate, but it is unmeasured and unlike anything in nature, so finding comparisons is difficult.

What followed was a peculiar exchange that bordered on distasteful between Kell Kressia and the Alfár. They embraced one another, in a familiar fashion, as if they were old acquaintances. There are rumours that the new ambassador is an old friend of Kell Kressia and was, in fact, the very Alfár who made the journey with him to the Frozen North. I have yet to confirm if the stories are true, because in the Pax Medina saga, it quite clearly states that only Kell Kressia returned. The rest of his companions died upon the ice. This is a well-known fact.

However, such minor details are apparently irrelevant. For in this new era of peace and wisdom, the distant and strange Alfár people will become allies and trading partners with Algany. From humble beginnings, and with guidance from King Marik, they will grow to become friends to all in the Five Kingdoms. We will raise them up, share our wisdom and experience, and help them to become a civilised people.

And under the leadership and guidance of King Marik, honoured be his name, it is inevitable that wealth and prosperity will follow for all.

ACKNOWLEDGEMENTS

With sincere thanks to all the people that helped me get here, to the end of this duology.

For my family and friends, for their ongoing love and support.

For my agent, Juliet, who continues to be my champion.

For the team at Angry Robot, for all of their hard work, and Tom Parker, artist extraordinaire.

For all of the fantastic authors who gave me great feedback and lovely cover quotes.

And of course, for you, loyal readers or maybe you're a new reader. Welcome. There are lots more stories from me, waiting to be told, but for now our time in the Five Kingdoms has drawn to a close.

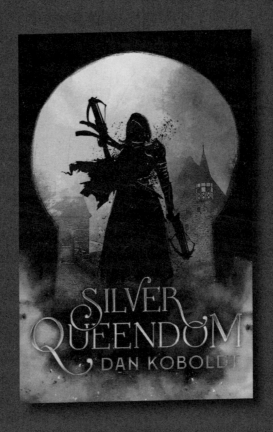

CHAPTER ONE
Uninvited Guests

Darin Fields never got invited to elegant affairs, but that didn't stop him from showing up.

Tonight's occasion was a gala hosted by the Duchess of Eskirk to celebrate the end of harvest season. Never mind that the Rethaltan nobles in attendance had little to do with the harvest itself. No, they had people for that. They packed the ballroom of the duchess's summer palace like colorful hens. The buzz of nervous conversation filled the air and, beneath that, a heavy layer of perfume. Neither was sufficient to dispel the salty-sweet odor of fear. After all, there was always a risk that the duchess might make an appearance at her own gala.

Only the blood plague killed more nobles than Her Grace's temper.

At least the plague could be avoided; its bright red pustules were hard to miss. The duchess offered no such warning, and the guests knew it. Their terror showed in how they snapped at one another like strange cats. How they didn't eat, but drank to excess. And not just any drink, either. Darin recognized the dark-wood barrel that everyone was looking at while pretending not to.

Imperial dreamwine.

Ounce for ounce, the most precious substance in the queendom. Dreamwine was an extravagance even for those born into prosperity. There were times in Darin's life when he might have afforded a glass. Brief times. But he vowed he'd never touch the stuff no matter what it promised. The nobles drinking it sat on plush divans around the edges of the room, their eyes glazed with hallucinated euphoria. The nobles who hadn't yet indulged hid their impatience poorly.

Thus distracted, they paid no attention to Darin as he slipped through the press and relieved them of their valuables.

The first coin was the hardest. He plucked it fair and clean from the purse of a fat lordling who'd already sweated through two layers of silk. It was a good coin, too: a queenpiece. He exhaled softly as he pressed the silver into his palm. The crowded room came sharply into focus. He moved more quickly now, cutting purse-strings with an invisible blade. Cajoling the coins into his pockets. Liberating the occasional necklace or jeweled brooch. He had a fortune of purloined jewelry secreted about his person, and fewer than ten paces to reach the exit, when he stepped on someone's boot.

"Watch yourself, you oaf!" a man spat.

Darin tried to ignore it, but someone grabbed his shoulder and spun him around. That shook something loose from the stash hidden in his jacket. Felt like one of the sapphire earrings. He whispered a silent prayer, and it fell into his breeches rather than clattering to the floor.

The owner of the trodden boot, unfortunately, was not so easily swayed.

"I called you an oaf," he said.

He was a highborn noble of the worst sort, young and fat-cheeked and angry. Darin wore the plain dyed woolens of a servant. It made him an easy target.

"Apologies, m'lord." Darin kept his body still, to minimize the clinking of half a dozen purses tied to his belt. "I was just–"

"Wipe it off."

Oh, wonderful. This flabby brat actually wanted a fight. Darin took his measure while pretending to think it over. *Soft* was the word for him. No callouses marked his hands. Big surprise. Men like this didn't work for a living. "Beg pardon, m'lord?"

"You scuffed my boot. Wipe it off."

His breath carried the mingled smells of wine and spiced meat. The least-capable member of Darin's crew could gut him like a deer. *But we don't have time for that.*

Darin made his voice cheerful. "Can't say I see it, m'lord."

"It's right there!"

"Never did have the best eyes, but I'll be certain to have them checked."

A wisp of a girl in a silk and taffeta gown tittered with laughter behind a tiny hand. She looked barely of an age to be husband-shopping, but the gems encrusting her bodice could serve no other purpose. Darin's fingers itched just looking at them. Yet another highborn. So that was why he was putting on this display.

Sure enough, the man's cheeks reddened even further. "Are you mocking me?"

"Wouldn't dream of it, m'lord." Darin tried to move around him, but the man shifted over to block his path.

"You're not going anywhere."

"That's terribly flattering of you, but I'm happily spoken for."

"You insolent little–"

"I wish I could stay and chat, but I've been sent to fetch wine for my master. He's not a patient man, I'm sure you understand."

"Who is he?"

The pearl and silver necklace threatened to spill out of Darin's left sleeve, so he thought it best to head this fellow off. So he spoke the name of the most dangerous and short-tempered man in Eskirk. "Lord Peyton."

Recognition bloomed in the man's eyes. *Oh, yes.* Even the most wine-addled fool would know to be cautious here. Peyton had challenged and killed men for the smallest of insults.

Harassing one of his personal servants would undoubtedly qualify.

"You've heard of him, I take it," Darin said.

"I should hope so." The brat wore a smirk that stabbed unease straight into Darin's belly. "After all, he's my father."

Of course he was.

Being around all these nobles made Evie want to stab someone, but since her mother had raised her better than that, she'd settle for robbing them blind.

She glided between the embroidered frock-coats and opulent evening gowns, trying not to look at any of their faces. Better to consider them strangers rather than the holders of names she once learned on her mother's lap. Better not to be recognized by anyone who would understand how far she'd fallen. Her plain servant's garb rendered her practically invisible among so much finery.

But not completely invisible, as the lecherous old Count of Sunbury's unwelcome hand in her skirts reminded her. She grabbed his pinky finger and bent it backward, rewarded with a yelp and the sight of the count spilling his drink on himself. He withdrew the offending hand when she released his finger. She moved on without a backward glance.

She approached a pair of women in luxurious silk dresses, one as green as a cut emerald, the other a deeper blue than sapphire. Exotic dyes both, and that spoke to the wealth of their owners. "Drinks, my ladies?" She held forth a silver tray with seven little porcelain vessels. A few brandies, a cognac, and a small assortment of other spirits. Fine offerings by most accounts, but both women refused.

"Come back when you have dreamwine," said the one in green.

Always with the dreamwine. Evie couldn't fathom their obsession with something so expensive, yet so fleeting. She dipped her head as they expected, then brushed her fingertips against the woman's side. "What a *lovely* bodice." She slid past, plucking two emeralds free and dropping them into her sleeves. Gemstones always brought good coin. A bit harder to move, perhaps, because you couldn't melt them down. Maybe that was why Darin often went for the silver instead. *Well, that's not the* only *reason.*

She hadn't wanted to come here. Eskirk's gala was the event of the season. In the not-so-distant past, she'd pleaded for an invitation. *Begged.* But only the elite got their names inscribed in silver ink on the coveted scroll. Half a lifetime ago, that might have included her, but no more. She knew it, and so did the castellan who managed the guest list. He was deaf to her pleas, but not entirely immune to her charms. He looked her up and down and offered her a job serving drinks during the event. She'd considered it just long enough to be polite, as much as she wanted to throw the offer back in his face. Serving those who were once her peers went beyond ordinary humiliation. Yet it was good she hadn't burned that bridge. The job paid far better tonight.

Now, in the moment, she realized it was foolish to expect that anyone might recognize her. The invited guests were too self-involved and probably too inebriated to look twice at the help. Besides, she needed to be here to keep Darin out of trouble. He possessed certain talents, but marks like these had their own culture. Their own vocabulary. Understanding them required a childhood in their world, and for Evie, that was all she had. Even now, the timbre of rising voices from Darin's spot near the door told her he'd gone off script.

She wove her way through the crowd to find him squared off with a stout lordling who could only be Lord Peyton's eldest son. She *tsked* to herself at Darin's impeccable ability to find trouble of the worst sort. She slid between them to present her tray at just the right level to draw his eyes to her cleavage. "Another drink, m'lord?"

A girl in silk and taffeta to her right stared at Evie and fanned herself vigorously, the equivalent of a snarl. Well, nothing she could do about that now.

"A drink? No," said young Peyton. His eyes slid up and down her as if sizing up a hog at the market. "Is that all you have to offer?"

Evie could almost sense Darin's blood rising but gave him a curt signal to stand down and giggled, touching Peyton's arm. "At the moment, m'lord. Perhaps later…"

The girl in taffeta gave her a look that would freeze imperial dreamwine. "He'll be busy later."

Peyton's gaze shifted from Evie to the girl and then to Darin, who'd begun to edge ever-so-casually toward the door. His eyes narrowed. "Where do you think you're going?"

"I was thinking anywhere but here," Darin said.

"You're a liar," Peyton said.

"An honest mistake, that's all." Darin offered a curt bow. "My apologies. I'll be on my–"

"Who are you?"

"No one of consequence."

Men in dark blue uniforms had taken notice of the confrontation and began working their way through the crowd. Evie gave Darin a tilt of her head. They needed to break this off and get out before the audience got any bigger.

But Peyton had other ideas. "I'll have your name." He took a step forward and shoved Darin in the chest. "Or I'll have you thrown in a cell."

Silk and taffeta girl gasped. Palace guards had begun to quietly assemble in a loose circle around the two men. Darin drew a deep breath, and Evie could practically see the wheels turning. She prayed that he knew better than to try plan B. Not with Peyton here and spoiling for a fight. But even as she whispered the prayer, she knew there was little point. The gods were too deaf.

Darin sighed. "Very well." He adopted a new posture, spine

straight, shoulders back. Evie caught his eye and ran two fingers through her hair – her own panic signal. It was too late, though. He'd slipped into the new role like a man tugging on his favorite jacket. "My father is Lord Delamere. Viscount of Harradine Fields."

Silence fell over those within earshot. Faces turned toward them. And then, whispers flew across the room like wildfire. Guests elbowed one another, nodding in Darin's direction. It was all in the bearing, the diction. And the careful study of long-forgotten noble lineages.

"You're a peer," Peyton said.

It might be Evie's imagination, but some of the ruthless bravado had faded from his voice. Still, this ruse made her nervous. Granted, the Viscount of Harradine Fields hadn't appeared in public for decades. No one here had seen him or knew much of his family. The duchess's clerk might dispute Darin's claim, were the man not passed out under a table near the back. Even so, by taking this step, Darin opened himself up to new avenues of danger. Ones he wouldn't understand or see coming. The worst part was, she couldn't wave him off any longer. He'd already spoken the name. She gripped the edge of her tray to keep her hands steady. She could feel the hilts of the daggers hidden up her sleeves. The cold steel was a comfort.

"My father wished for me to keep a low profile," Darin was saying. He'd settled into the casual confidence of a man born into wealth and privilege, like someone putting on a pair of favorite gloves.

"Understandable," said Peyton, through gritted teeth.

"If you'll excuse me." Darin put his back to them and faced the ballroom door once again. The full weight of his gaze fell on the two guards in his way. They stepped aside hurriedly, murmuring apologies.

"One more thing, Delamere," Peyton said.

Darin turned right into the slap of the glove. His cheek

reddened where it struck him; Peyton had put some weight behind it.

Knew he wouldn't see it coming, Evie groused to herself.

"I demand satisfaction," Peyton said.

Satisfaction would be meeting this man in a dark alley, with a sharp dagger in each hand. Evie elected not to say so.

Darin let out another sigh, a more theatrical one. Like a queen indulging a pleading commoner. "Tomorrow, at midday. Swords."

"There's no reason to wait. As it happens, I brought mine with me."

"You brought your sword to a gala?" Darin said.

Peyton's eyes glinted victoriously. "I like to be prepared."

A hawk-nosed guardsman with two stripes on his shoulder stepped forward and coughed politely. "My lords, Her Grace the duchess has a dueling green just outside."

Evie pursed her lips. Of course she did.

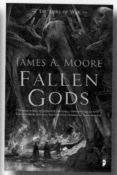
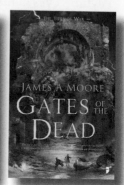

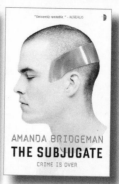

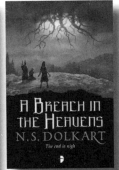

Science Fiction, Fantasy and WTF?!

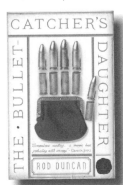

@angryrobotbooks 📷 🐦 f

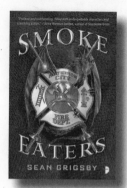

We are Angry Robot

angryrobotbooks.com